THE
NEXT
NEW
SYRIA
GIRL

THE NEXT NEW SYRIAN GIRL

REAM SHUKAIRY

LITTLE, BROWN AND COMPANY
New York Boston

Little, Brown and Company
Hachette Book Group
1290 Avenue of the Americas, New York, NY 10104
Visit us at LBYR.com

First Edition: March 2023

Little, Brown and Company is a division of Hachette Book Group, Inc. The Little, Brown name and logo are trademarks of Hachette Book Group, Inc.

The publisher is not responsible for websites (or their content) that are not owned by the publisher.

Watercolor jasmine flowers © Nanya/Shutterstock.com; jasmine vector © Vasmila/ Shutterstock.com; watercolor background © solarbird/Shutterstock.com.

Little, Brown and Company books may be purchased in bulk for business, educational, or promotional use. For information, please contact your local bookseller or Hachette Book Group Special Markets Department at: special.markets@hbgusa.com.

Library of Congress Cataloging-in-Publication Data
Names: Shukairy, Ream, author.
Title: The next new Syrian girl / Ream Shukairy.
Description: First edition. | New York : Little, Brown and Company, 2023. |
    Audience: Ages 12+. | Summary: The unlikely friendship between Syrian
    American boxer Khadija and Syrian refugee Leene reveals the pressures and
    expectations of the perfect Syrian daughter and the repercussions of the Syrian
    Revolution both at home and abroad.
Identifiers: LCCN 2022031749 | ISBN 9780316432634 (hardcover) |
    ISBN 9780316432917 (ebook)
Subjects: CYAC: Friendship—Fiction. | Expectation—Fiction. | Refugees—Fiction. |
    Syrian Americans—Fiction. | Muslims—Fiction. | Syria—Fiction.
Classification: LCC PZ7.1.S51797 Ne 2023 | DDC [Fic]—dc23
LC record available at https://lccn.loc.gov/2022031749

ISBNs: 978-0-316-43263-4 (hardcover), 978-0-316-43291-7 (ebook)

Printed in the United States of America

LSC-C

Printing 1, 2022

For Syria, the place of my heart

And for Mama and Baba,
who placed it there

1

Khadija

I pounce toward the man holding the round black targets.

Each explosive jab, hook, and uppercut fires my hostility at the padded mitts, whittling them down until they are scraps of neoprene and leather.

Lightning hands. Nimble feet. Stretched breaths. Every movement unleashes a pent-up emotion. My heart beats against my chest in a wild rhythm, my spirit uncaged from arguments with my mother and microaggressions with strangers.

"You're good," my trainer, Jerr, says, ending the session and resting his strong hands at his sides. My eyes trail the pads. "Take a look in the mirror. Your scarf is coming loose."

Reflexively my hands shoot up to my slipping headscarf and I stuff my light-brown bangs back in. Blood rushes to my cheeks from exertion. I train beyond my physical limits because wearing a scarf doesn't restrict me; it makes me train that much harder.

I'm the first and only Muslim girl to train at Jerr's Boxing Gym in the palm of Michigan's mitten. A healthy dose of post-9/11 hate, among other factors that give Muslim girls a bad rep, mixes me into an alt-American cocktail that's a little hard to swallow, but I own it. Because if I can't own my baggage, then it's only a matter of time before it's used against me.

I shadowbox a five-punch combination imagining the faces of my everyday opponents.

"Hey," Jerr calls out as I begin to unwrap my hands. "Twenty minutes on the bag."

I frown at it longingly, hanging there in its 120-pound black leather glory. "I can't, I have another...engagement," I say dubiously.

"No excuses. You told me not to let you leave till your two hours are done. They ain't done yet," he says as he helps a scrawny boxer with his wraps.

I swallow my pride and it drops down my throat like a bullet. "It's a thing for my mom," I mutter, desperately hoping he won't give me a hard time. Earlier, my mother asked me to swing by her friend's house for a small dinner tonight, and I couldn't wiggle my way out of it. I never can.

Embarrassment knocks the composure off my face when Jerr chuckles. "Best not be late for her, then."

Even Jerr knows the severity of an Arab mother's word. I contemplate ghosting her, knowing I'd suffer an earful of it later. I pull the ends of my hijab to tighten it over my hair again and stretch my DRI-fit shirt to loosen it over my curves.

Hijab—noun—he-jaab—/hē-'jäb/: the traditional covering for the hair and neck that is worn by Muslim women.

That's God-blessed Merriam-Webster's definition because they're about as deep as an oddly tinged kiddie pool.

It wouldn't have killed them to add the reasons that I wear it or that I don't have to wear it in front of women, male family members I can't marry, or my future husband. Not at home and *obviously* not in the shower. And it doesn't make me any hotter than everyone else on a blistering day in July. Something, anything more would have made this hijabi's life a lot easier.

Hijabi—noun—he-jaab-i—/hē-'jäbi/: invented Arabic-English blend word denoting a woman who wears the hijab.

Badass hijabi—expression—/bad-,as hē-'jäbi/: Khadija Shaami. Boxing beast. Me.

And with that thought, I roll my neck and loosen my muscles. My mother will have to wait. This badass hijabi has twenty minutes left of her workout.

"Khadija."

I know that tone. My mother's web-like mind has already

conjured a full-length lecture, not of why she is disappointed, but of how, if I lived my life differently, fate would be aligned in such a way that I would have arrived at this dinner on time. Then my mother would be content with my daughterly duties, and fate would change to be in my favor. And by fate, I mean God.

Mama leans over the passenger seat of my matte-black Mercedes G-wagon to shelter her white hijab from the rain. The indoor car lights shine on her pale skin, the chiffon fabric messily tied beneath her chin to cover her tightly curled hair. As soon as I'd put my car in park, she raced to meet me outside the dinner host's home, likely to prep me for how she wants me to behave inside.

"You're late," she chides me in Arabic. "I've been here for over an hour."

"Maybe you just arrived here early," I say, injecting cheeriness into my tone in the hopes that I'll get off easy.

"I told you this 'azima starts at five o'clock," she continues regardless.

"You also told me it was a small dinner," I groan. The lack of parking space out front suggests otherwise.

"You wouldn't have come if I told you anything else."

"So you tricked me?"

"Bala masskhara." She snubs me even though I'm not being ridiculous at all. "You've been out all day. I hope you prayed at that gym. I tell you all the time, that gym is not close enough to home. I don't want you to stop on the side of the highway for prayer when you run out of time. I heard a girl in Texas did that once and was attacked."

I grab my bag from the back seat to hide my eye roll. "Mama, don't believe everything you read on WhatsApp." The messaging-app-turned-Arab-news-forum is a great source of my pain. "Besides," I add, "I did pray. There's an area at the gym for salah for some of the guys, too."

With my mother, I always speak Arablish because, though she chooses to speak Arabic with me, our communication is a work in progress.

'Arablish — blend — aa-rab-lish — /a-rʌb-lɪʃ/: a kind of mixed language that switches between Arabic and English.

'Arablish with Mama — a conundrum — /a-rʌb-lɪʃ wɪθ mama/: yani she just speaks at me oo I can't get a kilma in edgewise.

I've tried it all. Straight-up English, straight-up Arabic, and once I babbled in French for an hour to try to convince her that she had broken me.

"I told you to stop fighting at that gym," she goes off again, mislabeling my boxing for the umpteenth time. I can call my boxing "fighting," but when she says it, it chafes my brain. She shudders. "And especially not with all those men. Find yourself a lady fighter or whatever it is you call them."

"Jerr's is the only gym I can afford," I remind her with a huff. "Since you won't pay for me to go to the gym in Rochester

Heights, I make do with what I have." For some chores and gym maintenance, boxers box at Jerr's for free. No need to charge Mama's credit cards.

"A proper Syrian girl doesn't fight," she insists.

"I guess I'm an improper Syrian girl then."

"You were raised by Syrian parents, so you are as Syrian as us."

"Technically I'm a half-baked Syrian girl who was raised in America." I shrug at her, the words pricking me in the sorest of places. Because no matter how much I can try to please Mama, she will always want me to be more proper Syrian like her.

So I stopped trying.

"I didn't raise you to fight," Mama reiterates. "I'm not pleased, Khadija."

"But it pleases *me* to box."

She turns up her nose. "You don't want to make your mother proud."

She means I'd make her proud if I were more proper Syrian like her. But if I give up even an inch of my territorial control, no matter how sensible, Mama would move on full offensive to ensure that I never boxed again. This weekly conversation barely travels from Mama's core principle: Her daughter, of all people, should not box.

My mother stares through me, her round hazel eyes speaking volumes. Finally, she tilts her head and I know she has elected to ignore the wasted exchange. She does a once-over of my appearance and smiles.

God bless. I was positive she'd hate my 'abaya despite its masterfully sewn black fabric adorned with dark glittering beads and pearls across the sleek shoulders and down the pirate sleeves.

"What are you wearing under your 'abaya?" my mother asks, practically beaming.

"Some sweats. I'll keep the 'abaya on inside. It looks nice," I reply.

"Terrific." Her excitement bubbles and she throws a gift bag that I didn't notice she'd brought out here into my lap. A smiling sun and laughing baby stare up at me. "I brought you a change of clothes just in case you came dressed like you usually do."

My hope plummets. "And how's that?"

"Like you're either going for a run or going to a funeral. Now get dressed. I've already told them I have a daughter with colored eyes and blonde hair, and they're excited to meet you."

"They?" I yell after her as she marches in the light rain back up to the 'azima. My grip tightens around the bag, and the baby's face wrinkles beneath my fingers. *They.* The marriage aunties for whom grand 'azimas are opportunities for young women to be paired with their golden-boy sons. They obsess over the genetic makeup of their future grandchildren that forms the stereotypical jackpot: white skin, colored eyes, and light hair. In response, my mom exaggerates the lightness of my features to fit their standards.

Exasperated, I throw the contents of the bag into my car and cringe at the peach-colored flare skirt and ruffled red blouse debased by tiny black cherries. Maybe I do dress like I'm always going for a run, but maybe I'm running to my own funeral. Cause of death: motherly smothering.

I slam the door shut and jump into the back seat, resigned to Mama's fashion choices. As long as I live under her roof, I have to follow her orders until I am married to a man who will then presume to give me his own orders.

With those old-school expectations, any boy of Mama's choosing would be in for one helluva ride. Naturally, my crushes are nowhere near Mama's sphere of influence.

I jump out of the car with my 'abaya covering the costume I managed to get my head and hips through. I make my way up the mini cul-de-sac to the house, and with the Arabic pop music pumping at this 'azima, I don't bother to knock.

House is a small word for this place, but *mansion* is presumptuous. A very large house, but a medium mansion, places like this are where most Syrians in Rochester Heights call home.

I push open the metal-spired, wood-framed glass door that looms in height. Stepping onto the marble interior, I try to slip in unnoticed, but my eyes catch at the mirror in the foyer, placed awkwardly at the bottom of a winding staircase.

The light bends and curves my reflection, and I freeze at the distorted mirror image. I am darker and taller, and my black hijab comes apart at my neck. My hand shoots up to fix it, but I feel the fabric still draped across.

I realize it's not my reflection. It's a girl with jet-black hair contrasting against a maroon-colored pantsuit, her bloodred lipstick and dark angled eyebrows stark against her muted skin. She remains motionless, her lips pressing into a thin line and her face becoming longer and more pained as time passes.

A chill stands my hairs on end. Turning away from her, I leave the image of the haunted girl at the bottom of the stairs.

Inside, I locate my best friend as quickly and discreetly as possible, pulling her into one of the rooms open for guests to get de-'abayaed. And yes, Merriam-Webster, that is now a real 'Arablish word.

"Do not laugh," I warn Nassima as I remove my scarf and 'abaya. Hijabs come off as soon as hijabis arrive at these female-only 'azimas.

'azima—noun—aa-zee-ma—/ʕa-zi-ma/: house party or event to which an invitation is extended.

Arab 'azimas—Arablish expression—aa-rab aa-zee-maz: over-the-top house parties that range from just coffee to full-on extravaganzas that put regular affairs to shame.

Nassima purses her lips to hold in her laughter at my

expense. "You look like you've run from the convent and this is your first night out."

"The nuns advised me to come to one of these 'azimas. They said an auntie might fall in love with me and let me meet her son if I'm lucky," I say sarcastically. She covers her painted smile with her hand as I tug at the alarmingly red fabric folds around my neck.

I flatten my short, wet hair in anticipation of the curls that'll seize as it dries. We wander through the marbled hallways lined with classically Syrian white sheepskin rugs, gawking at the estate's all but homey feng shui.

A wealthy Syrian home is like a bougie four-star hotel where sagging couches are strictly forbidden and the sound of guests banishes unopened mail and other clutter to unfrequented corners of the house. The luxury of the royal family and all nobility was re-created out here in Detroit among the Syrian American Women's Club of Rochester Heights.

Following the volume of the music, Nassima and I solve the house's maze to the end goal, the hub of all socialization: the kitchen. My sensory input would go into overload, but with my years of experience, I'm now immune to the effects of a Rochester Heights 'azima.

Rochester Heights 'azima—novelty: a goddamn Golden Globes after-party experience.

The excess of food skirts the line between indulgence and wastefulness, with triple the amount of cooked meat needed for the number of guests. Everyone looks like they have sticks down their spines to project a seamless image of etiquette while Louis Vuitton bags swing from wrists. The people who invented gluttony forgot to put a disclaimer that this display of wealth turns stomachs and makes it difficult to breathe.

Surprise, surprise, I've resorted to boxing and snapping at bystanders.

I pick up a gold-rimmed plate and circle around the island, which is blanketed with stuffed grape leaf towers, cheese and meat pastry arrangements, and vats of rice-filled intestines and beef ravioli floating in yogurt.

"Whose house is this?" I ask, starting my plate off with tabbouleh. All the estates and 'azimas started to blur together circa 2012.

Nassima shrugs. "I heard it's a get-to-know-you for a Syrian family that just moved here."

"Of course it is. You're more than enough diversity for them," I say. Nassima and I roll our eyes until they're underside our heads. These separatist 'azimas are meant for the families of doctors and engineers of select Levantine states: Syria, Lebanon, Palestine. Sometimes they'll include Jordan or Egypt, but God forbid they stray too far geographically.

Nassima sighs, finishing off her plate with red pepper and walnut paste. "I try my best to culture you, I really do."

I purse my lips in an air kiss. "Bah, merci, mon petit chou."

"Anytime, my little cabbage," she says with a smile.

Nassima is the only reason I've been able to survive this side of Rochester Heights. When I was little, I used to stay at her house for hours after school, and those years left me with a secret mode of communication that no one in my family could decode: French.

And though Nassima's family has the social standing, she's Tunisian, about one or two countries too southeast for the "in-group." But since Mama and I are close to the Abous, Nassima and her mom get special treatment that comes with a stream of gossip that follows them year-round. The women of Rochester Heights get catty when it comes to my mother—their queen—and her favor.

It really is even more petty than it sounds.

We pass by a horde of girls pulsating to the music in a mini rave bubble. Nassima and I share a chaise beside floor-length windows.

"Don't they ever get sick of it?" I ask, glancing over my shoulder at the girls and then flitting my gaze back outside the windows at a lake glittering in the moonlight. Every Arab house in Rochester Heights overlooks a lake as if it were regulated by the state's covert Arab American HOA.

"Sick of what?" Nassima strains her voice to be heard over the music.

"This high-society act we're fronting," I say. "It's always the same. Huge fancy houses, over-gassed luxury cars, slowly surrendering to diabetes."

Nassima's eyes crinkle. "The extravagance is how Arabs survive the Mild Midwest."

I laugh. "Well, I'm over it. I'm ready to see the real world."

"I'm on board. Europe and Tunisia with my bestie. A little bit of Turkey, see the sights—"

"Meet some Syrians who don't own at least two cars. The whole shebang."

"Exactly what we need to kickstart our post–high school lives." Nassima grins, then lowers her voice. "Except you've got your mom you need to convince."

"Khadija!" As if on cue, my mother's singsong voice fights its way to me through the music, the dancing, and the distance. She's as fine-tuned as a military radar. "Khadija!"

"God bless," I groan.

"I'm always praying for you," Nassima calls after me. She pouts on my behalf as I tear myself away from my dinner.

"Here she is." My mother has her superstar smile on as I approach the dining table, rows of occupied chairs surrounding her. Her friends all nod to welcome me, but I know the drill. I make my rounds, giving each auntie a kiss on either cheek.

"Assalamu Alaikum khaleh" is the standard greeting, a forced smile tagged onto it.

Khaleh—noun—khaa-ley—/xaːle/: literally mom's sister, one's maternal aunt.

Khaleh—title: missus or auntie, said before an older woman's name out of respect. Omitting it when talking to my mother's friends would be like wielding the axe at my own execution.

They carry on, and I don't interject even as the conversation shifts to me, knowing better than to give the hard-to-please khalehs more ammunition to criticize me with. Instead, I stand awkwardly while they discuss the merits of my studies and make remarks about my body.

"She's so skinny mashallah," someone says, intending it as a compliment.

"A little broad. It must be those muscles from all that fighting."

God bless.

They take turns comparing woes of raising teenagers in America. This is their Mothers Anonymous meeting, but I'm invited to sit in and nod. Mama has no anecdotes of her own, none that she would share, anyway. We are the 1950s nuclear family, no problems, no complaints. To disrupt that image is a felony.

I huff quietly, tilting my neck to the side, and I see an older woman teetering on a chair pulled up to the edge of the dining table. Though her eyes are observant, she tangles her fingers in the ends of her long hair, hinting that she's not listening. A wave of snickering ripples through the khalehs, waking the woman from her daze as she raises her eyes and catches mine.

Her eyes are hooded, under eyes permanently shaded. Sun

spots riddle her brown skin, and her hair is dull and frizzy in contrast to every other khaleh sporting heat-damaged curls.

"Oh, Khadija." Mama gestures to the woman who watches me from across the table. "This is Rana Taher. We're welcoming her to the community with this 'azima."

"Ah, this is your daughter," Khaleh Rana says, her voice raspy and thick with a Damascus accent. Her eyes brighten. "Thank you so much letting my daughter and me stay in your home for a while. I'm so grateful your mother could take us in while we get settled in Detroit."

My world freezes. I glance between Khaleh Rana and Mama.

Mama chortles. "Ah, Rana! I haven't even told her about that yet." Mama turns to me. "Looks like we'll be having new housemates! And it's great because she has a daughter your age!"

New housemates.

Khaleh Rana suddenly sits up in her seat. "Ah, here she is."

My mouth twitches as time resumes and a girl approaches. I blink at my earlier reflection from the bottom of the stairs. The reflection that wasn't really a reflection floats over to Khaleh Rana and sits in a chair beside her. Her black hair falls in straight sheets framing her cheeks. Her dark features paint her face in defined strokes, her olive skin strangely colorless in hue.

Like a ghost's.

Khaleh Rana gingerly holds her daughter's hand, but the girl doesn't swat or recoil, instead letting her hand rest in her mom's.

We hold each other's gaze. Goose bumps spread over my arms, and I can't shake the eerie shift in the air. It now feels as though time is rushing past us, as if hours and seconds and minutes could slip through fingers.

The girl recovers more quickly. Locking eyes with each khaleh, she doesn't extend her hand like I've been taught. Instead, in a voice as raspy as Khaleh Rana's and with a winning grin, she greets them in her nuanced Arabic artistry, "Assalamu Alaikum, I'm Leene. T'sharrafna. What a happy opportunity to meet you all."

My skin crawls as the khalehs practically coo at her.

My mother included.

2

Leene

The American girl doesn't sit. My instinct gnaws at me to pull a chair up for her and welcome her to the table. My curiosity begs me to ask her a thousand questions. My loneliness cries out to make her my friend.

Yet the American girl crosses her arms over her red blouse, a blouse I would have traded anything for a few years ago. She blends in with the wealth about her. Her short, light-brown hair makes her look sophisticated, though it frays as the curls dry. Despite the subdued light in this enchanting villa, her eyes shine a bright, icy blue. I'm taller than her, but her posture is faultless enough that it might make up the difference.

She is Khaleh Maisa's daughter, and Maisa, she is the woman who told Mama to check out of the motel at once and move into her home while we get settled in Detroit. She assured Mama, who doesn't speak enough English, that she will learn, that she will find a job, and she will be able to move on. And only when Mama moves on can I move on, too.

"I'm so excited to have you stay with us," Khaleh Maisa says to Mama and me, her voice chirping. She nudges her daughter with her elbow. "Aren't you excited, Khadija?"

The American girl whispers something to her mom, and Khaleh Maisa's expression turns sour.

"Don't be rude, we have plenty of space at home for guests," Khaleh Maisa says, dismissing her daughter. To her friends she whispers loudly, "Kids from America can be so inconsiderate. I'm sure there's so much Khadija can learn from sweet Leene."

I blush on the American girl's behalf. Mama would never call me out in front of all these people. The American girl drops her arms, balled fists at her sides.

"I only wish you had a son who could be friends with my Zain," Khaleh Maisa adds.

Suddenly, Mama's hand feels heavy in mine. My mouth twitches in the wrong direction, and I fear I've frowned instead of smiled. Mama jerks out of her trance, and I feel her grip on me tighten. I am holding her hand. Letting her know that at least I am still here.

Discomfort settles around us, and I squeeze Mama's hand to gauge her reaction. Thankfully, the American girl grunts and says something else under her breath, which procures another glare from her mother. It saves me from failing to come up with a cordial response.

Finally, Mama answers her hoarsely, "Well thank God I have Leene here."

I'm grateful for the time to recover, pulling myself forward from the dark corners of my mind. I flash a smile at the khalehs and lean my head on Mama's shoulder. "I'm lucky I have you."

"You two are precious," Khaleh Maisa trills, a gleam shining from her eyes. The American girl's face turns bright red, and her snake-like expression redirects from her mom toward me. I shrug reflexively. She tries to escape, but Khaleh Maisa grabs ahold of her wrist. She twists free of her and plants her feet down again, sighing dramatically. Perhaps she has somewhere better to be.

Khaleh Maisa shoots her daughter a look. "Thank God for our girls, right?" I hear a hint of sarcasm. "Our boys just give us headaches. We praise God when we get a boy, and when we get a girl we stay quiet, but the girls never disappoint. They're the ones that stay around to take care of us."

I nod, my mouth dry as I try not to dig my nails into Mama's palm.

The girl who was joking and laughing with the American girl strolls up behind her with her glowing brown skin and black hair that fans over her head in tight, shiny curls.

Khaleh Maisa reaches for her hand and mine. "Nassima, this is Leene. I want you three to be friends."

A warmth spreads in my chest. I hadn't expected to be welcomed like this by someone like Khaleh Maisa, whose world is so distant from mine.

Nassima's infectious smile falters as she catches the

American girl's eye roll. "Assalamu Alaikum," she begins. "It's nice to meet you."

Her Arabic is accented, and I try to place the dialect. "T'sharrafna. You're Algerian?" I ask.

"Tunisian."

"And I..."—the American girl ruminates for a moment— "am done standing in the line of fire." She drags Nassima by the elbow away from us.

"Go with them, Leene," Khaleh Maisa insists, waving me away. Dutifully, I follow after them.

The American girl narrows her eyes at me as I approach. She navigates this buzzing, rash world with a self-assuredness that quickly turns menacing. A heat from a fire within her that I may have helped ignite radiates toward me. Feeling a responsibility to extinguish it, I drop a classic Arabic phrase for tension defusing. "Haddi halek. I didn't mean to be a bother."

The American girl doesn't hear me, her eyes fixated on the table where her mother sits.

"I didn't mean to overstep," I murmur.

"You didn't," Nassima is quick to say.

Khadija snaps back to attention. "Listen, I'm sure you're real nice," she begins, sounding all but genuine, "but it's a lot to process."

Nassima nudges her. "Khadija—"

"It's going to be hell, you know," she interrupts, her voice hitching. She casts her gaze away. "Living with us."

We blink at each other, her face resolute, and mine furrowed with confusion. I know I should be the humbled guest and decline the offer to live at her house, especially now that she has all but spelled it out with letters that I am not welcome. I know that is what centuries of Syrian customs would have me do. But I also know that Mama and I have nowhere else to go. The cost of rent for us is unmanageable. We have to make do until Mama and I can find jobs and we can get ourselves on our own feet.

I chew the inside of my cheek. Michigan is my new start. Khaleh Maisa is our saving grace. I have no other choice.

This first impression took the wrong turn. This is the first potential friend I've met since arriving; she's my new housemate and I have already done a terrible job. Fear and doubt crawl up my spine. If all American girls are like her, then making friends in America will not be easy.

Contrary to my gloomy exterior, I crave the warmth and affection of friends.

Noting that her responses are a mix of English and Arabic and that my slick words didn't ease her worries, I offer, "Let's start over. And if you can't understand me that well, I can speak English."

Her eyebrows shoot up, and her cheeks flush. "No thank you, I understand Arabic perfectly well. I'm Syrian, too."

"I didn't say you weren't." Eyes wide, I realize I've called her the American in my head all this time.

"Masaa' il-khair." She bids me good night, sarcasm dripping off her words. She grabs her skirt in fistfuls and marches out of the room.

I stare after the puzzling girl named Khadija, plastering a cookie-cutter smile on my face to hide the fact that while I have a past full of ghosts, my future scares me more.

3

Khadija

*I*nshallah—expression—in-shaal-la—/ɪn- ʃaː- lʌ/: God willing; hopefully.

Inshallah (colloquial)—slang: we'll see; probably.

Mama's inshallah—negation: you better count your blessings because hell no.

Usage: I'll get through this night in one piece inshallah.

After the 'azima I drive home alone to my house of polished wood and marble floors and dustless countertops. A long
brick patio lines our portion of the same swerving lake's shore-
line. HOA regulated of course.

I drag my feet into the granite-and-mahogany kitchen
that bleeds into the high-ceilinged living room. My younger
brother, Zain, sits on a stool at the island, his thin frame
hunched over a bowl of cereal. Zain is a real-life boy with dirty-
blond hair and hooded blue eyes, a sophomore at Rochester
Heights High School, but at best, he is a life-sized Elf on the
Shelf. I'll walk into the kitchen and, appearing as if by magic

from his video game cave, he'll be cleaning a spilled soda or religiously downing cereal with bed hair and in wrinkled flannel pajamas. He's there one moment, then he'll be gone the next, hiding in the folds of this dimension until he decides to make another appearance.

And like a real elf, he seems to leave more or less no imprint on our world. Unlike a real elf, he wilts against the life around him. When I cross paths with him on the off chance that he has a cereal craving and he's in the kitchen, he always appears terribly, terribly sad.

Equally missing in action is my father the brain surgeon, on call at all hours, and in demand at all times. He comes and goes at random, more like a visitor than the homeowner, more like a grandfather than a father. I get little kisses on my forehead and a wad of cash every time we cross paths, but little else.

Mama keeps an eye on me, and Baba watches out for Zain, or so I'm told. And with that sort of family dynamic, the house is usually quiet and lifeless, weird and disjointed.

But it wasn't always like this. The start of the Syrian Revolution ended the biannual visits that my grandma—my teteh—used to take to stay with us, sometimes for a full year. "I'm getting old," she'd say, "and if I go to America now, I might never come back. I've lived all my life in the Midan and I'm going to die here."

Al-Midan—location—/ɛl mida:n/: est. in the second or

third millennium; the center of old Damascus, the oldest continuously inhabited city in the world.

Al-Midan—present day: a dilapidated metropolis still pulsating with life under soot and debris, severed pipes and blackouts.

I've stopped going into my teteh's room, the closest room to the kitchen because she liked to be where all the action was. Inside, the duvet and curtains have captured her scent, a mixture of jasmine and rosewater. In this house, the preservation of a memory is a miracle, but that's the power of a teteh. Her presence fastens itself to all that she touches, reminding me of our carrot and cucumber tea parties or transporting me to her herb garden in Syria.

Going into her room reminds me that I'm missing a part of me, and I won't dwell on that. So the door remains closed. The Shaami family keeps its routine of an absent baba, a bizarre elf who shies away from light, and my mother, who busies herself with being someone else's life coach.

"Khadija!"

Oof, and my personal governess, stern and stringent as hell.

"Khadija!"

My eardrums shatter. I hunker down at the kitchen table, readying myself for round two.

I stare at Zain, and he chugs the milk in his bowl, his butt half hanging off the stool.

"Will you be joining us to soften the blows?" I ask him, only cautiously hopeful.

But as always, Zain shrugs and gives me a sideways glance, gearing up to leave before it gets messy, abandoning me to the brunt of Mama's wrath.

Mama enters the kitchen and stops mid step when she sees her son. She gasps. "What happened to your beautiful hair?" She rubs his buzzed hair, a change that I hadn't noticed.

Zain slinks out of her grasp, avoiding physical interaction like it's the plague. He bows awkwardly like it's his version of the traditional "good night," and I wonder if he's said a word to anyone all day.

Can I blame him for wanting nothing to do with Mama's monologues and our arguments?

Mama watches him leave, worry across her face, then fixes her gaze on me. Her expression shifts to the offensive. Our shared love for American football makes the two of us experts at navigating our little games.

Her move. "Are you going to apologize?"

I'm used to this play, and my defense is to play dumb. "For what?"

"For acting like an ungracious host. Our guests haven't even moved in and you were ready to kick them out."

"Yes, let's talk about that." I turn to face her. "Am I supposed to be thrilled that I'll be living with strangers when you'd never mentioned it to me before?"

She pauses because I'm right, and it was a weak attack on

her part. "I hope you liked Leene," she blazes on. "You'll be spending lots of time with her from now on."

Third down and though it's a long shot, Mama prepares to hit me right where it hurts.

"It's going to be terrific," Mama gushes. "You can practice your Arabic with Leene, and she can teach you a thing or two about Syrian etiquette."

"She isn't going to be teaching me anything."

Mama's eyes are bright. "They're moving in tomorrow. I'll be prepping Teteh's room for them, so you need to pick them up for me."

All at once, my heart, which had been racing, slows down to a deadly rate. "Teteh's room? Since when did you put Teteh's room up as a hotel listing?" I ask. I don't even want to address her first comment: that Leene's abilities make mine negligible in comparison, especially in Mama's eyes. And Khadija Shaami is not negligible.

Mama, having predicted the deflection I'd telegraphed, charges on. "I worked it all out with Rana. I have friends in the Rochester Heights school district. I'll request for Leene to attend your school. They have an excellent ELL program for her there. You'll have breakfast together, go to school together, come back home together. You'll be like sisters."

My irritation skyrockets at Mama's delusional expectations. "They still can't have *Teteh's* room. That's like asking me to have Leene stay in my room."

Mama's brow quirks up. "That doesn't sound too bad actually."

If my ears could blow steam, I'd be whistling like a kettle. This is why I had been so harsh with Leene at the 'azima, why I have to draw boundaries before my mother begins mapping out plays. With the seconds of the clock ticking, my plays get crossed. "You don't need to solve everyone's problems." My voice sounds small.

"I'm being *helpful*. Aslan, this isn't up for discussion. They're already invited, and they're staying here until they can find a decent, affordable place, and that's that."

"You don't even know them."

"Rana is a friend of a friend, and we take care of our own," Mama snaps. "If you don't want to be a kind host then you can say goodbye to the fighting gym, Khadija. It's your choice."

Her interception has me reeling. "You can't take away the gym from me. It's free."

"But you can't go to the gym without a car," Mama threatens, and I swear she turns away from me to smile.

My heart drops in my chest. I have to choose both or neither.

So I switch to defense. "If you want me to go along with this, I require payment."

Mama shrugs like she flings wads of cash at others for fun. "How much do you want?"

I pull out my pitch. "No money. I want to go on a trip this

summer with Nassima. We're planning it all perfectly, the cities we want to hit, where we'll stay in each of them. Safe, pre-planned, no secret excursions. My price is your permission."

Mama's nostrils flare, and her brows slope until they're almost vertical, all warning signs that we're plunging into rapid-fire Arab-mom guilt tripping. "You're asking for me to pay you to help someone in need? Isn't my happiness enough reward for you? You want to go to Europe or wherever when people are dying in Syria? Do you know how many people get to make the requests like you do? You are so free with your wallet, so free in your privilege."

Oof, that word. *Privilege.* It makes me feel dirty. And when Mama throws it in my face like this, she makes me question whether I deserve to want anything.

Still, I persist.

"No one has to ask their mom for permission once they're eighteen. I'll be eighteen soon enough. Legally I can buy a ticket and travel alone. It's kinda like a courtesy to include you in my decisions." I throw the words out at high speed in hopes of getting away with some of them in this Arab household.

"People are dying, Khadija." It's my mother's blanket statement whenever I ask for something and she doesn't want to give in to me.

"Then let me book a ticket to Turkey, or Jordan, or Lebanon. Let me go help those people, my people. You say you want me to help. I can't help Syria from here, but I can volunteer in refugee camps with authorized organizations. There are hundreds of thousands of people who I can help if you would let me go."

My mom shakes her head. "It's not safe. You can't go alone."

"I'd go with Nassima." My voice quakes.

"Certainly not two girls alone—"

"But I can protect myself. I learned to box to make sure that I can protect myself, *and* for no one to question it." The escalation, my raised voice and negative tone, does not bode well. My mother waits for me to take it back. I rein it all the way in. "I need to see the world, Mama. Let me go."

She sets her fists down on the table. "You will be a kind and dutiful host. You will help Leene with everything she needs, and I can only hope that she rubs off on you."

I feel a pang in my chest for never satisfying my mother, for always being a disappointment. *Wrongfully*, I might add. I'm a girl with holes that I patch up with the scraps of the places I come from. I do my best with what I've been left with.

I can never be like Leene, a *Syrian* Syrian, not Syrian American like me. She knows exactly where she is from, exactly what expectations to fill, and she fills them out perfectly.

My face twists into a grimace. "I can't be confined to a small space with a girl like Leene. I know girls like her from the Midan. She's a basic Syrian girl who acts the way you and all the khalehs want her to."

Mama shakes her head at me. "You're wrong, Khadija. Think of this as an opportunity. I thought you wanted to help girls like her."

"She fled a war zone and got on a plane to America," I say. "Her luck landed her in our community, where people like you want to hand everything to her on a silver platter. Give her a chance to try the real world on her own." The better part of me cringes as I pass brutal judgment on a girl I just met, but it has to be done for my mother to understand me.

Because I do strain my ears to catch the echoes of my teteh's, my aunts', and my uncles' voices through the door of my mother's barricaded room. I've overheard the stories of how they try to pay for passage to live here, my cousins and aunts and uncles who would give anything to be here for a chance at a life, but the government refuses to grant them asylum. These days, Syrians play a delicate gamble with paperwork, visas, bribes, and chance.

It sounds bad, I know, but the fact of the matter is that Leene is one of the lucky ones and my countless family members are not. Leene's being here adds salt to my many wounds.

Mama frowns at me. "You haven't even had a decent conversation with her. You are so American, with your 'me, me, me' thinking." She says *American* like it's an insult, like it doesn't comprise half of everything that is me.

Except I remember the smell of cigarettes and fresh fruit in the streets of Damascus. I still hear the obnoxious honking and the vendors' booming voices listing the day's specialties. I see the faces of the cousins whom I love, but whom I am too ashamed to call because God chose me to be here and them to be there.

Yes, I am Made in America. Yes, I am Michigan born and raised. Still, I bleed the blood that streams down the low valleys of Halab, the rolling hills of Homs, and the crooked lanes of Damascus. My mother wants me to forget that. She made a new life with Baba in Detroit, and she'll be damned if I ruin her plans of the perfect Syrian American family who excelled under opportunities in the New World. All I want is to see the world for myself, to make my own choices, and to rejoin my body with the soul I left in Syria.

"Can't you just let me go?" I mutter. The memories dissipate quickly; as my time away from Syria grows, I forget more easily.

"Inshallah," she says, ending the discussion with her replacement for the word *no*.

There is no discussion, not now, not in ten years, not ever. But even this sorry excuse for a "discussion" is progress.

Some girls strive to surpass what their parents expect of them. Others act out to prove their worth to their parents when they don't meet expectations. Strangely, these contradictions perfectly describe my relationship with my mother.

Mama wants me to be her definition of the perfect Syrian daughter, someone more like Leene. To do that I'd have to stop the one thing I love that also allows me to protect myself. Boxing is the thing that makes me independent of her. Without everything boxing has taught me, I wouldn't survive one night out of my parents' house. I wouldn't make it out of the Rochester Heights bubble.

I fought my mother tooth and nail to start boxing a year ago, and I have yet to hear the end of it. When I cry and shout, I'm pacified with a car. I know, I know, first world problems. Except I didn't ask for first world problems. I want a simple existence. One where money doesn't define me and where my mother doesn't wield all the power.

The world begs to be seen, and if I have to slum it out to see it, so be it. Although slumming it out for her would be sleeping at the Hilton instead of the Four Seasons.

Before Mama can get up, shove the chair into the table, and march off with steam blowing out from her ears, muttering about how ungrateful I am, I play out the dramatic exit first. Except there is stomping instead of ungrateful muttering because despite all that she might say, there is some grace left in me.

4

Leene

I guess it's weird for a girl, but I love cars.

Sports cars, vintage cars, race cars. I can name every F1 driver in the last decade and the latest models of every major sports car brand. So when Khadija drives up to the bus stop by the motel in her sleek car, my jaw drops.

Now this is what I call a hot ride.

Mama and I put our lives—one suitcase and a half-filled backpack—in the trunk, and Mama gestures for me to take the passenger seat. Her look says, *Bond with Khadija.*

I get into her car, which is higher off the ground than it looks, with a grunt of effort. We exchange salaams as her car's heat embraces me. I do a little wiggle to get comfortable and don't hide my giddiness. The feel of the leather makes my chest feel fuzzy, and the new-car smell relaxes me. Khadija veers into the traffic. Her car zooms over the road like a hover-board, and I take in the bird's-eye view through the windows.

"This is what I'd call a Tank," I say, officially dubbing her car. I spread my hand on the dashboard, and Tank transfers its energy to me through my palms. I capture the humming sensation in my fingers. "There's so much power when you're this high up."

"That's a funny way to put it," Khadija mumbles.

"Well," I say, fumbling my words when I realize I'd spoken out loud, "it's because soldiers in actual tanks must need to feel powerful so they won't feel anything when they shoot people."

I can only imagine how much authority a real tank grants the soldiers who sit under the layers and layers of welded metal and steel that repel humanity and dispatch death.

"Uh..." Khadija stares at me in shock, and I realize too late that my digression didn't translate well.

"I mean," I say, scrambling for a more acceptable explanation, "it's normal. It *was* normal. Actually, I didn't even call them tanks. My dad didn't want me to be afraid, so we called them Lamborghinis."

Laughing nervously through my nose, I send a silent prayer that at least Mama cannot understand my half-English, half-Arabic speech.

Khadija only shrugs. Graciously, she does not ask questions.

She does drive like a madwoman. She glances my way sometimes, but the air is still, Mama purposefully quiet in the back. Mama said Khadija might need to adjust to our staying with her, so I should be extra respectful.

Bonding. I need to bond with Khadija.

"Do you have any music?" I ask.

"Is that okay with you, Khaleh?" she asks, looking in the rearview mirror at Mama, who nods. I detect a slight accent in her Arabic, but otherwise it's flawless.

She merges onto the highway and clicks on her stereo. She has a weird taste in music for an American. All her songs are foreign, and I recognize one of them as German.

"Oh, I like that song," I tell her after she skips a German pop song five seconds in.

She blinks at me and chews her bottom lip. After a moment, she plays back the song and lets it play through to the end. She doesn't understand the lyrics and can't sing along, but I can do both. I hold off on singing along, but I thank her as it comes to an end.

Outside the window, I spot two glowing eyes on the side of the highway. My eyes lock onto them. Scared and surprised, the deer waits to cross the road. Tank zooms past it.

And I remember Fulla.

Every morning for breakfast, Baba and I would go out for Mama's favorite ful dish, fava beans with tomatoes, garlic, green onions, and parsley drenched in olive oil and lemon, from my uncle's shop. As we left, we'd let Fulla, my calico cat, out of the apartment building with us for her daily excursions. Baba and I would buy a plate of ful before I went to school and before he went to work at the home appliance shop. Every morning I'd worry about the so-called Lamborghinis.

"The Lamborghinis," Baba would tell me, "they haven't been activated yet." He had convinced me for those first couple of years that there weren't people inside the Lamborghinis. He wanted me to believe no Syrian person would kill their own people.

Of course, there were soldiers in the Lamborghinis. I learned that the morning a bullet lodged itself into Fulla's gut and killed her. A soldier, a scrawny one who looked no older than me now, brought her to me in his bloody hands. He said he had watched me play with her before, then apologized on behalf of his friends for killing my pet for shooting practice. With Fulla in my hands, squinting from the pain of her last moments, I trailed the young soldier as he climbed back into his Lamborghini and drove away.

I wailed on the corner of that street with Fulla's corpse in my hands. Her normally soft and shiny fur was slick with blood and sticky with chunks of her guts. I must've cried for hours before Abood, his brows drawn on long like mine, his eyes the same shade of brown, pried her away from my fingers and took my hand. We walked to the end of the street, to the orange tree that shaded the ground year-round, and he buried her. He wiped my tears and helped me say a prayer for her. He told me I would live until I was so old that I'd have the chance to have hundreds of cats, but that I should never, ever forget Fulla because there would never be another who met an unjust fate like hers. A fate she didn't deserve.

Just like my Abood.

I push the memories away.

That happened ages ago, but the wound of losing Fulla is fresh. No other tragedy in my life had left me so broken until that moment, but that was when my family was still whole. Now, Fulla's death is a cigarette lighter's flame compared to the fires that followed.

I'm still in a trance when Khadija slows down into a neighborhood of storybook estates. She passes a diamond-shaped yellow sign that reads NO OUTLET. The snow-lined road winds down to a wrought iron gate. She circles a brick driveway at the front of the house and parks.

"Wow."

I stare at the mini castle, the grounds unfolding before me in stone walkways and pillars. The main house towers above me. I step out of Tank, the hot ride that brought me to this castle, as light snow begins to fall. I feel like I've walked into a movie. In the same day, I've ridden in a car that costs ten times more than my entire bloodline's life earnings and I'm about to make this castle my home.

Then I take my luggage, held together by three fibers of duct tape, and I'm sucked back into my reality.

This is temporary. This is a break from my exhausting life. This is a blessing.

I gawk at Khadija as she grows more grandiose and American than ever before. "Are you sure you're not an heiress?"

Oh, to be an heiress.

"I am not an heiress."

"I'm joking with you," I say, introducing a bounce to my step as we enter the house. I twirl to capture every detail. I relish in the marble columns, the intricate molding, and the floor-to-ceiling windows that shine light into the house. It's enchanting, and I am properly enchanted.

I trail behind her, dragging my feet and tilting my neck back to behold every exquisite ornament and trinket. I imagine myself in the salon, drinking tea out of the finest china, perched on the sublimely upholstered sofas. My meticulous adherence to etiquette would shine here.

"Welcome to my crystal penitentiary," Khadija mutters under her breath in English. I make a mental note that she uses English when she doesn't mean for me to hear things.

I touch the vividly textured paintings. "What is petinenten—"

"Penitentiary," she repeats. She switches to Arabic. "Yani prison."

"Why don't you say *prison*, then?"

"Because it sounds better."

I smile and catch up with her. "Do you know the word *Semantik*?"

"Semantik? Semantics?" Her brows are furrowed as we enter the largest kitchen I've seen in my life. All granite and wood and shiny metal.

"Semantics, yes." The next words come out stripped of my usual vibrato. "I learned about it in Germany because I love learning about languages. It means the meaning of words based on context. You say *penitentiary* and not *prison* because it changes the meaning. There's a reason for every choice."

Khadija stops in her tracks, and I body-slam into her. I didn't realize I was aimlessly following her to the foot of the stairs.

"What?" Khadija asks.

"Semantics?" I repeat with hesitation, a little disoriented.

She stares at me blankly. Then she points at my foot on the first step of the long, winding staircase to the first floor. I take a step back and firmly plant my feet on the ground floor.

I watch as Khadija runs up the flight of stairs, pushing her hijab off as she does, free in her element. I stand on the other side of an invisible threshold at the bottom of the stairs. It's an unspoken rule never to go up the stairs in a house that's not yours unless expressly asked to. It would be incredibly rude for me to break custom and follow her.

Maybe I got carried away with the excitement of being in a new place and having someone my age to talk to. But I don't feel the cold front of embarrassment. No, the warmth of this home holds me in a tight embrace.

I am happy, I tell myself, my chest and stomach tightening the more I try to release myself from my past. *I am happy here in America, seas away from Syria.*

And though I do my best to convince myself that I am, I really, *really* am, still I wait to see if Khadija might come back down. I have questions that I would want a friend to answer.

Where's the nearest library?

How do I apply for a job?

If I'm happy, really, really *happy, is it pronounced CON-tent or conTENT?*

The questions pile up, and I stand there until I hear her bedroom door close.

5

Khadija

The gym is my avoiding place. Now that Leene and Khaleh Rana live with us, I expertly dodge them at home. I pretend not to see them go into Teteh's room, but it's impossible. While Teteh's room is not upstairs with the other bedrooms, it's on the ground floor by the kitchen, so it's unavoidable.

Since Leene has seen where I live, the wealth and extravagance tag themselves to her mental image of me. Khadija: crabby but has a nice-ass house. I come to the gym to escape it.

In the center of Jerr's is a boxing ring that's usually occupied in the afternoons when the boxers get out of school, or earlier if they're cutting class. In the periphery of the gym is where the conditioning happens: Some guys jump rope, some bench press and lift weights, and beginners practice with trainers on mitts, punching bags, and speed bags in the Rookie Corner. At first, Jerr's didn't seem inviting, with its dim lighting and looming black interior, but one conversation with Jerr and the other boxers and I was sold.

Jerr's is a safe place. Here, I rarely worry about anyone staring or sneering at me because most of the boxers here know what it's like to be on the receiving end of unwarranted hate. There are always a few boxers who have it out for me, but I try not to give them any mental energy.

I hang against the ropes of the empty boxing ring after training. The ring should never be without its two boxers; its energy needs that elasticity that springs with every punch and sags with every draw back. I have an urge to take on any competitor just so the ring can be full again.

With wrapped hands I center myself in the ring, shadowboxing my competitor. I've done my second training session of the day, one before and one after school, but I always finish off a day at the gym by envisioning my fight. Voices in heated discussion pull me out of my imaginary spar.

"Would you take on Kadi?" one of the voices asks.

"Nope, 'cause she'd end me. Claw me with her nails and all that," says the other.

"Does Kadi look like she'd get those shit nails?"

"They're called acrylics."

Laughter. "How do you know that?"

"I'm a learned man."

"Yeah, learned from all the flirting you two do together."

Goose bumps spread down my arms, and I jump down from the ring. I put on boxing gloves and side-eye Gabriel for mentioning the f-word.

"I'm not flirting," Younes says, rubbing the back of his neck. I cut him a look for entertaining the conversation, but he flashes his adorable dopey smile that makes me forget everything I was thinking. Let's just say he's a major motivator to wake up at dawn to come to Jerr's.

He walks all six feet of himself over to me, offering me his wide smile that softens his intense brown eyes perfectly framed by his naturally curled lashes. Younes is built different; he's straight muscle and every bit of an athlete, but with a face that says he couldn't hurt a fly. His black hair is always on point, a mini afro with the cleanest fade.

Younes—yoo-niss—/junɪs/: [pictured: tall, dark, and handsome.]

My stomach flutters, and I dare it to settle down. Younes is my friend. Yeah, a guy friend, but just that.

"I keep telling you, Kadi," Younes starts, draping his arms on the ring ropes, the sinews in his forearms bulging, "you're always on offense."

"Because offense is more fun," I reply with a wry smile.

"I prefer defense. I wait for the perfect time to attack, and then pah!" He cuts a cross that whistles through the air. "Hit them when they least expect it."

I scrunch my nose. "Sounds boring."

He taps his temple. "Fighting with your mind sounds smart to me."

Gabriel, Younes's gym partner, shadowboxes lazily as he

follows along. "Yeah, less emotion, more smarts, Kadi." That's Gabriel's line because he thinks I need reminding of the stereotypes. He does it to get on my nerves, to get me to put more power into my next jab.

The always shirtless Gabriel is the wise man hailing from "Puerto Rico—where we have decent weather and tans," as he says. He's covered in the finest tattoos I have ever seen. He's a man of his own destiny. When no one else gave him a chance in high school, he chose boxing and adult school for himself.

"Ness and Gab always watching out for me," I say, suppressing a smile. They're the only guys who venture to talk to me at the gym since the hijab normally keeps people at a distance. There's this irrational fear that my Muslim will rub off on others, like my hijab is a beacon of piety and they don't want to be within the scope of its reach. That goes for most Muslim boys, too, but not for Younes. He doesn't see my hijab as a roadblock or an alien object. He sees me.

I knew it from the moment he approached me in the gym on my first day. He asked me if I'd ever boxed before, and I told him no, as if it wasn't apparent from my intense sweating. He asked me if I was scared, and I said yes. Pre-boxing me was much better at admitting her fears.

Then Younes told me he was scared of boxing at first, too. We were just strangers, but he confessed that he was scared every time he started something new because once he started it, he would have to do his absolute best until the end. His brain was wired to give everything his all, and that could be daunting. I felt that.

That conversation was only a year ago, but it feels like we were little kids, and now we're all grown up. He and I are seniors now, five months away from graduating. Every day we get closer, and every day I don't know what it'll mean if we get too close.

Gab begins skipping rope so fast it makes me dizzy to watch, while Younes takes up focus pads and holds them up to me. He looks at me expectantly. I glance at the clock.

"I'm not sure I have time," I tell him. Mama sent me angry texts ordering me back home since I've been sheltering here from her overbearing hosting. I've become a master at dodging because I have to savor this time before Leene starts attending my high school and messes with my Younes schedule.

Ahem. Boxing schedule, I meant boxing schedule.

"You should be flattered," Gab says. "This ugly champ is training you."

Younes grins at his friend, and I swear he's blushing. Proudly representing Somali Americans in the world of boxing, Younes is Detroit's very own favorite to win the Detroit Golden Gloves Championship in his weight class for the second year in a row. The Golden Gloves is the highest stage for amateur boxers like Younes and Gab. They do it because they love boxing; they don't care for all the Mayweather money and fame.

He leans over to me; a shiver travels down my spine very *non*friendly-like.

"We have lots of time," he whispers. "That FBI agent tagging you is on break."

"But yours isn't! He's right outside watching us conspire against him." I laugh softly. Ah, the FBI jokes are fresh, but the butt of these jokes always reeks of reality.

He shrugs like he knows and that we have to live with it. He holds up the pads and calls out combinations quickly, starting with jabs and escalating. I respond with a jab and left hook sandwiching a right uppercut. "Bust out all those moves you've been hiding from him, Dangerous Kadi." He keeps them coming and we're into seven-punch combos, and it's all about the speed of my punches.

"I'm not dangerous. My FBI agent files a report every day asking to be assigned to someone else. I hit a car in a parking lot and I leave a note on their windshield. I'm as good as they get."

He laughs, not buying it. "Sure you are. Doesn't make you any less dangerous."

I giggle, then play it off with a cough. There must be something wrong with me. I think dangerous is a compliment and a powerful punch is as attractive as red lipstick framing perfect white teeth. Aslan, I could pull both off.

My face feeling hotter than usual, I slide off my gloves and pull my hood over my gray cotton hijab.

"Have I ever told you that you look badass in boxing gloves?" he asks.

My eyes widen in shock, but I recover quickly with a smile. "Careful, Ness, I might start thinking Gab is right about the flirting."

Younes shrugs with his own sly smile. "Well, it's the truth."

"Why thank you," I reply, placing a hand over my heart hoping it'll make it beat less.

Okay, I admit it. I'm in the denial phase of my crush and it's not going so well. And maybe Younes has graduated from denial a little earlier than me.

We stand there looking at each other, our friendship feeling shakier and shakier with every moment. The flimsy label covers something bigger that neither of us is ready to confront. But more-than-friends with Younes would require dissecting relationship rules and the whole "no dating unless there is an intention of marriage" Muslim concept. I'm not ready for serious talk like that.

Since Younes approached me the week I started at Jerr's, we've been just friends. We see each other at school, and granted, he sits with Nassima and me at lunch in the cafeteria more than he did before, but that could just be a coincidence, right? It's not like he doesn't have his Anime Club friends or his soccer teammates or his childhood friends to sit with.

Damn, he really does spend a lot of time hanging around me.

When my heart rate returns to a *just friends* rate, I glance at the clock. "Uff, I'll be late."

"But I can help with your overhand," he offers quickly.

"I wish." I pout.

"You'll need it for the showcase," he says. "For when you show off all that training you've been doing."

The annual spring showcase is a contest of sorts where the audience votes for the boxer who impressed them the most. Usually, the boxers invite as many people as they know because they try to skew the votes, but it's a major attraction for boxing enthusiasts. And the prizes are always exciting. One year it was a stay at a resort in Florida, and maybe this year it could be my plane tickets out of here. If that's the case, I'll need to do all that I can to win.

"It's never too early to train," he adds, and matches my pout. The showcase is in May, and we're still in the thick of winter.

I should have more time with him—I mean more time to train. I thank Younes for his help and go to the locker room with the single shower secluded and separate for the girls. I dress in my usual sporty ensemble, an oversize long-sleeved shirt with ties on either sleeve over black leggings and black Nikes. I blow-dry my hair at warp speed and wrap my blush hijab with the skill of tying up a methodically messy bun.

I pull my coat on top and wave at Gab and Younes, each on a speed bag now, glistening with sweat in the dim lighting. As the glass door closes behind me, Younes's voice, light and cheery, follows me out with a sprinkled reminder.

"Fight with your mind, Kadi."

6

Leene

I look like I could be the lead actress in a Turkish drama.

I gape at my reflection in the floor-length mirror. At least my split ends bring me back to reality, because there's no logical way I'm standing here in this speckled white-and-gold-tweed dress.

Khaleh Maisa says it's Chanel. I say it's about the cost of my left kidney.

I twirl to get a good look at every angle, wiggling my toes into the silk rug beneath my feet. This room we're staying in, just like the dress, is also straight out of a Turkish show. Piles and piles of designer clothes cover the bed's silvery duvet, the room's accents are plush and shiny, and a furnished bay window opens to a stunning view of the sparkling lake outside.

Khaleh Maisa comes running from the closet with a pair of pale-pink heels. "I found them!" She sets them at my feet. "Ya-ii!" She oohs and aahs at my reflection. "You look beautiful. You have to take this one. Actually, take all the ones you like. I bought all of these for Khadija and she never wears them."

I blush furiously. "Really, Khaleh, I couldn't."

I let Khaleh Maisa drag me this far into these clothes, into these shoes, into this farce, when I usually try to be careful to stay quiet in this room. Thankfully, it isn't on the second floor where Khadija's room is, but it is central to the rest of the house, just down the hall from the kitchen. Still, this guest room is leagues beyond what Mama and I could have ever asked for. We had to assure Khaleh Maisa that Mama and I felt most comfortable sharing the same room so she didn't prepare another one for us. We're used to being in much smaller and worse living conditions than this, and we're used to being together.

So I can't help but feel like an impostor. My humility has abandoned me because deep down, pretty shoes and dresses make me weak. What's more, when I dress up like this as if playing pretend, I feel like this could be my life.

No, I tell myself. This life isn't mine, it's Khadija's.

But Khaleh Maisa is already at the pile of clothes on the bed. "Look at this dress!" She holds up a velvet dress dotted with a million crystals that looks like it costs more than my right kidney. "This one will look beautiful on you. It's Gucci—you kids love Gucci, right?"

Before I know it, it's thrust into my hands, and I'm being shoved into the closet to change out of the tweed dress and into the velvet one. Being Khaleh Maisa's dress-up doll is hard work. Being back in school would be less grueling.

Ah, school. Khadija has been gone at school all day and, if her daily pattern persists, she won't come home until late. I wonder what she does when school is over. Does she go to Nassima's house? Does she work? Does she study in the library?

My chest squeezes. I miss libraries.

When I step out of the closet in the velvet dress, I'm welcomed back by a round of claps. Not just from Khaleh Maisa but also from Mama, who has come back to our temporary room to rest. *Rest* being an interesting word choice here. Every night so far, I've twisted and turned so much that the moisture on my skin sticks to the silk sheets, tangling me in a filmy web. Most nights, I just lie on this bed fit for a queen, looking out the arched windows as the sun rises on the picture-book lake until my skin dries and I can detangle myself. I pray Mama has had better luck.

Khaleh Maisa clasps her hands together. "She looks perfect."

"My Leene."

"She's like a doll." Khaleh Maisa's eyes are even brighter than Mama's. "It must be so nice to have a daughter who wants to dress up like this. Khadija just lets it all go to waste."

Khaleh Maisa looks at Mama with what looks, impossibly, like jealousy. Mama only smiles a sad smile. A smile that has gone through too many hardships to be what a smile is to most people.

Too many countries. Too many losses. Losing my baba opened our wounds; losing the others ripped them wide open for our pain to grow a home inside. Memories from before flood forward, and my skin begins to itch before it catches fire. The overdressed room spins as the dress attaches itself to my skin, suffocating me. I want to claw it off my body, I want to throw out all the clothes on the bed, I want to stop playing dress-up in this castle by the lake.

Is this what moving on feels like?

No, it must not be. Moving on shouldn't hurt so much. It only hurts me because maybe, somehow, I could've prevented what broke my family apart. But in the end, there are some things that couldn't have been stopped, and so they should be forgotten.

I specialize in forgetting.

I hear my name far, far off in the distance. Is that Mama's voice? Or Khaleh Maisa's? Or is it—

"*Leene?*"

When my head rights itself, I'm staring into Khadija's piercing blue eyes.

Khadija glances around the room wildly. "Mama." Her

voice cuts through the air like ice. "What are you doing in here?"

Khaleh Maisa busies herself with fixing the collar of my dress. "They're staying in this room," she says.

"I know that," Khadija snaps. "I mean why are all these clothes here? Why are you having a little party in here?"

Khaleh Maisa rolls her eyes. "I brought some of those clothes you don't want so that Leene could try them on. Doesn't she look lovely in this one?"

"But this is *Teteh's* room." Khadija's tone is flat.

My shoulders seize up with the realization that, like the threshold at the stairs, this room lies beyond a threshold in Khadija's world, too. And I just pranced in without a second thought.

"This is your teteh's room," I start, flustered. "I didn't know, I—"

"It's just a room," Khaleh Maisa interrupts, "and now it's their room as long as they're staying here." She shoots Khadija a glare that says death. I internally cringe for Khadija, but she doesn't so much as blink at her mom's harsh tone. Then Khaleh Maisa grabs a rack of garments and rushes toward Khadija. "Why don't you try some on for us like Leene is?"

I sway under the awkwardness of Khadija's glance. "If this is your teteh's room, then I'd hate for you to be uncomfortable."

"Oh no, no, no. No one feels uncomfortable at all," Khaleh

assures me most unconvincingly. "Khadija just has an obsession with this room."

A scowl paints itself in twisted beauty across Khadija's face, and she steps away from her mom toward the door. I move to offer to leave, to stay, to become invisible, really anything to make things better with Khadija, when Khaleh Maisa glances over her shoulder at her daughter. "Aslan," she says, "I have no idea why you care at all. You never even come in here."

Khadija's shoulders slump for a moment; she thins out her voice until I almost can't hear her.

"Because if I do, it won't smell like her anymore," she murmurs.

She rushes out of the room and sucks out a powerful memory with her. I know what she means. When Khaleh Maisa brought me into this room on our first day at the house, there was a smell of jasmine and an olive oil soap that older people in Syria like to use. Laced together with a hint of musk and rosewater, it is undoubtedly the scent of a childhood surrounded by a loving grandmother.

The smell took me back to Syria for a brief moment. A beautiful Syria, a Syria that no longer exists, a Syria that is buried.

Khadija is as American as they come, but she must have experienced loss, too. Loss that might not have been met with kindness. And I can't help it, it's in my nature to fix. Whatever I've disrupted by coming here, I want to resolve. I want there to be a semblance of moving on, no matter how much it hurts me. But I have a feeling whatever is wrong between Khadija and her mother and the memories connected to this room, they have been wrong for much longer than I have been here.

7

Khadija

Mama forces me to have dinner with her and our new housemates. Dinner is a lean kofta loaf and melt-in-your-mouth lubya drenched in oil. My family owned an olive tree orchard in Syria, so when our neighbors were cooking their meat and pastries in ghee, my family was immersing every ingestible substance in olive oil. The earthy taste dances on my tongue.

God bless.

The taste almost makes me forget how the three of them looked in Teteh's room, like they shared some kind of secret that I wasn't allowed in on. Mama looked like she'd trade me in for Leene at the drop of a hat. Because Leene is a prim and proper Syrian daughter who enjoys dressing up in designer dresses and doesn't have a problem lounging in my teteh's room.

Sure, Leene shares more in common with Mama because she speaks her language better and knows more of Syria than my summers there could ever give me, but I don't want to be

Leene. I want to be me, just without feeling like an outsider in my own home.

I avoid eye contact with Mama while Leene and her mom interact like they're one person. Khaleh Rana sprinkles salt and pepper over Leene's food as she eats, and in exchange Leene takes the roasted tomatoes off her kofta and drops them onto her mom's plate. They're in tune with each other's wants without the need to express them. They are deft ballroom dancers while Mama and I are in the back stepping on each other's toes before the music starts.

They may be winning the Mirrorball, but Mama still cooks some of the best kofta on the planet and I'm not the only one who thinks so.

"This is delicious," Khaleh Rana says as she takes a big bite out of the kofta. "I'll have to make you my neighborhood specialty sfeeha. Maybe on a holiday sometime soon."

My eyes light up at talk of spiced meat pizzas. Then I remember I'm upset and reapply my brooding expression.

"America?" Khaleh Rana resumes her conversation with Mama. "It was so far from my mind that I never thought about it even as a young girl with big dreams."

"Surely you had considered it before," my mother tuts. Leave it to my mother to believe the USA is the end all be all across all people.

"I really hadn't," she insists, her long black eyelashes perpetually glistening.

"So how did you get here then?" Mama asks, intrigued.

Khaleh Rana's lips form a tight line. "By God's will. All our successes and failures since leaving Syria brought me here. For years I thought that God was testing me extra hard to erase my sins. Nothing worked out for us. From Syria, to Turkey, to Jordan"—her voice breaks—"to a brief pass through Italy, to Germany, then back to Jordan."

Excitement bubbles in my stomach, but when I look at Leene, the feeling vanishes. A pale yellow under Leene's skin returns, like it often does when the conversation is more than surface. I remind myself that they weren't traveling on vacation. They went to those countries because they were—or are—displaced.

"I spent my entire life savings on blasted train rides," Khaleh Rana continues. "And we were blessed because we still had our papers. They were water damaged, but at least we had them. Germany accepted our status, and Leene pushed for us to go."

"Your husband must have had his doubts. Men always have their doubts," Mama says very matter-of-factly.

"He wouldn't have believed that I made it here. He would have been so surprised that I attempted it without him, but he would have been so proud of Leene," she says with a small smile on her face. The corner of my lip twitches down. *Proud*. It's a nice word.

Leene and Khaleh Rana's faces are equally pale when they murmur, "May God have mercy on his soul."

Mama offers a slew of condolences that blanches any envy I had toward Leene and her world travels. I guess my mother assumed, like me, that Leene and Khaleh Rana were separated from their family but not by death.

"We're not the only ones," she recalls as though they're fond memories. "Nearly half the refugees I met were widows, especially in Turkey and Jordan. We were like a family of broken families. But I couldn't stay in Jordan. It was a bad place for me."

Her expression darkens, and a silence descends. Her eyes fixate on a spot far away, and she recedes from us to a shadowy place. Leene bites her lower lip and reaches to hold her mom's hand.

"You received news that you would come to America when you were in Jordan?" Mama interrupts Khaleh Rana's trance.

"It sounds easy when you say it like that, but yes. We were in Germany for a while, then Leene took us back to Jordan. She applied for asylum in America without telling me, and at that point I'd have done anything to get out of Jordan." Her revelation is both shocking and unsettling and I stare blankly at Mama. I can't leave the house to go down the street without Mama knowing.

"Is it because of Jordan? The place? The people?" I ask, unable to rein in my curiosity.

Khaleh Rana frowns. "There are memories in that place that I never want to revisit."

Her story doesn't echo pity; it rings of perseverance. Her retelling skirts sorrow but never embraces it. She doesn't crave sympathy. Or perhaps she's only told us fragments of her story. Piecing together my interactions with Leene, I infer the latter.

"How brave of you," Mama says to them both, but with dumbfounded admiration toward Leene. "I would worry for Khadija's safety, especially in a country she's unfamiliar with. That's why I like her staying where I know it's safe. Right here in Rochester Heights."

My face burns and I want to reject Mama's statements, but I bite my tongue.

"Anything can happen anywhere," Khaleh Rana heckles her sweetly. Wow. It's like she watched a video recording of my arguments with Mama. "Look at your daughter. God made her smart, strong, responsible." Khaleh looks at me and raises her eyebrows. "And I hope with a lot of common sense. She knows to stay out of trouble."

"The world is not safe for girls." Mama picks up empty cups to put in the sink. She's walking away from this discussion literally and figuratively.

"Khadija is a woman," Khaleh Rana says after her. "Khadija and Leene see all the bad that there is in the world every day on the news or in real life—they should see all the good in it, too. It's a great idea to show her the world if you have the chance and the means. Leene is ten years stronger from our travels."

Ouch, the jealousy hooks me hard in the gut. Leene has a strength that I strive for, and the acknowledgment I crave. My conjured-up image of her as the Damascene damsel needs a bit of adjusting, and it'll have to be at my ego's expense.

Zain trudges in for dinner, heading straight for the cereal cabinet, but when he sees the four of us, he attempts an escape. Mama jumps up to make him a plate, which he reluctantly accepts. Leene adjusts her hijab, and Khaleh Rana fixates on Zain, a frown tugging at the corners of her mouth.

"What a blessing it is to see your son grow up," she tells Mama, who nods in agreement, but without her usual vivacity. Mama and Khaleh Rana watch Zain hobble out of the kitchen, sadness welling in both of their eyes. Zain is like a phantom in the house, and Mama must imagine that there's something bubbling under the surface. But she just enjoys finding faults in her children. I bet if she stopped searching for our flaws, she might discover what's actually wrong with us. If I have a backlog of troubles, Zain definitely has no shortage.

The clinking of silverware fills the silence that follows. When I steal a glance at Leene, her brows are pulled together in contemplation and her skin is a pallid color.

Mama's eyes flit across the kitchen, and I recognize the look as the one she gets when her inner gears are churning a plot that'll surely frustrate me. She says, "Rana, why don't you allow me to host a party for the girls to get to know Leene? We need to properly introduce her to the community before she starts school next week. We can invite all of Khadija's friends, too."

My heart sinks. My mother throws around the word *friend* like it's nothing. Mama assumes that I'm friends with every Syrian girl in Rochester Heights.

I am most emphatically not. While they gush over purses and jewelry, I stand by with my top-of-the-line boxing equipment knowledge wondering how I can fit in a comment that doesn't feel forced. Since I have yet to figure out a way, Nassima remains my only friend.

Khaleh Rana and Leene exchange a glance, and then Leene looks to me. Her brows are furrowed as if she's about to ask a question, but I'm engrossed in dissecting my mother's intentions.

Khaleh Rana cedes respectfully. "I couldn't accept anything like that." How clever of her to have already learned to skirt around the autocrat that is my mother.

"No, we must," Mama insists sweetly.

"Really I couldn't—"

I step in on their behalf. "Mama, if they don't want it, we shouldn't push it."

Mama is quiet and doesn't look at me. I repeat the sentence over and over in my head, inspecting it for errors.

"Don't be shy about it. I want to do it to make Leene's transition easy. Leene is like my own daughter," Mama says.

Oh. Right. Leene is the type of daughter my mother would

have wanted. The last time I let her throw a party for me was in fifth grade, because she brought a Disney Princess role-play actress when I was at my peak Batman phase. She wants to have a daughter who can live out her fantasies. If that can't be me, I guess she'll find someone who can take my place. Maybe Leene is a good person, even a worthy friend, but when I'm beside her, all Mama sees are the ways that I'm not her.

My mother saves a date. She declares it a pool party at our indoor pool despite second thoughts from Leene. She plans the party like it's Leene's quinceañera. As Mama talks about this extravaganza, Khaleh Rana and Leene become more timid, and an awkwardness blooms between us.

"Khaleh," Leene interrupts. I glance at her, and Leene gulps. My anger at my mother is on full display, and Leene and Khaleh Rana will inevitably misread it.

"Yes?"

"I accept this party if it will make you happy," she begins, "but we've overstepped. When we first spoke about staying here, you said there was a guest room in the basement. I think it'll be much better if Mama and I stayed there, so we aren't in anyone's way. It must be weird for Zain and Khadija to be living with two strangers. Now that Mama started work at the masjid school, I will find a job, too. After all, this is only temporary until we find an apartment."

I watch as Leene's sweet Arabic prose weaves her to a position where Mama can't say no.

"Leene, habibti," my mother trills, "if this is about earlier, Khadija was wrong to—"

"It's not," Leene rushes to say, interrupting Mama's saying something that would have made my personal hell freeze over. "It's just that if I get too comfortable, I might never leave," she says with a small chuckle. "Mama and I need to keep moving on."

The conversation dies out once Khaleh Rana and Leene have properly convinced Mama to let them move their things down to the basement. The basement's guest room is no Teteh's room, but it's furnished and clean and has everything they might need down there.

We clear the table together in silence. I watch as they complete each other's actions wordlessly. They excuse themselves after Mama promises to hold up her side of the deal once the room in the basement is tidied up and ready for move-in. Mama stays in the kitchen after they've gone, and I can feel her negative energy stewing. I stick around to brood, but Mama doesn't sense my annoyance, too busy with her own to notice. But my thoughts aren't yet refined enough to tell her why I'm annoyed. If I spoke now, Mama would poke holes in my argument, and I'd lose.

Because I shouldn't be agitated that Leene and Khaleh Rana go together like cardamom and dates while my mother and I are like toffee and ketchup. See, even our analogy sucks.

I'm not happy that my relationship with my mother barely

exists. I try. I fight with her because I want to try. She's the one who tries against me. She's the one who would trade me for Leene.

The only game plan that makes strategical sense is keeping my distance from Leene. Without Leene around, I can stand alone, safe from comparison. My actual feelings toward Leene take a back seat to the other powers at play.

To Mama, Leene is docile and sweet: a perfect Syrian girl who abides by confining rules and doesn't take the reins of her life to create a path for herself. But I can tell there's more to her. A traveler, a survivor. I could give her some props, and a chance, but I remind myself that my mother is the queen of schemes. Though her surface intentions are to help Khaleh Rana and Leene, there's always a flip side. Keeping my head in Mama's game means resisting her plans of shaping me into Little Miss Teen Damascus. Sacrificing a potential friendship with Leene is just collateral damage in my war with my mother.

8

Leene

This fairy-tale life has endless perks and it's making me sick.

First it was allowing Mama and me to live in this home, then it was the clothes, and now it's this party that makes me feel like I'm stuck in another girl's body experiencing these luxuries. The Leene I was a year ago would not believe the Leene today exists. This Leene has moved on, and that one never thought there was a life beyond the endless sea.

Khadija's pool house booms with music, but I only hear the bass. Girls I don't know swim in the pool, shrieking and squealing, and my body shakes. As soon as people arrived at this welcome party, I banned Mama from the pool house because of the infamously low Taher family water tolerance.

I tune out the sounds as the trapped pool water jostles in waves, lapping the pool's tiled edges. Some of Khadija's guests, who didn't have much to say to either of us other than a quick hello, have clumped like magnets into cliques. Others jump into the pool, causing more ripples. A metallic taste coats the inside of my mouth. I'm bedridden with nausea as I lie stiffly in a recliner. I gaze at the clouds passing in the long skylights of the high wooden ceiling.

The jacuzzi is the worst. The water bubbles around the propellers—jets, they're called jets—making all sorts of gag-worthy noises. My stomach lurches.

Definitely a good idea to ban Mama from the pool house. I would escape this personal punishment just like her, but if Khaleh Maisa spots me inside the house among her friends, she'll try to get me into the pool with the others.

I cannot touch the water. After all the effort I've put in to forget the last time I swam, I can't bear the memories that lurk beneath the water. Control. I need to maintain control or the memories I block will flood back.

I twist around to see Nassima and Khadija huddled next to each other and hunched over their phones. Even from this distance I hear their booming laughter, years of friendship cocooning them and secluding me.

I sigh heavily. I check my email on my phone for the hundredth time today, but none of the jobs I applied for have asked me for a single interview. I am stuck in this fairy-tale world where I can do nothing to help myself.

Every single girl here hugged me and told me they were thrilled that I've moved here, to this town where I'm helpless. It's the moving that makes me wonder. As my mental blockades around my memories weaken, I begin to doubt how far I've really moved. Have I really moved on from the deaths that keep coming back to me like waves?

Girls splash each other in the pool, and I fight the urge to yell.

When I close my eyes, a memory flashes vividly. Bodies packed tightly together along a narrow deck. The taste of salt and metal on my tongue. Lights flashing over the choppy sea. Tiny fingers holding tightly to mine until they weren't.

I heave forward and force my eyes to peel open. My irises swim with the swirls of the water.

Concentrate, Leene. Concentrate on the lines in the tile. The water doesn't exist. The splashing and the bubbles are happy sounds. The girls are screaming from excitement, not terror. Droplets splash onto me, and I drop my head in my hands. My lips mouth the word *forget*.

Concentrate, Leene. Focus on the present.

9

Khadija

"You doubt me?"

Nassima raises a single eyebrow. "I'm supposed to believe you're going to get the plans rolling without your mom's say-so?"

I roll my eyes. "I don't need her blessing."

"I see. So you'd rather me use the word *permission*."

I wrinkle my nose. "Neither."

Nassima adjusts the red strap of her bathing suit while I recover from the massive cringe.

"So, where's the lady of the party?" Nassima asks, twisting in her seat. "Lady of the hour? Whatever that expression is."

I look around the room and spot her. Among the Syrian girls of Rochester Heights, she's not so easy to spot. The pool house is a rainbow of swim shorts and leggings over a one-piece or paired with a tank top. That's how the girls here turn up for pool parties. I'm no exception. I'm in a beige and black swooped-back one piece that I wear under a pair of black shorts.

I tilt my chin beside the pool as I pull out my phone. "Isn't that her lying like a corpse?"

Nassima squints. "Is she sleeping? She looks unwell." She glances at me. "Whatcha looking at?"

I lock my phone screen. "Nothing."

Nassima smiles slyly. "Checking Younes's Instagram again? It's your third time today."

"I'm not."

"You like him," she teases.

I'm blushing hard, so I flash a smile and say, "And so what if I like him, it's not like that'll change anything."

"Not unless you woman up and tell him."

"Yeah, that's not happening."

"How long have you been sitting on this crush?" Nassima postures. "Since you started at the gym?"

"It wasn't love at first sight," I mutter, throwing the word *love* around as lightly as I can. "We were just friends."

Nassima's eyes sparkle. *"Were?"*

"Are," I correct. "We are just friends."

"The way he stares at you, there's no way in hell he thinks of you as a friend."

"You're imagining things."

"I'm telling you, you're in denial."

"Okay, topic change, please."

Nassima gives me a flat stare that says I shouldn't be such a coward, but then drops it. She whips out her phone. "While you were daydreaming about Younes, I was brainstorming ways we can convince your mom to let us travel. Your mom can't say no to a good cause."

I nudge her playfully. "My bestie the genius."

She winks at me. "I made a list of orphanages and camps we could visit and help out or volunteer at. Most Syrian refugee camps have a bunch of laws and rules. Orphanages are more chill about volunteers."

We browse the links she's pulled up for volunteer sign-up pages, searching for the most credible opportunities.

"This one's simple and easy. It's in Mafraq, Jordan. It's called Ibtisami Ya Shaami Orphanage for Syrian Children," Nassima reads. The orphanage's name contains my last name in it, but here it means "smile, my Syria," whereas my last name means "of Syria." My name is literally Khadija of Syria. It's a tag that I can't seem to live up to.

Nassima turns her screen to me. Two boys and a girl stand in front of a termite-riddled wooden frame door. The girl flashes a toothless grin, but her gaze is fixed beyond the lens. The older of the boys hooks his arm around the younger one, who stares directly at the camera with his dark-brown doe eyes.

The little girl's face is sandy, but she has that beautiful Syrian kid tan that I used to have from being out in the sun at all hours of the day. Her brown hair has golden highlights. The older boy's face is covered in soot, and his hand clutches the younger boy's shirt. It's the ashen-faced, doe-eyed boy who commands the camera's attention. His right eyebrow is sliced by the memory of a scar. His round lips are in a natural pout, and he clenches his hands into fists. He is neither toddler nor old enough to be a boy, and he holds tightly on to his friend like he's holding on for survival. He sets his cheek against a dirty blue blanket.

He looks lost. I wonder how many, if not all, of the children at Ibtisami Ya Shaami are waiting to be found.

Nassima stands abruptly, phone in hand, severing my line of sight.

"You'll swim?"

Nassima flips her hair. "Hell no," she says. "I'm gonna ask Leene if it's safe to be that close to the Syrian border. I have to have a comprehensive plan if I'm bringing this up to my mom."

I watch her leave and glance at Leene. She's in one of the recliners by the pool, bent over with her head in her hands. Seems the migraine from the old-school Tamer Hosny beats is making its rounds.

I pick at several carrots and peep at Leene's curved back. Nassima crouches down to her. Knowing Nassima, she's charming her way into a segue rather than getting straight to it. She turns her phone to Leene with an amiable smile on her face.

Leene's shoulders straighten up and, reflexively, mine do, too.

Nassima stands from her squat. When she glances at me, her smile melts away. I rise from my seat to come to my friend's side.

Leene raggedly rises from the recliner and heaves, her chest expanding and deflating rapidly. Nassima reaches for her, face full of concern, but Leene evades her, bringing Nassima's phone closer to her face. Her fingers swipe at the screen haphazardly. Nassima waves at me for help at the same time that Leene's body turns.

Years of pain etch themselves onto her face, weighing her expression down. Her dark eyebrows slant like ski slopes and her eyes are foggy.

Leene isn't present.

"Okay, breathe," Nassima instructs. Leene's breathing is jagged and her chest rises and falls irregularly. A sob mounts in the back of her throat.

"Leene," I whisper, reaching for her arm.

She steps back from me, gripping Nassima's phone like her life depends on it.

"Careful," Nassima warns.

I step toward her, and like a partner in a dance, Leene's foot pulls back. Arms trembling, she shifts her weight over and over, struggling to get out any words. Her soul appears to dissociate from her body in an excruciating exorcism.

Leene takes another step back.

Her heels teeter on the edge of the pool.

I lunge at her swiftly to lend her my stability, but she jumps back from me.

A strangled sob escapes her lips as her feet seem to hover above the pool, probing for the ground. One arm writhes in the air toward me while the other pulls the phone over her heart.

Her back strikes water.

10

Khadija

The girls laugh at first, but they didn't see Leene's face like Nassima and I did. They didn't see the anguish, like the translucent face of a ghost who roams the world haunting the life of a loved one. She wasn't pushed in; she was pulled in by an unseen force.

My knees connect with the tile, and I submerge my arm in the water, lengthening my body to reach for Leene's ankle.

"Can she swim?" Nassima's question lingers in the air. I dunk my arm down to my shoulder and submerge my neck and ear, still unable to grasp her. Disturbed, Nassima whispers, "She can't swim."

The voices subside and panic sweeps the pool house as comprehension settles in. Leene doesn't struggle to the surface. The sound of jets echoes through uninterrupted space.

I've listened to Nassima's analysis long enough. The water swallows Leene's body like an anchor sinking to the bottom of the pool floor. A cloud of black hair is all I can see of her. If she is drowning, she isn't attempting to save herself.

The girls evacuate the pool in a frenzy as if the water has been bewitched into sucking the rest of them in. Our Arab genes have everyone yelling instructions over each other so that I can't think a damn thing.

I take a staggered breath and dive into the pool. Needles sew into my exposed skin as water surrounds me. The change in temperature forces my body to suction in on itself.

Peeling my eyes open, I swivel my body deeper and deeper, the pressure bearing down on me. When I crash into the blob that is her unmoving body, she sinks farther away. Water swallows her into the depths.

I wrap one arm around her torso and kick off the bottom, but our ascension drags. I'm pulling deadweight. My arm flails around me as I thrust my feet in the viscous liquid, trying to gain traction against the water.

Hands thrashing above stretch miles away. The vibrancy of the surface doesn't filter down to us. I squint my eyes, willing the rays to reach me, to brighten the dimming syrup of the pool.

I tighten my grip on Leene against all logic because she isn't drowning, she's sinking.

My body and legs contort to propel us up.

My free arm stretches for the surface. If I let her go, I can make it. I hold on to her wrists despite my survival instincts.

Fingers latch on to me.

A palm grips my elbow.

A dozen hands haul me over the edge.

Surrounded by air, my diaphragm contracts violently and my lungs cave in rather than expand. I spit up the trapped water that I involuntarily sucked in. My lungs burn as I gasp for air. My body convulses as it resets itself.

I flop away from Leene, whom they hoist over the tiles. I fight against the exhaustion to inch closer to her, but no dice. I turn my head. Nassima's face is by Leene's purple mouth.

I read my best friend's expression. There's something wrong. I cough and sputter as I search for an explanation.

Everyone yells instructions but no one acts.

"She's not breathing!"

"We need CPR!"

"Move, move!" Mama appears out of thin air, pushing girls aside and kneeling beside Leene. She sets her hands on top of each other and over Leene's chest. She compresses Leene's chest rhythmically.

Limp. Wet. Dripping. Pale. Leene's body rebounds in an unnaturally weak oscillation.

I shut my eyes and turn away. When I open them again, Khaleh Rana kneels in the doorway to the pool house, clutching another khaleh's clothes for dear life.

The seconds pass in a vacuum. The sound of pounding soulless flesh quiets the room. Then, like a jammed door breaking open, the unsettling scene shatters as Leene coughs up a gallon of water, her body jolting and retracting. The awful noise is drowned out by numerous directives to call an ambulance.

Leene fails to sit up. She grips her body as if to check that it's there. Her silence is punctuated by her sudden wails, and my bones tremble at the sound. Long and agonizing cries that no living person should ever hear. She acts through the motions of tears that don't materialize.

Mama cradles Leene through whatever grief has taken over while Khaleh Rana remains frozen in place by the door. Nassima leans over me and pulls me into a hug, and we peer at Leene.

"What is it?" Mama leans over and puts her ear by Leene's mouth. But Leene's wails don't subside. Her hands are locked across her chest as she stammers.

I wriggle my arm to hold Leene's hand, to let her know she wasn't left to drown, that someone brought her back. I touch metal. I feel its rectangular body and pry it out of her vise-like grip.

Nassima's phone. Through her debilitated state, Leene gripped that phone within an inch of her life. The little girl and two boys stare back at me from the wet screen.

The water in my ears muffles the gossip rippling through the guests.

I hyper focus on Leene's face: her shadowed eyes wide

and unblinking, her stammering jaw and her body's tremors. A string of sounds pours off her tongue, the end of the last and the beginning of the next blending into each other.

I catch the name as she manages to pronounce it clearer and clearer.

"Mustafa."

11

Leene

WINTER 2017
1 YEAR AGO

The fishing trawler plummets back down to the sea with every choppy wave. Wave approaches, trawler rises, wave passes, trawler crashes, and the Mediterranean Sea splashes buckets on us. I can't complain though because I deserve the worst this terrible journey can give.

I let that Jordanian brother scam me. Family compartments? A four-star ship? I'm as stiff as a board, sardined between Mama and an old teteh on the deck of a dilapidated vessel. I threw away good money on this self-proclaimed cruise out of the country. I should have thrown all our money away on three plane tickets instead of making my family endure this boat.

But how was I supposed to know? I may be the newly self-appointed Woman of the Taher House, but the scammers coming from every direction are hard to keep up with.

I turn over and give a tiny smile. It's nowhere near ideal, but at least our days in Jordan are long over; we are hours into the sea on our way to Europe.

Europe.

The promised land. We'll be in Greece, Italy, Crete, or wherever we dock in some odd hours. I don't care where we end up as long as it's not where I've come from.

Jordan was a hellhole, not unlike this trawler we're sandwiched on. Most of us here are Syrian, but we have some Palestinian brothers and sisters who ride the wave of increased smuggling that came with the influx of Syrian refugees. We ride hellish waves out of Jordan, a place where we were only welcome until it was decided we'd overstayed.

I'll be damned before I get caught overstaying anywhere ever again.

This trawler stinks. I sniff again. Nope, that's just the teteh's underarm that I cannot evade. Shifting and squirming is useless. I freeze at the old woman's cold stare, but I can't help but laugh.

"Nothing about this is funny," Mama chides, adjusting her life vest. She fidgets with the zipper that won't zip to the top and yanks up hard. Her wet fingertips lose their grip, and she smacks herself in the chin.

"Blasted shop owner ripped us off. This life vest can't keep a watermelon afloat." Mama giggles, too, and I laugh harder from the crazies of an extreme lack of sleep. We hear a small cry and a fuss, and we swallow our laughter fast.

"Shhhh." Mama and I clamp our mouths shut. Wrapping the light-blue baby blanket tighter around Mustafa, Mama kisses his forehead to feel his temperature. He sighs jaggedly and smacks his lips, twitching like he does in deep sleep.

Mustafa: my younger brother, my last brother, and the only soul on this trawler in REM sleep. I pray that at three years old he won't remember our dangerous trek out of Syria, the discrimination we encountered in the towns of Jordan, or this blasted boat trip on our way to a new life. I pray he doesn't feel the cold and that I do enough to shield him from the sea sprays.

"It's my turn to sleep." Mama coughs and I hear the phlegm in her throat. It's a terrible time to be sick. She nestles her head by Mustafa's and flutters her thick lashes closed. Mama and Mustafa would be twins if it weren't for the scar slashed through his eyebrow and the dark tinge of his skin that mimics Baba's. Mustafa also shares the Taher boys' black curls that Baba and Abdul Rahman once sported. Other than that, Mama's and Mustafa's features are identical.

The salt in the night air reminds me of field trips I used to take to Tartus, the seaside city where the Syrians speak lilted, the days were hot and humid, but the evenings were heaven. Except in Tartus, I only ever watched the boats, never sailed on one.

I hear retching on the far side of the vessel. Passing the peak of a monstrous wave, the boat heaves forward and the sea chucks water across us. We hammer into one another toward the bow. Mama's head and mine crash into each other.

Strange lights scatter across my vision; I think I must be imagining them.

Yet searchlights really do shine against the windows of the captain's quarters. I'd gotten used to the sounds of the crashing sea and the rhythmic motor and propellers, but a roaring engine disrupts what my mind had warped as normal.

I raise my head to see over the trawler's edge, wrapping my frigid fingers around the rusted railing. It's all that separates me from the impressive ship, twice as long and tall, manned by men whose pastimes consist of smoking and bulking.

They take turns cursing at us.

"We have some dogs here!" a pirate in an Egyptian dialect yells, his voice carrying over to us in the pitch-black sea air. "Sons of bitches think they can leave their country through our sea!"

Frantically, Mama pulls my head down, and I force my frozen fingers to release their hold on the railing. "Stay down and cover Mustafa," she orders. We lean over him, shielding him from the hailing planks of wood hurtled onto our deck by the pirates.

"God save us. Lord protect me and my family. God save us."

I force my eyes open just as the screams begin to erupt.

The pirates' hurled pieces of wood and metal find their targets. All around me, dark syrupy blood fills widening gashes and drips from foreheads. The passengers hold mashed fingers tightly to their chests or frantically cover their wounds to stop the bleeding.

A log flies through the air and cracks against my calves, stinging the skin and bruising bone. I yelp, and Mustafa wakes with a sharp jolt. He joins the babies' cries.

"Mama! Mama! Mama!"

"Lord, oh Lord, oh Lord."

"Stop!" one of our smugglers yells across. "Leave us be. We'll get out of your way!"

"Syrian dogs!" another pirate bellows back. "You should have died in your country!"

The others on our trawler send off a chorus of "goddamn yous." The volume of the engine soars in acceleration. I shut my eyes in anticipation of what is to come.

One, two, three. The pirates laugh.

Four, five, six. The smugglers plead.

Seven, eight, nine. The refugees pray.

Ten.

The noise of the earth splitting reaches my ears. Their ship rams into ours.

The trawler rocks us violently, and Mustafa's body bobbles against me. I spin my head, discerning what I can in the low light. The stern is cut clean off, leaving an entire family dead upon contact from the pirates' vessel.

The howling wails torture us before our inevitable deaths.

The trawler tilts, and from that single ram, the end scene of *Titanic* unfolds. Stern first, propellers hastening, water sucking us down family by family.

"We have to jump, Mama," I cry. I use whatever balance I have left to cocoon Mustafa in his blanket and secure him under the crook of my arm.

"Leene." Mama bares weakness in her voice, and I sense the grief that grips her into inaction. When she lost Baba, she lost her authority. When she lost Abdul Rahman, she lost her spirit. At the possibility of losing Mustafa or me, Mama loses her will.

She won't lose anyone else. Not today. Not if I can help it.

I grab hold of Mama and force her up. The sea is open and black, inviting us into its cold embrace. The sun won't be up for some hours. The unknown of the water and the waves dare me to jump in. The screams are muted as prayers lift up to the sky. I try to pray, but my mind won't settle on a single supplication.

The lights from the ship and the trawler shine into the water, a sign telling us to take a leap. The smugglers throw the single lifeboat and jump into the sea after it. Screams sound from the sinking side of the trawler and my eyes follow them.

On the far side of the boat, white foam near the propellers swirls red. A girl in pigtails falls off the boat and hits the water. Her pink blouse is sucked closer and deeper until—

"We're jumping, Mama!" I cry, the fear of God in me.

"One…" I know how to swim. Mama too. "Two…" We have life vests. Awful ones, but we have them. "Three!"

I fly through the air for an eternity. I left Syria to find freedom. I bought my way onto this boat to escape Jordan in my quest for it. Flying through the salty air, I feel raw, uncharted freedom and wonder if this is what I always wanted. What nations of people die for.

Our bodies crack through the seemingly solid layer on the frigid sea surface. I poke my head out as my life vest fills with water. The Jordanian man didn't just scam me. He sent me away with life vests that are a death sentence. If we didn't know how to swim, we'd be sinking to the bottom of the sea.

Treading water, Mama and I slip out of the weighted vests, and I help Mustafa out of his. He complies without a single sound, his eyes closed and his small nose quietly squeaking with effortful breaths.

A passing plank of wood floats beside us, and my arms cut through the water as I swim to pull it over to my family. Lifting my arms with incredible effort, like icy chain mail is weighing them down, I raise Mustafa out of the black sea and onto the plank. I can only hope that his winter clothes underneath the blanket are half-dry, because the quieter he becomes, the more I worry.

The trawler sinks rapidly, and the pirates don't wait to see it off. Their ship turns as they prepare to ride off.

"You should have died in your country, you dogs." They spit at us. "That would have been the honorable choice."

My eyes sting with anger and my numb fingers grip the wood. Mama's teeth chatter as she damns them to hell.

A quarter of the voyagers we began the journey with float alongside us. The sole lights in the vast blackness of the Mediterranean Sea accelerate out of view as the pirates leave us for dead. But God shines His light on us by shifting the clouds and letting the full moon shine bright. *We are not alone*, I remind myself. *God is with us.*

With that blessing comes the witnessing of the aftermath. My memory preserves images of revolutions and war crimes that only a victim's eyes can capture. Mutilated corpses and limbs drift past me. The ruby-red water. The smell of salt and metal and death. The sound of mourning and of the patience resounded through prayer. I always saw prayers as peaceful, but I'd never heard a prayer from a man who has stared into the eyes of death, or that of a mother who has seen her son sucked into razor propellers, or of a newly wedded wife losing the love of her life moments before.

Desperation leaches into every word.

Fights breaking out over the buoyant items end the time of supplication. People shove each other from fear. Those who can't swim beat their arms against the water to save themselves from drowning. I hold our plank of wood tighter. Mustafa can survive this cold if he stays on the plank as dry as he can be, I tell myself.

My sweet little baby brother lies motionless on his bed in the sea. Time has no place here; we are both floating forever and for only one moment.

"He's blue," Mama laments. My heavy lids fall on Mustafa. His eyes are wide open, and his tiny mouth is a perfect blue O. His breathing is labored, and he is so cold he can neither speak nor cry. His baby-blue blanket cocoons him in an ice coffin; his name embroidered on the top corner in red thread is his tombstone.

I will those thoughts away.

The water laps against me and the waves swell around my legs. Seconds spread into lifetimes. Mustafa curls into himself and his round black eyes roll back as he drifts into a bitter cold sleep.

Mama pleads with him to stay awake. A fog creeps in like the angel of death. Somewhere a mother weeps for the death of her child. I pull the plank closer to me to create distance between him and Mama's unfurling hysterics as she suspects the worst. I place my forehead against his freezing hair.

Mustafa should be lying on his chubby belly in front of the television in our warm home. And our home should be whole, not the pile of rubble we narrowly escaped. He should be singing along to cartoon songs with his heavy lisp.

Mustafa's eyes shut. I do not shake him. If this is his last sleep, it will be full of love. I sway him softly as I sing him his favorite song.

The bunny rabbit said to his mo-om,
"Will you let me go out and play, Mama?"
She told him, "No, oh, Mama,
"The wolf might come for you, oh oh oh, the wolf will come
for you."

The beat is all wrong. The freezing air and my craggy voice strip the rosy tune down to a haunting hymn.

The bunny rabbit shook his shoulders,
And didn't listen to his mother's words.
He went out to the pen
To pick some flowers and smell them.

I cannot hear Mustafa's breathing. Tears freeze in my eyes. My voice cracks.

The wolf saw him and attacked!

I shield Mustafa's pale purple body from my mother's eyes.

The wolf saw him and attacked!

I can't remember any other words. There's no hiding from the wolf, no running back home to Mama, no surviving, no safety, no lesson, no moral. That's the end of the story. The wolf sees and the wolf attacks and the wolf kills. The Lamborghinis, the Mediterranean Sea, the wolf.

Hours pass before a cargo ship brandishing a foreign flag sails near enough, and by the time their dinghies begin to rally up the few survivors that include my family, I have no more hope.

I help Mama into the dinghy first. The sailor reaches his hand out to me, and I take it.

"Wait, Leene," Mama rasps. "Pass me Mustafa first."

The cold winter is unrelenting. My frozen face twists and my sob comes out dry and painful.

The bearded sailor glances at Mustafa and then back at me. He pauses before reaching for the oars. He cannot bear our anguish. The weathered lines of his face twist with sadness, but he knows as I do that there is no point. The dinghy can only hold so many, and it cannot transport the dead.

So Mustafa will remain on this plank of wood, his final bed floating into the secrets that live and die in the endless sea.

"Leene, get Mustafa!" Mama demands, and she continues to even as we row away, her shrill screams rattling the few of us left.

Her screams travel up into the black sky and shatter stars.

The oars separate our family with silent distance, but my heart rips with Mama's howls and cries. My eyes linger on the tiny blue blanket until sailors carry me onto their ship. All night in a cot on a foreign boat, I pray the waves float Mustafa back to Syria, where he can rest at home.

12

Khadija

That night, when Mama is with Khaleh Rana and Leene at the hospital, I pace nervously in my room. It's been a little over three weeks since they've been living here and I'm no closer to understanding them.

The terror clinging to Khaleh Rana as she watched Leene's limp body being ushered into the ambulance keeps me up late into the night. I lie in bed and stare at the photo on Ibtisami Ya Shaami Orphanage's web page. I zoom in on the faces of the two boys. One of them is named Mustafa, and Leene recognized him.

Eventually, I fall asleep.

I drift to the last night of my visit to my parents' homeland. Every summer of my life since birth had been spent in Syria with Mama, Zain, and sometimes Baba. But that summer would be different, and though I didn't know it, I could sense it.

The entire family was packed into the roofless inner

courtyard of my grandfather's old-style Syrian house in the Midan. The summer night was cool, and the smell of jasmine wafted down from the creamy white canopy of flowers.

A total of seven aunts and twelve uncles and a hundred cousins and second cousins once or twice removed set aside bad blood and sibling rivalries for a farewell party. They sang songs by Fairuz and Umm Kulthum, my uncle maintaining a beat on the goblet drums. They snacked on roasted black watermelon seeds and my older cousins served black tea with ma'amoul, date- and pistachio-filled cookies.

Mama and Baba distributed the final suitcase of gifts. My cousins and I played with the RadioShack trinkets, flashlights, and shockers in the poorly lit streets until we tired out. Our feet pattered the cobblestones as we zoomed past closed shops, sparklers in hand illuminating our wicked grins.

The night crept closer to dawn, and the kids and I returned to the house, where the adults drew team lines and set up Syrian card games that had more at stake than all the money in TV poker. I studied their plays, teaming up with my aunts to learn their strategy as they fought for their pride. One day, I dreamed, I'd hold my own set of cards.

The summer of 2010 in Syria, I opened my heart to everyone in my family. Our humor, our habits, our love languages were the same. It was easy to love them and let them love me.

Mama laughed harder with her sisters than with anyone else in her life. She was soft and kind, the love of her own mother contagious. Baba took off work to be there. Zain never stayed cooped up in a room. He played soccer and swam and shot fireworks with our cousins. He was himself. I relive them this way nearly every night, in my recurring dream born out of a memory.

Then it was time to say goodbye. Our time in Syria had come to an end.

I wept like a baby that last night. I weep in my dream, too. My cousins comforted me with teasing smiles and glints in their eyes. "Stop crying, you'll be back next summer," my aunts and uncles said. It was a promise. A guarantee. Yet that year their words didn't comfort me. Maybe in the back of my mind, I knew it would be my last time there.

That's where the memory ends and the dream turns into a nightmare. In that courtyard surrounded by my family, they disappear one by one. First my cousins, then my aunts and uncles, and finally my teteh and grandpa fade away, too. Their absence rustles the leaves. A fog in the night erases my family, and I begin to sob.

In my nightmare, Baba and Zain vanish as well. My mother prevails in the end, standing with her arms outstretched under the spindly lemon tree. I let tears sear my cheeks and my tight throat choke my breath, and I do not embrace her.

That is when I wake up, as I always do from this nightmare, with a stone in my gut, blaming my mother for making them leave me. Poof. Just like that. Why else would she be the only one left?

"Wake up, habibti!" This time, it's my mother's high-pitched voice that rips my eyelids open. The light from outside singes my retinas. She's already opened my velvet floor-length curtains and begun to gather my gym clothes off the ground.

"Rise and shine! A morning of blessings! The Prophet said those who rise early are blessed!"

"I sleep in one day of the week, Mama." I turn over and pull the duvet over my face.

"Don't be lazy!"

So much pep. As if we didn't witness a traumatic episode yesterday. My mother sweeps everything that isn't perfect up and away.

Mama is nimble, and she pounces on clutter. I think clutter adds character. She thinks it's a reflection of the mind. I don't see the problem. She starts rummaging through my drawers.

"I woke up at seven o'clock and guess who was awake? Zain!" Way to let me guess. "We sat and ate breakfast together and I was so thrilled."

"Zain ate breakfast with you?" I grunt in disbelief.

"Well," Mama says, "he ate his cereal next to me while I drank my tea."

"Next to you?"

"Well, not directly next to me, but nearby. He sat at the island, and I was at the dining table, and even Baba walked in for a few minutes before he went to work! We *talked*, too!"

"You talked?"

She's checking under my bed, and her voice is muffled. "We exchanged some words." She pauses. "Don't doubt your brother, Khadija."

I want to say I doubt her and not Zain, but I think better of it. Also, she's swallowing my sheets up in her arms while I'm lying on them and it's dragging me off my bed. I refuse to get up, so I slide off the sheets but keep my duvet with me. I groggily reach for my pillow, but she seizes it just in time.

"Khadija, I'm worried." She sounds enthused, though. "Dana told me she caught her son smoking in his room. You know her son. He's in Zain's grade. And not sheesha, the real stuff that they wrap themselves."

"Mama, they roll it, not wrap, and it's all real," I inform her. "What if Zain was smoking sheesha? Is that okay?"

Mama hesitates. "I'd understand why he does it. All the boys think it's cool. Some of their fathers do it, too."

"What if I smoked sheesha?"

There's a pause and I raise my mop of a head to catch her reaction. Mama's grip on my pillow tightens. She squints at me, probably replaying my behavior over the last year through her mind to see if she missed something. Finally, she says, "You'd be grounded for a month, and I'd blame it on all that time with boys in the gym."

"Double standards!" I cry, and now I'm up because my mother doesn't have the self-awareness to admit it.

Mama latches on to my wrist. "If you see Zain doing

anything weird at school, dating, drugs, that kind of stuff, you tell me, okay?"

"I never see Zain at school. Like ever. He probably avoids me like I do him, and we're both really good at it because we never ever see each other."

"I'm worried about him, Khadija," Mama says again, but this time stoically, eyes deep in thought.

"There's nothing to worry about," I reply, picking out the cleanest gym clothes from Mama's laundry pile. "He's too shy to do anything dangerous."

She shifts her gaze to me, and words threaten to leap off her tongue, but she holds them back.

I raise an eyebrow at her. "Unless there's something going on with Zain that you're not telling me about."

"Mama?"

We both flinch when we hear Zain's broken voice from the hallway. Mama alters her worried expression to light her face up like a Christmas tree for her son. "Yes, habibi?" Her grin attempts to lure him in.

"Come in," I offer. "Apparently there's a family meeting in my room this morning."

But Zain just rubs his hand over his recently buzzed hair, always so elusive.

"Someone's at the door for you," he says to Mama, his voice terribly shaky, like it's out of practice. I blink and he vanishes from the room as soon as he delivers the message.

"Thank you, habibi!" Mama yells after him, watching him go with extra pride for relaying the simple message. Her apprehension ricochets to fascination anytime Zain breathes in her direction. Mama's eyes find mine again and she tosses my greasy curls with a frown.

"Who's here this time?" I ask with an audible sigh.

"Enough," Mama tuts. "First, I want you to go check on Leene downstairs. I made them a simple breakfast because I'm sure they won't have the energy to make anything for themselves. We should give them privacy right now, but it's a nice gesture."

"It's your nice gesture. Why don't you take it to them?" I pose the question like a genius suggestion rather than with the dread of having to confront whatever emotions were unlocked yesterday.

Mama waves me away. "Fix your hair, take the Tahers' meal downstairs, and then join me for breakfast. We have a visitor."

God bless. I can't have a single morning in this house to myself without someone coming over to discuss renovation plans or charity work with Mama. And she'll drag me into it for a salaam and make me sit by her side like a proper Syrian daughter, a puppet in her play.

I didn't mentally prepare for socializing this morning, so plotting my escape I say, "I'm going to Jerr's."

"Laa, the fighting gym is closed on Super Bowl Sunday,"

Mama chirps on her way out. God bless. How does she know that?

I throw my short hair up into a ponytail but stay in my jersey because I'll always rep my quarterback, Dak Prescott. No Rolls-Royce–driving khaleh strutting into this house can change that.

I scavenge for a pair of socks and sweatpants that survived Mama's detection and grab my keys and a scarf. Even with Mama's hyper cleaning, my room is still mostly me. While my mind is mapped out beyond our red, white, and blue shores, I will always have two all-American loves: boxing and football.

My closet is stuffed with Muhammad Ali, Mike Tyson, and Cowboys posters and memorabilia, but I don't stick them up in my room. *They aren't appropriate for you*, she would say.

That didn't sit well with me at all. So, with many swipes of my conceding mother's credit card, I converted my room into an ode to Syria. A jumbo Syrian flag covers one wall—the revolution's flag with the three red stars and not the two green ones. I have burned the other flag on occasion. Adorning another wall is a mosaic of tiles imported from Turkey but made by Syrian textile workers who were driven out of Halab. Floor to ceiling, they create a backdrop to my hanging plants identical to the ones my aunt has hanging by the fountain in the courtyard.

On the third wall hangs a canvas painting of the Umayyad

Masjid, the Great Mosque of Damascus, where we would pray after an exhausting day at the souk, a neighborhood mosque that is also a historically revered structure. From its minarets to the detailed arabesques in the stone relief to its rows of arches and courtyard of white marble, the mosque commands presence in my room. Above the painting, in ornamental Arabic calligraphy, a verse from the Qur'an in light-beige paint: *And be patient over what befalls you*. It's what I first see when I wake up from my nightmare.

My room is my Damascus in Detroit.

I shut the door and sneak downstairs. The voices of Mama and her friend travel through the house from the foyer. Pulling some stealth moves that Younes would be proud of, I slink into and out of the kitchen unseen. And since I am not the worst daughter on planet Earth, I stop by Teteh's bedroom and knock. When I don't hear an answer, I knock again, then crack the door open to give myself a peek inside. The bed looks perfectly made, duvet and throw pillows expertly placed as if by Mama herself, so I stick my head in farther.

The room is empty. I let the door swing open. It's freshly vacuumed and dusted, the air settling back into the stagnance since Teteh left. My chest constricts at the sudden absence that floods in the place that Leene and Khaleh Rana occupied. Again, like my family, it feels like Leene and Khaleh Rana had never been here, completely erased by one of Mama's magic erasers.

My chest feels strangely empty, too. But Mama had asked me to bring them breakfast. They're still here, and by downstairs she must not have meant the ground floor, but the basement. Mama kept her side of the deal to move them down there when it was ready. If I didn't feel so funny, I'd be surprised. I turn away from the room, but not before I notice the faintest smell. Teteh's smell. Of jasmine and rosewater.

I pause with my hand on the doorknob. My eyes linger on the room, as if the subtle smell could procure her from nowhere. Finally, I carefully close the door to Teteh's room.

Delivering the tray of jibne and zaatar mana'eesh to the top of the stairs leading to the basement, I stare below but do not go down.

On my way out of the house, I see Leene's and Khaleh Rana's shoes at the door. There isn't the usual flare of irritation at the image.

I get into my car and shut out the brisk February chill. As I turn out of the driveway, my chest slowly fills up again.

A lot has been taken from me, most traces of my family wiped as if by magic, but at least Teteh's room is the same. Still like jasmine and rosewater.

13

Khadija

I drive everywhere I can think of, from ranting at Nassima's house to frowning at a glittering lake in the frigid cold to aisle surfing at the Prime Sports on Dye. As my gas gauge flirts with *E*, I give in to driving myself home, but my mind brings me here. The one place I know is closed on Super Bowl Sunday.

I put the car in reverse, when my eye catches on movement in the gym. I park and launch myself out of the car, tapping on the glass until Younes's quizzical expression meets mine. His slanted smile appears as fast as his right cross.

He opens the door and hurriedly shuts it behind me to keep out the cold. "Kadiii." My name is lax on his tongue, and my chest squeezes as I hang my jacket on the hook wall. He's got his usual workout attire on: an oversize shirt and black joggers. Today, his shirt is a deep green, my favorite color on him.

"I thought the gym was closed today. Breaking and entering

isn't a good look," I say while securing my left glove around my forearm.

"Jerr gave me the keys to train in exchange for some cleanup." His voice is close. I look up, expecting him to be across the room finishing up whatever he was tidying, but he's an arm's length away. His eyebrows shoot up as he looks at my jersey. "You traitor."

"Traitor?" I repeat incredulously.

"The Cowboys, even on this sacred American holiday?"

I laugh, feeling light for the first time in a while. "The Cowboys every day so long as I'm breathing on God's green earth."

Betrayal paints itself across his face. "Oh, that may be a deal breaker for me."

I smirk while fastening the other glove with my teeth. "Why, what are we negotiating?"

"I'm negotiating with myself," he says, then takes my other glove in his hand. His fingertips flit against the thin fabric of my shirt as he helps me with the glove. "Trying to see where to place you."

When the glove is secured, I stiffly retract my arm, distinctly remembering what Nassima said about the way he looks at me. Is that a sparkle in his eye or just the lights in the gym?

I frame my face with my gloved hands and grin. "You can't place me anywhere. I go where I want."

He chuckles softly. "I guess that's the problem. You like walking straight into hearts."

"Into hearts?" I reel. Dammit, maybe there *is* a sparkle in his eye when he's around me. "Are you sure you got the right girl?"

"You are Khadija-is-actually-soft-under-all-those-spikes-Shaami, right?"

"Never heard of her."

Younes rolls his eyes playfully, jumping into the ring. "You wanna spar?" he asks.

I jump in after him and raise my gloves around my head. I try to gauge what Nassima sees, but all I see are his kind eyes looking at me like he does everything else.

"Would you call this fair?" I gesture to the difference in our height.

He leans into his boxing stance, the sinews of his muscles tightening, his angles dripping with assuredness. "If you play it right," he replies.

I smirk. "I meant fair for you."

Younes lets out a laugh. "There's that Kadi confidence I love."

The butterflies in my stomach flutter. Younes finds it so easy to use words like *love* and *hearts*, and I'm left floundering. He is open while I am tightly closed. It's a good thing he likes a challenge.

We skirt around each other. He slips from my jab. I dip at his cross that I see coming from a mile away.

I narrow my eyes. "You're acting slow. Is this how you compete?"

"Won't happen again. Promise." He bumps gloves with me. Such a tease.

I throw a cross and a hook that he evades with ease. His speed lands him a five-punch combination that he executes lightly on my shoulder, torso, and side of my head. It's over before I realize I've been hit.

"You're going easy on me," I say.

"I'm not going to hit you," he answers while circling me in his enviable boxing stance. "I drop guys weighing in at one eighty. And what are you? Like a hundred pounds?"

I laugh so hard that he manages to graze my chin with a fake uppercut. "A hundred pounds?" He wouldn't know, he doesn't have any sisters. He's the oldest of three boys—I must be an education for him. I wipe the corners of my eyes, pretending to rub off tears of laughter. "We need to get your eyes checked. And maybe take you to a nutrition class."

He chuckles to himself. "Is that not realistic?"

"Not even close."

"Still not going to hit you."

"Why not?"

"Because you're not being realistic, either."

"I can take a hit," I say defiantly.

"Oh, I know," he taunts me, tapping his gloves over my shoulders, dragging them over my hips, tracing my curves. I shiver. His gloves travel back up, falling around my shoulders, pulling me close to him. My face burns, and I swear on the Qur'an he's blushing.

I throw a weak jab that misses its mark. He twists my gloved arms in his own. His arms are strong, and though I'm nervous as hell in this disjointed gloved embrace, I feel safe. It's been so long since I've felt safe with someone. A moment when I'm not feeling attacked.

Right now the only things attacking me are my feelings.

"What are you—"

"Close the distance when your opponent is bigger than you. If you keep your distance, I can land my punches, but you'll be swiping at the air." He releases me from his glove hold, but I don't pull away. "Stay close, and my long reach is useless."

I lift my eyes to his, flushed that I'd been staring at his chest as he talked. I wish there were no gloves.

Muslim crushes are the worst.

The intimacy of having close male relationships is kind of counterintuitive to the whole "only date to marry" Muslim concept. Younes and I have been friends all this time, so it's not a big deal. Jerr's is also a buffer halal zone with plenty of people always around. But if this becomes more, I don't know what to do.

I try to step back, but I stumble over my own feet, and Younes's arms are there to catch me. When I look up, our noses are almost touching. I stare into his eyes, which are such a deep brown I forget that I'm hanging there in his arms. I straighten up out of his hold, putting a little distance between us. We stare anywhere but at each other.

He breaks the silence first. "Do you know why I like you? Because even when the odds are stacked up against you, it's like you don't even see them. You just see your goal and you go for it no matter what."

"Y-you like me?" It's like my brain stopped at those words.

"Someone had to say it first," he murmurs. "We can't be flirting gym buddies for the rest of our lives."

I choke out laughter because he took such a hard left out of the friend zone that I'm suffering whiplash. What can I say, I laugh when I'm in pain.

"Why are you telling me this now?" I ask, always cautious in the ring.

He takes his right glove off with his teeth, and then the other. "You know that I put my all into everything I do, right?"

I do. He takes AP classes and participates in more clubs than I can remember. He maintains a high GPA, and everyone that knows him can rely on him to show up for any event or function for support. On top of school, extracurriculars, and boxing, he always makes it to his younger brothers' soccer games or piano recitals. I know Younes puts his all into everything he does, but he also carries the burden of it all and hides it from others. So I say yes even though the expectations he puts on himself are too much for a kid.

"I like you, Kadi, and I'd like to give you my all," he says, a smile on his lips. "The Cowboys and the Lions aside."

My mind races, trying to rework his confession, to find the punchline of a joke that I'm missing. But I stop myself short. In my life of complications, I want this to be simple.

Younes is right. I never let the odds get to me—I only see my goal. In many ways, Younes is like me. Competitive, ambitious, blindly confident. But in other ways, he's everything I want to be. Open, free, abundantly compassionate.

And I like that about him.

"I like you, too," I say breathlessly.

Younes grins his wide smile that hides nothing, and I won't lie, I feel a little sick, but I think that's just a side effect of speaking feelings into the world. That's how I know they're real.

And now they're something I need to protect. Which means I need time to warm my mother up to the idea of this so that I can keep it.

Okay, think, think, think, Khadija. One can never be ready for when her first crush makes a move, and my skills lie in repelling others, not attracting them. If he starts this with me, I don't know what comes next. If I have a more-than-friendship with Younes, I'll have to deal with my mother's opinions about us. Relationships with boys of my choosing aren't in Mama's rule book. Or they're in her locked files, and I'm not at that level yet even though Younes just expedited the process.

Until now, I played the long game with Mama. Little by little, I tried to gain her trust and to be respected for my small choices, but I feel the pressure from wanting a halal relationship with Younes, wanting to travel with Nassima, and to not be compared to Leene. Maybe there's a way to fly under her radar, unquestioned about my choices because she's already happy with me as a whole.

And there's one person my mother is so deeply pleased with that, with her help, I can balance the scales.

With Leene in my corner, I can get on Mama's good side. The only winning side.

14

Leene

Since arriving in the United States, I have never felt more like my old self.

Pain and grief are my longtime companions. For the three weeks that I've been living in this fairy-tale castle, I've kept them at bay. But they didn't vanish when I pushed them to the corners of my mind. I wasn't prepared for when they resurfaced.

In this room in this basement, I have all the space in the world. The bed is enormous, clean water runs from the faucet, the walls insulate the heat that flows endlessly from vents. On the first floor, amid the luxury, I allowed myself to forget for the sake of moving on. But in this room in this basement, with its prim furniture and simple window that overlooks a corner of the snow-covered garden, I have no distractions. In this room in this basement, I have no choice but to remember.

The grief didn't return in stages. It burst through a cell-phone screen in a picture that shouldn't be real.

Seeing the little boy in the blue blanket on the orphanage's site gives my world a whole new filter, and I don't know how to live in it. Mustafa's blue blanket, Baba's curls, his scar, the resemblance to Mama. Akh, how he has aged. At an orphanage, alone, he aged.

No matter how I turn the semantics over in my head, an orphanage is a place where children without families live. Children who've lost their families, or in Mustafa's case, children whose families lost them.

The probability that Mustafa hadn't been dead as we rowed away from him, the proof in the picture that he lived beyond the sea, changes everything. By the waves of my misfortune Mustafa can't and couldn't have survived. Yet the photo of my little brother in Jordan means he's out there. He, impossibly, survived the sea.

But he's not here with me, and it's all my fault. I left him there thinking he was dead. When I placed my head by his mouth, I felt no air. How could he have been breathing so quietly, undetectably, that I was confident enough to leave him? I must not have been in my right mind.

No. A child as cold as ice should not have survived that sea while healthy young men and women didn't.

Yet here he is, on my screen, a full year older.

I should have held on longer. Mama felt it in her bones. Her wails were justified.

In the sea, I had to make a decision. I chose wrong.

Did a sailor go back and notice something I didn't? Did he get sick? Could he be healthy after freezing? If he got on the cargo ship with us, why did we not cross paths?

Why does the world insist on being cruel?

In this room in this basement, I feel the weight of the house crush me. I did not move on; I could not move on. This was only temporary, a lapse in my nightmare, a moment where I thought I could dream. I turn in my bed, the sheets too soft, the bed too comfortable. I shut my eyes, willing myself to sleep.

It must be midday because Mama is getting dressed to go out for a training for work. She tells me I should get up and eat something. She tells me the doctors said I am okay now and not to worry. She can say this because she doesn't know what I know. And Mama can never know, because if she knew, she would not be able to look at me. Because I am the girl who left her brother alone in the cold sea and dared to move on.

15

Khadija

When I get home the tray of food is still at the top of the stairs to the basement. And maybe it's divine intervention or just big-brain thinking, but not for unselfish reasons, I take the tray and go down to Khaleh Rana and Leene's room.

The basement is like its own apartment. It has a living room area, a guest room, and a kitchen with the essentials. The house is on a little hill, so one side of the basement has a few windows to let in light, making it more than homey. I notice a few new plates in the kitchen, maybe because Mama revamped the place or because Khaleh Rana went out for some things after work.

I reach the guest room and rap the door twice. No answer. When there isn't an answer the second time, I pause to reconsider.

Then it really must be divine intervention because it compels me to open the door and peek in.

No one's inside. I let the door swing open and place the tray on the dresser. Mama really held back on the interior decorating in here. There's a bed, a dresser, a nightstand, a lamp. It's clean and simple and it could be anyone's room except their luggage sits in a corner with a pile of folded clothes. I turn to leave when my eyes catch some pictures on the nightstand.

I should respect their privacy, but my curiosity wins over my manners. I take ahold of the pictures frame by frame, the edges of each photo cracked, the colors blanched. In one picture, there's a stretched smile I recognize as Leene's and an older boy who shares her eye shape and dimples. An older man who could be her dad waves at the camera from behind them. Another shows a much older Leene in hijab holding a baby in a barely blue blanket in her arms. My mind wanders to the people in the photographs, the man who had to be her father, the boy who could be her brother, and the baby she carried with such pride in her arms. But Khaleh Rana had said she had no sons. Maybe they're Leene's cousins, memories that she wanted to keep close to her chest like I do with mine.

The light-blue blanket around the baby gives me pause. I stared at that photo from the orphanage for what felt like hours last night. The blanket in that picture looks like the same one around this boy, and the scar is strikingly familiar. Which could only mean...

I bring it closer to get a better look, but my mind is racing fast. Too late I realize that the sound humming in my head is the faucet running in the bathroom. It cuts out.

I freeze. The bathroom door opens and Leene steps out, face freshly washed. Her expression, already exhausted, crumples as her eyes shift from me to the picture in my hand. Guilt grips me. Leene rushes at me, snatching the picture from me and scooping the remaining photos into the drawer. She shuts it and wedges herself between me and the nightstand, guarding the drawer with her life.

Her eyes brim with tears, and worry paints her face. She looks like she's hiding something. She looks as guilty as me.

Any curiosity I had abandons me.

This isn't a museum. It's not a place open for viewing. I trespassed into her life, into a safe place where she hides her secrets from the world. I should know best about the secrets Arabs keep within the walls of their home.

I don't know why I came down here. It wasn't plain curiosity or an innocent gesture. Maybe I wanted proof that Leene isn't the Miss Teen Damascus that Mama has built up in her head. That just like me, Leene has her own secrets that make her imperfect. But aside from finding the proof that we are more alike than different, I discover the product of my spite.

I retreat to the door for a shameful escape.

16

Leene

*W*ait." My voice cracks. The growing distance between Khadija and the photos I conceal from her allows me to breathe easier, but the easier I breathe the less strength I have to hold in the tears. The secrets the photos could reveal grip me with fear, and yet I don't want her to go.

I want her to know, I realize, and the walls around my heart crack. I want this American girl who knows nearly nothing about me to know my deepest regret.

"I should go." She recoils, her expression stony and her voice clipped. "I shouldn't have barged into your room."

Her eyes dart to the nightstand again, and my hands begin to shake. I want to stand watch over it, guarding what is inside forever. A good hostess would pull out the photos, talk about them and ease the atmosphere, but none of the stories hidden there have that kind of power.

I open my mouth to speak, but a strangled cry escapes instead. Khadija's eyes widen in horror at my outpour of emotion. My ingrained etiquette orders me to rein it all back in, but all I can think about is Mustafa.

I am surprised that Khadija stays until I find my voice. "I need your—"

Help. The word tastes bitter on my tongue, and I can't say it to Khadija. The hope that Mustafa may be alive out there has paralyzed me, but it's not the only reason I struggle with the word. Leene Taher used to be a need-no-help girl. The word used to not come easily onto my lips.

Baba used to heckle me into using training wheels to learn how to ride a bicycle, but I refused. I wanted to learn to ride a bike without the help, so I got on that two-wheeler every day and fell. I never did learn to ride it, but at least my pride remained intact.

My journey out of Syria broke that part of me.

The more help I accepted, the more of me washed away.

When I ask for help, I accept my status as refugee. When I left Jordan, I vowed to stop describing myself with that label. *Refugee* implies the need for aid, and I'm too proud, as many refugees are, to ask for help.

I'm Syrian first, and Syrians always figure a way out on their own with what they have. When Baba and Abood were gone, I had to get Mama, Mustafa, and myself out of Syria. I did, and I did it without any guidance. But look where that got Mustafa.

By the time we were planning to move to America, the

problems were too big for me. I had to yield and accept help. I became helpless.

The Mustafa situation is no different. There is no more hope for moving on. I need to unpack this monster of a problem and Khadija is my only option because Khadija doesn't give a damn about anything, and definitely not me. She isn't going to pity me and cry about my story. She might have a mental breakdown if even a tear falls out of her eye. At least, that's what I hope.

Because if that's the case, then I can tell her about Mustafa.

But first, wiping at my eyes and clearing my throat, I buy myself some time. "Do I make you uncomfortable?"

Khadija's eyebrows hike up, and she crosses her arms over her chest. "Why would you think that?"

"You avoid me," I say. "I thought we would be friends when I saw you, but you don't seem to want that."

Khadija shrugs. She's guarded. We both are.

"Is it because I'm a *refugee*?" My voice dips at the word.

Though I would like to believe that I'm more than a refugee despite what it means, the word still tastes sour on my tongue. As a refugee the assumption is that I'm pitiable, and a reminder of other people's entitlement. I don't want to be that for Khadija or for anyone. It's what I call self-scapegoating.

"Maybe," she says lightly, "you're just not as likable as you think."

I try to smile, but it feels like a grimace.

Khadija shifts uncomfortably. "But what about that semantics crap you were talking about before? Doesn't the word *refugee* mean something different to everyone? Context and all that?"

I blink at her, tears stinging my eyes for another reason. I am a refugee. A refugee skilled in Syrian etiquette and nuanced with my language.

I am also a survivor. A daughter. A possible friend.

I lower my mask in front of her. My strained politeness won't work on Khadija. Her forced indifference won't work on me, either. I can trust Khadija, this American girl with a glint in her eyes that emanates reliance.

I open the top drawer of the nightstand. My hands tremble as I clutch the simple wooden frame over my chest. I turn the picture up to her. Baba's fat mustache takes up one-third of the picture because of the wide smile underneath its curtain. My black hair and thick bangs that I sported at eight years old are smushed against Baba's cheek. Ten-year-old Abdul Rahman, my older brother, my Abood with his head full of curls who goofed off just as much as he tried taking care of others, poses like a praying mantis behind us.

The girl I used to be is on full display in this picture. Mustafa was the end of this girl. Abood was the beginning of her. I'm not ready to tell Khadija about Abood, but Mustafa cannot remain a secret.

"I'm from Douma," I begin. "In the outskirts of Damascus. It's infamous because of the revolution. Now, it's a ghost town. When we lived there, Mama would often get this grippe where she would get ill and not be able to leave bed for days. Sometimes weeks. She didn't want to leave Syria, but I knew we had to if she was going to get better. She couldn't be in a place where we lost so much."

Over time, I'd bartered some sanity for closure on Baba's and Abood's fates. And Mustafa's death, until now. I pull another picture out of the drawer. I'm in hijab several years later, and I cradle Mustafa, wrapped in his embroidered baby-blue blanket. The scar that slices his eyebrow is clear. It was taken a few weeks after a glass shard from a shattered light bulb slashed his brow and a few months before we set sail on the cursed voyage.

I pass the photo to Khadija and hold my breath.

She grabs her phone, pulling up the orphanage's site. She glances between her phone and the photo.

"Is it the same blanket?" she murmurs, eyes focused. "Are you saying this is him?

No pity, no pity, no pity. I gulp, and my eyes well up. Thankfully, she doesn't touch my arm or ask if I need anything. I don't want any empathy. That's why Khadija is the perfect person. She'll soon learn that I left my baby brother for dead in the heart of the sea, and she'll call me out on my sins.

I cry into my hands, and I unleash all the water that has built up from the heartache of the last forever. A scalpel has been cutting into my heart for years. The master surgeon specializing in heartbreak performs the perfect incision into my heart. The image of my baby brother provided the surgeon with the final push to rip through the cold heart that left Mustafa floating in the sea.

Khadija lets me cry.

"Without a doubt, it's him." I choke out the words. "He isn't a doppelgänger who's just meant to torment me. He is my brother. He is Mustafa."

Her eyes flit between mine as she tries to find words. "But how?"

There's worry in her expression. The look doesn't suit her. She's been the strong American girl until now. Her shift gives me courage.

I cover my face with my hands, and my brain filters nothing. I tell her everything, from the second that we got on the fishing trawler all the way until the sailor's face that gave me the false courage to leave my brother floating on the plank of wood, and the clarity with which I made that choice.

"The sailor and I were so sure. He was blue and still as the dead. He looked exactly like the other dead children floating in the waves except he was on that wooden plank. I put my cheek by his face and felt nothing. I thought he was gone. Those aren't excuses. I'm not excusing myself. I'm a monster for leaving my baby brother. I should have felt it in my bones that he was alive. Mama felt it. I should have, too."

I take the picture from Khadija's limp hands. Her eyes fixated on the wall, she looks deep in thought. "Why—"

"Why did he survive?" I complete her question. "I'm trying to figure it out. When I play it through my head, the sailors returned to the wreck and rechecked the victims again and noticed something that I didn't. The ship was so large, if he made it on, if he went to the infirmary while I was with the cargo, I could never have known. How he got sent back to Jordan, how we got separated by countries, I'll never really know."

We'd completed the voyage together only to be separated on land.

Khadija tilts her head. "No, why are you telling me this? I mean shouldn't you tell your mom? Tell my mom? Someone who can actually do something about this?"

I shudder. "I could never tell Mama. Unless Mustafa is in my arms, it would break her before she could accept it."

"But this is proof."

My gut twists. "I know, but I know Mama. I know Mama better than anyone else. And I know that if she found out that we left him, she won't be able to live with herself. She lost so much already. I never thought she'd make it this far. She's finally found peace with herself after all that we went through. After Mustafa, in Germany, she couldn't live with herself. If I show her that she didn't have to lose her baby, I fear what will happen to her."

Quiet settles around us. Impossibly beneath this fairy-tale house, I feel lighter.

"So what will you do?" she asks, straight to business. And while I am not done beating myself up about losing Mustafa, it helps that Khadija is not dwelling on my mistakes. "We can tell my mom," she suggests. "She knows people. She can help you."

My heart drops, and my voice comes out gruff. "Laa. Please no. She won't keep it a secret. And I already feel like a burden."

She purses her heart-shaped lips as she thinks. "So then you want to find him on your own? Do you want my help?"

Help.

There's this stereotype that Syrians have of the Western foreigner ever since the war started. The foreigner finds our pain and suffering fascinating and walks through our streets that they call a war zone in a bulletproof vest, taking pictures at a distance. When they go back to where they're from, they share their discoveries, and everyone applauds them for being cultured and brave. The foreigner takes a snapshot of the story they want to tell about Syria.

There will always be this fear that when we tell our stories they won't be the whole truth. But Khadija heard what I did, and now when she thinks of me, she'll see me in the context of my errors. She'll project her understanding onto this version of me that I live every day regretting.

That's the thing about semantics: It shows that we only ever have a part of the story, and no one sticks around long enough to hear the rest of it. Maybe Khadija won't be like others, and I have to trust that she will be here until the end.

Khadija sighs and makes her way to the door. "I can help," she says simply. "We can figure out the details later. But for the love of God come upstairs and watch the Super Bowl with us. It's the Syrian thing to pretend everything's okay and perfect. Don't want our moms to get the wrong idea."

Then she goes off ahead of me and I breathe in and out for what feels like the first time since the pool yesterday. Because I was right. Khadija does not have spare pity to offer me. Out of everyone, she is the only one I could trust with this secret. Khadija the American, the stranger, the brash and bold girl who doesn't care what anyone tells her. Khadija, my possible friend.

17

Khadija

"What the hell!" Mama's the one who says it, not me. "Does he have butterfingers? He can't catch a football!"

"Our quarterback is too slow in the pocket." I tsk at the screen.

"Wallah, you're right," she agrees.

"I don't understand. Bowls, quarters, backs, butter, fingers. Pockets? You're not making this up, are you?" Leene murmurs from the armchair.

I smirk. Football craps all over Leene's semantics. She lounges on the armchair close to the television, her face as pale as ever. We exchange a look, and it says it all. The knowledge that she's acting and we're the only two in on it takes away any uncertainty I had toward her.

Her attention ping-pongs from the game to our mother-daughter commentary. Her presence instantly improved Mama's mood. We haven't fought once. We even chose the same team to root for since the Cowboys aren't available.

"They're football words." Zain's low voice comes from behind me. I jump and so does Leene. I should really stop being surprised when I see him here. After all, this is his home.

Leene's expression softens. "You can sit with us," she offers shyly, pointing to the armchair beside hers.

Zain obeys instantly. I gape at him, aware of the fact that he wouldn't have blinked twice had it been my invitation. Mama leans over to me. "See how she's aware of others? Very considerate mashallah."

I swallow my words, a very choice comeback that rhymes with "I don't give a ship," but then I remember Younes, my mother's acceptance, and my freedom.

"Fourth down, dammit!" I redirect her attention.

"Dammit!" Mama parrots after me.

I giggle. Football is our middle. Too bad it's the end of the season.

After an impressive fourth down conversion and a tackle so intense that the mics pick up the sound of collision, Leene turns away from the television. Her face is paler than usual, and I wonder if she's seeing another memory.

I lean back out of her view and nod along to Mama's grumbles about the defense. I hear Leene introduce herself to Zain.

"You don't like American football?" she asks.

"No," he responds at a surprisingly human speed. His departure from sloth reactions halves my attention between the game and the two of them while Mama remains absorbed by the television.

Leene launches into an interrogation, gaining strength from Zain's presence. "You go to Rochester Heights High School? Do you like it there? Will I see you there when I start school tomorrow? Will you drive with us to school tomorrow?" That catches my attention and Leene glances my way nervously. Us? She did say *us* just then, right?

The confusion must be plastered all over my face because she glances at me and retracts. "I just thought I'd go to school with you because, well, I thought, but maybe not, I—"

She's not wrong; Mama will lump us together for school rides. I fix my eyes on the game. "No, he doesn't go with *us* to school. We're not those kinds of siblings," I murmur, not looking her way and grateful that Mama's consumed by the game from the opposite couch. "He made me late so many times last year, and now we don't do that anymore."

"If I had a brother, I'd do everything I could with him," Leene whispers. A week ago, I would have perceived that as a jab, but now I know better. My chest folds in on itself in response.

Leene pesters Zain with nonsense questions about school, classes, hobbies. She almost passes as totally fine, and I have to admit I'm impressed that she's an expert at pretending. She could be an actress, but she's really just a skilled Syrian girl.

Classic Zain masterfully evades further questions by keeping his mouth shut and miming responses. Mama nudges me again.

"What?"

"See how she tries with him? Take notes," she advises, her eyebrows arching toward Leene and Zain.

I turn my head away from her before I roll my eyes. "Does it look like I have a pen and paper?"

"I'll get you some," Mama replies, and leaves the room. I wish I had any more disbelief to spare, but my mother's perseverance knows no limits.

Then, shockingly, I hear Zain ask Leene a question: "Where are you from in Syria?" He pronounces *Syria* with the heavy American *R*, and I cringe. But I have to give kudos to Leene for breaking through his caveman-signs-and-grunts barrier.

"I'm from Douma," she says. "Do you know it?"

Zain and I nod. Douma is the city where Bashar Al-Assad dropped chemical weapons on his own citizens to stop them from protesting his oppressive regime.

Bashar Al-Assad — politician — ba-shaar al-as-sad — /bə'ʃaːr ɪlɛsɛd/: crooked man who inherited the Syrian presidency from his father in 2000.

Bashar Al-Assad — aka the bane of my existence: Syrian dictator who uses any means of silencing opposition against his family's reign of forty-seven years and counting.

Douma wasn't the first city he attacked. Sarin gas spread

over the city, infecting everyone without judgment. Men, women, old, young, grandparents, babies. No one came away from the attack untouched. I wonder how Leene made it out alive.

"You guys are from the heart of Damascus, the Midan, aren't you?" she asks.

Zain nods, then mutters, "Do you think you'll go back?" I'm enraptured by the attention he bestows upon her, but then again, she did skillfully coax him out of his shell. I glance back at her.

Leene's gaze is intense, unfocused on me, yet piercing through me. She's eerily still. "There isn't anything to go back to."

I make the mistake of glancing over at Zain, who broods with his shoulders arched and the collar of his shirt crushed between his fingers. Syria is a touchy subject in the Shaami household. It's not about the Syrian customs or identity that we're supposed to claim, it's the times that we spent there that are sacred. We remember those times, but we never *ever* discuss them. Back then, Zain used to smile every time he entered a room. He laughed at everything, even when it wasn't particularly funny. These days I can't remember the last time he looked me in the eye, let alone smiled around me. He's changed so much.

"Turnover!" Mama claps dramatically at the television as she reenters the room. She takes her seat quickly, fumbling to hand the pen and paper over to me. I take them from her with all the grace of handling raw chicken legs.

I try to return my attention to the game, but thinking about Zain has me in a mood. I don't remember when he stopped watching football with Mama and me. What's worse, I can't tell if he's actually stopped or if I just no longer noticed he was around, sitting with us silently, neglected in the background.

And I never minded when he withdrew. Maybe Mama is right. Maybe I'm not inherently good like Leene is, and maybe I never will be.

Leene does a one-eighty, opening up a conversation about her favorite movie. She tries to relay it to him: A girl dates the Joker for the sake of her sister's social life, an overprotective father giving pregnancy advice, and love born from intense hate.

It sounds like *10 Things I Hate About You* lost in translation, and Zain sits through Leene's entire replay. Zain's being around lifts Leene's spirits tenfold, and my brother, who shies away from everything, doesn't shy away from her. A thought creeps up on me: the knowledge that he wouldn't sit through a story narrated by me.

Because even with my own brother, Leene is winning. She must've forgotten what it's like to have an annoying younger brother or doesn't know because Mustafa was so young when she lost him.

I never felt responsible for my own brother, but maybe that's because Zain is right under my nose. Rochester Heights is a guaranteed safe zone, so Zain doesn't need my attention. He's not in any danger, though sometimes his hollowed cheekbones, colorless skin, and thin frame give me a fright as I pass by him wherever he's placed by Elf on the Shelf magic.

One day if my mother forgets to set him out, he'll be gone.

18

Khadija

*E*arly on the first Monday of every month, I join the other boxers around the ring, our heads tilted at Jerr with his clipboard. He assigns us our tasks for the next four weeks. God bless the new change. Last month, I was on toilet duty with one of the middle schoolers and I will never be the same. I pray for an upgrade for the month of February.

The gym is cheap, and some of the kids coming off the streets don't pay anything, so they, along with us regulars, pitch in to help Jerr with maintaining the place. This month I get paired with Younes on mats. He nudges me and half winks, half crinkles the side of his face, showing off his dimple. My heart does a little flip, and I feel like my cheeks are on fire. Just yesterday we said the three words to each other, and Younes has gone headfirst into full-on shameless flirting.

"Our annual showcase is in three months," Jerr announces. "Same rules apply as last year. We have tickets, so get out there and sell 'em." May will sneak up on us before we know it. The gym is free, but it relies on the showcase to bring in money and donors.

"What do we get out of it?" someone calls out.

Jerr glares in the boxer's direction. "It ain't about the money. It's about bringing people in. Last thing on your mind should be the prize money in your weight class." Someone agrees with the burn and there's snickering, but Jerr ignores it. "Show Detroit that boxing's about discipline. About your mind before you throw the punch."

"Told you," Younes whispers with a cheeky smirk. *Fight with your mind, Kadi.*

Jerr regroups. "You'll all be separated into your weight classes, and there are no coed fights. I only have enough in the reserves for one prize, so the boxer who is voted by the crowd as the best performer of the night across all weight classes wins the grand prize. Maybe that'll get your lazy asses to sell more tickets. It won't be prize money, but if you got ideas, come to me with 'em."

My overgreased gears shift into high gear. Best performer doesn't mean best boxer. Essentially, Jerr has created a popularity contest. If I sell the most tickets to people who I know, then they'll vote for me out of loyalty, and I'll have a chance to win the prize. Because if I don't, then Gab or Younes will wow the audience much more than me. We have a diverse gym with boxers from all kinds of backgrounds, but the crowd, like with a lot of sports, is always overwhelmingly white.

Jerr breaks the meeting, and I'm already up in the ring with him.

"Plane tickets."

He looks up from his clipboard like I didn't speak English.

"The grand prize should be plane tickets for this summer." My tongue practically trips over itself. While I'm still very much obsessed with this summer's trip, not talking Jerr's ears off with it might pay off in the long run. I continue when he doesn't seem keen, "I think everyone here would go for a pair of tickets."

"Then what?" Jerr drops out of the ring, and I follow him. "The kids won't have a place to stay. A ticket to Los Angeles gets you four days sleeping on the street."

I rework it. "Advertise it as a trip. All expenses paid. Then when one of us"—me—"wins, we plan the trip according to the cost of the ticket, housing, all that."

Jerr ponders it, and he even sets down the clipboard on meeting morning, which means I struck the right chord.

"Okay, I heard you, now get outta here."

That's as close as Jerr will ever get to saying yes straight to my face. That's his version of inshallah.

"I'll figure out the details for you," I say after him excitedly. "I'll make a spreadsheet and flyers and everything." Jerr not yelling at me to slow down seals the deal.

If I win a pair of tickets in my own right, I can loosen my mother's tight grip on buying and planning a trip. Even if I do pull this off, she will not lend a cent to me. But if I won these tickets, then Nassima and I could go anywhere.

And maybe while I'm at it, I can help Leene find her brother. The thought has occurred to me more than once since she told me he was out there.

I start to head to the showers, but the clock says I'm already late and I head for the front door. I gather my bags for what will be a stinky day at school.

"Why do you look so happy?" The voice is thick with judgment and sucks the spirit from my step. Whitney Sutton is, for all intents and purposes, my rival. Since Jerr doesn't encourage cross-sex boxing, Whit is my only competitor at the gym in my weight class. She pulls off judgy-yet-sweet white girl exceptionally well with her pixie cut and tiny upturned nose. She's totally nonmenacing until she slams you with a mean left hook.

"No reason," I bite out, willing her away.

"Looks like I'll have to put up the performance of the night. Say you'll help me," she requests with a pout on her thin lips.

"Your competitor makes you look your best in the ring if you're winning." I smile back without a trace of sincerity. "I hope you bring your game so I can show off my skills."

"Don't forget this is your first real match."

She's always reminding me she's the veteran. She stalks off to the showers before I can remind her that she can't even be in the women's locker room with me alone and now she'll have to be in the ring with me. You'd think the guys would get weirded out by your scarf more than the girls, but some girls cannot fathom a hijabi having the same parts as them. I will never forget how Whit stared at me when I first took my scarf off in the locker room. Some girls compliment my hair to break the ice, but she gaped at me like how-dare-I-be-normal.

I'm going to have to bring my A game to beat her.

I struggle to close my gym bag and I'm steps away from the door when I remember I didn't come here alone.

"Hey, Kadi." Younes approaches me, relaxed because he doesn't have class first hour and doesn't need to be across town in fifteen minutes. "Is she KGB?" he asks.

I follow his line of sight to the front door. Leene walks in wearing her gray coat and royal-blue hijab, taking in the energy around the gym with wide eyes. I agreed that she could snag a ride with me to school so long as she wakes up early enough to come along with me to my pre-school workouts.

My chest kind of deflates. "That's Leene," I tell him, "and if she is KGB, she's got one hell of an in into our lives." My mother will spill all of her top-secret family recipes and we'll have to live off the grid.

"Let's say hi." He's already walking over to her.

I catch up and for reasons beyond rational control, I try to stop him. "She's not—" my friend, I don't add. "We don't—" have that type of relationship. The words don't want to leave my mouth. Almost like they aren't true enough to be said anymore.

"Salaam." He waves at her and doesn't extend his hand. Smooth Ness. He knows what's up. If a hijabi extends their hand, then it's okay to go for the handshake. Leene doesn't, which is cool; I don't like to, either.

"Salaam." Leene smiles. Give this girl an Oscar already. Since the morning she's been wearing this warrior mask over her face. Only I can see the seams that hold her together. Still, she's cool and collected even in the gym. The first time I came in here I was sweating buckets and that was before the workout.

"You're Kadi's friend?" he asks.

"Kadi?" Leene looks between us.

Younes and I point at my face, but when he does it he smiles and squints at me like we're the only ones in the room, and I want to melt away.

Her face transforms with understanding. "Yes. I'm friends with Kadi." Her accented English can charm a snake, but I raise my eyebrows at her claim. It's a bit of a stretch. "Sorry, I didn't mean to come in," she says with a yawn. "You said you would be done by now and I was worried we'd be late for school."

"You go to our school?" Younes asks, gesturing between us. "RHHS?"

Leene nods. "Today is my first day."

"Well, don't sit in the car while you wait for Kadi," Younes says. Then he glances at me and pouts. "You didn't tell me you had someone waiting in the car for you."

"Because I tell you everything?" I ask, directing an arched eyebrow at him now.

"Sadly, no," he says with a mischievous tilt of his lips. "I'd like to know everything, though."

See, totally shameless. I blush, but hope it just looks like after-workout glow. "Too soon."

Younes's gaze slides toward Leene. "You should come in if you're with Khadija in the mornings. You don't need to box— there are other training sessions you can do."

Leene smiles. "Then I can be a boxer like John Cena?" She leans over to me like she's sharing a secret. "I loved watching John Cena in Syria."

My jaw drops, and my hand lands over my heart, simultaneously hurt and touched. "Leene. John Cena is a wrestler."

"I didn't know there was a difference," she says innocently.

"We can teach you the difference," Younes says with a chuckle. This boy can make friends with a mannequin if you leave him with one long enough.

I will him to stop. I may be slowly accepting Leene into my life, but the gym is my place. Our place, if I may be so bold.

"I don't know . . ." Leene peeks at me for a sign, and I widen my eyes as if to tell her no. I shake my head minutely.

"Stop that." Younes elbows me, catching on to my little signals. He looks back at Leene. "You should come. I'll help you with some self-defense. Kadi knows Jerr wants more people at the gym."

Leene hesitates because I stop with the signals. "I can't, I don't have money for it."

We're all nodding now, all for different reasons. Younes refuses to speak. He nudges me. I raise my eyebrows at him.

"The. Gym. Is. Free." He feeds me lines under his breath.

"You want to train KGB?" I whisper back. He nudges me again and we might as well say our vows and he may kiss the bride because this is way more touching than is normal for me. If he nudges me one more time Leene will assume we're secretly married, and my mother will find out and I'll have to join a convent and I'm not even Christian. He isn't having it, so I succumb: "The gym is free."

Leene looks around, and I don't blame anyone who walks in here and wants to start punching something immediately. The energy intoxicates. "Okay, I'll do it."

"I'll get you started," Younes offers, kind and welcoming as ever. He brings a sign-in sheet and gives her a quick tour. She even meets Jerr. Leene infiltrates my space, and I don't rage about it. I sense the runoff exhilaration of seeing the gym for the first time through Leene's eyes.

When she throws me a corny thumbs-up from across the gym, I can't help myself from smiling back at her. Of course, Leene could use this distraction. I need time to win those tickets, and we need to be smart about locating Mustafa. In the meantime, she can at least try to be normal.

For the first time since we met, I feel we aren't on opposing lines, just two girls passing each other and realizing we're on the same side of the battlefield.

We hurry out of the gym. In the car, I turn on my concoction of German and French songs, blast it through the speakers, and peel out of Jerr's parking lot. Through the light snow, I turn into a drive-thru.

"Just a quick detour," I say, swerving into the lane for my ritual after-training coffee and bagel. I lower the music, then switch it altogether to the local radio.

Stalled, my senses zero in on Leene's foot tapping against my bag at her feet.

She sighs softly. "I hope we won't be late."

"Don't worry, I time my mornings perfectly."

She must be nervous. I raise the volume on the stereo because background noise always helps me when I'm nervous. Wrong move. The news anchors immediately shift from the robberies on Elm to the topic of the Syrian Civil War, and suddenly I feel like I am under a magnifying glass.

Back in 2011, when the world made better sense to me, the Syrian people revolted against the dictator, Al-Assad, and his regime. What began with tear gas at protests escalated to snipers, bombs, and chemical weapons on civilians. Forcing people out of their homes with whatever they could grab before their building crumbled to the ground. But at least there are civilized discussions about it on the radio, so it's making a difference. Right?

My brain splits from the morning debut of these thoughts. I need coffee. The car ahead inches closer, and we listen to the anchor's voice. "The Supreme Court recently upheld the Muslim ban, which disallows Muslims from entering the country from select Muslim countries." The anchor's voice fades, and another declares, "Donald J. Trump is calling for a total and complete shutdown of Muslims entering the United States—"

My hand fumbles with the switches on the stereo, and I'm still messing with it when the lady hands me my breakfast. I pay her while the anchors begin to discuss the statement.

"Can I help?" I hear Leene only marginally.

The next station: "The proposed refugee ban blocks refugees from Middle Eastern and African countries like Egypt, Yemen, Syria, Libya, South Sudan, and others, like North Korea, from entering the United States—"

I juggle my bagel and coffee, smacking all the buttons on the stereo. Leene reaches to the rescue, and I jerk away just as the stereo shuts off, spilling hot coffee onto my thigh. I bite my lip as my leg spasms at the gas pedal and—

"Watch out!" Leene screams.

Booming honks startle me, and when I lift my head with a gasp, the hood of a truck fills my field of vision as my car barrels dangerously closer to it. I brake hard, my body surging forward before my head crashes back into the headrest. Leene lets out a disturbing sound that twists in the hot air.

My car narrowly misses their truck door, and the two white middle-aged men, riled and infuriated, roll their windows down, their heavy breath immediately condensing in the frigid air.

"Hey!" Their middle fingers gesticulate in my direction. Leene wastes no time unfastening her seatbelt, sliding off her seat, and assuming the fetal position on the floor of my car. I manage to throw my hands up, waving them around and placing them over my heart in shameless apology.

"Go back to your country!" he barks. "Oppressed bitch!" My face burns up, boiling to the top of my head, and I worry the temperature will cause my hijab to catch fire.

"Give them what they want," Leene whimpers.

"I don't know what they want!" I swear angrily. I only know that my body repels how they make me feel so small.

"Look at the goddamn road! That's why they don't let you drive in Iraq!" I want to correct their ignorance, that I'm not Iraqi and even if I were, women can drive in Iraq. The driver with the sports sunglasses floors it and pulls up next to my window. Despite my panic, I'm itching to start a fight.

"Drive away!" Leene demands.

Their faces glowing red with rage are all I see. They motion for me to roll down my window. A voice in my head that sounds an awful lot like Mama's alerts me that they might have a gun.

Leene clings to my damp leggings. "Get us out of here." Her eyes bulge out of her head, the fear in her voice surreal. "Drive!"

I slam my foot on the gas and drive off, wildly checking my mirrors as the distance between my car and theirs grows. All those years of mental training and discipline are rendered useless. Their hateful words paralyzed me when it mattered most. I spew a slew of curses in Arabic at them. When I'm angry, only Arabic curses hit the spot.

I park a few blocks down and wait for the coast to clear and my nerves to subside. When my heart finally sinks down my throat to settle back into my chest, I look down at Leene, who has yet to begin her recovery. Her head remains between her knees, and her labored breathing is pitched.

"We're safe now," I say, though my voice wears sympathy like an impostor. Fear sits at the bottom of my throat, distorting my tone.

Leene lifts her head, her face bright red and lined with sweat. She raises herself to peer through the window, gasping and ducking at a passing minivan. She reassumes the fetal position, her back to the door.

"What if they followed us?" She gulps as her chest rises and falls rapidly.

My hands tremble, and I clasp the steering wheel to cover it up. "They didn't. I checked."

"I thought…" Her jagged breath takes her words away. "Y-you're hurt."

I look down at my leg. Thanks to the adrenaline I can't feel the burn, but my sweatpants are soaked. "Shit. I can't go to school like this."

I jump into the back seat and rummage through my gym bag for a spare pair of pants. My hands shake. When I hop back into the driver's seat, the residual sweats kick in. I start to push the entire encounter to the back of my mind. I want to feel like myself again.

But Leene didn't get the memo. Instead of backing down, she asserts, "You froze."

I whip my head in her direction.

"Why didn't you drive us out of danger?" She sounds furious, though her knees are pulled into her chest like a baby, jaw chattering. Whatever my body is doing in response to fight or flight, her body is doing double.

"Well, you fell apart." I throw blame because I don't know how else to respond. My chest adjusts to the unfamiliar pain of allowing others to strike fear in me.

"Because I was scared," she mutters plainly.

"And I was just chilling?"

Leene bristles, "You don't have anything to be scared of. You're practically one of them."

"*Them?*"

She flinches at my incredulity. "You're American, too."

"Obviously not." I grit my teeth to cover up my uneasy voice. "Just because I'm American doesn't mean we're alike. Sometimes it doesn't mean anything."

Leene's silent, and her lack of acknowledgment strikes a nerve. Mama and her friends must think Leene and I can bond over our mutual Syrianness, but it's not so simple. If Leene sees me as American like those men then she doesn't see the real me. Leene will always be Syrian and I will always be Syrian American. The difference is like the sun and the moon. Their essences might be the same, but no one confuses one for the other.

Leene lifts herself onto the seat with immense effort. Only now can I see her body's tremors.

My runoff panic takes a turn from hostility. It's plain curiosity that makes me ask, "Why'd you freak out like that?"

"I don't know." She shudders. "Isn't it a normal response?"

"This isn't normal."

"You wouldn't understand." She shudders.

I serve her a look. "But you understand me perfectly."

American, like them. I've never felt less American than right now.

Leene looks me straight in the eye. "For kids like me, it's normal."

I bite my tongue. After all that I learned about Mustafa, I should know better than to judge her triggers.

Electing to move on from this particular patch of humiliation as quickly as possible, I bend to mop up the coffee mess in the car. Leene leans forward to help. Hell-bent on taking care of it myself, I swerve away forcefully while her arm jerks up with a surge of purpose.

Smack!

My jaw connects with a loud crack against her knuckles, and my bottom lip rams deep into my teeth.

19

Leene

*Y*a Allah! I didn't mean to—you moved out of the way—I was only trying to help—" I blubber more excuses that don't abate the bleeding.

Khadija, the American girl who says she's not as American as I think, tips her head back and attempts to block her open wound with papery napkins. "I can't believe you punched me." She pauses, eyes widening. "I can't believe I let you."

"I didn't punch you," I counter, adrenaline blazing through my veins all over again. Technically she slammed into my fist when I was trying to help. "I'm *so* sorry."

"Whatever." Decidedly unruffled by the angry men, Khadija drives off with one hand on the wheel, the other pressing against her lip, the picture of American vogue.

She raids the glove compartment, though her shaking hands struggle to find what she's searching for.

"Are you okay?" I ask.

"I'm fine." This time, I hear the vulnerability in her voice under the fake bravado. Was she scared, too? She pulls out a package of baby wipes. "Thank you, Mama, for being a neat freak." She tosses them into my lap.

I look down. Crimson tissues glisten in the sun. Her blood on my hands turns chalky as it dries. A trembling spreads to my fingertips. The smell of coffee nauseates me so much that my stomach caves in on itself.

My veins drain of adrenaline. The energy to keep myself upright depletes, though my heart rate spikes. My chest tightens like a vise, squelching my breath, doubling me over.

"Is my face red? I feel hot." My voice is far away.

"What's going on?" I hear her say over my wheezing. "Are you okay? Should I stop the car?"

"Keep driving," I say with a croak. A warm tingle spreads in my hands and feet, and my chest compresses with a stroke of terror, a panic attack. Control. I've lost all control, and the memories I constantly block flood back.

With the hot flashes, I feel the warmth of blood spread from gunshot wounds I'd sealed with my hands.

The nausea brings forth the smell of waste and corpses wafting from hospital doors and spilling into the street.

My body chills and I'm back on an open sea, gripping Mama's hands, shielding Mustafa between us.

Tank glides over the wet highway, and I haltingly regain control of my breathing. I need to talk through the rest of the episode.

"Your car," I rasp, "reminds me of the huge tanks that rode down my street in Syria. I told you my dad called them Lamborghinis whenever they came our way so they wouldn't frighten me. On our way to the shops, he'd tell me not to run if I saw one coming. Only people who did something wrong ran from them, and I wasn't doing anything wrong by walking down my street. He said I should slide into the closest alley and knock on the door of any house. Anyone would help me hide in their home until the coast was clear. We all wanted the same thing: to keep out of a Lamborghini's way."

Whether we called them Lamborghinis or tanks, it didn't matter.

I shut my eyes to convince myself that my irregular heartbeat is all in my head. My hands smooth over the dashboard that hums with the song of the engine.

"I like cars. It was the thing that I shared with my baba. Every morning before school we'd buy ful for breakfast from down the street. We'd point out the models of all the cars. Sometimes we were lucky and we'd see a new BMW or a Mercedes coming down the street. That stopped after the tanks started coming. My baba said the tanks were the newest Lamborghini models to keep things fresh." A smile forms on my lips when I remember the enormous beat-up frame of the tanks and their nonexistent resemblance to the actual polished machine. A frown tugs on my smile's corners. "I'd never seen a Lamborghini before so I went with it. It became our inside joke."

I shut my eyes as a croak bubbles in my throat. "One day, I didn't go with him to get breakfast. Mama and I waited that morning and I missed school waiting for him. When you wait for a dead person, the seconds go by like hours. A bullet from a Lamborghini shot Baba, and his heart stopped in seconds. He was on his way back with our breakfast. He was two buildings away, the ful for our breakfast splattered on the street when it fell from his hands.

"I had seen that same Lamborghini on our street every morning on our walks. They never shot while I was in the street. Maybe that means they had some humanity. Maybe it means that if I was with him, I don't—I don't know, maybe Baba would be here right now."

I exhale into hiccups that slacken the chest compressions. I let my eyes close, utterly exhausted and awaiting my body to restore itself.

"Do you get panic attacks often?" Khadija whispers. I only hear curiosity in her voice, and the lack of pity lends me strength.

"They really don't happen that often," I murmur. "I didn't always have them. They started when…" I let my voice dwindle.

"When you lost Mustafa?" Khadija completes my sentence.

I look out the window. "Mustafa wasn't the first."

"When you lost your baba?"

"Baba wasn't the only one."

Mercifully, Khadija doesn't ask more questions.

I let the world passing before me act as a distraction. An uninhabited strip of homes teeters on leftover foundations attached to rotting patios. Dead vines coil around windowsills, and front doors are torn out, revealing fossils of homes. Streets like these exist even in America.

The hot air blowing through Tank dries the sweat from my body and clothes. I tremble violently, and I clutch the door and seat.

"I should take you home."

"No." I swallow hard. "By the time we get to school I'll be fine."

"You still want to go to school?" she asks, sucking in a harried breath.

"I have to keep going. This is my first time getting to be in a classroom in a long time. I want to go," I affirm.

Khadija makes a turn, and we whiz past another America, the one I've seen in the movies. Big houses, long green lawns dusted with flurries, Valentine's Day balloon decorations, owners in puffer jackets walking their dogs. My eyes roam over the Audi-, BMW-, Jaguar-, and Porsche-filled driveways.

Traffic thickens as teenagers in backpacks jump down from parked cars, though I don't see a school, only a brick cathedral-looking building with a clock tower and mini turrets. The cars file forward into the parking lot before I see the sign out front: ROCHESTER HEIGHTS HIGH SCHOOL.

I have to catch my breath, but this time it's from the astonishment. I swivel my head around in amazement; the excitement that buzzes from the students as they walk into their school dulls the final traces of my episode.

Khadija parks, saying, "My mom will kill me if she finds out I didn't get you help when you needed it."

"I don't need help," I manage with a squeak. "I know how to control this. I was surprised is all."

She observes me carefully. I try to snatch at her phone, but her reflexes are too fast. She widens her eyes at me.

"Please don't," I plead. "I can't be left alone at home with nothing but my thoughts."

Khadija rips the crusted tissues away from her lip. Etched into the bottom right of her lower lip is a ruby-red V-shaped cut, rough and conspicuous. She looks like Lara Croft from that movie Abood used to let me watch when Mama and Baba weren't around.

She checks the gash in the mirror. "What's in it for me?"

"You don't tell either of our moms and I won't tell anyone I gave you that busted lip." I'm half-serious, but I have to commit to the threat. This is most unlike me. "Or those second-degree burns," I add weakly.

Khadija scoffs very American-like. "I distinctly remember you were scared shitless."

"At least I'm still in one piece."

"Touché," she says, which I don't understand. Her lip

twitches into a lopsided smile that she quickly obstructs, but I catch it. A faint sign of friendship clicks my world into place for a fraction of a second.

"I can't decide if I respect you more or less now," she sighs.

I clamp my mouth shut hoping it's the former. I cough for a minute, my body attempting to expel the demon I call anxiety. Khadija assesses me one last time, and from the mess of soiled napkins and exploded emotions, I hope she can see me as more than just an outsider infiltrating her world.

"But we have a deal," she says. "I won't say a thing about your panic attack, but you need to do another favor for me since no one will believe you did *this* to my face." At "*this*" she dramatically motions to her injured face. "I guess we have to get used to these deals if we're going to be partners in getting Mustafa back."

My face falls. "It's weird to hear you talk about him."

"Get used to it," Khadija says. "You made your choice to trust me, so you gotta deal with me. Not the watered-down version of me—*all* of me. You'll have to look at me through rose-colored glasses because God knows I look too harsh through regular ones."

I tilt my head. "You look fine to me."

She smirks. Khadija may be unpredictable, but being by her side beats being alone.

With no one to help me find Mustafa. No one to walk by my side as I enter my new school. Not like how Baba would in the narrow Syrian streets as we picked up breakfast from the ful shop, not like my brother who shared my brows and my smile would when we walked home after school, not like Mama would when visiting our friends' houses on Eid.

Alone. A feeling I am too acquainted with. I haven't had someone to hold my hand literally or metaphorically in a life-time. Maybe Khadija, she can be my hand to hold.

A girl can dream.

I nod, confirming our pact. She extends her hand for a shake. When I move in to take it, it falls away, evading me at the last second.

She opens Tank's door and jumps out. "Great. Catch you after school."

"Wait!" I call out, scrambling out my side. I scan the students entering the red brick school. There are so many Americans, but not American like Khadija—Americans like the ones in the dubbed shows I watched. They all look different, all dressed nicely like Khadija, except these are American Americans.

I catch up with her, sidling my lethargic body beside her. My body trembles involuntarily. She eyes me suspiciously. "We're gonna be late."

A question itching at the back of my head springs to the forefront. I catch up to her again. "But what about those two men? Nobody needs to know what they said to us?" I hesitate. "It's . . . okay?"

She stops abruptly and I nearly slam into her. She holds my gaze with a fiery intensity. "It is not okay for strange men to yell racist things at us in a parking lot and follow us in their car. It might be normal, but it is *not* okay."

"So what happens now?" I ask.

Khadija fidgets with her hijab. "Now, we never speak about this morning again. Not about those men, who will get away with what they did. Not about this busted lip I got from training this morning. And not about your secret panic attack." Then she adds, "Friends are for keeping secrets, right?"

Friends.

"And Mustafa?"

Khadija stares forward. "We work on finding information first. We can start after school today."

Before I can say more, Khadija marches into her school, hijab fluttering behind her. I take a deep breath, concentrating on the positives of this ill-fated morning.

Hot air and voices smack me in the face when I enter the building. There are lockers and linoleum floors and kids who laugh and joke with one another. There are Americans whose families come from all over the world, and they don't stare at me in the halls, they don't point fingers or ask me questions about where I'm from, and I don't ask them. I'm still new here and I haven't figured what *American* can mean in all these new contexts.

Then there are the other hijabis. Khadija dresses sleek and sporty, but these other girls dress as though a fashion editor chose their clothes to expertly match their neutral-toned hijabs. They drip with American finesse like Khadija does, personalities blazing and mascara smoking. I look down at my two-year-old coat, single pair of jeans, and worn-out sneakers.

What will they think of me?

Maroon-colored lockers line the hallways of RHHS, pressed up against stone walls supported by intricate buttresses. Posters are pasted around the hallway and students walk with their teachers. The girls carry purses instead of backpacks and the boys have haircuts that are short on the sides and voluminous up top. I lock a target on a group of hijabis that look less intimidating based on my Khadija scale and take a deep breath. Then another, and another, siphoning confidence to approach them. But a high-pitched bell shepherds them into the classrooms to their individual desks, and I miss my chance.

I explore the empty halls until I find the main office. Like most of the students, the staff also looks like they have never wanted for a thing in their life. Phones ring off the hook and secretaries answer while sifting through files. They all move with such purpose that my arrival doesn't earn a second glance.

Breathe, Leene. With my heart pounding, I approach the counter and wait for the man to get off the phone.

"Hello, I'm new," I say in my accented English.

He points to the desk across from him and picks up the next call. An older woman delivers me my schedule fresh off the printer.

Overcome by the unknown, I take a look at my schedule. It reads *Taher, Leene.* I find my first class: ELL, McCarthy, D., E208.

I press down my nerves. The office alone might be half as big as my old elementary school, but I can do this. I fought to get my family out of Syria. I trekked with my mom across Europe and led us to America. I can find my way around a high school.

Breathe, Leene. I find a medium-sized map pinned to the wall, and I carefully twist off the pushpins to remove it. This is a game, just like *PAC-MAN* on the Atari. Navigate the halls, eat the fruit in my path, avoid ghosts, and conquer.

20

Khadija

"Ça marche," I say, giving Nassima a thumbs-up for her little art project. A week since the accident in the car and my face still throbs when I make most facial expressions.

Nassima paints CRÊPE DU JOUR in giant red block letters on a club event's poster. As the French Club president's unofficial bodyguard, I'm on duty when Nassima is. And since she doesn't have any enemies, I mostly serve as a distraction. While she works on her project, we discuss the summer trip, currently imagining eating éclairs on a café terrace in France.

Nassima clicks her tongue. "I also need pictures at all the sights. At Notre Dame, the Champs-Élysées, l'Arc de Triomphe, la tour Eiffel. Oh, and we have to see the Louvre. I need to see the Mona Lisa."

"Could you fit any more clichés in there?" I ask, practicing my hand wraps with some boxing tape I found at the bottom of my bag. My French homework is splayed out on my desk, but I can't do any more conjugations.

She grins. "I can fit *all* the clichés. That's what a high school graduation trip is for."

"Sounds like fun," I grumble.

Nassima notices my shifted mood. "I'm sure it'll work out. No matter what your mom says."

I glance up at Nassima's misreading of the situation. Yes, Mama is the queen of objections, but recently I've taken up more pressing concerns.

Nassima continues, "We can have my mom convince yours. She just doesn't want your mom to hold it against her if she sides with us on this girls-only trip."

"That's because your mom has rational fears."

"My mom thinks it'll help us grow," Nassima says, ultra content. "Plus, I have family all over France and some in Belgium. Everywhere is close together in Europe. We won't find ourselves alone no matter where we go."

I nod slowly.

"Imagine: country hopping and nonstop culture shock that peaks as we cross over from Europe into Asia."

My wraps get all knotted the longer Nassima speaks.

The topic dies as her imagination takes her to warm nights by the Bosphorus, a tiny cup of steaming Turkish coffee in our hands. It's a picture-perfect image. Yet the lighting on this image is all wrong.

Instead, my mind wanders to where I was last year when

Leene leapt into the Mediterranean Sea not knowing what would happen to her.

I was fast asleep in my bed in my roomy Cowboys jersey. Or I was fighting with my mother for the umpteenth time, decidedly miserable despite the roof over my head, warmth tingling my toes, and food cooking in the oven. Or I was planning an escape, probably dreaming of the summer trip of a lifetime that makes me a little sick now. Or I was sitting here in class after school, staring at the conjugation of *pouvoir* and *vouloir* and getting the subjunctive all wrong.

No matter where I might've been, I know I was complaining about my life of privilege.

I open my laptop and pretend to search for subjunctive forms of verbs. I click on one of the hundreds of open tabs. The picture of Mustafa flashes onto the screen. My eyes dart to Nassima. Thankfully, her tortilla-looking crêpe illustration commands her full attention. I have yet to tell Nassima all that Leene told me, and the more I wait, the less I want to. Nassima is an appendage of me: If I know something, it's a given she will, too. But Leene's terrors are her own, and I can't casually let them slip in an RHHS classroom.

I scroll through the orphanage's site and find a sponsor page. When I put in my debit card information and pledge money, the site gives me a list of children I could potentially be sponsoring at the orphanage. There are at least four Mustafas on the list. It must be a huge orphanage, or the staff may never update its list. I scroll down endlessly. I give up and click the contact page.

As I write a letter to the orphanage director, I remember a couple of years ago when a man in Cheeto-shade foundation thought he knew two shits about Syria and, standing behind a podium with cheeks full of melted marshmallows, tried his best not to drool.

"Did you ever see a migration like that?" he'd slurred. "They're all men, and they're all strong-looking guys....And I'm saying to myself, 'Why aren't they fighting to save Syria? Why are they migrating all over Europe?' Seriously."

He spoke like he was all-knowing, but he's ignorant as hell. They're all men? This page listing hundreds of children at a single orphanage begs to differ.

To quote Khaleh Rana, she didn't even think about a life outside of Syria. Douma was her whole world. Only until the government Chernobyled her city did she accept Leene's pleas to leave. Yet there are men in red ties and blue suits that think Syrians brought the killing and torture unto themselves in order to migrate to Europe with those left in their family. In 2010 there was such a thing as visas and college exchange programs. Now it's become more impossible than ever to visit family abroad.

Syria had been an oasis. A country of gardens and streams no one needed to leave. Then the thoughtless spray of bullets and remote release of barrel bombs descended upon the country, and time froze. Family ties without reinforcement fell apart. Those who were lost remain lost.

"There you are." Younes's voice comes from the doorway, and my fingers seize up over my keyboard. He grins at me as he drags a chair next to me, sitting on it backward to drape his arms over its back.

He gives Nassima a salute but leans over next to me, and I try my best to hide my lip, though he's already seen it. It's been a week since the incident, but somehow it looks worse with every passing day.

"Whatcha doing?" he asks.

I slap on a *Sincerely, Leene Taher* to my email and nearly break the return key to send.

"Nothing exciting," I say, pulling up French conjugation charts.

He shuts his eyes as though the verb tenses blinded him. "I've looked at enough hiragana, katakana, and kanji charts for a lifetime, thank you very much."

I roll my eyes. "You just had to go off and take four years of Japanese."

"One day, when we go to Japan together, you'll thank me for learning Japanese."

My jaw drops at the assumption we'll go abroad together, but ever since the confession, he says things like this just to see me get all flustered. I recompose myself. "Did you come to gloat?"

A phone's shutter sound snaps me out of my banter with Younes. My head whips toward the sound and Nassima grins at her screen at the photo she just took of me.

"Delete it!" I screech, completely mortified and balling up the wraps to throw at her, but they're all tangled. I'd been knotting them all over again as Younes spoke.

Nassima holds her phone in victory. She tuts, "You and your busted lip are gonna be my lock screen so I can wake up to it every day. I never thought I'd see you look like this, Ms. Badass," she says with a laugh.

Younes raises a hand, cheeky as ever. "I am equally shocked, but it does look badass."

I bury my head in my hands, careful not to aggravate the bruise and scar. They both know that it goes against all logic that Leene, who couldn't possibly lift thirty-pound dumbbells, wrecked my face like this.

"Are you both here to torture me?" I mumble.

Younes lets out a small laugh. "Yes, but I'm also here because I saw someone who looks a lot like Leene standing outside in the cold."

"Leene," I groan, and a pain shoots down my chin and tightens in my chest. "I forgot I have to take her home."

Not used to the routine of driving to and from school with Leene, I'm always forgetting about this added responsibility.

Nassima, her cool brown eyes hooded by thick eyeliner, watches me as I scramble to unravel my wraps and stuff them in my bag. Nassima and Younes follow me out as I skid down the halls to the entrance.

The snow falls down hard outside, and the beginnings of a blizzard brew. I search for Leene in the corridors, but when I crane my neck outside, the lavender color of her hijab contrasts against falling snowy-white sheets.

"Hey!" I call out. Leene has her hands stuffed in her pockets, and her nose and cheeks glow bright pink. "Have you been out here all this time?"

Nassima follows me out, breathless. Younes is last to join us, walking at a steady pace with his long legs.

Leene smiles. In this cold, flakes melting against her skin, she smiles. God bless. Where does she get that good nature? "This is where the students go after school is done." Her teeth chatter and her lips quiver.

"They come out here because their rides are in the parking lot," I explain. "It's freezing. Do you want to get hypothermia?"

Nassima warms Leene's hands in hers. "You'll get sick," she says, her voice thick with concern.

I stare at their hands. Nassima always knows the right thing to say and do. Nassima says her salaams to us and scurries off to her car. Leene and I start off toward mine. Younes gives me a long gaze as if trying to tell me something before going his way, too.

Jumping into the car, Leene huffs. "You know I've slept through snowstorms worse than this."

I drive, unsure what she's getting at.

"I can take a lot," she continues, her voice icy, "from the world, but also from people. I like to say I see the good in people. That's how I know you're a good person even though you try not to show it. But one thing I can't stand is when people underestimate what I can take."

I purse my lips because she has a point. "My bad, I'll keep the underestimating to myself."

"Or don't underestimate me at all."

My jaw nearly falls open. Leene is really clapping back. Go Leene.

She moves on quickly, giving me a play-by-play of her day as is her daily routine. From what I gathered from our car rides in the last week: RHHS is the most beautiful school she's ever seen, she adores her classmates, and she excels in her German course because she spent the longest time there of all the countries she's lived in.

"I have so much in common with one of the girls in my class," she tells me. "Her name is Amal. She's in my ELL class and she's Syrian, too. Do you know her?" She takes her hands from her pockets and heats her fingers on the vents.

"Not all Syrians know each other."

"But she wears the hijab like us."

I roll my eyes. "And not all hijabis know each other."

She talks to me with ease, like we're childhood friends from Syria and we're reconnecting as teenagers, and I don't hate it.

But it still feels strange. It's like she forgot about Mustafa. We haven't seriously spoken about him since before the Super Bowl.

"Leene."

"Yes?" she responds quickly, the corners of her mouth turning up.

I glance at her then back at the road. "I sent an email to the orphanage asking about Mustafa."

When I glance to the side, her face pales immediately. She shakes her head like she's mentally reorienting herself. I don't know what my email on Leene's behalf will uncover. Even with the picture proving Mustafa's existence, I'm not sure if it's worse knowing he's helpless out there or accepting that he was gone. All I know is that without any answers, Leene could spiral the longer she thinks about imagined Mustafa scenarios.

"Oh, I've been so distracted, I totally forgot."

Confused, I ask, "Do you do that a lot? Just forget?"

She places a shaky hand on her forehead. "I—I guess I learned to block things out."

And I see it, the beginnings of a spiral. We're off the highway, so I turn into a parking lot and stop the car. I reach out my hand and grab hers, copying Nassima. It feels weird, no, weirder than weird, because I've never been one to comfort others. Leene stares at me with wide eyes.

She rapidly devolves. "What if they say they have him? What if they ask me to go get him? I don't have money. I shouldn't even be staying at your house. I need to find a job. I need to find Mama and me our own place, get us on our own two feet. I don't know what I'd do if they tell me he's alive and he's there and I—"

"It's going to be fine," I say, and pull my hand away. This whole touching for comfort thing is phony. She doesn't need comfort; she needs a way out. Though he can't materialize in Detroit, these emails can give her a distraction until I win those tickets and earn my freedom from Mama. Then who knows what'll come after that. I search for more solutions. "If you don't want to stay with us anymore all you have to do is ask. I'm sure Mama can find a way to get you your own place."

Leene shakes her head. "How can I help Mustafa if I can't even help myself?"

I stare at her, surprised. Again, I've misread her. She's not looking for handouts. She's stressed out that she can't stand on her own. Like me.

Leene clamps her hand on her mouth. "Ya Allah, I'm so sorry. I didn't mean to sound ungrateful. I'm so rude, please ignore me."

"No, I get it."

We drive home in silence. At the front door, Leene throws her hand out to stop me from entering.

"Wait, let me make sure the coast is clear." She's been on the lookout for me so that Mama doesn't see my lip. She goes in and after a minute, pokes her head back out. "She's cooking in the kitchen. You're safe."

A warmth spreads in my chest, a feeling that only comes from being around Nassima or Younes. This feeling certainly never happens at home, not since Teteh last visited. And yet I feel it now because someone here is watching out for me.

As I pass her in the doorway, I wonder if she feels the same.

21

Leene

$\mathcal{E}$very day in Tank, on our ride home, I tell Khadija every last detail of my day at school to distract myself from asking her about Mustafa.

Khadija sends more emails, and we wait. The waiting will kill me. It's been two weeks, but it feels like it's been years.

Khaleh Maisa insisted I take an old laptop of hers, which means I can read and reread Khadija's futile emails to the orphanage and fall asleep to Mustafa's less-round face and longer limbs. With every second that I am away, he is changing, growing, dissociating from my Mustafa and becoming his own. And becoming his own means distancing from us. I tap the faint red stitch at the corner of his blue blanket, the thread that I lazily hand stitched his name with on an exceptionally long day in Ramadan.

In her emails, Khadija explained that we recognized Mustafa and his blanket. The orphanage director must know that blanket belongs to him—the proof is in the frayed red-thread embroidery of his name. Mustafa stayed at the orphanage long enough to get his picture taken; surely records show that. Then again, the orphanage must receive thousands of emails from mothers, fathers, sisters, and brothers asking about a lost little one.

How could I, anyway, think my tragedy is so extraordinary that the orphanage's efforts to find my brother take precedence over hundreds of others?

I have to switch to work mode so I don't feel helpless.

"I got a job," I tell Khadija. "My friend Amal has one at a restaurant called Falafel Guys, and they asked me to work because they always need more waitresses who speak Arabic. I did some math and if I'm going to get Mustafa back—"

"*When* you get him back," she interjects.

I inhale sharply. "Aslan, I'll need to get there to get him back. For now, I can work on getting there."

Khadija is quiet for a while. I wonder what she's thinking. "When do you work?" she asks.

"Three weekday nights, and evening shifts on the weekends. I took as many hours as they would give me. Today's my first day. I'm going to take the bus from home."

"I can drop you off."

I stare at her, but she purposefully keeps her eyes on the road. I'm learning about her slowly. She has a warm heart, but she doesn't like anyone pointing it out.

"I would love that," I respond.

Falafel Guys is on Rochester Heights's Main Street, where I'm told all the best restaurants are. When Khadija drops me off out front, I am surprised at how new and popular it looks. Red brick facade, huge open windows, fairy lights, and neon signs. There are a lot of American Americans at the tables, and there are a good deal of hijabis and Arab boys, too. I smile at everyone that makes eye contact with me, already feeling like it's my job to welcome them. This part of the job comes naturally.

Amal is already here; she sees me when I enter and she's already at my side. She's a round person: round cheeks, round eyes, round face. Her eyebrows are dark and thick and her eyes are a deep brown. Her smile is like an invitation—she's eager to be friends with others, even if that makes her a little bit of a people pleaser. If she weren't a refugee like me, I would think she is naive about the world, but I know that isn't the case.

"You're early! Mumtaz, I'll show you around." She takes me to the back and hands me a black waist apron that has an animated, mustached falafel wearing a chef's hat. It's identical to the one on the wall, so I assume it's the restaurant's logo. She puts me at the food bar behind the counter. Here, I have hot pita bread; a tray of falafel straight from the fryer; every vegetable topping, pickled or fried or fresh; and an assortment of sauces. Laban with olive oil, laban with tahini, laban with a tahini, cilantro, and shatta mixture. Basically every version of a laban sauce imaginable.

The customers come. Some speak to me in English, some

in Arabic. I make their customized sandwiches. I send them to Amal, who rings them up. Sometimes they ask for a specialty sandwich that the chef makes in the back, and Amal takes it out to their table. My mind is nothing but the smell of crisping falafel and perfecting my technique to fill the sandwiches with as much food as possible because, as they say, I'm not filling them from my father's house. The more I can give, the better.

After a few hours, we get a break in the wave of customers. Amal slumps against the counter. "Akhiran," she says with a big sigh. "Ah, look at the time, you're almost off work."

I check the time and, to my disappointment, she's right. This four-hour shift at $9.45 an hour doesn't get me much, but over time it will.

"Can't I work more hours?" I whine.

She frowns. "There's another part-timer who takes the next four hours."

"But you get to keep working."

"I got this job first, and the boss knows I'm the only one who works in my house, so I get the eight-hour shift," she says proudly. "It's good for me that we close at midnight."

"When do you get any homework done?" I ask, impressed at her work ethic.

Amal shrugs. "I don't. Wallah, it's a miracle I go to school at all."

"You do sleep through our classes." I giggle.

"It doesn't matter," she begins. "I'm not going to college. My English sucks. I'll get my high school diploma and I'll keep working here or I'll get married and take care of my kids. God knows all I do now is work to take care of my younger siblings."

My jaw slightly drops, but I turn my head away so she doesn't see it. "I doubt your parents would want that."

"My mom died in Syria and my dad can't speak any English at all so he can't find stable work. He'll be happy if I find someone who will accept me when I come from nothing."

My tongue tastes metal. Amal is from Homs, and I know this because her consonants slant with the Homsi accent. It's my favorite dialect in all of Syria. But no matter how cute she sounds, her words cut like a knife.

"I didn't know about your mom. Allah yerhama," I say, giving her my condolences, reaching out to touch her forearm.

But Amal continues wiping at the counter with disinfectant. "It was bad in Homs. We should've left earlier, but there's no use in regretting. *All* of us should've left earlier."

Her eyes pass over all the uniformed kids in the restaurant, including me. It clicks. Everyone who works here is a refugee.

A boy our age walks into the restaurant in a waist apron like mine. I'm suddenly embarrassed I asked for more hours, because just like Amal and I need the money, he does, too.

One day, the $9.45 per hour will add up to more. It'll take

more days at this rate, but eventually it will. Not only for me, but for all of us.

⟡

Apparently, filling falafel sandwiches is tiring. After work, I take the bus home and collapse on my bed. I take a mini nap before waking up to do my homework. This has been my routine for the last few days. Since there are more part-timers than positions at the restaurant, my shifts often get switched to accommodate the extra workers. Today, they hired someone new, and I had to give up some more hours. I couldn't complain.

I use the extra time to apply for government programs that will give Mama and me affordable housing. I keep myself busy because the Mustafa leads are meeting dead ends.

There's a knock on my room door, then Khadija's head pops in. Her lip is still swollen, but the cut is done scabbing over. The hit was bad, because it's been weeks and it's still bruised an awful shade of purple green. She's in her gym clothes and holding her duffel.

"Our moms are upstairs getting ready for the 'azima today," she whispers.

"That's today?" I look at my planner. The days are blurring together with work.

"Yes, it's today and I need Mama to be distracted while I go upstairs and cover this up." She gestures at her face. I've been helping Khadija evade her mom at home while her lip heals, but this 'azima seems unavoidable.

On the first floor, Khaleh Maisa is throwing clothes at Zain and has a closet full of her 'abayat displayed in the hallway as she picks what to wear. I approach her with Khadija trailing close behind. I make a big fuss over a brown 'abaya embroidered in gold to give Khadija an opening to run upstairs without her mom seeing her.

"Leene!" Khaleh Maisa beams at me. "Come, come, I have just the thing for you." She vanishes into Khadija's teteh's room and resurfaces with a long burgundy shirt, black slacks, and a silk hijab. Designer names dot the fabrics.

"This outfit is for you, and the one I have inside is for Khadija," she says. She cranes her neck to look around me. "Where's Khadija?"

"I think she's already changing upstairs," I say meekly as I rack my brain for how to refuse her generous offer.

Khaleh Maisa puts a hand on her hip. "Akh, Khadija. She's always one step ahead of me. It doesn't matter, you can wear this and show her how nice the clothes that I pick out are."

My cheeks flush. Khaleh Maisa has an affinity for making her daughter sound bad. "I'm okay, Khaleh, I have some clothes for fancy occasions."

I hurry away before she can stop me, my cheeks burning with embarrassment at refusing. At the end of the day, I'm a guest here, and a guest respects the host no matter what.

Once I'm changed into a flowy cream skirt and pink pull-over, I rummage through the drawers.

"What are you looking for?" Mama asks, exiting the closet dressed in her only proper coat, the one we bought when we first arrived in America because her other one was badly soiled. She looks boxy in it because it's a size too large, but in my eyes, she looks like the most respectable woman in the world. I give her a quick hug.

Pulling back, I ask, "Have you seen my hijab from Baba?"

Mama, who always knows where everything is, pulls it out for me. I take it out of the clear plastic wrap. It's still crisp and creased from the packaging. Just a few months before Baba was shot, he had gone out for work when unexpected protests spread in the city. Most times the government sent in soldiers to stop them with their bullets. That time the government dropped bombs. Before long the neighborhood whisper network made its way to us. They told us Baba's workplace was hit.

When that news arrived, all we could do was sit and wait for him to come back. If he didn't, that was answer enough. We didn't sleep for waiting up. Around midnight, someone knocked on our door.

It could have been Baba, but it could have also been someone bearing the bad news. I didn't answer the door and neither did Mama, who held baby Mustafa tight in her arms. Abood, my strong brother, answered it for us.

And there Baba stood, holding bags of gifts and groceries. He'd left work early to go to the shops. He gave Mama a necklace, Abdul Rahman a soccer ball, Mustafa a teether, and me this hijab. The hijab that saved his life.

Only for so long.

I iron it out and lay the silky cream fabric over my hair. I look like a strawberry creamsicle from the dukkanat below our home in Douma.

Mama kisses my cheek. "You look so beautiful."

My stomach flips, not from the compliment, but feeling like I don't deserve it from her.

We join the others upstairs, where Khaleh Maisa is adjusting the fabric of Khadija's clothes. Khadija found an impressively huge black turtleneck that swallows her chin and most of her mouth. She tucks this into high-waisted checkered pants. Their attention snaps to us.

"Ya Leene, I love your outfit," Khaleh Maisa compliments. "Leiki Khadija, she wore a skirt. You should wear one, too."

Khadija averts her eyes from both of us. I wish that Khaleh Maisa would not look at us under a microscope, grading us against each other. Khadija's face deflates every time she does this.

"I think Khadija looks great, too," I say to cheer her up.

Khaleh Maisa scrunches her nose, and my chest tightens for how Khadija must feel. "You look so much more put together, habibti." Then to Khadija she says, "You know the khalaat always have something to say about how you dress. We don't want to let them talk."

"I'll give them something to talk about," Khadija grumbles, pulling down her turtleneck for a second as she passes me. Her eyes twinkle mischievously with a hidden smile.

I smile back, feeling a special kind of joy knowing I'm in on one of her secrets.

22

Khadija

God bless turtlenecks. In the passenger seat beside me, Mama side-eyes my outfit again and at one point even tries to tug on the lip of my knit turtleneck.

I did my best with some concealer and powder, but it's still beyond help. The stress of Mama's imminent freak-out that I'm swollen and green under my turtleneck is enough for me to floor it to this 'azima. I whip past trees and dent pavement.

Mama grips the door handle and flattens one hand on the dashboard. She braces herself like I'm driving a tractor at seventy miles per hour. The melodrama.

The car dives and snaps, dipping again and jostling us around in our seats. Okay, I may have hit a pothole. Or two.

"Driving like a 'afreeteh," Mama says, exasperated.

'Afreeteh—noun—aa-free-tay—/ˈɪfriːte/: not to be confused with ifrit, a demon in Arabic mythology.

'Afreeteh—as used by Arab moms: a wild girl who lives without morals or rules.

When she calls me this, it reminds me of my teteh telling off her own daughters when they acted out and didn't wear slippers in the house. While walking around the house barefoot was as bad as my mom and khalehs would get, I'd say I'm a different breed of 'afreeteh.

I glance in the rearview mirror. In the back seat, Khaleh Rana and Leene wear identical greenish filters on their faces, and Zain pulls off his tie.

"Zain," Mama chimes. "Keep it on, Zain."

Zain gulps and doesn't respond but continues to fiddle with it. He's a mime, and not a very good one at that.

"Zain." This time Mama turns the warning levels of her voice all the way up.

Though he stops tugging, he hides his face from my view, but I glimpse his tie askew. He mutters, "I don't want to."

Saaaame. I want the vibes to spread through the car to him. My heart feels heavier in my chest as his brows knit. Zain must want to make his own choices, too. Mama's superpower of coercion exhausts us both. Neither of us wants to come to this 'azima, but like hell we can stay home with Mama's powers at work.

"His outfit will look good without the tie." I sow the seeds of doubt in Mama's head. "It's not that formal of a 'azima. He wore slacks and a vest for you. I think we can give up on the tie."

"You wouldn't know, Khadija," Mama reproaches. "Dr. Shaami's son will be the best-dressed boy at this 'azima."

Dr. Shaami, who was entering our driveway in his Bentley as I was exiting it, is an expert at just missing us. I suppose I had to inherit my skills of avoiding others from someone.

Zain's eyes meet mine in the mirror. I offer a frown that he cannot see and surrender. At least I tried. His light eyes cloud over, the thoughts behind them monstrous, but I can't read his expression. Before I gather that there might be something wrong, he averts his gaze back out the window. He fidgets with the tie the rest of the ride there.

When we're at the front of the house, grand and superfluous and bordering an HOA-regulated lake, we enter without ringing because the sheer number of cars outside says that there are too many people to care about another guest's arrival. We slip off our shoes and add them to the sea of shoes already in the marble foyer.

As soon as we enter, a crowd of people accept Mama into their throng. Leene and her mom get swept up by another khaleh, and Leene stands attentive, nodding and smiling as needed.

I slip away, watching as Zain goes off to the men's side, where he busies himself with the food table on his own.

And suddenly I'm alone as I watch today's episode of *Muslim Girls of Rochester Heights*.

It's a cringey show that plays out every time I come to one of these 'azimas. The cameraman zooms in on the females obnoxiously flirting, but then Camera 1 zooms on the males, who commence their mating calls involving deep-throated boasting of muscles and academia. Camera 2 zooms in on the other females drooling, swerving, one-upping, or accepting their part in the dance. Camera 1 zooms out to capture the amateur games afoot.

That's what flirting is like at these 'azimas because of the fact that it is a family-friendly atmosphere. Who openly flirts in front of their parents and friends' parents? Hence the cringe fest.

My mother explicitly warns me not to partake in it; therefore, I'm not a member of the cast, but more so an extra in the background. Zain is one, too, though he might evaporate from the social strain of standing in the background.

All the interactions feel rehearsed. Everything about it feels unnatural to me. Suddenly it's as if no one has ever seen the opposite sex before. Everything becomes formal and disjointed; even our clothes feel stiff.

Rather than continue with the dramatic social commentary to myself, I throw on a fake smile and embrace all the girls my mother calls my friends. They smile back at me, and we catch up and talk about school. But there's a hurdle in our friendship I never manage to get over with the other Syrian girls of Rochester Heights. There's the expectation that our shared background determines our high compatibility, enough to make us the best of friends. But besides that bare minimum, I have little else in common with them.

I push those reservations aside for my new motive. I invite anyone with ears to come to the fight at the gym. If enough of them come and vote me best boxer, then in just a couple months, I'll have my hands on two tickets that will zipline me out of here.

After I tell everyone and their mothers about the fight, I push through more of the 'azima. Since Nassima wasn't invited, I navigate between people in hopes of finding Younes. I walk around the congregating boys, wondering why Zain isn't among them. He looks like he would fit in with them, and I even recognize some of them as his friends, though they pretend not to know me. They joke and laugh as if everyone wishes they were a part of their banter.

My stomach growls for the hundredth time since I arrived. I look wistfully at the food knowing that I can't eat without exposing my injury. Then I see Younes at the food table picking at the chocolate-dipped dates filled with an assortment of nuts.

Younes catches my eye and grins. He's dressed in plaid beige trousers and a long button-down with a band collar. I forgot how good he looks in non-workout clothes. We both start toward each other and meet in the middle of the 'azima; the background fades away as I look up at him.

"You're here," I say with a smile, my eyes doing all the work because my mouth is swallowed by my collar.

"You sound relieved," he says smugly, popping a chocolate-covered date into his mouth.

"I was starting to think I'd have to make small talk with the others," I mock whisper as my eyes sweep the room.

"Isn't that what you've been doing?"

"You were watching me?" I act hurt. "And you didn't save me?"

"You don't need saving."

I hold my elbows, wondering why it feels weird to hear him say it. I know I can save myself, I'm used to saving myself, but I don't want him to say that.

"What's wrong?" he asks, and I realize my gaze has drifted off.

I glance back at him. Suddenly I want to lean on him, lean on the boy who said he liked me. His brow furrows with concern, and I wonder how much he's hiding from me. He takes on a lot of responsibilities, and for as much as I like to poke fun at the Muslim boys and girls of Rochester Heights, the baggage that all of us have to unpack is a full-time job on its own.

"I think we all deserve at least one person who's allowed to save us," I say. "I think that's fair."

He crosses his arms, surely thinking of the next cute thing he'll say to torture me. "Hmm, if we can only choose one, can I choose you?"

And there it is. "I'm a mess," I say half-jokingly. "Do you really want to choose me?"

"You're the only person who doesn't need me," he says, his voice low. "And I don't want another person to need me. I just want you to want to be around me. To want to be with me."

My voice catches in my throat. "Well, someone has got to teach you about boundaries."

His lips spread and his dimples deepen. "That's why I choose you."

Mama, Nassima, Younes, Zain, Leene. Whom do I choose, and who chooses me?

One of Younes's friends calls his name, and he saunters off after winking at me. Before I can process how bold Younes is and that we've become another pair on the flirting show, I'm jerked back to the reality of the 'azima by my growling stomach.

I go in search of a corner where I can stuff my face when Leene materializes with a plate of kibbeh. She passes me one. "I'll cover for you."

"God bless you," I say, turning to the wall and stuffing my mouth.

"This 'azima is funny," she says, and I realize she looks out of place here. Like an outsider looking in. "I feel like I'm back in Syria like ten years ago."

"Who would've thought we'd re-create Syria here," I say sarcastically, my mouth full.

"It's nice, though," she says. "Because this kind of stuff definitely doesn't happen over there anymore."

"What do you mean?"

Leene hands me another kibbeh, all casual. "I mean half this food is impossible to make because it costs thousands of lira for a pound of meat. Plus, there's no way this many people can gather in one house without the whole party getting shot down."

"You mean shut down."

"No, I mean shot down."

I swallow my bite of kibbeh. It goes down dry.

"Do these people even really care about us over there?" Leene asks flatly.

Her question strikes a nerve. Not only because she talks like she's a part of an *us*, which implies that I'm a part of *them*, but because her question is valid.

Do I really care about Leene? Just a month ago I was hating on her because of Mama's pressure. When I pledged to help her, what really made me do it?

Because when I remember how many people are dying or have died, people with the same blood as me, Syrians like Mama, Khaleh Rana, and Leene, I feel guilty. It's the guilt of knowing Leene has gone through things my nightmares cannot conjure. I, along with the rest of us here, live in bliss while our family members, friends, and those who look to us for help are going through the unimaginable.

"Oh, your mom was looking for you," Leene says with such an ease that it erases the weight of her previous question. She makes it so comfortable for the others around her to move on, when I know her mistakes freeze her in the past.

God bless. I look to her. "Will you come with me?"

"Leene Taher, at your service." She salutes me.

I make sure my turtleneck is in place and we make our way over to Mama's posse.

By ignoring the khalehs so far, I've violated every one of Mama's rules and my better judgment.

"Here she is! Khadija, come say a proper salaam!" I hear Mama's irritation loud and clear.

I drag my feet, tucking my neck between my shoulders. As I approach them they smile at me, one foot over the other.

"Masaa' il-khair," I say loudly, though the fabric muffles the greeting. My mom smiles her fake smile too hard and mimes for me to lower my collar. I shake my head minutely.

"I heard she was hurt," a khaleh on the periphery mentions.

"Yes, my daughter told me something about that," another adds.

Khalehs and their kids can be such tattletales.

"Are you?" Mama raises her brow at me, and I know she'll be annoyed that her friends know something about me that she doesn't. They must have discussed me more than they let on because Mama and I fight about the state of my turtleneck with our eyes until Mama voices her chagrin. "Why are you wearing your sweater like that? You look ridiculous. Pull it down."

"I'm cold." I give a forced laugh, and my lip throbs.

"Khadija." Mama's voice is livid. Leene tenses beside me.

I fold down the turtleneck collar, which has wiped nearly

all the concealer off my face. My swollen green lip elicits a chorus of faint gasps. *You asked for it.*

"That is the most unfortunate looking thing."

"I wouldn't know what to do if my daughter came home looking like that."

"How terrible, and on such a delicate girl."

"I think it makes me look badass," I murmur to myself and Leene. She nods dutifully.

Mama sighs. "I tell you not to go to that gym." She turns to her friends. "It's that fighting that she does."

Khaleh Aisha, our host of the night, tsks. "I know so many women who would love to have your looks and coloring, Khadija. You should think harder about that before putting yourself in danger. Wasting away your beauty in a fighting place. Putting it at risk of being tainted. Just look at Leene all clean and feminine. She's a perfect example for you."

The kibbeh feels like stone in my stomach. I'm about to excuse myself when Leene clears her throat beside me. "Actually, khaleh, Khadija hurt herself by slipping on ice." Leene's tone is light, but a sharpness edges into it.

The khalehs stare at her, likely weighing whether or not to accept her lie as fact. Mama clearly doesn't buy it. If that were true, I would have told Mama about it, but since I didn't, naturally Mama's mind will conjure up some elaborate deception on my part.

Then, ever the actress, Leene launches into a whole story

about how we were walking in front of the school, and I saved her from slipping on a patch of ice in the parking lot and fell instead, hitting my lip against the side of my car. The khalehs are enraptured by the retelling that makes me out to be a hero.

When I glimpse her again, Leene looks like she's from a world both so close and yet so far from mine. A world where I am lumped together with Leene at times, and at others we barely fit in the same mold.

The conversation shifts away from me as Leene takes the khalehs' complete attention. They love her. She answers their questions like a magician, every response drawing out this illusion that Leene is whole and perfect.

And here's the thing: These khalehs exist in a microcosm, a Syria in Detroit that cocoons them in their prolonged delusion that an unbroken Syria can continue to exist overseas. And they try their best to fit me and their daughters into their microcosm, but we can't fit into a mold that wasn't made for us. Girls like Leene give them a sense of hope that they'll succeed, but even Leene can't fit their expectations. She may have been born and raised in Syria, but it's not the same Syria they remember.

And their daughters and I are all a mélange of Syrian and American that doesn't fit into their neat boxes, no matter how hard they try to remold us.

Mercifully, Mama wants to head home soon after. In the car, the silence points out all our faults post-'azima. My bruised lip feels enormous, Zain and his missing tie look awkward as hell, and a dark cloud hovers over Leene's and Khaleh Rana's heads.

"How did that happen to your lip?" Mama finally asks. "And don't lie to me."

"It was an accident" is all I divulge. She humphs and I brace myself for the worst. Instead, she frowns, and I think she may actually be concerned. God bless. My cold heart softens. "I didn't mean to embarrass you," I add.

"You didn't embarrass me." She meets my gaze. "I don't like them talking badly about you."

In that moment, our feuds cease to exist. My breath fills my lungs completely, and a tender feeling stretches across my chest. It feels like the roots of an understanding, the remnants of a memory, or a connection between us sprouting again. I feel like I used to, when Mama and I didn't argue all the time, and when I didn't disappoint her with every one of my choices. Then I have to look back at the road ahead of me.

"They always talk about how bad your fighting is. You came up looking like that and you give them more to talk about. But only I can talk about your fighting. No one else."

I glance at her again, and our eyes crinkle, though our mouths don't smile.

"But," Mama says, "you are forbidden from entering that gym until that completely heals."

The tenderness between us vanishes.

"What the hell, Mama."

"What is this 'the hell'? Is that how you talk to your mom?"

"No," I mumble sheepishly, the word coming out in tiny font.

"Then that's that," she says. Mama looks over her shoulder to the back seat. "Thank you for saying that story about Khadija, Leene."

Leene's gaze locks with mine in the rearview mirror. "Of course, Khaleh."

"Even if it was a lie," Mama adds.

My heart skips a beat. "What the hell, Mama!"

"Stop it with 'the hell,' Khadija. You have a long way to go."

23

Khadija

Dear Ms. Taher,

Thank you for your sponsorship. Your donation will be utilized for the children's food, water, schooling, and shelter maintenance. In terms of your inquiry, when children arrive at a young age without family members and without papers, we are unable to recover their given names for accurate record keeping. Often, their exact ages are unknown, and their background cannot always be ascertained. Since that is the case, we cannot guarantee that your brother is among the many children that share his name at the orphanage.

Unfortunately, I cannot be of more help. If you are able to identify a child in any other way, by picture or in person, Ibtisami Ya Shaami Orphanage is open to foreign visitors and volunteers at all times of the year.

I wish you all the best in your search,
Charlotte Ra'ee-Harris

When I see the email during lunch period, a full month from when I sent the first email, the cafeteria zooms way out. It's addressed to Leene, but it's in response to my email, so I technically don't have to share it with her. The email is electronically signed with addresses from London, England, as well as Mafraq, Jordan. For all I know, Charlotte Ra'ee-Harris is an intern for the orphanage organization in London and has as much of a clue as I do about what's going on at the orphanage.

I send Charlotte a follow-up email, attaching the screenshot of Mustafa's photo from the site's front page. I will send follow-ups to my follow-ups until I receive any substantial information.

But if I have to face reality, we can never really know for certain unless we visit the orphanage ourselves.

The right thing to do is to let Leene know. The right thing is to forward this email to her and put her in the loop. But I can't. I stare across the cafeteria to where she's eating lunch with some girls from her ELL class, linking arms and snapping selfies with Amal. This news would devastate her. I can't bring myself to share it with her. Not yet.

Last night, my recurring nightmare that begins in Syria and ends with only Mama shifted. As usual, my family members began to vanish until Mama was the only one left, but the nightmare unfolded further. The topaz-tiled fountain in the courtyard was filled to the brim with water, and then the water overflowed as Leene's body, bloated and facing up, floated in it. My sweat licked my sheets as I failed to pull her out, unable to save her. Thrashing in my sheets strangled me awake.

Nassima peeps at my phone and then follows my gaze to Leene. "Everything okay there?"

I lock my screen quickly as Younes slides in beside me with his lunch. "Fine."

"She's probably just nervous about the showcase," Younes guesses, a cheeky smirk on his lips.

"Not nervous," I say.

"Whit has been getting better," Younes teases.

"Khadija's better," Nassima says, coming faithfully to my defense.

"I'm just saying." Younes holds his hands up innocently. "She trains like she's going pro. She's obsessed with beating you."

I'd been so distracted that I didn't stop to think that my win isn't guaranteed, and the showcase is only two months away. "I'll swing by Jerr's more," I promise him. "I'll take extra lessons from you. I'll even sit through your lectures about patience and fighting with your mind and all that."

He chuckles. "You really want to win those tickets, huh?"

"I *need* to win those tickets."

Nassima grins. "Don't worry, we'll be backpacking through Europe before we know it."

Europe.

Younes takes a huge bite of his pizza. I look down at my sandwich, and I don't say anything. My heart doesn't beat faster in anticipation of a summer of memories waiting to be made. No, instead, my heart sinks in my chest.

"Ness," I start, "what would you do with the tickets?"

He chews with purpose for a moment. "I don't know. I don't really want them. I just hope one of the scouts in the audience wants me to train at their gym and I can keep boxing. Take me to the next level, you know?"

"You can't do that at Jerr's?" I ask.

"Not really," he replies. "Jerr doesn't train any semipros. I want to box for a few more years and make money to pay for college, but to do that I need to go semipro."

Semipro. Younes knows what he wants, not just today or tomorrow, but a year or two from now. For me, I can barely see past the end of my nose.

Because if I won the tickets, would that mean anything besides a nice summer on a riviera? Does saving Mustafa really fit into all my plans with Nassima?

"Don't look so sad," Younes teases. "I'll still come to Jerr's all the time."

"I'm not sad." I correct whatever face I made while deep in thought. "You should leave Jerr's if that's what you want. You won't catch me holding anyone back."

He smiles at me, and I roll my eyes as I banish the thought from both our heads.

"Okay, listen up." Nassima pushes my lunch platter away and gets down to business. "I made a slideshow presentation detailing the days we have in each country. I even put in some Turkish refugee camps that are more developed than the others. They have short-term volunteer programs. I penciled in some time at the camp of our choice."

"Refugee camps?" I ask, an itch at the bottom of my throat returning. "What about the orphanage?"

She shrugs. "The orphanage is in Jordan, and it turns out it's far out from the city. We won't be able to do that in the few days we have at the end of our trip."

"Only a few days?"

Is that enough? I'm going to intrude on people's lives for a few days, observe what my Rochester Heights' eyes subjectively choose to, pass out care packages to children, and call it compensation. The few days will humor my guilt while I float in the baths of Budapest in my burkini.

"I catch you staring."

I blink away from Leene and back at Nassima. "Not staring."

"You are staring," Younes concurs. I bite my lip, outnumbered.

"You've been watching her all lunch long," she adds. "We can invite her to sit with us or if you want to start a fight, I can arrange that."

"I don't want to start a fight," I mumble.

She swallows the rest of her pizza. "Good, because I

thought you guys were getting along better now. No more angry Khadija."

I widen my eyes at Nassima's word choice. "I was never angry with her. Just curious. People love her as soon as they meet her—she must be some sort of magician."

"I liked you as soon as I met you," Younes says all matter-of-factly.

"God knows why," I retort.

"Well, you act like you don't care about others, but really you'd lay down your life for the people you care about. You're unrealistically confident and also weirdly cute and—"

"Yes, yes, Khadija is amazing," Nassima interrupts as my cheeks flush red, "but we're psychoanalyzing her, not complimenting her right now, Younes. We need you to focus."

"Right, sorry." He looks at me. "So, you're jealous of Leene?"

"Uff, no. My problem isn't with Leene; it's with my mom. Always comparing me and wishing I was more like her." Even saying the words makes me feel bad. "But I'm not jealous of Leene. She's just caught between us."

Jealous crudely simplifies the situation.

"I bet you two have loads in common," Nassima says.

"Yeah, right." I wince because yeah, *right*. I can't say I don't enjoy her company. I do, but every time I feel like I can let my guard down, the world reminds me that I'm not good enough. I press my lips together. "Maybe it's for the best that we don't get too close. Leene is too nice for me. I'd just hurt her feelings eventually."

Nassima narrows her kohled eyes at me. "You're nice, too."

"Nice comes out all wrong when I do it."

"Mm," Younes manages through a mouth full of food. I cut him a look, and he swallows quickly. He holds my stare in his big brown eyes. "Who said nice is always better? You're honest and real, Kadi, that's what matters."

Nassima agrees. "It is physically possible to be friends with her."

Is it not impossible? Leene is quick-witted yet likable. She's gone through the worst and survived. She's a genuine Syrian Syrian girl, yet not the Miss Teen Damascus my mom wants to make her out to be. She's everything that I'm not. She's the parts of me that time has taken and I can never get back.

Am I jealous of her?

Younes's question echoes in my head. Jealousy is too convoluted. I don't want her life, and I don't want to be her. I follow a rigorous regimen and abide by brutal rules, my own and my mother's. I strive for the best, placing strenuous expectations on myself, yet I'm never enough. Leene, on the other hand, always seems to be enough, even with what little she has.

"Do you think I resent her?" I ask them.

Nassima tilts her head from side to side as she thinks it over. "You have issues, mon petit chou. Talk to us, unload it all."

So I do. Leene isn't a Syrian clone who got the easy way out like I first thought. She's more than that, and she deserves more. She lived through a rocky revolution. She's a war survivor. She's a refugee who lost her brother and didn't let it tear her apart. All that pain and suffering would have shown my doubters, my mom, that I'm capable. It would have proved my tenacity, my independence, my backbone. If I overcame just one of the challenges that Leene was up against, I'd have all the respect and trust that I crave from my mother. I'd be free to take on the worst that life can throw at me and that life has already thrown at Leene.

"I wish I didn't sound like such a jerk."

"Hell yeah you do," Nassima finesses. Nassima. My best friend. Keeping it real.

The weight on my chest fractures into lighter pieces, but I keep a secret I'm not ready to admit to Nassima or Younes.

I'm not jealous of Leene; I admire her. I fear others will compare us, but I compare myself to her first. Like kryptonite, my Americanness diminishes my Syrianness, whereas Leene is confident in her identity. My Arabic is childlike next to hers. My memories of Syria fade more every day while she has ownership over her past, mistakes and all.

She's complete, and I'm not.

And when I'm with Leene, I'm made aware of it. When I'm with Leene, I feel less.

I can't avoid it. Mama's comparisons don't follow me. Over time, they've become a part of me. And that's not Leene's fault.

Nassima and I look at each other, and her thickly hooded eyes turn down, urging me to do what's right. I remember in eighth grade when all the other girls thought I was too serious, too aggressive, and too proud because I was passionate about the Syrian Revolution. In ninth grade when I tried to make a club called Foundation for a Better Syria, they all feigned interest and then left me in the dust when I approached the principal with my plans. But not Nassima. She has always been my fiercest supporter, standing right there with me even when we had no chance. Nassima will be front row at my fight. I have a Nassima. I wonder who Leene has.

I can be there for Leene. I can win those tickets and use them for the both of us to travel to Jordan to find Mustafa. I would have to put the graduation trip with Nassima on hold, but I can do that. The decision feels right. And I don't need Mama's blessing to know that much.

24

Leene

I'm doing English homework in my room when my phone dings with a text from Khadija.

Come upstairs!

Khadija doesn't usually text me, so that could only mean one thing. I go upstairs to the ground floor to search for her. She's not in the kitchen and not in the living room. I check everywhere.

I'm about to text her back when she calls my name. I follow the sound to the stairs. She's looking down from the railing.

"Come up," she calls.

I walk to the first stair and pause, staring at the step that feels like a looming wall of separation. I stand on the side where strangers are allowed—beyond this step is for family and the closest friends. I've seen Nassima pass over this stair a dozen times without a second thought. Once I pass it, I'm in new territory. As I step onto it, I'm underwhelmed when the barrier vanishes.

I skip up the steps two by two. Following the sound of French music, I make my way to her room.

"Welcome, welcome," she says as I step in.

I almost fall back from glancing around her room. This is not how American girls' rooms look like in the movies. In the ones I've watched, the girls either have makeup and pink stuff everywhere or comic books and scary-looking band posters on the walls.

To think that I called her American in my head when her bedroom is a shrine to Syria. She listens to foreign music and dreams of going to faraway places with Nassima.

"You can close the door and take off your hijab," she says. I do this, fluff up my hijab hair, and look around, but there's nowhere to sit other than at her desk. Khadija, sporting two short French braids, is sprawled on her bed with her homework fanned out around her. She glances up at me like it's normal for me to be in here. "Oh, come sit by me."

I walk over and sit on the comforter, careful not to disrupt too much. She hands me her phone.

I read the email slowly. I'm not the fastest reader in English and my vision blurs, but I get to the end eventually. For a long while after, even when the screen turns off, I stare.

"So that means they don't know if Mustafa is still there," I rasp. "It means they can't help us."

Khadija frowns. "Their email isn't really helpful. They basically just said that they have unreliable records, and we'd have to find him ourselves. We won't know for sure unless we go."

My eyes sting with tears. Ever since I saw the photo, I have thought of Mustafa at this orphanage just waiting for me to get him back. But what if there's a chance that he was just passing through? What if I go all the way there and don't find him?

"But not to worry because I have a plan," she says, giving my shoulder a shake. "You know my mom thinks I want to go on a summer trip with Nassima, right? She already knows that I want to go abroad, and I'm on my way to convincing her. Maybe we can go look for Mustafa on our way. Or what if we go to find Mustafa instead?"

I set my face in my hands, my eyes brimming with unspilled tears. "I can't have you change your trip for me. I have to go myself."

"Without your mom getting suspicious?" She raises an eyebrow at me. "And how? With school and your job? We might not be able to go until we graduate in June."

She's right, it's almost April, but June feels like a lifetime away. Still, the image of bringing Mustafa home gives me so much hope that it tightens my chest until I can't breathe. Mustafa coming home means coming here.

I've gotten too comfortable. My hands shake. "Mama and I need our own place to bring him home to. I've already been looking at apartments and I submitted an application for government rehousing."

Khadija props herself up on her elbows and slides her laptop over to me. "Can I see what you found?"

I go through all of them, and the places that we could afford are definitely a downgrade from living here, *downgrade* being an understatement, but it's our first step on our own in America. Aslan, home is a place that is created from context, and without context, home is just a place. As long as Mama is there, and if we could find Mustafa, I will have my family and anywhere could be my home.

But Khadija doesn't point out all the faults, she just nods and makes comments like "Nice, that one has a washer-dryer" or "Is that mold?" and she says it all without a tinge of sarcasm. I feel safe sharing these with her. Once the affordable apartments run out, the climbing prices hold me in a vise. I have to click away.

I hold my breath. "So we're going to find Mustafa. This is real."

Khadija cracks her knuckles. "Soon as I win those tickets and walk across the graduation stage, we're going to find him."

Maybe I should feel relieved, but mostly I feel scared. What if I don't find Mustafa? What if I *do*? What will Mama think of me? What will Mustafa think of me?

I look at Khadija, who flips onto her stomach and continues her math homework while humming to herself. At least she doesn't judge me for this. Surprisingly, she's the only one who knows what I need and is willing to help me, no questions asked.

I chuckle softly to myself, getting a look from her.

"What is it?"

I laugh shallowly, rubbing my nose. "I can't believe we're hanging out up here like friends."

Khadija's gaze falls off.

She shrugs.

A glint in the corner of her room catches my eye.

"Is that ibrik qahwa?"

The most intricately embossed gold dallah coffee pot sits on a lowered pedestal behind her desk. The angular spout is too curved, its hourglass body too accentuated, altogether inflated in ornamental glamor. It's the fanciest one I've ever seen in my life.

"Yeah, I thought it matched pretty well," Khadija replies.

"It does, but shouldn't it be in the kitchen?" I say. I've never seen an ibrik qahwa displayed like a piece of art in a bedroom.

"It reminds me of Syria just like all this other stuff." Her words nearly evaporate before reaching my ears.

"That's a silly thing to remind you of your country."

"Why's it silly?"

"Because something with a function doesn't carry memories. It's used for its purpose and that's that," I say. I feel weird explaining that to her. Maybe I don't get it because it's an American thing or a rich person thing.

Something flashes behind her gaze. "Well, I also keep the prayer beads from my teteh's broken misbaha in that jar there. And I have empty ketchup chip bags in a photo album. And I still play cards with the same water-damaged deck that I used when I was learning to play all the card games with my family in Syria." Something that looks like longing, a painful feeling, piques at the center of her forehead and spreads to the rest of her face. "But maybe you're right. I'm dumb to keep this junk for so long." Her voice catches on the word *junk*.

"You aren't dumb," I say, realizing that I might have crossed a line. "You're just different."

"*Different?* What does *different* mean in this context, Miss Semantics?" she asks with a long look.

"Nothing," I say, and her look deepens. "Wallah, I just meant you're different from me. It's not a good or bad thing."

"Are you sure *different* doesn't mean less Syrian than you?"

"I never said you were less Syrian than me." I don't tell her that maybe at some point I had thought it.

"Everyone else says it plenty," she says. "People love comparisons. They love putting you and me side by side and ticking off boxes on who does what better."

I think of Khaleh Maisa's remarks in the car and around the house asking Khadija to be more like me. It was uncomfortable, sure, but it's not anything new.

"My family used to love comparing me to my cousins," I tell her. "My looks, my skin color, my grades. Even after the revolution started, they would bet on which of us would be able to marry abroad and get out."

"That's disgusting."

"That's being Syrian."

Khadija shakes her head. "It's not fair. I bet you and I could've been friends a long time ago if it wasn't for my mom trying to clone me into you."

"Trust me, you don't want to be me."

"I know that," she says. "I love being me. I'm not upset with you because you're everything I'm not or everything that the khalehs want me to be. I'm frustrated with where I fit in between. I wish they'd accept me as I am."

"It wouldn't hurt your chances if you smiled more," I start, teasingly, "but that doesn't make you fit in any less than me. If you could even call whatever I do 'fitting in.'" I raise my eyebrows at her, addressing the gap between my lifestyle and the ones being lived around me.

"But that's what's implied when they treat us that way. Especially when my mom acts like I'll never be enough so long as I'm not like you. It makes me bitter." Khadija bites her lower lip and sighs heavily. "Uff, I hated saying that."

Khadija's divulgence breaks down a barrier between us and I capitalize on it. "Just because I have the patience to talk to a khaleh about her day doesn't make you any less Syrian. It's not like I'm more entitled to using that ibrik qahwa over there."

Khadija crinkles her nose. "I wouldn't know how to make Arabic qahwa anyway."

"Please," I say with a snort. "If only you saw me in the kitchen! I literally have the cooking skills of a five-year-old. And that might even be offensive to some five-year-olds."

Khadija laughs.

"I'm just so sick of hearing that I'm not good enough, not Syrian enough, not American enough," she lists.

I shrug. "I'm not American at all."

"It's not hard to be American," she says. "You just have to look the part."

I remember all the American faces at school. I super-impose the features on her. "You look American to me." Khadija with her blue eyes and confident airs and in clothes with authentic brand logos.

She reaches over to her nightstand for a scarf. She wraps it around her head in one sweeping motion. "Do I look American now?"

"I see."

Khadija throws it off her head, and she levels her gaze with mine. "My mom and her friends don't think I'm Syrian enough and the world doesn't think I'm American enough. So I have to find a way to be both in perfect sync."

"You're both, though," I say. "I can see that now."

Her eyes are sad, but her lips turn upward in a smile. "But it doesn't matter what one person thinks when everyone else has already made up their minds. I didn't get enough time in Syria. You got more time there. You have more of a right to it than I do."

"Time doesn't give me the rights to it," I tell her. "If you love Syria, if it was once your home, that's all that matters."

Khadija's eyes soften, and they're soon bright and swimming. "Thanks for saying that."

I open my arms for a hug. "Friends?"

She makes a face at me, but I throw my arms around her anyway. She swats at me, but I don't let go.

"I'm tapping out," she cries, slapping her hand down on her bed.

I let go and we lock eyes and there isn't any mystery sentiment behind it. I knew we weren't destined to be enemies. I knew she was worth it.

Khadija, the first Syrian and American friend I've made in America.

25

Khadija

$\mathcal{I}$n what feels like no time at all, Leene's government rehousing application goes through, and their place is ready for move-in by mid-April. God bless America, I guess.

She texts me the news as soon as she gets it. They'll be able to move into their own place in a couple weeks. She sends me a sequence of emojis that make no sense alone, but perfect sense together. Her texts come staggered.

Having breakfast with our moms

We can tell them together!

So nervous

Ahhh

I lumber down the stairs and into the cutthroat kitchen. I glance at the counter where all the car keys sit in a bowl and count all the keys except Baba's. Checking the counter is a habit I've had since I was a girl, and when his were there, I'd be overcome by happiness. As I got older, those moments became fewer and fewer, and now, on the rare occasion his keys are in the bowl, I feel nothing.

A complete Syrian breakfast is set on the dining table: side dishes of yogurt and cucumbers, olives and pickles, honey and butter, handpicked apricot and quince jams, and a stack of pita bread. My mother gossips with Khaleh Rana over a main dish of lemony, tomatoey, oily ful.

Leene catches my eye and grins. Mama follows her gaze and leaps up to usher me over to the table.

"Ah, Khadija, I love to see you," Khaleh Rana says in her voice that's identical to Leene's. She continues, "Leene only has the best to say about Khadija. You should be proud, Maisa. You raised a wonderful daughter."

I gape at both Khaleh Rana and her daughter. My mother beams.

God is too good to me.

Then, as I serve myself ful, reality strikes me down. "If only she'd listen more, then she'd do me some good," says Mama, ever my devout humbler.

"I think she's doing a fine job," Khaleh Rana, bless her soul, insists.

"It's the fighting," Mama says with a shake of her head.

Leene clears her throat. "Did Khadija tell you that I signed up at her gym?"

My mother side-eyes me.

"I tried to stop her," I say with a heavy sigh, not without

humor, and in hopes of recompense from Mama. "But she's stubborn," I joke to Khaleh Rana's delight, "and now she'll learn the hard way. Through sweat and tears and bruises."

Mama turns up her nose. "Both of you should stop going immediately. You'll damage your bodies and you won't be able to bear children."

I roll my eyes. "That's why you won't let me get a cat, either. You think they'll stop me from having kids. As if I want kids."

Leene purses her lips to stop herself from laughing. Laughing would definitely aggravate the situation. She's racking up some serious points with me. But the "cat conversation" catches on and Khaleh Rana is in total agreement. It's Syrian lore that cats obliterate fertility and it's a thorn in my side every time I stalk kittens on the internet.

"A friend of mine," Khaleh Rana begins in all seriousness, "had a cat when she was younger and had such trouble conceiving. When she finally had a daughter, the baby was as hairless as a fish!"

Doubtful, but definitely a myth Arab moms would invent to get their way. I look over at Leene, whose lips are nonexistent, and her faint dimples are deep from suppressing the laughter.

"Hairless?" I repeat. "If a cat is gonna save me from my foresty armpits, I'll take one today."

Leene cracks up first, and it's a domino effect. She reaches over the dishes for a high five. I hesitate, but then think a perfunctory *what the hell* and reciprocate it. Khaleh Rana chuckles quietly, but Mama gazes at me in awe. It's more smug than amazed.

It gives me the perfect segue. "Actually," I start, "Leene has some news."

I pass the mic to Leene. She drops her pita bread and presses her lips together. "I applied for an apartment through a government-funded program. We can move into our own place in a few weeks."

Leene and I beam at each other, but to our surprise, the news is met with silence.

"Leene…," Khaleh Rana starts, her brow creased with worry.

"Was this your idea?" Mama asks me, her voice hard and her glare deadly.

I frown. Mama is mad. Why is she mad?

"It was my idea," Leene says quickly. "I wanted to be more independent, and I know we can't stay here forever. We've already outstayed our welcome."

"Outstayed your welcome?" Mama repeats incredulously. Her wide eyes twist toward me.

At Mama's tone, I drop the pita bread. I've lost my appetite. I would never say that Leene outstayed her welcome, but that doesn't matter when Mama is already convinced that the version of me in her head would.

"That's ridiculous," Mama says. "You two are welcome here for as long as you need."

"And I'm thankful for that," Leene replies. Then she turns to her mom. "But, Mama, you know we can't stay here forever. If we have this chance, we should take it."

Khaleh Rana wipes her mouth with a napkin. Doubt colors her face. "I don't know if we're ready to be on our own."

"We are," Leene insists. "We have to be."

Leene glances my way and I know why. Her mom needs to be ready because if Mustafa is out there, if we can find him at the orphanage, then she has to be ready for more than just moving out.

Reaching her hand to cover her mom's, Leene says, "We're going to be okay, Mama."

I look at Mama's hand, a fist on the table, and then down at my own, clenched just as hard.

My mother serves us after-meal black tea with peppermint. I can't escape her piercing glare. I burn my tongue downing my tea in seconds. As I do the dishes, I hear Mama's polite talk become increasingly curt. She's already strategizing for a fight.

Khaleh Rana and Leene excuse themselves in a cluster of gratitude and head downstairs, but I can't turn around to face them. Not with my mother back there, too.

"Khadija."

I shut the water off and turn, pressing myself back against the kitchen counter.

Mama's hands rest on her hips, and I roll up my sleeves. It's my turn to be on the offensive.

"I did nothing wrong." I replay the breakfast. Nope, nothing. I did nothing wrong. I get to be angry with her for making me sound like I was trying to get rid of Leene, not the other way around.

Mama blows out her cheeks. Her voice quakes with irritation. "How could you ask Leene to leave?"

My head spins. "What? Who said I asked that?"

"Why else would she suddenly want to move out?"

I put my hand on my chin. "I don't know, maybe because Leene wants to have her own place. Maybe she doesn't want to feel indebted to you."

"Who would mind living here?" Mama asks, exasperated.

"Not everyone wants what you have, Mama. Some people treasure their ownership and independence more than all the material stuff in the world. Did you think to ask Leene if she wants to keep living here?"

"Why would I, Khadija?" Her voice rises and plows onto the football field, leveling any semblance of an organized match. "Why would they want to leave unless they felt uncomfortable? I bend over backward to make them feel comfortable. The only person who could make them feel unwelcome is you."

My jaw is tight, and my throat constricts. "You're blaming me?"

"I'm trying to get them on their own two feet in time. Rana isn't ready to be on her own."

I scoff. "You don't know that."

"I'm trying to make them feel normal."

"W-what?" I stutter. "Not letting them move on isn't normal. You're controlling them because you're obsessed with control."

But Mama doesn't hear me. "I see you laughing and joking with Leene, and you're finally branching out and making a new friend besides Nassima. For a second, I think you've made progress. It doesn't hurt that Leene is someone I would love you to be like. Then what? You've found a way to kick them out of the house? I'm shocked you'd be so cruel, Khadija."

My eyes sting, but I don't dare shed a tear. Why cry when Mama's words are so untrue?

But she doesn't stop there. "It's you who neglects others and their feelings. It's you who can't be a caring friend. You're selfish, Khadija."

My eyes blur. *Selfish* is a pathetic translation of the word my mother uses. The Arabic language is rich, and it packs a punch. *Ananiyah. Ana.* I. The word she uses is *conceited, egotistical, self-centered,* all in one sound bite.

I squirm when I hear it.

"Ananiyah?"

"Yes, ananiyah. You think about yourself first and last and always. I'm helping them start a life here and you're too busy trying to live your life all on your own to notice how bad you've become. The only time you want my input is when you need something from me. So watch yourself, Khadija, and don't start that traveling talk at all in this discussion because I won't listen to it."

Discussion. This is an argument in a huge kitchen in an enormous empty house in which every atom attracts toward us and bounces off between us. The tension is stifling, and I want to break through it. A fight between Arab women is always high stakes. A wayward spark can blow a massive explosion. One of us, if not both, will suffer injuries.

"No." I have my voice under control, but it's injected with pure rage. "You can force Khaleh Rana and Leene to live here forever, but I am talking about that trip. It's this summer. I will win the tickets myself at my gym at the fight that you won't be going to because you hate it just like you hate everything I love."

"I do not."

"You do! Boxing, my Arablish, my love for Syria, all of it!" And now I'm screaming. "You hate everything about me because it'll lead me to leaving you. When I'm eighteen—"

"Eighteen doesn't mean anything."

"It means I can travel on my own without your permission." I'm walking toward her and fuming, my jaw locked. "And I will. I won't need your money; I won't need Baba's money. I will go this summer. Bring all the Leenes into my life, but it won't change me, and it won't stop me. It definitely won't stop everyone from abandoning you, because I'm the only one who bothers to show up for you anyway."

It's a low blow I know, but it's also true. From Mama's perspective, this house is long and empty and cold. She is alone with Zain isolating himself and Baba working away all hours of every day. I'm the only one she has, but she'll never be satisfied with me as I am. If I let her get used to me by her side, I'll never be able to leave.

My mother is quiet for a long time, and I realize my cheeks are hot with tears. I never cry, but now that I am, Mama's looking at me like I'm the eighth wonder of the world. Finally, I've let her see how much pain she puts me through.

When Mama finally speaks, she sounds sickly angelic. "I am looking out for what's best for you, Khadija. You wear the hijab. You need to live knowing you're a target. People will hurt you. Eventually, something bad will happen to you if you don't live cautiously."

Hijab isn't a source of weakness for me like Mama thinks it is. It's the reason I strive for more strength every day.

"I can't stop living my life because people will attack me for what I wear. I *won't* stop living my life because you're afraid. I learned to protect myself because I'm sick of being scared. I box so I can defend myself if anyone comes at me. I box so you don't have to worry about me."

Mama frowns. "Khadija, I only want you to be safe and happy."

"You can't guarantee both of those can coexist." I wipe my tears. "With me, I don't think you can guarantee both of those at the same time ever."

I glare at Mama, neither of us relenting. I want to stop there, but that word, the indicting word that she used earlier, feels like it's stamped on my forehead. It doesn't shame me or make me furious. It makes me hurt.

"And I am not ananiyah," I whisper.

Mama reaches to touch me, but I recoil. I don't want her comfort. Not in my dreams, not in my nightmares, not anywhere. I don't know who this person is in front of me who criticizes me, blames me, and then cares for me in ways that make me feel neglected. Mama doesn't want me to be happy—she wants me to be exactly what she wants. Whether that matches what I want from my life or not.

Shutting myself in my room, I don't remember the last time I let my mother hold me.

26

Leene

"I'm having a jalta." I grip my knees, breathing like an over-worked mule.

"You are not having a stroke," Khadija says. She leads me back to the black bag of my misery, acting as the strings to graze my puppet hands against the bag. "My cousins used to make fun of me for saying I was having a stroke every time they scared me." She smiles as she looks away, remembering.

"I give up." I wheeze. My face feels the color of saffron.

"You wanted to get your mind off things, right? This is how I get away from the pressure of life."

"You torture yourself to clear your head?"

"This isn't torture." She punches the bag so quickly my brain spins. Everyone here moves their bodies in impossible ways; it's unclear to me how they wake up the next morning in one piece. Khadija turns back to me. "Arms up."

I barricade my face behind my fist as she instructed, and I begin again, though my body begs me to stop. My arms fall at my sides. "I think filling a million falafel sandwiches a day might be my exercise limit," I say, out of breath.

"Don't give in," Khadija whines. Even though she completed a full workout, her hijab is fastened to her head like glue. Mine clings to my head by a few hairs.

"This isn't how I expected to spend my Sunday," I cry.

My arm wobbles in her direction in my weakest attempt at a punch all morning. Khadija comes to my side and instructs me on proper form again. She has to raise her voice over the loud rap music that is almost as distracting as the thudding of fists on leather bags. The other boxers don't really look my way, but I notice they don't act like most people do around me. The others work out beside me—they don't pick the farthest bag away from me like the students who take the farthest seat from me in class. The only thing that makes it obvious that I don't belong here is my inability to stay standing for longer than two minutes without Khadija propping me up.

Yani, it's clear I wasn't born for this. It doesn't suit me like it does Khadija, but it's hard to catch her at home since she's been practicing extra hard for her match. So I tagged along. After signing up for the gym months ago, I'm finally here. Rapidly wilting but here.

At least at the gym the muscular athletes and loud music make it harder to overthink. About Mustafa and about the big move. Since I told Khaleh Maisa that Mama and I were moving out, our room has been a tornado of clothes and boxes. In the past few months, Mama and I have accumulated a ridiculous amount of stuff because Mama has returned to her old hoarding ways. I won't complain, though, because I'm finally seeing signs of the Mama I had before the revolution broke her.

A few punches later, I can't keep my arms up. A water bottle nestles into the nook of my hand.

"Take a break." This man, whose tattoo-covered muscles bulge through his navy T-shirt, doesn't speak to me. He sidesteps me and locks eyes with Khadija. "You're going to kill her, Kadi."

"A stroke…," I mumble in English, nodding my head and guzzling the bottle.

"Don't put that idea in her head, Gab," Khadija complains.

"The idea of a break?" he asks with an amused look on his face. I wonder if his hair is slick with gel or with sweat.

"Yes, break time!" I exhale. I don't bother moving. I flop on the ground since my body, once of bones and organs, has thawed to liquid.

"No break time." Restless, Khadija paces in front of the punching bag.

"Never?" The man named Gab wiggles his brows. He leans against a tower of weights. "I thought I'd never wear a shirt at the gym again, yet here I am."

Khadija points at him as though warning him for next time, but her look unfolds into a smile. "Touché."

"Oh, there's your boyfriend. Come here and distract her," Gab calls out. Khadija glares at Gab and punches the bag so hard the gym music cuts out in my ears.

Despite becoming one with Jell-O, my head whips around the entire gym. I want all the details about Khadija's "boyfriend" as soon as possible. I'm not a gossip, but I am Syrian, and it's in my blood to sniff out rumors.

I keep looking for Khadija's mystery man when Younes approaches me. He nods a hello at me, ever the gentleman he was when I first met him. I squint at him from the sweat bleeding into the corners of my eyes and stinging.

"You're training even on your birthday?" he asks, grinning at Khadija.

My head whips over to Khadija. "It's your birthday?"

Khadija shrugs. "According to Nassima's one thousand happy birthday texts, yes, yes it is."

"And you didn't tell me?" I ask, feeling like a useless friend.

"She was too busy abusing you," Gab says.

"*Abusing?*" Khadija interjects before I can formulate a response. She kicks the punching bag weakly and her voice drops. "I'm destroying every cell in her body to make new ones. Stronger ones."

Somewhere in my gelatin brain, I tuck her words away.

Younes turns away from me and faces her, and from afar they look like they're about to square off. Younes may argue back, and punches may or may not be thrown. Except he doesn't say what I expect. "True," he agrees, "that is the hardest part on the road to greatness."

Khadija laughs lightly. "You're so full of it."

Gab sits up. "So full of shit," he corrects.

"Just 'cause I whooped your ass," Younes rebukes.

"On today's episode of who's more macho." Khadija pretends she's one of the presenters on John Cena's show.

"You won that title, luchadora." Gab smirks.

For a full ten seconds I forget all of my mistakes. I'm a normal teenager still looking for my friend's crush and tuning in to Khadija's everyday banter.

Younes and Khadija tiptoe around each other until they are separated by the length of the boxing ring. Younes leans toward the ring, draping his arms along the bottom of the rope.

"Oh, I got it." I slip into Arabic from the shock of my realization.

"You got what?" Khadija responds in Arabic, skillfully ejecting Younes and Gab from our conversation, though they listen intently.

"You and him." My chin minutely motions toward Younes.

"Me and him what?"

"What your other friend said." I refer to Gab but can't risk another head tilt.

"And he said what?"

In Arabic, the word for *boyfriend* is also the word for

someone's lover. I know even before I say it that she's going to take it the wrong way.

I inhale sharply, tilting my neck toward Younes and lowering my voice. "Your habibi."

Gab and Younes crack up. Khadija's fists clench, and her brows slant like one of the villains on *Spacetoon*, Arabic-dubbed anime that I used to watch on Syrian television. "He is not my habibi," Khadija says in English. The tension in her body releases in one frame just like in anime.

"I could be." Younes winks at her. Apparently, everyone knows what *habibi* means. I blush on Khadija's behalf.

She rolls her eyes, flipping one end of her hijab over her shoulder like the ladies do on those Pantene commercials, except without the hair.

I can't help but gape at their coy exchange. Khadija pushes my jaws together. "Uff," she says, reverting to Arabic and unable to hide her playfulness. "You can't tell my mom about Younes. Deal?"

With that, we seal a sweat pact, which is as unbreakable as a blood oath. If this is what it is like to be real friends with Khadija, I have to be on my toes at all times.

"English, please," Younes blatantly gripes.

"Jealous?" Khadija teases. Younes scrunches his nose, prompting Khadija to chuck her gloves at him, which smack him squarely in the face—they ricochet off his eye. He flinches and doubles his hands over it in pain. She scurries over with a slew of apologies.

"I'm sorry... but it's your fault," she gripes.

"My fault? Why are you throwing things at me?"

"You're making faces at me!"

"What can I do with my face to not make me a target?"

"I was overwhelmed," Khadija stammers. "I don't know what to do with your face."

"You love it." Younes flashes a smile at her, left eye squinting.

"Stop that."

"Stop what? I'm just looking at you."

"Then stop looking at me like that!"

There are definitely sparks between them.

I toss my gloves aside and reach for another water bottle.

"Leene, you're coming to the showcase, right?" Gab asks me.

I look at Khadija to gauge her reaction like I used to when I didn't want to overstep. But she doesn't lend an ear while she continues to banter with Younes.

Khadija and I are friends. So much so that I can be in her gym, in her bubble, and I can answer without tiptoeing around her. I guess this gym provides me a break from reality, too.

"Of course," I reply as Khadija and Younes return to our

world again. "I wouldn't miss Khadija's fight for anything." Khadija's expression softens, an invisible string tethering us tighter together.

Gab smirks. "Good, then you'll be there to watch her get her ass—"

Younes chucks a pair of boxing gloves at Gab's gut before he can finish his sentence.

27

Khadija

*A*fter training with Leene, I drop her off at her work and come back to the gym. And not just because I need more practice for the showcase that's just over a month away.

I let out my frustrations on the bag until I'm all sweat and body aches. When I get home I'll knock out, and I know Mama won't ask for me because we're at a stalemate. Happy birthday to me, I guess.

The day we've been fighting about has arrived. I'm finally eighteen. I don't feel any different.

I land a right hook that reverberates through my glove to the rest of my body.

"Need a live target?"

My shoulders seize up at the sound of Whit's steely voice. "Are you volunteering?"

We jump into the ring. She's shorter than me, so she'll try to come in close since I have the longer reach. She's stubbornly offensive, even more so than me, so I'll have to lie back and wait for the perfect opportunity. We circle each other, and I analyze the fight like I'm outside the ring: I evade and evade and evade. Still, I see no opening.

Then, all at once, I see stars. My ear throbs and I hear ringing. I shake my head and Whit, who is looking more like three Whits, is wearing a smirk. I didn't know she'd hit me until after she did.

"Come on," Whit pouts. "If it was going to be this easy to beat you, I would have trained half as hard."

My mind was elsewhere. I abandon all thinking and go full offensive, closing the gap but missing all my punches. They're too long, too sloppy, and she's too close. She takes the advantage and I'm stuck in a corner protecting my face, my arms taking the brunt of her hits.

The ding-a-ling of the front door sounds and my heart lurches for a break in her attack.

"Playing without a ref?" Younes's voice is loud and clear. Whit stops her barrage of punches, and I send silent thanks to Younes. He narrows his eyes at Whit. "That's against the rules."

"You wanna ref?" Whit challenges.

"I wanna talk to Kadi," he says curtly.

Whit jumps down from the ring, throwing off her gloves, and heads to the locker room. "He saved your ass," she calls back at me. "There won't be any of that at the fight."

I hold back a comeback because she's right. I accept the beating and leave the ring with my head down. I lie on a bench in the corner of the room, and my body aches with pain.

Younes walks over and looks down at me with furrowed brows and a lopsided smile. "You came back to practice? Are you overworking yourself?"

His words do something to me. My nose stings and crinkles, and my eyes water. Maybe his voice is too soft. Maybe his eyes are too warm. Maybe the answer to his question is yes.

I sit up and cover my eyes with my hands. It's times like this that I wish I wasn't wearing hijab so my hair can fall over my face and hide me. I've been caught feeling feelings red-handed.

Younes scoots next to me, twirling his keys in his hands. He doesn't say anything, and I'm left not only with my feelings, but with my thoughts.

I have to win those tickets. Per the rules, if the people I've invited come to the showcase and vote for me based purely on loyalty, I win. I could book a trip to Jordan. I could help Leene find Mustafa.

Mama might think I'm incapable of empathy, but if I make a difference for Leene, if I help her, then I can prove that I'm not the selfish monster she thinks I am.

I hide it well, but I spend countless hours cinching dates and calculating the cash in my bank. I try to parse together a plan where my trip with Nassima and one with Leene can both happen. But the more I think about it, the more I'm uncomfortable with the idea of eating at a street café on a cute French street or strolling down Las Ramblas in Barcelona knowing that I could have done more for Mustafa. For kids just like Mustafa.

I blink back tears of rage. They're the kind of tears from when you sing along to a new song that unloads so many emotions you never thought you had. Remembering my hellish relationship with my mother in the midst of the other roadblocks threatens to break me.

My eyes dry up, and Younes nudges my knee lightly. I look up at him and put on a fake smile. "I'm fine."

"Are you?"

I'm not. I wedge an axe between the ties in my fragmented little family a little more every day. I tear apart. I try to build bridges with a sledgehammer. I tried with my mother. Even with Leene and Nassima, I feel I will have to break one of their hearts when I choose one over the other this summer. And if I can't bring my family together then how can I expect myself to reunite Leene's?

"You're not okay." Younes reads me. He's kind and thoughtful and he's everything I don't deserve.

There is a villain inside me, the part of me that I hate, the part that I need to tell the world about.

"I'm really not." My voice comes out harsher than intended so I abate it. "I am rich and spoiled and I have never had to ask for anything other than having more of what I already have. My parents give me everything and still I obsess over the little things I want and say it's insufferable when I don't get them."

I think of the psychological torture that Leene must have

gone through—that she must be going through. "My friends have lost more, and left so much more, but they blame themselves. I have everything and all I do is blame others."

I'm holding myself, as the Arabic saying goes. I'm holding myself from releasing all that is within me and unleashing the guilt that I've stored since 2011.

I need someone to hold me, and Younes must notice it. The electricity buzzing around us with emotion pulls at me like a magnet. We both acknowledge that the physical barrier between us exists for a reason, and we respect the rule. A single touch on a night like this could crumble the wall we've built between us. A wall protecting us from an unknown that can take us anywhere.

I spread my hands on the edge of the bench and clench them. Over and over. "Why do I feel so guilty all the time?"

"You're not guilty of anything," Younes says with heart.

"But I am," I reply weakly. "Any one of my cousins is more deserving of being here, where there's clean water and a warm home and life and change. Not sleeping to gunfire or dropped bombs. Not imprisoned or enslaved to the army. Not frozen in time. Not stuck in 2011. Not in Syria. I should be there, and they should be here, then I'll learn to be grateful. I wouldn't avoid my mother like a snake. I'm guilty of hating what I have and throwing it all away because I can't hug my mother and tell her I'm sorry. I'm guilty for wanting more when others don't have a fraction of what I have.

"That's why I want to win the trip from the fight. I need it. I want to run far away from all the money and protection and see the real world and then help my people. There are people who are more deserving of this life that I take for granted. I can't live with it anymore."

I stop blabbering to let Younes tell me how I'm being hard on myself and that my woes are circumstance. He sees the glass half-full, whereas I smash the glass so I can demand another one that's filled to the brim. I want to lean my head on his shoulder, to feel his energy and his understanding transfer through me.

But Younes turns his knees away from me. He says, "Every day I drive by Ford Middle School before I come back to the gym after school. It's on the other side of town. After the final bell, the kids find their groups and they stand around school until dark. Shit goes down at that school. Really heavy shit. So, after I get out of class at RHHS, I stop by and play basketball with them. One guy stopping by for an hour after school and telling the kids to get their asses on the courts can end all the shit they're passing around, and it keeps them busy. It doesn't change everything for all of them, but it changes enough for some of them. As you know, Kadi, I always like to be doing something, so I like to be there for the people who need me. Sometimes it's overwhelming—the number of people who ask for my help is way more than the number that I can ask to help me when I need it. But it makes me feel like I'm making a difference right where I am.

"You know," he continues, "it's been a long time since Somalis have been leaving Somalia because of flooding or famine or war. But I don't feel the same way that you do about going to Somali refugee camps to help."

"So what are you saying?" I ask, craving an answer. "Are you saying I have some savior complex?"

My question sounds a little harsh, but it's because I want a hard answer. I don't want him to sugarcoat anything for me anymore.

"If you go," he adds softly, "don't expect you'll make a big dent in their lives. You'll touch a few lives, but the war, the hunger, all of that, they don't begin and end with you. If you're going because of that guilt you're putting on yourself, then don't go."

I blink at him, stunned at how he can make such brazen comments gently. He has no idea. I can help Leene. I can make a huge difference in her life. Just because she's one among millions doesn't mean helping her find Mustafa isn't worth it.

But when I return, successful or not, will I commend myself for doing what little I could, pat myself on the back, and move on without a guilty conscience?

And if that's the goal, who am I doing all of this for?

"I shouldn't go?" I repeat.

His brown eyes bore into mine. "Don't go. Your guilt is your personal problem. God chose you to be here and them to be there for a reason. Feeling guilty about it is another excuse you make for yourself when you don't put in the work. It drains all your energy and justifies that helpless feeling you have, and that won't get you anywhere."

The hairs at the back of my neck stand, and I'm up on my feet. "You think I'm helpless?"

"No." Younes stands, too, reaching for me, but his hand falls away a moment later. "I mean maybe you think you are. You can't use time and space as an excuse for not acting here and now. You being there for Leene is noble, too. I don't think you realize how much it means to her that you're her friend. I see the way she looks at you like she wants your attention."

"She does not."

Younes levels his eyes with mine. "I would know, Kadi. I want your attention, too, and you don't seem to notice that, either."

I frown. "I just feel like I'm drowning all the time."

"So do I," he says with a sigh. "But when I'm with you, I get a break from that. I like the way you're sucked into your own world, and I get to be there along with you. But sometimes, you're in your world, and you don't let anyone in. You won't even leave it occasionally for the rest of us."

I nod, wondering if maybe that's how Mama sees me, and I'm the oblivious one.

Younes must see me spiraling because he continues. "My only point is, why go abroad when you have a community here that needs your help? Other families like Leene's. I think seeing a refugee camp and volunteering for a few days is a way for you to be free of your guilt about a crisis that's happening but that you can't see. Isn't it more about you than about making a difference in their lives?"

"I get it." My throat constricts, and his faces eases. "I'd be useless to them. My reasons for trying to help my people are completely selfish." My hands are shaking and clammy. It's that damn word that follows me. Ananiyah. I step away from him as he steps forward.

"I never said that." He's apologetic, and his arms stretch out to me to steady me. I push up against a padded wall. I know I shouldn't add to Younes's worries and problems; I don't want to be another person on his list of people who need him.

"You're right," I whisper, "you're right." He takes too many steps closer, calling my name on an exhale, sucking out the air between us. I search his warm eyes and find his vision of me, a defeatist whose self-inflicted guilt provides for her a lifeboat in a sea of blood and loss.

28

Leene

"Could you went to Syria? I could...went? Can you go to Syria? I can't go? Right?" Amal sighs heavily beside me. "Why is English so hard? Practice with me."

"Can you go to Syria?" she asks.

"I can't."

"Could you went to Syria?"

"I couldn't."

Amal folds her homework papers. "Complete sentences." She wants the answers.

I could tell her those are complete sentences, but my life is a fog of exhaustion. Moving is more work than I thought, and I stay up at night wondering if Khadija's plan will work and we can go to find Mustafa. What if her plan falls through? There are too many variables, and if one falls through, then I'm getting nowhere. Mustafa will still be in the orphanage thousands of miles away.

Or what's worse, we could go all the way to the orphanage

and not find him. Mustafa could be lost forever. Not in Syria, not in Jordan, and not gone, just lost.

And lost is worse than gone.

Can't, couldn't, whatever. I would fall apart, and I can't, couldn't, wouldn't anything.

"I can't go to Syria," I answer for Amal. "I couldn't go to Syria."

Amal clasps her hands together. "I couldn't go, that's right. You're right!" She doesn't know how wrong I've been. She ponders for a second. "But you could. You could before."

If I don't find Mustafa, I can't, I couldn't, I won't.

I can't, I couldn't, I won't be able to live with myself.

I can't, I couldn't, I won't face Mama. I'll hide away forever. She doesn't deserve her heart to break a second time.

I can't, I couldn't, I won't forgive myself.

We arrive at the ELL classes in the hall at the back of the school. I turn in to our classroom and pull back out to save myself from Amal's grammar dissection, but also because I must've seen wrong.

I peek my head back around the corner, and it wasn't a trick of the eyes. It's Zain. Zain in my ELL class. He sulks in the middle of the classroom surrounded by other boys I have never seen anywhere near our hall. They make obscene jokes in English and guffaw obnoxiously.

Zain slumps in his chair and brings his face inches from his paper. He writes with extreme care, thinking full seconds before moving on to the next word. Suddenly, the boys snatch his paper from him.

One of them, the shortest one, with flappy ears and dark curls pulled back from his forehead with a headband, clears his throat and straightens his imaginary bowtie. "My Most Memorable Memory, by Zain Shaami," he reads. For some reason this is hilarious to the other boys. As they cackle, Zain shields his face as though they are the sun brightly shining rays of embarrassment at him.

The flappy-eared boy continues with his reading, this time with a long face and solemn voice: "The last time I went to Syria was in 2010. It was summer and the weather was very hot. Every day I played soccer in the street with my cousins. Sometimes we played next to huge ditches and survived. I learned the names of more than a hundred family members. My dad has eight brothers and five sisters, and my mom has four brothers and two sisters. On the last day, I visited my grandfather's house. The whole family was there."

The boys snicker with every word, then Flappy Ears determines the essay doesn't yield a somber tone. My heart drops when he acts lame and delays his speech and speaks as though he wears dentures.

"Uhhh—the fam-ily gathered at the—uh—house to say good-bye. It was a ce-cel-uh-b-b-br-uh—"

Another boy leans over and shoves his friend. "It says celebration. Well, he tried to spell celebration. How are you even reading this? Half of it is misspelled." The others chortle at Zain's expense.

Zain could be a turtle, his head nestles so deep into his shoulders. He pulls his hood over his head. His embarrassment is contagious, but I can't, I couldn't, I won't help him. I'm gripped by the fear that this might be happening to Mustafa, and I can't, I couldn't, I won't be there to stop it.

Flappy Ears goes on, reading louder so that even Amal on the other side of the room is audience to his act. "We p-played games and sang songs. I will ne-ver forget that good-bye. The next y-year in March, the rev-o-lu-tion hap-pened."

I try to tune out Flappy Ears's cruel interpretation of Zain's writing. I listen to the words, falling down the rabbit hole of Zain's thoughts. "I can't see my cousins anymore. We can't play soccer in the streets together and prank each other. The streets were like a playground for us. I beat anyone just by telling them that I was from America. I beat them all for real when I used to play, but I don't play anymore. My cousins can't play anymore because it is not safe anymore. I don't think I can play and live happily when they can't, either—"

My eyes burn. *I can't live happily when Mustafa can't, either.*

Flappy Ears stops and his eyes peer down at the shrunken lump that is Zain. He throws the papers down on the desk. "This is effing depressing." In single-celled-organism fashion, the boys pick up and leave, filing past me as I glare at them.

I count to twenty in my head and walk in. When I do, Zain tentatively picks up his pencil. I sit a few chairs away from him and muster some fullness in my voice. "Salaam, Zain."

He flinches, then glimpses me. "Hey." He drops his hood, and the words spill out. "I'm just finishing an essay for the teacher. I'm not—I'm not—"

I nod to stop his attempted excuses. Just from the reading I can tell he belongs in this hall. We have the same assignment: most memorable memory. I can't bring myself to write it because I'm still living the most memorable nightmare.

I do say, "I saw some boys in the hall I've never seen here before."

Zain gulps. "They're my friends."

An arrow to the heart. No they're not, Zain, they really are not.

"How do you know them?"

"They're my mom's friends' sons." His voice sounds disjointed.

"Do they bother you? They seemed pretty loud," I say, pushing gently.

"That's just how guys are," he mumbles. "They tease me because we're friends."

I want to disagree, but I can't bring myself to it.

"What are you writing about?" I change the subject, aimlessly questioning him in hopes that a regular conversation will bring some color back to his face. Who am I kidding? I can't manage regular, either.

There's a long pause. Our words carry no meaning compared to the silence between our voices. Our exchange is like two species of birds lobbed out of their habitat and forced to sit together. The words mean nothing—it's the pauses and the tones that carry all meaning. Fear, sorrow, regret.

"It's about Syria."

I would never have thought Zain felt this deeply for Syria, just like I thought about Khadija. Where Syria is always just "loss" for me or "a crime against humanity" for the men in suits, it is a place of summers of everlasting escapades for Zain and Khadija.

It is childhood.

I always seem to be wrong. Khadija is more Syrian than I could have ever believed. A baby floating in the freezing Mediterranean Sea can survive against all odds and all my doubts. Zain's memories and days in Syria surpass my preconceptions tenfold.

Yet I have no energy to comfort him and tell him I wish that I'd snapped at Flappy Ears and made him feel ashamed, because I have no will to do anything anymore. I can't ensure the security of my own brother, so I can't pretend to have any influence over that of Khadija's brother.

"Would you go back to Syria?" I ask him, losing to my curiosity. "If you had the chance?"

He swallows, his pencil floating above his paper. He looks sick. "Wouldn't you? It's still your home."

Home. Home is just a place if it weren't for context.

Douma is all heartache for me. It's where I lost Baba and Abdul Rahman. The last place where I was happy with them and with Mustafa.

The stinging in my eyes surrenders to a welling of tears. Would I go back? Before Mustafa came back from the dead, I would never. But now that I know he exists, returning to the front lines of a war zone to be with him seems possible. Would I go back to my personal hell for Mustafa?

I can't, I couldn't, and yet…

"I would."

29

Khadija

*G*od bless moving day.

Mama is busy with her khaleh knitting circle, so I can walk around the house freely. Leene and I pack my car with their belongings and some extra things they've collected and have been gifted for their new place. It's loads more than what they came with, but it only takes us ten minutes to fit their entire life into my car.

I hop into the driver's seat and turn to Leene next to me. "I was finally getting used to you."

"Kattar khairek, took you long enough," Leene teases.

"I'll miss you like I'd miss an annoying little sister," I say, turning on the engine.

Leene sticks her tongue out at me. "My birthday is in January, so I'm older than you."

"Semantics," I say all pishposh-like.

"Ya Allah, I shouldn't have taught you that word."

Snickering, I put the car in reverse.

"Wait," Khaleh Rana calls from the back seat. "Let's say salaam to Zain."

I brake and see Zain standing in the garage watching us. I hadn't even noticed him. Leene waves him over.

"We could use your help," Leene tells him.

He glances my way. I point to the back. "Hop in."

Several miles out of Rochester Heights, I follow my GPS to a Motel 6 and an identical building across the street with the word APARTMENTS painted over what used to be a motel sign. This motel has clearly been repurposed as apartment housing.

I park my G-wagon between banged-up compact cars on fuel-stained concrete and gravel. On the side of the building is a steaming dumpster, and the parking lot is littered with broken beer bottles.

If my mother knew I parked on this side of town, she'd have a stroke. But that's why Mama is not with us. When we get down from the car, it's not so bad. Just a case of a gray and gloomy spring.

Michigan is not just lakes, suburbs, and estates. It's got other sides to it, and while not all of it is what Mama makes it out to be, it is still beautiful.

On the second floor of the complex, we reach number 23. Khaleh Rana unlocks the flimsy door. It swings open like a prop, and she flips the light on.

The apartment has the bones of a motel room, but it's been repurposed as a studio. There's a kitchenette with a white oven stained yellow and brown. The stove has two burners, but at least the kitchen sink is newly installed. The apartment is furnished with two twin-size bedframes with naked mattresses in the far corner while a couch sections off the first half of the studio. Wind drifts through the poorly insulated walls and I suspect everything is sticky.

While I hesitate, Leene kicks off her shoes and walks past the beds to the other side of the room. She looks into the bathroom and shuts her eyes and the door.

"We need to bleach every surface in here," she says. She places her hand on her head, clearly stressed. Syrians are obsessively clean and there's a lot to clean here.

Khaleh Rana nods, all business, then sighs heavily. "Yee, we forgot the cleaning supplies."

"I can get them," Zain offers. My eyes widen at him. He's never so much as offered to lift a finger around Mama.

"Okay," Leene says, her voice rumbling. "Mama, you can go with him, and Khadija and I will stay here and get started."

With Leene on the verge of breaking, I hand off my key to recently licensed Zain.

"Be careful with her," I say, sending a prayer for my car in his hands. He nods, and they're off. They leave the door cracked to air out the room. I open the window, hoping the smell of cigarette smoke will dissipate. When I turn to the room, Leene isn't there. I look down to where she's crouching, her shoulders shaking.

"Leene?"

She sobs with her entire body. Holding her up by her arms, I help her over to the bed.

I grab a toilet paper roll from the luggage because Arabs never forget toilet paper when they pack. I hand it to her, and she takes it. She cries for a long while and I sit beside her, wordless.

"Don't mind me," she mutters in Arabic, sniffling.

I clench my fists. She's being the polite Leene even when she's on the brink of a breakdown. I place my arm on her shoulder. "Damn," I begin, "I'd cry, too, if I finally got to rest in my own home."

30

Leene

My own home.

A cry bubbles to my lips. "I haven't had my own home since Douma."

Khadija sets a hand on my shoulder. "You don't have to talk about it."

I don't, but I feel myself coming undone and talking always helps. "Have you seen the videos of Douma after the chemical attacks?" I ask, and Khadija nods. They're the videos of naked bodies that had been tossed into empty warehouses, an attempt to contain the carnage. A massacre without wounds and without blood. Starved bodies lying limp beside hundreds of others that were dumped into mass graves, never to be claimed. "That's Douma. That was my last home. When I was there my family was so much bigger."

I open my phone and pull up a picture. My eyes water all over again looking at it. This picture isn't of Mustafa—it's of me and Abdul Rahman. My Abood. My older brother and I holding identical peace signs in front of the iron gate to our apartment building.

"It was just me and him for the longest time. Abood and Leene. The bossiest little sister and the kindest older brother. He used to eat my tomatoes because I hated them, and he would hold my hand when we jumped into the pool because I was scared of the deep end. He was my best friend long before Mustafa came along and stole my heart."

I swallow the ball in my throat. "He wanted to be a pilot. He told me he wanted to be a pilot so that he could show me the world. I told him to see it by himself, because, you know, I was a brat." I manage a weak laugh. "But he didn't let it go. He said he wouldn't want to see it by himself, because it isn't about where you go, but who goes with you. And he wanted it to be me."

A sob claws its way up my throat, but I push through it. "Before they dropped sarin gas on our city, Mama and I left with Mustafa to visit my grandparents at their orchard. I wanted Mama to get better because she was always sick after Baba died. I told Abood to come with us. I told him that after Baba was killed, we should stay together. He didn't listen. He said he had to go to work to make money to provide for our home. *Our home.*

"Mama got better at my grandparents'. Mustafa got to play outside in the sun there. I told Mama we should just move out of Douma and live there. Abood could find a way to go to work in the city, but we could start over again at my grandparents'. Then the news came that they dropped chemicals on our city. Sarin gas. The stuff chokes you from the inside. When they dropped the sarin gas on our city, I didn't tell Mama. I *couldn't*. She found out on Facebook from the videos. My older brother faceless among them. She had only enough energy to forbid me from returning home, but I didn't listen. I had to see Abood for myself; so long as I didn't see his name on the lists on Facebook, I clung to the hope that he was alive, but Mama felt it in her bones." Just like she sensed Mustafa's soul in the sea. I can't bring myself to say that to Khadija. "When I got home, he wasn't there. The city was a ghost town. The only people left were counting the bodies piled high at the hospital. They wouldn't even let me search for him among the corpses."

I wipe under my nose, my entire face a bloated mess. But I feel lighter for saying this. Now everything I have hidden is not only mine to bear. Still I can't look into her eyes; I can't see how she sees me.

"How—how did you survive all of that?" she asks, surprise coloring her voice.

I hold my breath. "Sometimes I wish I didn't."

Then we look at each other and Khadija's watery eyes widen in surprise. "You feel guilty."

"How can I not?" I ask, throat tight. "How can we all not feel so guilty? Sometimes I feel like such a coward for running away. For trying to make this place my new home."

This is my house, but home is not this place. My home is where I can be with Mama and Baba, Abood and Mustafa. Moving on in this new house is supposed to make me happy. I got Mama this far even through her sicknesses. But most of my family is gone, and they were taken from me needlessly.

My baba and Abdul Rahman weren't on an opposing front line. They weren't even protesting. Abood had been living his daily routine, trying to make a living to support our family after we lost Baba. And Baba, he was buying breakfast for us when he was killed.

They are victims, but no one uses the word *victim* when the narrative is war. Victims die in attacks. Casualties fall in warfare.

My baba and my brothers aren't casualties. My baba and brothers should be here.

The door creaks and Khadija and I snap our heads toward it. The wind blows in, and the door is light enough that it flies all the way open. Behind, Zain peers in, his face pale, his eyes turned down, and his frame looking like it will fall over at any moment.

I don't know how long he's been standing there or if he's heard my entire story. Khadija squeezes her eyes to get rid of any tears, and I give her some toilet paper. She adjusts to make us look natural.

"You came back quickly," she says with a nervous laugh that doesn't sound like her at all.

Zain steps in, and we lock eyes. "You look like you've seen a ghost."

"Not a ghost," I say tepidly. "A memory."

Khadija holds her breath. "Aren't those the same for us?"

We glance among each other, the unlikeliest trio who share more pain than happiness.

Mama comes in soon after, hands full of cleaning supplies, breaking apart the tension in the room. Khadija gathers her things, gives Mama a kiss on either cheek, and collects Zain to leave. She takes two steps and freezes in the doorway. I stop behind her with my hand on the hollow door frame.

Before I register that she's turned around, Khadija throws her arms around me and I feel like I'm in a headlock. I stand stiffly before I return her embrace.

"You can say what you want," she whispers, "but you were brave."

I've heard it a thousand times as a refugee, but always in the present, the "you are brave" tag. The trophy compliment. It's a given when it comes to refugees like me, except I am not brave. I don't feel brave.

So when Khadija says it in the past tense, maybe I was not the monster I believe I was. I want to believe what she says. I want to believe that once I was brave.

31

Khadija

The moonlight shines through the kitchen windows, spattering shadows of scraggly branches. It creates a spooky pattern, very fitting for the past few days in the Shaami home. Life at home has receded without Khaleh Rana and Leene. With May approaching, I spend my days and nights training at the gym. Soon, the showcase will determine my plan for the summer.

I enter the kitchen, check the counter, and blink twice at the extra keys in the bowl. Baba is home.

I stop short at the sound of voices from the living room. I lean over the counter to get a glimpse of the glistening liquid black lake, eavesdropping. But, just my luck, a lull of silence wades its way back to me. I tiptoe through the kitchen and past the dining table and poke my head around the corner.

The fluorescent lights rain down on her in shafts, darkening her hair and bleaching her complexion, making her appear regal. A queen, most likely, somewhere in her bloodline. Her thumbs press against her temples and her fingers shield and shadow her eyes and face. Or maybe she is a statue of a queen. Not breathing, unfeeling. I approach the back of the couch and settle my hands on it, keeping it between us as a precaution.

Her hand lifts slightly and her forehead creases. "And did you just come home?" Mama asks, her voice laced with pain. It is pretty late. "Nice to know you're still a part of this family."

God bless. My lips press into a tight line. How many young girls have lost their mothers like Leene lost her father? I have mine, and I can still set things right between us. Whether there will be bloodshed is completely up to Her Majesty the Queen Maisa. I enter the ring where Mama is my competitor. "Who were you talking to?"

Mama slides her hands over her hair. "I was talking to your baba."

"Where is he now?"

"Asleep."

As always, we miss each other. "What were you talking about?"

"You're curious today." Mama's irritation rings clear.

"No." I force myself not to give up on this conversation. "We just haven't talked in a long time."

"Because you want to leave me." Her voice hitches on the word *leave*.

Now, I know that I've said that many times, and we've had

our fights about it, but this time Mama won't show me her face. Other times, I act coy or go off on a larger-than-life tangent and Mama hums me away. This time, her tone frightens me, and it lands like a mean left hook.

"That's not why I want to go—"

"You want to be free of me."

The synapses in my brain fire like a whip. "It's not about you." I bite my lip. "I do so much to please you, Mama. Look at my friendship with Leene. It happened eventually. You got what you wanted."

Mama kisses her teeth. "I wanted you to be friends because I want you to be more like her. She takes care of her mother. She doesn't want to leave and forget all about her family."

My face burns red. "Traveling isn't to spite you. It's for myself. It's not to forget you and run away from my life. No matter how unhappy I may seem to you."

Mama isn't listening as her battle is with herself. Her palms press into her eyes. "When you leave, you leave me. Baba will keep working, and Zain will stay in his room, and I'm the fool who tries to fit the mismatching puzzle pieces of this family together."

"You're not a fool," I murmur. The tassels of the pillows are knots in my fists.

"I am. I restricted my son's future when I didn't get him help for his learning disabilities. I ruined my relationship with my daughter. I have no words to describe your father. With all that we have, we're supposed to be fine. My life wasn't supposed to be this hard. My family wasn't supposed to feel broken." She removes her hands from her face, revealing puffy eyelids and cheeks.

No matter how much my mother and I disagree and the mountain of fights and insults we've exchanged, she has never cried. She's broken me, sent me into hysterics, but I've never gotten to her. Of course, I've never wanted to—that's messed up. So messed up that when I see her recovering from tears, no couch or coffee table can separate us.

"Are you okay, Mama?" I slide in beside her, but I'm afraid to touch her, as though she's a Swarovski Leaning Tower of Pisa. Untouchable.

She sits up straighter, acting as though evidence of her breakdown isn't all over her face. She recedes into herself, so I try something new. I stretch my hands out like Younes did to me, and she slinks away as I did.

I knew I shouldn't have tried. I pull my arms back to my chest. "I want to help you."

Mama frowns deeply, and I search her face for answers. She avoids my eyes, staring at the ground. "I need help" is not in my mother's vocabulary. It's an age-old Syrian trait to be too proud to ask for help. A phrase that so many use easily with her is one I have never heard her say.

Mama's head is back in her hands. "I want my mom," she says.

My heart sinks. "Did something happen to Teteh?"

"No, no," she murmurs with a grateful prayer.

"Then call her." My advice is infantile.

She frowns deeper. "It's not the same. Instead of visiting her when I could, I wasted all my time building this house so I can live in it alone. You're the only one I thought would stick around for me, and now you want to leave me, too."

"I'm not leaving you forever."

"You can leave me," she croaks. If I wasn't distressed, my jaw would hang open. "You can leave me because I was a daughter like you once. I wanted to leave Syria and come to America to marry your baba. Your baba, who takes one evening off every year and uses the time home to nag Zain about his grades. And Zain's face. You should've seen Zain's face, Khadija. He wasn't even devastated. It looked like nothing mattered to him anymore."

I can only imagine Zain's hopeless expression, a hollowed-out version of the person he once was, and the image moves me to hold her hand in mine. Whatever was said, however she feels about it, she shouldn't have to go through it alone. If I had been there, I could have defused some of it. I wonder how I became the only one person she really has. I make a terrible companion; I can only imagine how lonely it is for her.

She's my mama, but she's a daughter to someone, too. She is naive and inexperienced to at least one other person in this universe. I've always only seen Mama, but for a second, I see Maisa.

We stay there under the pale white lights, and I'm compelled to make a peace offering. "My match at the gym is a week away. I'd like it if you came to see me."

"Your fighting," she mumbles, her lips tugging upward. She looks away from me, ashamed, as I observe the woman who is my mother. "I'll leave boxing to you." She pats my hands and places them back in my lap.

She called my fighting boxing. The word *boxing* came from my mother's mouth.

She stands precariously, like she's stone breaking out of a spell. When the coffee table is between us, she turns halfway to me. "Khadija, habibti, if you do leave this summer, I'm not going to be pleased. If you are confident you can travel without my rida, then fine."

Rida—noun—ri-da—/rɪdʌ/: parental blessings and satisfaction.

Rida (weaponized)—used in parental threats: taking away rida invokes massive fears; resulting feeling equivalent to the end of the world.

After throwing that knife in my back, she leaves, slumped shoulders and all. Mama is a queen, yes, but also a lioness, lying in wait, fierce and majestic, attacking when I am most vulnerable.

She raised me to believe that without her and Baba's rida, my plans will undoubtedly fail. The plans of this summer, whatever they are shaping up to be, may have a green light and a full tank of gas, but Mama's rule ordains that the road leads to a fifty-story drop off a perilous cliff. If I survive the cliff, I am free to go.

Even at her lowest points, Mama pounces. We're alike in that way.

But I'll be jumping off that cliff with my parachute. It's all a matter of whether or not it'll open.

32

Leene

 $\mathcal{J}$ find a seat among the visitors at the gym for Khadija's showcase. Rows of chairs surround the boxing ring where Khadija's fight will be. Temporary professional camera lights shine down on it this May afternoon. I feel like I'm on a movie set. I'm just a face in the crowd, but soon Khadija will be the star.

Checking the time again, I alternate between searching the crowd and glancing at the door. I'm the only hijabi here so far, so sometimes a baby will fixate on my head, and I have to make silly faces to alleviate the awkwardness with the parents. The baby gets a laugh out of my dumb faces, whereas the parents try to shield their baby from me.

It is strange: The audience looks nothing like the boxers at the gym. Other than some couples and families, there are many white faces in sportswear and some white men in suits. I scan the crowd again, searching for Nassima. A swath of black fabric—Nassima's hijab—grabs my attention. I swivel out of my chair and make my way over to her.

"I was with Khadija." Nassima points to the far side of the room, where the boxers bob and bounce to music. "I made sure she wasn't psyching herself out."

Sometimes I nod even though I don't understand their English phrases. This is one of those times. I scoot closer as the seats fill up. "Where are Khadija's other friends?"

Nassima cranes her neck distractedly. "Which friends?"

"The ones she said she invited."

She clicks her tongue. "Those friends don't come to these things."

"Why not? Friends support each other."

Nassima's face stretches into an exaggerated smile. "Friends should do that. That's very good, Leene."

I count back the weeks I've known Khadija and then count down to weeks that consisted of actual friendship. Yet I'm here, and her other friends whom she's known for years aren't. It's one Sunday of the year. I wonder if they have something better to do. Feeling very protective, I convince myself that they better have something more important to do. Or else. (Or else nothing, but it sounds like the right friend thought to think.)

"How about Khaleh Maisa and Zain?"

She answers with a sigh of laughter.

"I didn't know there'd be so many strangers here," I say.

Nassima glances around. "Oh, these guys? They're hard-core boxing fans. They follow the Golden Gloves and all that. Some of them are scouts, too. Taking amateurs to the big leagues or whatever. I barely know sports."

The words go straight over my head. *Golden, gloves, scouts.* If I've learned one thing since coming to America, it's that sports words have very little to do with the actual sports.

A microphone screech squelches all other questions. The old gym owner swoops into the ring and atones for it by beginning the show.

"Thank you all for coming out here today. We have some excellent fights for you, and I won't talk your ears off, so we're gonna get started. You got a ballot under your chair to vote for the night's best fighter. The grand prize is a paid trip for two. Or a better trip for one for our lonelier boxers. I'd box for that one myself if I had any chance." He chuckles, then introduces the boxers, and the first rounds commence.

I flinch for the full six minutes of one boy landing punch after punch on another. Finally, Jerr, who judges the fight, stops it and announces the clear winner.

I don't understand the premise of boxing. Lots of hitting too fast for my eyes. The bell dings and they go to their corners and start again. And again, and again.

All I understand is that for Khadija to win the prize vouchers to purchase the plane tickets, she doesn't need to win against her opponent. The winner of the tickets is decided by a vote. At the end of all the matches, the audience votes for the boxer who impressed them the most. It could be because they boxed spectacularly or showed inspiring potential or growth. According to Khadija, these rules are supposed to discourage unhealthy competition, but to me, it just sounds like a popularity contest. And I hope Khadija is really, *really* popular.

Finally, Khadija takes a corner, and her friend Whit takes the other. Or maybe not her friend—I'm not good at judging others' friendships. Khadija is in all black with a gray hijab tucked into a long-sleeved sports top and baggy shorts over tights. She shakes her shoulders out and loosens her neck.

"Do you say break a leg?" I ask Nassima, racking my brain for idioms I learned in ELL class.

Nassima giggles. "Not really, but you can say whatever you want."

"Break a leg!" I yell, and Nassima cracks up and sinks into her seat. Khadija doesn't hear it, but everyone else does, and if there was no indication before, I've revealed myself as a fake fan.

The woman beside me scoffs, displeased with my lack of boxing knowledge. She pulls her coat closer to herself and edges away from me. I smile to help her relax. It's only boxing.

At the ding, Khadija and Whit dance around the ring. For a while, neither throws a punch. Whit lunges and Khadija retreats and punches aimlessly. The first rounds pass with few touches. Each in their respective corners, I spot Gab advising Khadija as she glares across the ring.

Another ding and Khadija immediately starts off with a right hook to Whit's head. The force makes Whit stumble, but she dances around the ring with a buzz. Khadija moves with purpose, imposing her dominion over the ring from that first punch, and though I know nothing of boxing, her strategy shows. It turns out she doesn't punch senselessly. Her punches are few and far between, but they are quick and deliberate and powerful. Her precise moves elicit gasps.

The crowd is quiet for the first time since the start, in awe of Khadija's performance and waiting for Jerr's final call because Whit is barely holding on. She retreats twice to the ropes and her arms shield her face from Khadija's punches.

"She's unnecessarily aggressive," the woman beside me says.

"Jerr needs to keep that girl in check." This from someone behind me, leaning forward to tell everyone around them.

"Excuse me." Nassima's voice rumbles like it originates from deep under her surface, where a volcano has been dormant. My perception of the eerie silence transforms from awe to displeasure.

The crowd is upset. The comments persist in faint murmurs that ripple through the crowd.

Another round dings out and they retreat to their corners. Gab hands Khadija a water. She looks out at the audience as her chest rises and falls with effort. She leans toward Gab and whispers to him, and he analyzes the spectators, too.

I look around me. The overwhelming number of sheet-white faces glower and grimace at Khadija. The disgruntled murmurs multiply and rise in volume. Then the white man behind me stands.

"You gonna stop the fucking Arab when she knocks our girl out cold, Jerr?" The gym echoes with his words.

I feel a little woozy, and my body temperature flips between extreme cold to extreme heat.

Nassima hisses a curse. Whit bites her inner cheek. Jerr frowns. In a swift motion, Khadija undoes her gloves with her teeth. Gab faces Khadija looking furious, but Khadija won't leave her corner for the next round.

"Why are they angry with her?" I ask, my skin feeling prickly as the stares grow more intense. The boxers' families and friends ignore the angry members of the crowd, but we are outnumbered. "Is it over?" I check with Nassima, but she slides off her chair and rushes over to Khadija.

Gab speaks to Jerr while Whit struts over to them, holding her head high despite having taken a beating. Nassima is flushed, speaking heated and fast. She picks up the gloves and shoves them back into Khadija's hands. Khadija takes them but swings her legs over the bottom ropes and ducks underneath and out. She falls back into the ranks of the other boxers, leaving the ring—in which she had performed so impressively—empty.

Jerr raises Whit's arm and declares her the winner by forfeit. The crowd, a moment ago so mute we could hear a pin drop, applauds loudly considering the victor's performance. Whit accepts the applause and slips out of the ring without a word or a smile.

Nassima flops back into her seat.

"I don't understand," I say with a bad taste in my mouth. "It's just a game."

Nassima shuts her eyes. "It's never just a game. If it was just a game, what does it matter if she wins? Everything has to be personal."

"Khadija lost because she wears the hijab?" I ask, confused.

Nassima shakes her head. "No," she says, "she was going to win. One more round and she would've. But she stopped."

"She forfeited? She gave up."

Nassima's eyes flash open. Narrowing her eyes at the grumbling crowd around us, she mutters, "No. She didn't give up. She didn't have any other choice."

33

Khadija

Three-quarters of the spectators had come to Jerr's to see Younes's fight. Boxing enthusiasts who saw a young man become a champion at the Golden Gloves paid homage to the gym that honed his talents.

Younes is good—no, he's one of the best—and today he was exceptional. Scouts approached him after his match; everyone's attention was on him. His winning was only natural.

For them, the boxer performs, but the boxer never permeates the ring. Not unless they're one of the greats, like Muhammad Ali. So when my victory threatened to puncture a vulnerable bubble of belief in which they were comfortably nestled, hell rose and my fists fell.

Obviously, I didn't want to throw the fight. My skin crawls when I think about choosing not to continue. But it wasn't like I had much of a choice. The audience was close to jumping in the ring to keep Whit from taking another hit. I was racking up points, I was keeping my distance, I was landing every hit. But when I looked into the crowd, I didn't feel like I was winning. I was suddenly scared to win if it meant an angry mob in the gym.

I played by the rules. I played by the rules, and I performed well. I should've won.

If I was as good as Younes, maybe the crowd wouldn't have been as angry. When the spectators get high off a boxer's adrenaline, they don't care about the color of their skin, their language, their accent, their money, and, in my case, my hijab. Maybe since my hijab is new to the spectrum, every day is groundbreaking territory. Maybe, in front of this crowd, my hijab isn't allowed to win.

Huffing in frustration, I slam the folding chairs shut and stack them with a vengeance. This is the first time I boxed competitively. I refused to put on a show for spectators who wouldn't bother smiling at me at the supermarket. There's nothing wrong with that.

This is not the last time I'll box publicly. I never felt anything like that. The energy I feel in the ring is magnified by a thousand in front of a crowd. But next time I'll be ready. Next time, I'll perfect the act. Boxing, after all, is a performance.

Younes performs the act masterfully. Of course, he's likable that way. I mean, what isn't to like? I steal looks at him and his dimples over at Jerr's official ballot-counting table. The audience voted for their favorite performer and since none of my invitees came, I have no chance at winning. I send a long look at the table. With a roar of laughter, Younes holds back a boxer we call Little—a nickname that is an antonym to his stature—who demands a recount by resorting to his fists.

Now that I've graduated from self-inflicted guilt, I skirt around the gym avoiding Younes and his truths at all costs. At school these past couple of weeks, I was sure not to look him in the eye.

A still-fuming Nassima and her polar opposite, Leene, charge at me. Leene throws her arms around me. "Mabrouk!" she congratulates me.

"For what?" I shrink from the embrace, shooting Nassima a puzzled look. Nassima rolls her eyes, but I catch traces of a smile.

"For being up there." Her eyes are wide with admiration. "You did so amazing."

"I didn't win." I pout.

"But Whit was done for," Nassima says through gritted teeth, displaying her ardent loyalty.

"Done for," Leene says with a giggle. She links her arm in mine and I let her stick to me. The Damascene friend habit strums a long, silent chord of nostalgia.

An upheaval at Jerr's table attracts us closer. Younes dangles an envelope above his head and all the younger boxers jump for it. The older ones grab their bags and head out, unconcerned, as if they heard exactly what they expected to hear.

"Did he win the prize, Gab?" I ask. Gab nods but says nothing to me. He's angry with me for forfeiting. He doesn't understand it. If Jerr had raised my arm and declared me the winner, the audience would have revolted. They watched me winning the fight with such contempt I couldn't bear their reaction if I'd won. "Don't be like that, Gab," I tell him.

"Quitter," he grumbles.

"Am not."

Younes swerves away from the youngsters and rescues me from piecing together a wretched recovery retort. "Ah, ah," he baits the whining boxers, "I said I don't want the tickets because they belong to someone else."

He steps backward and faces us, a wide grin on his face, eyes falling on me. Gab claps down on his thighs in frustration. He glowers at Younes and then peers at me. Gab and I glare at each other for a solid twenty seconds.

"These," Younes announces, making me flit my eyes to him, "are for the best boxer." He steps toward me and I'm acutely aware of Leene's tightening grip on my arm. "And that wasn't me…not today at least." He presents the envelope to me with a grin.

My blushing physically pains my cheeks. I curb my giddiness. "No way," I say, declining. "I didn't even win my match."

Gab's eyeballs do cartwheels. "She—didn't—even—lose. She—gave the—up." My mind automatically censored that. There were too many f-bombs for so few words. Leene is mortified.

Younes ignores his friend. "She fought with her head. But that's not why she won. Anyone who pisses off that many white people without finishing a fight wins at everything."

I watch Gab struggle to accept this, and he finally concedes. "They *were* shitting themselves." Gab's creative tongue affronts Leene into a statue.

The clouds part, and Nassima's mood lifts. "They were going to start throwing chairs."

"It's yours." Younes offers me the prize again. "For fighting with your mind. And to keep the peace."

My smile falters as I remember our conversation. "No, really, it belongs to you."

"You have to."

"No—"

"Really." He grabs my hand and a shock surges through me. He shoves the envelope in my hand and drops it fast. The rush of electricity chokes me up. God bless.

Nassima cocks her perfectly arched eyebrow.

"At least go out with the guy." Gab groans.

"Hold up—" I start to object, but Younes looks at me like he's waiting.

Younes shrugs with a smile. "I won't say no to a date."

Nassima tugs at my shirt, and Leene sucks in a breath loudly. I open my mouth, but my words get tangled in my throat. I rack my brain for a comeback or a deflection, but nothing fits. Younes chuckles. "I'll take that as a yes."

It was about time that my comebacks ran out.

"Hey."

The five of us look at Whit at once.

"I hope you know I didn't want my dad to defend me like that during the fight," Whit says to me. So the man who called me a fucking Arab was her dad. Whit swallows her pride. "I wanted to finish it. For real."

Gab mutters something under his breath.

"I would have knocked you out," I reply.

"I know," she admits. "Maybe we can train together more often."

"Yeah, maybe." I'll deal with Whit never.

"That was the worst fucking apology I ever heard," Gab says with a scowl even before Whit is out of earshot.

Leene nudges me proudly. "She knows she would've lost."

I smile, clutching the envelope in my hands and pulling it to my chest. I look up at Younes. "Thank you."

Younes grins, clearly ultra-pleased with himself. "I got a date out of it. Plus, I would have wasted them on Disneyland with Gab," he jokes. Gab flicks him off. "Holding hands by the castle with Mickey Mouse ears and all that sh—" He glances at the ever-innocent Leene and thinks twice about his word choice. Younes's eyes crinkle. "You're going to do great things with them. I know you will."

"I will," I promise.

"Yes, we will!" Nassima throws her arms around me. I feel

undeserving of her affection. Nassima still imagines us carefree on a European playground. Having our pick of delicious food at foreign supermarkets. A few days to snap photos of orphans, single mothers, and hills of encampments, plus the souvenir of a guilt-free conscience.

When she pulls away, I don't have the energy to plaster a smile on my face that matches hers. She notices that my excitement is dull in comparison, and her lip twitches. Her brows furrow just barely. I have to look away.

I hold Leene's gaze as she dons her "I'm happy for you" smile, but I know she's holding out hope that I'll use the prize to cash in for tickets for us. She wears the facade for everyone else and it deceives. It worked on me from the beginning, but now I know. There's worry and guilt in her smile, and not like my faulty guilt. Her guilt is pure and damaging.

I'll have to tell Nassima that Europe isn't enough. Europe will always be there, but Mustafa might not be.

34

Leene

A hundred and twenty-four dollars. That's the number in the bank account after the bills paid on the first of the month decimate Mama's and my hard-earned money.

Two hundred dollars. Those are the two bills in a plastic bag taped to the bottom of my nightstand.

Three hundred twenty-four dollars buys me a quarter of a ticket to Jordan. The four-digit numbers and dollar signs blur into the bright white screen that bathes me in iridescent light in my dim, mildew-ridden home. Retrospectively, this is a downgrade from Khadija's basement but a massive upgrade from my living conditions before. And still, it must be hundreds of times better than the orphanage where Mustafa is. Or isn't.

I blink back tears. Mustafa is there, inshallah. God protected him this long. My baby brother waits for me to return for him.

There's just one problem that blares at me like a neon sign every time I shut my eyes. Three. Hundred. And twenty. Four.

I hear the familiar jiggling of keys and slam the laptop shut. The creak of a door and a great sigh later, Mama walks in, kicking her shoes off immediately and allowing a cool May breeze to sweep through the room.

"Good evening." She smiles widely once she sees me. "A thousand good evenings."

"Really?" I mimic her cheery tone with immense effort. A thousand of anything is a big deal. "Good day at work?"

"Work is work, alhamdulillah, but tomorrow is a special day." She slips her hijab off and begins boiling water on the stove.

I think. It's not my birthday and it's not hers. Syrian Mother's Day has already passed. Think, think, think.

"Twenty years ago today, your baba and I got married. Twenty years."

I do the math. Yes, Abood would be nineteen this year. I lean over and grab the cluster of photos that survived our journeys. I find the one of Mama and Baba, her in a silky white dress with puffy sleeves and classic Arab blue eyeshadow and red lips. Baba is half the size in width and a few inches more in height than I remember him. He has his same old bushy mustache; even so, his tuxedo lends it some sophistication.

I bring the photo over to her by the stove. She takes it willingly, but her smile trembles. "I thought we'd be married forever. For sixty years or more. I really did, even though I used to complain all the time. You remember?"

I nod, a smile playing on my lips. I change my voice to sound just like Mama's. "We've been eating dinner cold for the last twelve years; I can't eat cold dinner for another fifty years with you! I can't and I won't!"

We chuckle and Mama rolls her eyes. "His love for football made for too many cold dinners."

"You always made them hot."

"And he always had them cold."

Our grins suddenly ache and our mouths slacken. Mama averts her droopy eyes. "After fifteen years, we called it in. Never did I think we'd have Mustafa. When we had him it was good. Everything around us was falling apart, but Mustafa was good. Baba had him for so little time, but still…"

My chest constricts as I hold my tongue. Mama's nostalgia threatens to break the fortress around my secret.

I should tell her Mustafa is alive. Keeping it a secret makes me feel foul. But I convince myself to hide it for longer.

"I had Baba for fifteen years, and we had all that time with Abood. Your baba and I shared our baby Mustafa together for only a few months. I can barely remember it."

If I tell Mama now, maybe the weight on my chest will lift. Telling her that her baby is alive is only right.

"Mustafa my baby, the light of my eyes." She sniffles.

No, revealing that we left Mustafa in the middle of the sea, heart beating faintly in that small chest, may be what's right, but in this cruel reality, must I do what is right? I can't tell her.

I will hide it for her sake. Until I can reverse Mustafa's fate, I will hide it. She would never forgive me. And she'd never forgive herself for trusting my judgment on a freezing-cold night in the middle of the sea.

"I'm sorry." Mama gazes at me.

I should be saying those words.

"For what?" I murmur softly, a lump forming in the back of my throat.

"For all that time that I wasn't there," she says. She encases my unresponsive body in her arms. "I was present, but I wasn't there. I lost your baba and then I lost Abood, and I didn't know what to do with myself. I prayed and I slept. I didn't care to eat or drink. I couldn't even bother washing myself. You took care of me even though you were still a young girl. You should have been playing with friends, watching movies, going shopping." She pulls back and looks just as I feel, pain streaking our faces. "After Mustafa, in Germany—"

"Mama, it's okay," I whisper. We don't like to remember Germany.

"It's not." She cups my face in her hands. "In Germany I wasn't a mother. I wasn't a friend. I wasn't a person. I was in this waking coma, and you must have been so alone—working, going to school, all the while trying to be a kid."

Mama might as well have been dead the months after Mustafa died—so that's how I viewed her. She didn't speak, and she barely lapped the liquids that I spoon-fed her. She wasn't my mother. In a foreign land of a foreign language, I was the worst type of alone. Being caged with a loved one who cannot love carves complicated scars.

The revolution did not only take away my baba, my Abood, and my Mustafa. It took away the child I would've been. It left only wounds.

Those wounds scarred and have since scabbed over, and I have learned. If I tell Mama that Mustafa is out there, my current agony is nothing compared to the torment that will grip her. She can know her baby boy is alive when I arrive at our doorstep hand in hand with Mustafa and his blue blanket.

I'm more than ready when Khadija calls to pick me up to hang out at her house. When we get to her room, she blindfolds me.

"This is silly," I gripe, though my heart pounds with excitement. I'm always searching for another distraction so I don't fall into the claws of my worries about Mustafa.

"It's for the effect," Khadija says. I hear her typing on her computer, but the blindfold blocks out my strongest sense. "Spin."

"Why?"

"Come on." Her bed squeaks and she seizes my shoulders to send me twirling again. "Keep spinning."

I do. "Why am I spinning? And you can't keep saying it's for the effect."

"Sorry, but it's always for the effect." She clicks away. "It's not a surprise graduation gift if there's no ritual prologue."

"This is ridiculous. You don't need to gift me."

"I'm not gifting *you*," Khadija corrects. "I am *giving* you a gift, to be exact."

"Are you really correcting my English? You blindfolded me and now we're doing grammar? What is this, torture?"

Khadija giggles, and I hear the door creak open. My heart rate spikes, and I slap my hands on my hair and hit the floor. Khadija guffaws. "It's my mom."

I laugh nervously. With difficulty, I grip the bed posts to stand.

"What are you girls doing?" Khaleh Maisa asks, and I hear her questioning our sanity. Khadija doesn't respond verbally since her laughter seizes her, and I'm a donkey in a blindfold, so I stay quiet. Khaleh Maisa sighs heavily. It sounds sad. "Food is ready downstairs."

As the door closes I call out my thanks while Khadija recovers at sloth speed.

"Not funny," I say, and start another spin cycle. "I thought maybe Zain or your dad came in." I try to calm the frazzled nerves of a hijabi.

"Zain never comes in here," Khadija says with a "whew," thus ending her laughing fit.

I know I shouldn't ask why, but I do anyway. I seesaw on my two feet waiting for her reply.

"Just because," Khadija mumbles. Several more seconds pass. "We used to be cool with each other, but he changed after we stopped going to Syria. He doesn't talk anymore, doesn't try. I can't even remember the last time I saw him smile. He changed into someone I don't recognize."

Tension spreads across my shoulders as I remember the day I saw him in my classroom. "Is Zain in ELL?" I ask.

Khadija pauses and I nearly take off my blindfold from the curiosity. Then she replies tepidly, "He's in remedial English, but it's the same program at RHHS."

"Why is he behind?" I try to assert my voice, but it insists on fragility. I'm met with more silence, so I backtrack. "Sorry, I don't want to pry."

"It's whatever." I assume she means about my prying. "He has dyslexia, but my mom wouldn't accept it for the longest time. She thought he was slower than the other kids so she waited it out. When she finally listened to the teachers and the specialists, he was in fifth grade and could barely read or write. He's been behind in everything since then." I hear an edge in her voice.

His slow strokes and acute concentration. His effort to craft those simple sentences. His essay may have been simple, but his writing was real.

"Why are you asking?"

I shake out of the memory. "I saw him in my class the other day. There were these boys with him. He said they were his friends."

Khadija grunts. "I wouldn't be surprised if my mother has a monthly payment plan to have them spend time with him."

She must know about Zain's bullies. I probe further. "So you know they tease him? A lot?"

"Boys will be boys." Her voice sounds disinterested.

"He who is born an ass can never become a horse." I deliver the Arabic proverb, my voice gruff.

"Exactly."

"So only he changed?"

"No, I did, too. Less social, more aggressive. More fights with my mom." She pauses. "You probably don't know how that is."

I lean to my right side, then seesaw again. "Mama goes silent when life gets hard. She'd worry about the smallest things when she got desperate but never did anything to change them. She stayed in her room and didn't come out. She wouldn't notice if I was there or not. She'd wake up screaming from her nightmares and I would sit with her until she fell back asleep. I wanted to tell her that I'm her kid, that I'm the one who needs *her* to comfort *me* to sleep. Instead, I sat and sang her Mustafa's favorite song until she dozed off."

Khadija's typing stops. I'm comforted that the blindfold gives us a sense of privacy. I continue, "But I stuck by her side because she's my mom. She's the last person in my family. No matter what she does, she's still my mom. She won't be here forever, but my memories will be, so I have to make them good.

You must know how that is. You might never see your family in Syria again, but their memories live with you forever. Even if they're on the other side of the world or if you can't stand to be around them for very long. They know exactly what to say to hurt you most, and that's why you can hate them the most. But they also get your jokes better than anyone else, and they know the deepest parts of you, and you can't give that up for anything."

When she says nothing, I go for another twirl. "It's easy to say everything on my mind when I'm wearing this blindfold."

"It's easier for me to come clean when you look like Cyclops from X-Men, too," Khadija says. There's movement, and then, "Okay, it's ready."

She guides me to her desk and yanks off the blindfold. The adjustment from dark to light discombobulates me. My eyes focus on Khadija's laptop. I read the text under my breath.

"'Dear Leene, below is a list of documents required upon your arrival. Passport or green card, visa…'" Khadija doesn't let me finish before clicking on another tab. Detailed itineraries from Detroit to Amman airports. June 16. Taher, Leene. Shaami, Khadija. She clicks another tab, a reservation for a hotel room in Jordan. She clicks back to the first page, the email, and I check the signature. Charlotte Ra'ee-Harris. The director from the orphanage.

"Say wallah," I demand, asking her to swear. My voice is a squeak, and my heart rate slows down so much that I have to check several times to make sure I'm breathing.

"Wallah," she swears with a goofy grin on her face.

"You didn't, Khadija!" My hands are shaking. "Tell me the truth. Don't lie to me. If you lie to me, I will never forgive you."

"After our graduation, we're getting on a plane, and we're going to find Mustafa."

I'm up and twirling again to stay one with my spinning brain, and I shut my eyes to keep the four walls of Khadija's room from zooming in and out of my vision. My entire body feels like pins and needles.

"I don't do things 'for the effect.'" Khadija's voice is full. "I prep my victims before I blow their minds."

I stop. Mustafa, my Mustafa. No more staring at the bank account and wishing for a couple more zeroes so I can hold my brother again.

I don't believe it.

"If this is a joke…"

"I would never joke about this."

"What about Europe?"

"Europe can wait. Mafraq, where the orphanage is, is ten miles from Syria. It's time I go back to my second home."

"What about Nassima?"

Khadija lowers her head. "I have to tell Nassima that I changed plans. I had to budget even with the prize trip vouchers from the showcase."

"Is she going to be okay?"

She sighs. "I don't know. I know she knows something's up

because we haven't talked about the trip in forever. She's not responding to my texts at superhuman speed and she hasn't video called me every six hours, but this is my choice and I have to deal with the consequences."

I bury the polite, sweet girl in me. I cannot give Nassima her dues. I have a right to this ticket, too. It is my ticket. It delivers me one step closer to facing my mistakes and saving my brother.

"We're going to Jordan. I'm going to get Mustafa." I repeat it until I believe it. My heart skips a beat. "Does your mom know?"

"I'll tell her," Khadija says. She pulls her hood over her head.

I gulp. "Don't tell her about Mustafa," I request, and Khadija considers it. "I can't let my mom know about Mustafa. I'm not ready." I pause. The excitement wears off. Whether I fail or succeed, my mom will have to learn the truth eventually.

"I'm scared," I tell her honestly.

Her gaze falls to a spot in the distance. "Me too."

35

Khadija

Since Mama vehemently objected to my trip, I've been feeling like I'm playing with an injured Achilles and that too much movement could tear the tendon. I'd be out for a full year. Whole seasons and trade deals could be shattered.

So I've finally stopped waiting for the blessing that was never coming. I'm officially booked for my international mission.

I pass through the kitchen to the living room—noting Baba's keys infamously missing from the bowl—where Mama is watching the news and sipping her black tea. She sits in her same spot, alone.

The fear of one's mother is an irrational fear. So irrational that even the index of phobias doesn't list it. I've searched it. Extensively. You can fear your stepmother (novercaphobia) and you can fear your mother-in-law (pentheraphobia), but you cannot fear your mother.

When I get caught in her crosshairs, I'm like a cat who's

just seen another cat for the first time in ages. My body puffs up, my hair stands on end, and I'm frozen in a suspended reality where her existence threatens my own.

"Hi, Mama."

"Hi?" She narrows her eyes. "What is this 'hi'? What happened to 'masaa' il-khair' or 'assalamu alaikum'?"

"Okay…masaa' il-khair," I tell her, praying it will be a good evening.

"No manners," she mutters with a tiny smile on her face. She could beat up a koala, then without guilt testify that it wasn't her fault it looked too much like a stuffed animal.

I set my open laptop in her lap and flop into the couch adjacent to hers.

Mama chokes on her tea and I bolt to grab her a cup of water. She won't need it, but I definitely can't wait in the vicinity of her stank eye.

"Who said you can go on with this?" Mama's voice is like steel. She scrolls through the tabs on loop.

"You did." Stay civilized.

"No I didn't."

The timer on my civility meter starts. "Yes you did. You told me I could go, but you wouldn't be pleased with me. So I'm going with that as permission."

"Akh, please, Khadija." Mama slides my laptop down the couch toward me repugnantly. "That means no. Of course I shouldn't have assumed you'd heard it that way. You don't take extra care to make your mother happy." I don't want to fire back so I take my laptop and hypnotize myself into silence by staring down the flight dates and times. "You're not going," Mama resolves. She's chosen the offensive, but I want to be on offense, too. Two offenses make a mess of a fight.

"Yes I am."

"No, you're not."

Our bickering is a broken record, each time one voice rising above the other's. We yell at each other, our warrior stances mirrored in the glass windows around us.

"I am!" I shout.

"Kill me first!"

"Stop being dramatic!"

"You'd walk all over your dead mother's wishes?"

God bless. "I'm not your prisoner. You can't control me because you have no control over anyone else. Your loneliness doesn't mean I have to be lonely, too, confined to this prison you built yourself."

She doesn't hesitate. "This isn't my prison. It's my kingdom. You aren't leaving it."

"I am," I say. "The tickets and reservations are right here."

"So?"

So? So, so, so what? "I'm going, Mama."

I hate the sound of my voice. It gives away how deflated I feel.

"So you could get yourself hurt? No, definitely not."

"Haven't I proven I can take care of myself?"

"Like at that boxing fight? There will always be someone ready to say or do hurtful things to you, Khadija, on the inside or from the outside. I'm trying to protect you."

"Protect me?" I repeat, rage bubbling beneath my skin. "*Protect*—Wait, how do you know about the match?"

"I have my sources."

My eyebrows part with realization. "You were there."

She juts out her chin and doesn't respond. And I know.

"Would it have been so bad to let me know that you were there supporting me?" I ask, wiping the snot from my upper lip.

"I—I didn't—I—I thought—" Mama stutters, then closes her eyes. I didn't think Mama *could* stutter. She sighs. "I can't support your actions if they're putting you in danger. You could do anything you want in this world, Khadija, so long as it's safe."

I blow out hot air. "Nothing I do will ever be safe enough for you. Nothing except for sitting beside you forever. And I can't do that. I'm going, Mama."

"We both know you aren't."

"Let me go." My voice is small, begging. Mama refuses. She leans back into the couch and unmutes the television. My nightmare is realized. Except this Mama does not want to embrace me.

"Why?" I whisper to myself. I say it again louder, but it's no longer a question. My questions are truths. "Why. Why do you delete everyone from my life. Are you scared. Do you think I'll choose someone else if you let me be with them. Because you know I'll want to run off to Syria in the summers and be with them again. Is that why I can never speak with Teteh or my aunts and uncles. You're so worried for yourself because no one ever chooses you. I chose you for years, Mama. I was here for you because Baba and Zain weren't. But I can't choose you anymore. I can't choose my warden."

I stand up to leave, but Mama clasps her fingers around my wrist and whips me around to her. She mirrors my anger, and I wonder if it's as frightening on me as it is on her. "I am your mother, Khadija. Do not blame me for your short-comings. I haven't stopped you from interacting with your teteh or with your cousins or with any of our family. You have a phone, too. Call them up yourself if you can't bear to be near me long enough to take my phone from me. 'It's too hard for her,' 'It makes her too sad,' 'She misses you too much.' I make those excuses for you. I do it because I'm your mom and I know it's hard for you. But they don't know that, and they don't have any explanations other than my excuses for you."

I don't believe her. Of course she blames me. Her defense technique is diverting. Mama sighs and releases my wrist. "Until you take responsibility for your mistakes and you don't need my excuses, then I will be your 'warden' and maybe then you'll be mature enough to travel across the world all on your own. Until then, you're not going."

"I am. You said I can. I have the tickets here."

She shakes her head. Her jaw is set.

"Baba will let me go. If I have to go to the boss man himself, I will," I threaten.

Mama's eyes flash with fury. "I am the boss man."

Without another word between us, I leave her in her glass sitting room, accompanied only by her tea. Our offenses failed. All that's left is to give up on the game. To give up on each other.

No itinerary in the world could secure my seats on that plane. Mama couldn't care less if all that money I spent, from my own and from Younes's prize vouchers, burns in hell.

Mama conjures that literal and metaphorical cliff and then blocks me from driving off because she thinks I won't bulldoze through her.

But she doesn't know that my promise to Leene ranks higher than her obstacles.

36

Khadija

Impossible is just a big word thrown around by small men who find it easier to live in the world they've been given than to explore the power they have to change it. Impossible is not a fact. It's an opinion. Impossible is not a declaration. It's a dare. Impossible is potential. Impossible is temporary. Impossible is nothing.

—Muhammad Ali

The tension at home mounts. With Nassima giving me the cold shoulder since I dropped the ball on our trip without so much as a heads-up, I turn to my other safe place. I end up at Jerr's.

Saturday mornings are the busiest mornings, but this Saturday not a punch slices air and not a weight clinks metal. Instead, a disconcerted air unsettles the boxers and the ring.

Guys cram into and crowd outside of Jerr's office, where he blasts ESPN's Muhammad Ali eulogy special. Two years since his death and this day hasn't gotten any easier for Jerr and the older trainers. For them, this is the day they lost their idol.

A single boxer's jabs cut through the air and interrupt the sound of television. Younes. I pace the floor across from him, then climb up into the ring and circle it to defuse my nerves, which ravage me like an unreachable itch. I lean against the ropes and stare up at the ceiling and the lights.

Muhammad Ali is the champion: the champion in the ring, the champion of words, the champion of justice. His existence had brought me steady comfort I hadn't felt until a harrowing absence replaced it two years ago. After his death, I was hit with the realization that Ali had unknowingly protected me from the brunt of the hate; he was my break from it all.

In a rapid lash-out, Younes ditches his gloves and climbs into the ring next to me. He opens his phone and scrolls through his social media, letting me peek over his shoulder. Twitter and Instagram are refreshing feeds of Muhammad Ali quotes and tributes. Black and Muslim Twitter and Instagram explode with reminders to pray for him. Ali retired from the ring years ago, but to all of us, his youth, his evasion of the draft, it all feels like two days ago. We're still recovering today from his game-changing actions. I stretch my neck to get a view of Jerr's office television, where a montage plays of Ali's interviews and fights.

"...falling under the spell of Malcolm X," the voiceover reports, "and converting to Islam." Younes and I don't bother acting puzzled at the word choice. The report pivots to the Vietnam War, omitting any religious affiliations or motivations for evading the draft.

Younes pockets his phone and shakes his head, annoyed.

"So typical," I say, equally irritated by the report. I ramble, "People listened to him, you know? After all that he went through because he was an outspoken Black Muslim and because he didn't want to follow the status quo, he finally became someone people had no choice but to listen to. He had the chance to say all that we never could. He said something about hijab once, and he's the only one who could talk about hijab in a way people could listen and accept it. They say our fathers, brothers, and husbands oppress us, yet they only listen when it's mansplained to them. Maybe it should make me mad that men only listen to men about women, but I can't be angry at him. No one would have listened if I had said what he did, and someone had to say it."

"What did he say?" Younes leans against the ropes across me, the weight in his gloves accentuating his tense muscles, glistening with sweat.

"I can't remember the details," I admit. "He said that everything that God made valuable in the world He covered and protected. Diamonds are hidden deep in the ground, and pearls are at the bottom of the sea in shells. Gold is deep in mines, encased in layers of rock. He said that women are more precious and valuable than any diamond, pearl, or gold, so God made it a part of our religion for us to cover. To protect our bodies from the elements that want to violate us. That's how it's supposed to be. If it's that reason or any other reason, it's my choice, and it's all me. I shouldn't get hell for it. I shouldn't get hell for choosing what part of me is too precious to show to others. When I heard him say that, I was even more sure of my choice. Mine."

That is what Muhammad Ali means to me. My hijab, the way I dress, was reaffirmed by my boxing father figure. Ultimately, every match, jab, and hook is redefined by my hijab, but I wouldn't have it any other way. It is my choice. It is my first line of defense.

A few weeks ago, the spectators at the fight gawked at me as if my skill in boxing reflected a barbaric tendency deriving from my hijab. Their terrified faces replay in my mind as I peer over the edge of the ropes. I catch Whit's ponytail bouncing across the floor before she squeezes her way into Jerr's office. I shudder, thinking how humiliating it was to forfeit and how I didn't feel there was any other option.

"Ain't no nun being called oppressed," Younes says, and he offers a shadow of a goofy smile.

"Ain't no nun." I giggle faintly.

He pushes off the rope and slips on his gloves, proceeding to land one hell of a right hook on an unclaimed zipped bag left in the ring. My heart rate accelerates and my palms line with sweat. Shoot me, but troubled boys make me feel right at home. "You have a vendetta against that bag, Ness?" I muse.

Younes huffs, shutting his eyes. He shoots me a mischievous look. "You wanna spar?"

I hold up my naked fists. "I'd leave you to your hormones, but I worry about public safety. And you." I hiccup, but Younes doesn't look twice. Being together might not be as complicated as I think.

"I don't think," Younes starts, his voice low and shaky. "I don't think I can keep going without an answer, Kadi."

"An answer?" I repeat, my tone more playful. "I didn't realize there was a question."

The corners of his lips don't so much as twitch. He's in no mood for jokes, let alone a good spar. He closes the distance between us so that the ring feels enormous and the space between us nothing. We stand so close together I can feel his breath. My body stretches in every direction because I want to run away, but a stronger force commands me to stay. Younes tips his head slightly to give me a lovely view into his dark, creamy eyes. It feels as though an hour goes by while I'm staring into them before he inhales sharply and—

"I'm tired, Kadi."

"Tired?" I blink at him. "Did those scouts not call you back? Listen, it's not the end of boxing for you. You can't give up—you can just train harder. I'll stay longer hours so you don't get bored at the gym, trust me—"

"Khadija." My full name sounds foreign coming out of his mouth. I freeze. He gestures between us. "I'm tired of this. I feel like I'm chasing you, and you never stop running away."

I pout. "We're going on that date, aren't we?"

"Do you even want the date?" he asks, and I'm taken aback by how hurt he sounds.

I widen my eyes innocently. "Obviously I do. But it's just one date. The logistics of a relationship are too much."

"You mean keeping things halal? Who cares about technicalities? You're always going headfirst into everything except for this. You keep me at a distance. I'm not asking to marry you. I don't know how the hell this works, but I do know I want to go out with you," he says. I rack my brain for another poor joke, but his thickly lashed eyes don't have an inkling of a smile. They're full and honest and hopeful.

"But," I start, hating the sound of my voice, "but you know how it goes. One date, then dating, then…"

I can't say the steps that follow in a halal relationship. Engagement. Marriage. Maybe even love. In my mind, those things are worlds from me, but Younes is an arm's length away.

"You're overthinking it," he tells me.

I am. For months I've been stalling with tasteless jokes and terrible timing. And yet. "How can you not?"

"I like you a lot." He is sure. "More than a casual thing. More than being with you at Jerr's. I want more, and I think you want more, too." He is so sure.

Then time stops because Younes cradles my face in his gloves, the leather and dense padding barely buffering the electricity between us.

"I feel so young." I hyperventilate.

"Me too. But let's date and be young. Go on one date with me, and then another if you want and more after that. But I'm done chasing you. I'm always running after everyone else in my life. Going to that event or dropping off that brother or all the other things that make me feel like I'm already grown. I want to be young with you."

My face fits perfectly into the nook of his gloves. Impossibly, I feel the warmth of his hands on my cheeks.

"I want us to do it the right way," he adds like an afterthought. His voice is so damn soft. "Slow and steady, but right."

I know he means the halal way. Dating in an engagement period of however long we choose with the caveat of intending to marry. But thinking about all of that is harrowing.

He senses that I'm done melting in his arms because he releases me. There isn't a sucker I wouldn't punch to wipe the confusion off his face.

"We're both eighteen. We're both adults. Whatever that means." He and I both know that age and adulthood have no correlation in our respective cultures. "We don't have to think about the marriage part. We can take our time. We don't decide anything until later."

Suddenly, my skin feels like it's not mine. "You know that I live in my mom's dollhouse. I'm her porcelain doll that she forces to sit this way or do that thing. I'm still a child to her. I don't know if she'd want this."

Hurt, Younes takes a step back. "This isn't about your mom."

But I feel suffocated. "It always is."

"I'm not formally asking for your hand. I'm asking you, Kadi. You're who matters to me. You want to go out with me, don't you."

He doesn't phrase it like a question, and I don't want to question it.

My voice buries itself at the bottom of my throat. My choice, my voice, matters to him, and I can't seem to find it anymore. I wait for someone else to speak up for me. My mother, Ali, the white man in the pickup truck who calls me oppressed. I need anyone to tell Younes what I can't.

Yes.

"Did I misread something?" Younes's voice sounds dilapidated.

I recount all our conversations and I find myself shameless in my affections. "No, no, everything you said is true."

"Then what is it?"

"Nothing," I say, faltering. "But maybe it's not the right time."

"It was only a question." His doe eyes, moments ago naive and hopeful, are wounded. "When's the right time for an answer?"

He's right, the way our world works, matters of love are complicated enough, and I shouldn't convolute it. Do I want to be with Younes? Right now, yes. Do I know what that entails?

Hell no. Does love wilt away until it's some form of my mother's disjointed marriage with my father? Is there ever love?

"When I'm back from Jordan," I start, and his crestfallen gaze buries the words in my throat. In an intricate mess of heartstrings, I owe it to the ring for separating us. Though I want to comfort him more than ever, he's the one wearing the gloves, not me. I hold my elbows tightly. "I promise you'll have your answer when I get back, and it'll be the right one for both of us."

"You owe me a date, Kadi."

I can't look him in the eye. I don't know what one date could lead to, even with the best of intentions.

Though the butterflies in my stomach swirl a storm and the word is on my tongue, I leave Younes hanging. I cast a longing, apologetic look at him and drop out of the ring. Always, I surrender from the fight.

37

Leene

What if we miss the flight? Does the airline reschedule or are we stranded?

What about the connection? Traffic, delays, they could upend all our plans.

What if there are no buses to Mafraq? I would go on foot.

What if I arrive at the orphanage and they don't believe that I am Mustafa's sister?

Do we still look alike? How much has he grown? Will I recognize him? Will he recognize me?

I toss and turn, the mattress squeaks, and the iron bed post thumps against the wall. Mama grunts feet away from me, throwing her sheets off the side of the bed. I wipe my clammy palms and cautiously take up my phone.

I type up my nightly text.

You're sure we're not forgetting anything?

She texts back immediately.

Khadija: **Yeah...don't worry and go to sleep**

I can't. I explained that to her the first time I texted my freak-out with live updates by the second. Then, it was about not having a suitcase that isn't pieced together by duct tape. Today, I graduate from the step-by-step game play of Operation Retrieve Mustafa. Today, my mind wanders to other unresolved issues.

Did you tell Nassima?

A minute passes.

Khadija: **Did you tell your mom?**

I told her I'm traveling with you on your international trip.

She trusts me so she's fine with it

Khadija: **Lucky you**

You're dodging my question. What about Nassima?

Khadija: **I haven't yet. I forgot**

Lies!

Khadija: **I promise! I have too many things on my mind**

I sigh. She does. But she's avoided Nassima for so long, confronting her best friend about cutting off the plans they've been working toward for years can't be easy. My thumbs dart across the keyboard.

You're an angel, you know. You and your mom both

Minutes go by without a reply. I type a follow-up.

Except you're the devil when you're hungry.

My phone buzzes quickly.

Khadija: **Devil sounds about right**

I let my phone fall against my chest as a placid quietness

distills me. It feels like peace plus a dull pressure of my potential doom. It is an uncomfortable stillness with the humid air unbending and my dense thoughts clogging my brain. *Limbo* is a word I learned today, specifically to describe this feeling. Perhaps I am perpetually stuck in what Americans call limbo, or perhaps I am finally finding my way out of it. Either way Khadija is not with me wherever I am.

We are going to be okay, right?

Her reply is quick: **No border no ocean no cliff is gonna stop us from being okay**

Inshallah, I type. God willing.

Khadija: **Inshallah** 😈

38

Khadija

I promise to make no more promises.

God bless. No promises. I'll have to stop using that word until I learn the weight of it.

My promises have led to Leene's paranoia that something will surely go wrong, and it already has where my mother is concerned, but I'd rather not break her spirit and feed her paranoia. My other promise has me counting down to when I'm out of Rochester Heights so that I can consider what to do about Younes. And the biggest promise of all is the one I made with Nassima. I put off booking tickets with her, so much so that she has gone radio silent and all our talk about coordinating graduation outfits has gone in the dumps along with our European getaway.

At this rate, I'll have let down more people than I've helped.

"It's your graduation tomorrow. You pick a movie for movie night," Mama says, snapping me out of self-loathing while she pops popcorn on the stove. "Look, Zain's watching with us."

She grins, dropping her voice as Zain walks into the kitchen with a box of DVDs. Sometimes I forget what year we live in.

"This one." I pick the movie right on top. I slide it across the counter. A golden Denzel Washington gazes off into his epic football victory. *Remember the Titans*: an American classic and one of my all-time favorites.

Mama balks at my movie. "What about *Titanic*? Or *Singin' in the Rain*? Those movies are fun."

"*Titanic* only gets good once they hit the iceberg."

I didn't say it; Zain did. I gape at him, and my mouth loosens into a smile. Okay, okay, I see you, Zain.

"Nothing more fun than a ship full of rich people sinking," I add.

"Might I remind you two that you are wealthy," Mama says, trying to hide that she's ecstatic. Zain ripping a joke is like witnessing a meteor shower. It's rare, it's astonishing, and it leaves us wondering what he might have or has yet to destroy.

Zain rummages through the DVDs and, with meticulous compulsivity, arranges six movies on the counter for us. The *Lord of the Rings* series followed by the *Hobbit* trilogy.

Mama beams at him. "Great idea, Zain!"

I groan. "I thought it was my choice. My graduation, my celebration, my choice."

"Don't be difficult—you love these movies, too," Mama warns.

I lift *The Fellowship of the Ring*, and Aragorn's stare defeats me. Still, I muster a fight against it. "You hate these movies, Mama. You spend the entire movie grumbling that it's all witchcraft and devilry!"

"No I don't. I love this movie," Mama defends. "Don't I, Zain?"

Zain looks between us. "You pretend you love this movie for me."

I grin, leaning over to my little brother to face off against my mother, my lips tight and smug.

"Not true," Mama says pretending to mope, but I hear her excitement that her kids are doing a shared activity with her. "I like the first one."

"So we're watching it?" Not waiting for an answer, Zain takes the movie and strolls into the living room to insert it into the DVD player.

Mama is in a stellar mood thanks to Zain. I take a deep breath and brave the mild front that has calmed my mother's bitter winter.

"My flight is in six days." My voice barely breaks through the *Lord of the Rings* opening music.

"Will you be going to the airport?" Mama asks, her tone friendly.

I'm taken aback by her question, but I tread on. "Yeah, yeah I am."

"Good." She picks up the bucket of popcorn.

Surprised, I reply, "Good."

She pounces. "You'll get a good view of your plane passing over your head. Don't forget to wave at the passengers—you'll be just like an ant on the ground, but maybe the pilot will see you and wave back. I imagine they may do that sometimes."

I simmer for the first quarter of the movie, festering over her attack. I sit on the farthest armchair away from her while Zain sprawls on the ground between us and falls under the movie's spell. I wish I could let myself go into their adventure, but my mind is a web of tangled thoughts.

"I don't understand." Again, Zain shocks me by speaking. His glossy eyes are fixated on the screen.

"I don't, either," I reply, biting hard on my lip. "Why doesn't the Elven king join the fellowship? He kicks butt, he's powerful, but he doesn't offer anything to them. He's all 'you have to go to Mordor' and he knows how to get there, but he doesn't help them get there." As I say the words my mother morphs into the Elven king.

Zain doesn't say anything. I need distractions from fighting it out with Mama. I try again. "Or you don't get why everyone in this movie has to be white and a dude because I don't, either."

Zain goes absolutely mute. I don't try with him for this reason. He says something or inserts himself into a conversation and then vanishes. The goblin scene plays on the screen.

"What are those, Yajuj and Majuj?" Mama whispers, and

I sync my lips to it. Yajuj and Majuj parallel Gog and Magog. This is where her commentary usually begins.

"You say that every time," I point out.

"Well," she rebuffs, "it is devilry and witchcraft!"

"You don't have to watch it." I will her away. She leaves after making a sizable fuss and bidding Zain good night while disregarding me. Zain sits up, his head turned to where her perfume lingers. Frodo and his buddies cry on-screen and suddenly it cuts. Zain ejects the DVD.

"Hello?" I protest. "I was still watching." Zain wavers, then closes the DVD in its case and hands it to me. "What is wrong with you? Can't you say something? Would you like to mime to me?"

He stops with the coffee table between us. He's a new recipient of this angle, appearing small in the huge frame of the room where Mama usually towers.

"I want to be homeschooled," Zain says, avoiding my questions.

I shake my head at him, confused at the sudden request. But I'm not a fan of Zain being at home more than he already is. "Nuh-uh. School is good for you. You see people at school. You get out of your room. There's no reason to leave it."

"I have summer school," he mutters.

"You always have summer school."

"I don't want to go to school."

"It's not your choice, Zain."

God bless. I sound like my mother. My palms sweat. Rewind. "Why don't you want to go to school?" I ask.

He thinks for a minute, his hands locked in claws. "It's not easy for me," he finally says, a bit louder than anticipated.

"School is a little cruel for everyone."

"N-no," Zain stammers, and his swimming blue eyes find mine. "It's not easy for me to talk to you. When I do, I remember how it was before."

"Before?"

"You know what I mean."

Before. My dream is before. Our family surrounding us, sparklers in our chubby hands, no one asking us to do better, to be more. Mama, Baba, Zain, and me together. A time when we were enough.

As he gathers the courage to speak, his voice cracks. "Do— do you ever think it would've been better for everyone if we weren't here?"

I feel the color drain from my face. "What do you mean?"

He clears his throat. It sounds effortful. "I just mean that one of our cousins would be able to do so much more with what we were given."

I reach for an objection. I can't find the words.

"I fail. Every day," he whispers. "I fail."

I lean back in the armchair. Zain is a stranger again despite his hair having grown out into his five-year-old curls, reminding me of when we used to play on the rooftop of my family's house in Syria with each other. This Zain's eyes are rimmed in shadow and his skin is lurid gray. I'm not sure what I'm supposed to say to this boy I don't recognize.

"You're not alone," I tell him, but my words fall flat. Ever since we stopped going to Syria, Zain has only ever been alone.

He turns his head, staring at the dark TV screen. His words lodge in his throat before breaching the dam. "Frodo gets a whole fellowship to help him go to Mordor, but in the end Sam's the only one he needs to get there. Sam never leaves him, even when everyone else gets caught up in their quests. He just needed one Sam to make it."

"Is this still about Frodo?" I ask him, weighing his cryptic reply. An itch nestles itself in my brain. It strums an unsettling nerve, disturbing a dormant worry. I want to scream at him to translate himself into words I can comprehend so I can give him a helpful response.

"I don't see the point anymore," he whispers.

"The point of what?"

"Trying."

The unease in his voice, the way it shakes then drops, needles a terrible thought into my mind.

What if, one day, he stopped trying?

I'll be the first to admit, I'm not the best sister. There are days when he's right in front of me and I'm too sucked into my own world to notice. But I never do it on purpose. After all, I'm also trying to survive.

The speculation stifles me, so I pivot. "You're coming to my graduation, right? I don't know if Baba will make it, but you will, right?"

Zain's expression turns to stone, but it quickly returns to the Zain I've come to know, the one who has stopped caring and trying, the one who blends into the background.

He slinks away, and when he's gone, it's as though he was never there.

39

Leene

I never thought this day would come. After transferring schools, self-teaching to stay at my grade level, learning to feel safe in a classroom again, I finally made it.

I, along with my graduating class, a cloud of dark emerald robes and white tasseled caps, stand for the final declaration of the Class of 2018. Hands reach up and caps fly high like Frisbees before plummeting back down. A communal breath suspends in our lungs. On the collective exhale, the school band comes alive.

Clutching my empty folio where my diploma will rest in a few months, I push myself through my former classmates. I've officially graduated. My tumultuous relationship with school has come to an end. I've dissected enough German sentences for a lifetime and repeated the impossible pronunciation of the word *murderer* more times than I'd like to admit. I've attended too many schools for RHHS to stick with me, but it will.

I walk aimlessly to locate the reason why I care for this school more than any others. The robes steadily disperse, with graduates waving to friends on their way to find their families. The school's auditorium roars with celebration. Mama waves at me wildly from her raised seats where she sits with Khaleh Maisa.

"Mabrouk habibti!" Mama congratulates me. We beam at each other. Khaleh Maisa passes her a bouquet of flowers and Mama dangles them down to me from her seat on the bleachers. I jump to snatch them, and Mama gestures that they'll get down and meet me on the auditorium floor.

I take a big whiff of the scentless grocery store flowers. Just five more days. My mind wanders to Mustafa's kindergarten class, who his teachers might be, whether or not he made friends, what he's learning. I imagine standing in the bleachers cheering him on as they call his name when he graduates from my alma mater. Mustafa at eighteen. I was sure that day would never come.

In a corner of the auditorium, a group of boys and girls with their caps pinned to their scarves gather. One of the parents among the group blasts dabkeh music from a portable speaker, leaded with heavy bass so any fool with an ear and a bit of rhythm can catch the beat. My classmates link hands in a line and dance in a circle by following the dabkeh leader's fancy footwork. I clap along to what becomes a performance, a stomping dance spectacle. The dabkeh spreads in the auditorium, and there are more raised eyebrows than at Khadija's boxing match. Just barely.

Someone strikes a goblet drum and begins competing for sound waves with the band's trumpets and clarinets. A tap on my shoulder breaks me from my hypnosis and Mama materializes behind me. She throws her arms around me, and my chin connects with her shoulder.

"First one of my babies to graduate," Mama says gleefully.

She marvels at me. My every breath is a blessing to Mama, so today is a miracle.

"I did it, Mama." My eyes fill with tears. I almost didn't get the chance to hold this diploma in my hand. Many of my friends from grade school won't be able to because the odds are stacked against us. Some can't bear to be in a classroom anymore, others need to work to survive. School is a luxury. I know that.

Khaleh Maisa kisses me on the cheeks and gives me her congratulations. She waits patiently as Khadija takes pictures with Nassima, but the tension between the two girls is palpable. Khadija's smile is stilted, and Nassima, who is usually so warm with her friend, enforces distance between them.

Mama and I join them.

"One, two, three!" I snap shots of Nassima and her family. Nassima is a creaseless, glossy North African queen. They separate. I snap pictures of Khadija and her family of two. They unhinge their smiles and untwist their arms like they're two pieces of an IKEA bookshelf that don't fit. Before Mama pulls me in for pictures, I clinch Khadija and Nassima into a three-way embrace.

"Isn't this exciting?" I ask, grinning like a complete doofus.

Khadija lets out a shaky breath, and Nassima squeezes my shoulder. She pulls away from Khadija first. The ecstasy of celebration fizzles out around us as Nassima steps away and retreats to her family.

I lean over to Khadija, who looks dejected at Nassima's frigidity. "Not even Zain?" I whisper to her, shooting a sympathetic glance between her and her mom.

Khadija shrugs as she shoots a sad look at Khaleh Maisa, who stands ever straighter, filling up space where the rest of her family should be. The diamonds in our eyes turn lackluster as our smiles fade. More often than not smiles are for cameras.

Then Khadija does a double take. "What is he doing?"

"Who?" I glance around.

No living creature could stand in Khadija's way as she charges for Younes, who looks dapper in his robe with cap in hand. I chase after her when she comes to a halt, and she holds out her hand to stop me. Khadija is miming all sorts of signals, but Younes arrives at his target first. He gives his salaam loud enough for us to hear it.

Khaleh Maisa sizes him up like he isn't a foot taller than her. "Wa alaikum assalam."

I actually hear Khadija exhale. Khaleh Maisa stares at her daughter throughout Younes's introduction.

"Yeah, wa alaikum assalam," he says with a furtive smile. "I'm not sure if you know, but I box with Khadija."

"God bless," Khadija mumbles to me behind an open palm. "I'm getting killed today."

Khadija hides her face and clogs her ears for the effect. She does a lot of things for the effect. "It's not so bad," I tell her.

"She's never told me about you," Khaleh Maisa says inquisitively.

Younes cocks an eyebrow. "Really?"

"Well, it is nice to meet you. Though, I'm sorry, she's never mentioned you before."

"Yeah, that's okay, she probably—" he begins, interrupted by Khadija sending him the peremptory Arab sign for if-you-take-the-wrong-step-someone's-going-to-die. Thumb to index finger and at least three inverted hand wags. A light shines in his eye like he's playing a game, then he adds, "I wanted to meet you anyway."

Khaleh Maisa raises an eyebrow, a single action that asks a dozen questions.

Khadija's hand travels to cover her pained yet entertained expression. Younes perks a bit. "You know, because you're Khadija's mom. I wanted to see where she comes from."

Khaleh Maisa glances at Khadija, who shrugs dramatically. "Why?" she asks.

"Most people aren't born with her confidence and impossible conviction," he says, making Khadija blush.

"Most people can't handle it," Khadija mutters to me.

"It's got to come from somewhere," Younes adds.

Khaleh Maisa smiles, tight-lipped. "It's not from me." She looks at Khadija proudly while Khadija gazes at Younes like she's seeing him for the first time.

"Who else, then?" he says with intentional charm.

Khaleh Maisa laughs from the flattery, multiplying the volume of Younes's head.

"Did my mother just laugh?" Khadija needs to steady herself from shock. "I'm not going home tonight."

Younes glances between Khadija and her mom, not bothering to mask his confusion. He gives Khaleh Maisa a farewell salaam, then lazily salutes Khadija and me, shoots a congratulations, and saunters off.

"Why did Younes do that?" I can't hold in my curiosity.

"Five more days," Khadija murmurs, ignoring my question and staring after Younes.

40

Khadija

*F*ive more days to get my shit together. Fumbling with Younes's proposition, his introduction to Mama at my graduation a message that the ball is in my court now. Sorting out Zain's riddles and wondering why he wasn't at my graduation earlier today. Breaking off from Mama. Post–high school life is hitting me hard, and I've only just walked across the stage.

Yet dealing with it in Nassima's bedroom with a movie and snacks feels right. Even if I had to force Nassima to let me come along, because she barely looked at me all ceremony long.

"Sleeping here, Khadija?" Khaleh Leila peeks her head into the room at midnight. They're replicas of each other, except Khaleh Leila's curly black hair has deflated over the years. She smiles at me with her motherly smile and kind eyes. I glance at Nassima for an answer, but Nassima won't tear her eyes off the screen. Khaleh Leila takes that as her response.

She pauses to leave, then stops the door from shutting all the way. She peeks her head in again. "Khadija?"

I look up at her, wondering if her mother's intuition can sense my anxieties. Because she is thoughtful and patient. She knows me and my mother and my life. And I can be quite pitiful when I want to be.

She says, "Habibti, you are always welcome here and I'm not saying this because anyone asked me to, but it must have been hard for your mama to be the only one at your graduation. If you sleep here, you'll both be okay, you're always okay, but your Mama wants to celebrate you, too. Even if it's just you and her. It would mean a lot to her if you spent some time after graduation together."

A storm of emotions swirls in my gut. All at once I'm grateful for Khaleh Leila and Nassima, angry at my actions toward Mama, yet tired of her need for my companionship, and apologetic to them all.

Like Zain said in his odd style and delivery, yet encompassing all that we feel: We all need a Sam.

Nassima knows my predicament. Khaleh Leila cares, but more importantly, she has a point. It's not Mama's fault that she only has me. Circumstances of revolution and tangled priorities aren't her fault. Our social standards permit Baba's absence because of his demanding, prestigious career. And God forbid Zain is ever to be blamed. So I am all that's left for her. I didn't ask to be, but I'm Mama's Sam, and Nassima is mine, derelict promises aside.

"I'll think about it," I finally say, which satisfies Khaleh

Leila. I've thought about it. I turn my phone off, freeing myself from Leene's paranoia and deactivating what is effectively an ankle bracelet to my glass prison.

Here I am, calling Mama and my home a prison when I lock myself behind the bars of my twisted promises. If I'm taking the leap in five days, then this is my running start. No more talk of prisons.

"Is it okay with you if I stay the night?" I ask her tentatively. When I invited myself to her place afterward, it may only have been because she felt bad that Baba didn't show up to my graduation that she allowed me to follow her home.

Nassima hits the space button hard. Her back still to me, she speaks toward the wall: "I can't tell yet. Maybe you can tell me why I shouldn't be upset with you after you basically ghosted me about our summer trip."

Straight up, Nassima will knock you down, no fists involved.

"Okay. First, I'm sorry."

Nassima gasps sarcastically, "A Khadija Shaami apology? What for?"

Rip it off like a wax strip to the upper lip.

"I'm sorry because I'm bailing on our graduation trip. I'm breaking the promise I made to you about our trip. I don't want to make excuses for myself."

Nassima turns in her bed, squinting at me. Moments pass before she says, "That's it? I told you I wouldn't hold that against you, Khadija. Your mom wasn't having it. It's not your fault."

A lump forms in the back of my throat. "That's not it. I am taking a trip, but not the one we had planned."

"What, with your mom?" Nassima's voice is hopeful but suspecting. She may sound optimistic, but she levels it with a stoic expression.

"No, I'm going on a trip with Leene."

"Yeah, right," she scoffs.

"I'm a terrible friend. I'm so sorry. "

"Wait, you're serious?"

"I'm not taking her on our trip. I'm traveling with her to help her out."

Save for her eyes, she is chiseled stone. After a silence, she speaks. "Tell me why."

Mustafa. His name is at the tip of my tongue, but I can't give him as an excuse. Leene's secrets are her own to spill, not mine.

"I can't say. It's not my story to tell. It's not even my journey to take. It's Leene's. I'm only helping."

Nassima's eyes moisten, and she blinks rapidly as thoughts filter through her head.

"I should've told you earlier," I say. "I got caught up in everything that was happening and then I felt like crap for breaking my promise to you. I put off telling you for too long."

She stops blinking. "Okay."

"Okay?"

Nassima sighs and says, "I don't blame you. I know you, mon amie. You wouldn't ditch me for no good reason or even a plain good reason. This has to be something important. And I don't know, I'm kind of grateful to Leene. She's the one that helped bring back the Khadija that doesn't hit or pounce at the nearest moving target."

Any worry from earlier dissipates into nothingness.

"I don't deserve you, mon petit chou." I spread my arms out for a hug.

She accepts it. "Yeah, yeah, but don't you ever keep secrets from me again."

Nassima, always keeping it real.

A ringing interrupts our reconciliation. Habit draws us each to our phones, but my phone is black. Nassima scans over hers; her thumb wavers. She twists the screen to me.

My mother's name lights up the screen.

"Allo?" Nassima answers. I hear Mama's voice yelling through the speakers. A million regrets course through me. Khaleh Leila was right. Panic spreads across Nassima's face. "Wait, wait, I can't understand you," Nassima pronounces loudly over Mama's voice. "Yes, she's here." Nassima holds the phone to me like it's a bomb about to go off.

My heart sinks. As soon as the phone hits my ear, Mama's tone cleaves the cords of my heart.

"Where is he?" Her voice hikes.

"Who?"

"You don't know? No one knows? Ya Allah. Zain is gone. He took his pills and he's gone!"

41

Khadija

$\mathcal{I}$ slam my foot on the brakes.

"Stay here." I keep the engine running.

Nassima reaches over and turns the car off. "I'm coming with you."

The parking lot of Heights Mall is desolate. The ancient streetlamps filter a yellow light on the two broken-down vans. Darkness envelops the deserted building, darker than the cloudy night sky.

I scale the perimeter, leaving Nassima in the dust. Graffiti covers old signs of shop names and department stores. This shopping strip was abandoned years ago. Well past midnight, the mall feels like it's crawling with ghosts.

My body moves forward while my soul beats itself further and further into a rabbit hole. *Why would Zain come here?* My pace quickens. I smack my dry lips together. I think the worst of all possible scenarios.

"Did you hear me, Khadija?"

"What?"

"Why would Zain come here?"

I try every door I pass. I bang on them, and without an answer, I charge into them with my shoulder. I don't know why he'd be here, but I'm not stopping until I search everywhere.

Nassima repeats her question.

"I don't know. I don't know." I'm beyond shaken. "He's nowhere he might be. He's nowhere."

"Don't talk like that." Nassima grasps my shoulders. "We're going to find him. We need to think about where Zain might be. I don't think he's here."

I numbly allow Nassima to draw me back to the car. Once inside, my forehead thuds against the steering wheel.

"What have I done?"

"Nothing. Nothing has happened yet," Nassima maintains.

I punch the dashboard, releasing no frustration. "I don't know where he could be." How could I? Zain feels like a stranger to me. "Did I do this? Did I make him feel alone? What kind of sister am I?"

"It's not about you!" Nassima grabs my fists and shoves them into my lap. I blink at her. A terrible sense of déjà vu waves over me. "We're looking for Zain. Now drive us out of this parking lot."

I force myself to regulate my breathing. I can't. Fear has me in its grip.

"What if finding him is worse than this?"

I think of Leene and of not knowing. Of how much knowing the truth can hurt more than assuming the worst.

"We're going to find him." Nassima believes it fully, and my brain fires and my muscles react. I start the car when my phone rings. My heart shrivels in my chest. This could be the call. Cowed, I pass it to Nassima to pick up.

"Allo? Yes, she's here, she's driving," Nassima says. I anchor myself with the slick steering wheel. Nassima listens, she glances at me, eyes etched with exhaustion. "She's fine...one second." She holds the phone to her chest. "Leene is asking if she can help with anything."

Leene. My gut twists. "Tell her I'm fine. My mom won't want anyone to know."

"She was with your mom before. She knows something's wrong," Nassima says.

"Does she know it's Zain?"

"I don't think so."

My jaw locks. First rule of Mama's household: Reveal none of your personal problems to anyone.

Tonight, as my whole world hangs out of balance, I take my first action of many.

I put the car in drive. "Tell her to be ready in ten."

He's nowhere.

I throw myself back into the driver's seat. My emotions torpedo inside me and pull my nerves into taut tendrils.

Mama and I haven't seen him since our movie night before graduation. His car, my hand-me-down Mini Cooper, is still at home. None of it makes sense.

Zain did not run away. If he did, he would have had to plan it out, take some of his belongings or his legal documents, but everything is still at home. He didn't leave Rochester Heights. And if he is in Rochester Heights, he will be found, but my imagination has already convinced me it'll be worse to find him. The police have been informed. Does Zain's name get tacked onto the bottom of a missing persons list? Is that the end of his story?

It would've been better if we weren't here.

What did he mean? I want to yell it over the rooftops. *What did you mean?*

He couldn't say it to my face, whatever it was; he couldn't tell me, and my mind contorted his inability into his routine failure.

My heart throbs.

Leene's and Nassima's knocking on the car windows intensifies. I unlock the doors and let them in. Leene takes the back seat in sweats that she threw on half asleep, and Nassima sits beside me, taking my hands in hers.

"Did you know?" Nassima asks me, and in my peripheral vision I see her stare at me intently. I keep my eyes fixated through the windshield, on nothing in particular. I don't need to look at her to know that her resolve is gone. She knows it too now.

"Did I know what?" I murmur, my dry vocal cords barely vibrating.

"That he was taking those pills."

I swallow nothing. "No."

"Did you know he was depressed?" I hear Nassima's question as if she's on another side of a thick glass window.

Fiery whips of emotion snap against my skull and my skin stings. My silence is response enough.

"Do you think..." Leene's voice dissolves in the thick air. She finds it again. "Did you check the school?"

"Yes."

Leene leans forward and pokes her head between Nassima and me in the front. "He had bad friends," Leene says. *Had.* "I saw how they were around him. They weren't real friends. They bullied him. I always thought if I'd die anywhere it—"

"Don't talk like that," Nassima says, bridling Leene. She reaches over and places her hand on mine. "It's going to be okay," she says.

Leene shuts up. I close my eyes. It's not about me. "Where would you have died, Leene?"

Leene clears her throat. "I'd have died in Douma. I'd have died in the one place that stripped me down of everything that ever meant anything to me. The place where I was weakest. Either there or in the sea. Floating side by side with Mustafa."

"The school is Zain's Douma."

She nods, determination replacing sadness. "We will find Zain. You're crossing the world with me to find my brother. You made sure I didn't give up on Mustafa. I won't let you give up on Zain."

Nassima's hand falls away from mine. We lock eyes and I see a wave of understanding rush over her.

I must find my brother.

Leene's jaw is set. "Let's go to the school again."

42

Leene

"Zain!"

I know he's there. I feel it in my bones, and this time it's not a lie.

Save for our echoes, the school grounds are silent and unforgiving. We circle the outside of the main building, looking in from the glass exit doors into the dimly lit hallways. Khadija and Nassima's desperate calls reverberate against the stones. I run past the outside of the halls, and while Khadija looks into each hall with peeled eyes, I call them forward.

I turn to the back stretch of RHHS's main building. The back of the school is lined with entries to more halls, each with its own impressive archway. The very last archway leads to the ELL hall. My nerves buzz and my lips loosen. I look over my shoulder at Khadija. "He'll be here."

Khadija skips a step and breaks into a run. I do, too. My apprehension escalates as the contours of the archway swallow the hall entrance in darkness. Nassima and I are steps behind her and with every footfall, the walls eat up our shadows.

I turn to see into the lit hall through the glass doors.

What did I expect to see? My brain obviously wouldn't conjure a picture so peaceful as him sleeping there with a backpack and a train ticket. The blood and death I've seen paint a terrifying image, but we're met with nothing and no one.

The deserted red brick archway and hall relieve me of the negative images. I ransack my brain, trying to think of where else he could be if not on the school grounds. Even if he's inside, the school should be locked after hours.

Khadija doesn't stop to think.

She charges at the glass and metal double doors that frame the ELL hallway. She pulls back her fist, and a crack splits our ears and reverberates against the glass, unable to shatter it. Her shoulders shake with a sob. With a heave of her shoulders, she collapses to her knees.

"I'm so sorry. I th-thought—I was so sure he'd be here…" I stammer.

Nassima kneels beside Khadija. "This doesn't mean anything. We'll find him. Or he'll come around eventually. Inshallah. It's going to be—"

"It won't be okay," Khadija cries. "It won't."

"Don't say that." Nassima waves me over, but I'm looking around as if Zain might walk up to us any second now.

Khadija leans her forehead against the door's metal bar and releases a shuddered breath. She pushes against it, and the metal bar inserts, budging the door open and drawing her in.

The door was unlocked. Someone is in here.

We stumble into the hallway, whipping our heads wildly.

Khadija barges into the cracked open door of the nearest classroom. No more than three feet from us, the images in my mind take on reality. Sprawled on the linoleum floor, Zain's inert body lays at the foot of the desks and chairs. His floppy hair covers his face. No light, no shine, no movement. His back curves and his shoulders slope into each other.

"Zain?"

Khadija's knees hit the ground by Zain's side. Her cries reduce to hiccups and she turns Zain's body over. His yellow skin is as lifeless as a sheet of old parchment spread across his skeleton. His dry mouth hangs open.

I have seen many dead men, women, boys, girls. I have seen my little brother turn the color of a grape. I will the image of Zain to detach itself from those thoughts.

"Oh no, no, no." Khadija shakes her brother as gently as her nerves allow. "Come on, Zain. I'm here. I'm sorry. It is better. It'll always be better that you're here."

Nassima prays as she fumbles with her phone. Her other hand trembles despite clutching Zain's limp arm. She lets herself cry. "Emergency," she says into the phone, her voice catching.

I lean my cheek by Zain's mouth and wait patiently. Khadija rocks beside her brother.

"Is he breathing?"

All I feel is the air sucking in and out of my own body and Khadija's desperate rocking.

"Please."

I press my ear to his mouth. I look down at his chest.

"Zain, please be here."

I feel his breath. His chest barely rises.

"Oh no, he's—"

I grab Khadija's arms. "Stop," I snap. "He's alive. Barely, but barely alive is better than not at all."

"Ambulance is on its way," Nassima cries.

"Where are the pills?" Khadija asks. She searches her brother's pockets and Nassima checks the classroom.

I run down the hall and into the boys' bathroom. With today having been a half day because of graduation, he may have been here long after everyone went home. I check the sinks, the stalls, the urinals, and then I dive into the trash cans. There, in an empty little orange casket, air fills the space where there was once medicine.

I take the pill bottle with me back to the room.

"I'm going to wait outside for the ambulance." Nassima exits, and I hand her the pill bottle on her way out.

"He didn't throw up," Khadija says, some sense of control finding its way back to her. "That stuff is still inside him." I rub my hand on her upper back. Her body trembles beneath my palm.

"All we can do is wait now," I tell her softly. I hear the faint sound of sirens and pray it's for Zain.

Khadija wipes her snot with the back of her hand. "It's my fault. He tried to tell me. I should've known, I should've helped him."

I blink back the tears. I look at her like I'm looking at a mirror of myself. I see myself as I rowed away from Mustafa in that sea. Maybe she also sees herself in me because her blue eyes widen, and she wails. She cries into my shoulder, her body heaving.

"He'll be okay," I murmur, hoping beyond hope. "You'll still have your chance."

The doors clatter and a team of medics bursts into the classroom. Hands and arms and voices overtake the scene, and tubes and masks and straps fling over Zain. They lay a stretcher in front of us and instruct us away until we're bystanders, watching them work on Zain's thin, unmoving body.

"Name? Age?" someone asks.

"How long ago were these ingested?" another asks, screening the pill bottle in and out of our field of vision.

"I don't know," Khadija answers.

"How much did he ingest?"

"I don't know." Her teeth chatter. "I don't know my brother."

Four of them transfer Zain from the ground to the stretcher. They unhitch the stretcher and begin wheeling him—

"Wait." Khadija speeds after them. "I'm his sister. I need to stay with him."

Their departure sucks all the pressure out of the room like a vacuum in space. The nerves of the night, the precarious matter of life and death, the composure that I upheld for Khadija, all come crashing down.

I keep myself upright, my palms pressing against a desk. My nails dig into the edges on the wood and my chest constricts. As I'm no longer needed to comfort Khadija, the reality that we might have been too late for Zain hits me like a bus. I begin to pray.

I pray that Khadija has a second chance with Zain.

I pray that she can tell him that she said those words: *I'm his sister. I need to stay with him.*

And I pray that I'll forgive myself for never saying them to my brother.

43

Khadija

I write your name, oh love, on the old poplar,
You write my name, oh love, in the sand on the street,
And tomorrow when it rains...
Your name will remain, oh love,
And mine will be erased.

—Fairuz

The ICU of Baba's hospital smells of antiseptic and musty cleanliness, if such an oxymoron exists. The white and beige hospital surfaces give off a blunt gleam. Anything brighter would sear the retinas in my tired eyes.

It's also on one of the top floors. I don't like to dwell on that particular detail. "Closer to heaven," an old man in the waiting room told me as he waited for his wife, who had suffered her second stroke. He thought telling me this would cheer me up. I could only stare back blankly.

Entering the ICU is the life-size experience of sticking your hand in the crevices of a couch and not knowing where it'll reach or what it'll touch. Sticky and obscure coupled with a legitimate fear that you'll never come back the same.

Nurses aid the patients in the ICU with their every movement. Patients' beds face the hallway so that as I pass by, open or closed, the glass doors give me an unobstructed view of the patient and their condition.

All of them are old. Some are so frail they can't raise themselves from their beds. One woman stares at her nurse like he's the angel of death who, out of courtesy, is checking her vitals. Most of the patients rest next to their beeping machines attempting to recover from the near-death experience that rendered them in need of intensive care.

I imagine a lot of them have been sick. Their minds and bodies need rehabilitation. They need rest under highly monitored conditions. The words *suicide* and *overdose* are no strangers to these walls.

I cross a corridor to the edge of the pediatric ICU, where Zain's room is.

The nurse's desk has an optimal view of his room. They switched out Zain for another patient by orders of Dr. Shaami himself.

Of course, Zain's name is just Zain on his card. Nothing should taint my father's reputation at his workplace. Zain lies on the wide hospital bed, sleeping like a rock, a hint of color returning to his pallid skin. His body and mind are physically exhausted since they revived him by pumping his stomach. I couldn't watch as the nurses frantically moved him through the emergency. Mama drove like a madwoman to arrive at the hospital at the same time as us, and she had been absolutely hysterical.

That was then and this is now. Mama smolders in the armchair by Zain's side. Her eyes droop and sink into dark shadows. Her hijab slips back waywardly, allowing her bangs to escape.

"Did you see Baba?" Mama rasps. The crying episodes have sanded down her throat.

I shake my head. "I met an army of nurses, though. One nurse said he'll be done with surgery soon and come up." I plop into the armchair, with Zain between us.

"He can't postpone a surgery." Mama sucks her teeth disapprovingly. "Not even for an emergency like this. His son almost..." She can't say it, and neither can I.

Mama loves Baba, more than she loves anyone else, even her own children. She must since she left her entire life for him. Her hostility is simply an outburst, and the silence confirms that her slipup means little else than mild grievance.

Time ticks by as we wait for Zain to wake up. What do we say when he does? What do I say? Will Mama pretend everything is perfect again?

I can't be around her if she does that.

Nearly an hour and a half passes as I contemplate my first words to Zain. He is reborn on this day. His second birthday. I need to shape up and be there for him. Just as I descend into my black hole of thoughts, a miracle happens. My father arrives.

"Yes, just checking on the new patient." I hear Baba's accented English and immediately straighten up. I look down at my day-old sweats and snotty hijab. Usually, I try to look more presentable around him.

He squeezes into the room and pulls the curtains closed before turning to us. All of a sudden, the room feels cramped, and I am acutely aware that the four of us haven't been in an enclosed space together in months, maybe even a year.

Baba has the ultimate Syrian grandpa look. Bald head, white beard, bushy white eyebrows, soft hazel eyes. His face lines form canyons in his white skin. He has a Syrian dad belly and gravelly voice. His every trait reminds you of a teddy bear and demands that he be hugged.

He sighs heavily. "My baby Khadija," he says, and his million-dollar surgeon hands reach out for me. He kisses the top of my hijab and holds me in a tight embrace. I reach one of my hands to his forearm to reciprocate the hug. I feel nothing. "My best girl Khadija." He releases me.

Baba says salaam to Mama and pats her on the shoulder, an incredible amount of affection for my parents. He barely glances at Zain; he doesn't reach for his hand. He picks up his chart and checks the doctor's notes.

A question grates on me like a bad itch.

"Did both of you know he was depressed?"

Mama doesn't react, but she studies Baba's every movement. His eyebrows lift, and I suppose he peeks at me. "Of course, baby."

"So why did no one tell me?"

"We didn't want to upset you."

"I'm his sister. I should have known."

"Don't worry about that. You have school, peer pressure, all of that. We don't want to make growing up harder for you."

I look between my parents in utter disbelief. Mama picks lint off her skirt. Baba makes a disapproving sound at the clipboard.

"What is harder than this?" My voice rumbles. "I found my brother dying on the floor of his classroom because I didn't have all the facts. What if I said something to him that made him do it? What if I could've been there for him to prevent this? I'll beat myself up for years over this. And why? Were you afraid I'd tell someone? That word would get out? We don't need to be perfect. We need to be real. Zain needs us to be real. A real family."

My parents' gazes fall to their son. They don't bother responding to me. My message is wasted on them. Mama frowns and she shifts so that her body slants up at Baba.

"Did you know the antidepressants could do this?" Mama asks, an edge to her voice.

Baba shrugs. "You told me the psychiatrist was concerned about self-harm. I talked to his doctor; she said she'd prescribe

SSRIs. Children should be carefully watched two to three months after starting medication because it could increase the likelihood of this happening."

"So you knew and you didn't tell me?"

"I did tell you," he says at the clipboard. "You see it when you pick up the prescriptions. In a way, you should've known if you were paying attention."

Mama glowers at him. "If I was paying—" Then she lays into him. "You don't show up to Khadija's graduation, I excuse you. You don't remember their birthdays, I remind you. You don't see your children, I cover for you. Why do you think Zain is here? Maybe he thought you'd come around if he ended up in the hospital. No, I know that's what my son was thinking. Does Khadija need to get hurt too for you to be with her for more than a few minutes? I thought you were there for your son. You always said, 'You watch out for Khadija, and I'll watch out for Zain.' I watched over Khadija, and I neglected Zain because you said you have it under control."

Mama raises her voice higher. "Oh, that's right. You wanted to hear that. You want me to say it's my fault that I didn't take care of Zain enough so you can be free of all sins. You have an image, Doctor Surgeon, sir. I need to help you keep up your image. The rest of us whom you bless with your presence every so often are to blame. See this?" She gestures all around us. "This tragedy we are in? I could've avoided it all if I had dealt with the signs on my own without waiting for you. This is a product of *our* neglect."

Baba's calmness in the eye of Mama's fiery storm is inhuman. He drops the clipboard at the foot of the bed. "You are blaming me?"

"God forbid," Mama remarks sarcastically.

"I love my family, Maisa," he recites as though he's reading off a script. "I'm taking care of us financially. I'm working all my waking hours to support us."

I stop rooting so passionately for Mama when he says this, but it doesn't faze Mama. "Support us? We aren't living in that studio over the butcher shop anymore. You're not a starving student. We have enough 'support' to retire right now. No more excuses. I will take care of my son. I raised Khadija to be good and strong, and now it's time to care for Zain. I have complete authority in the matter. You will sit here until he wakes up. You will be the first person he sees. You will be the charming man and father that I fell in love with and that your kids believe you to be. I won't allow their image of their father to be tainted."

I'm stunned and enraptured by her ferocity. Then, as if by a light switch, she fixates on me with a kind tone: "Khadija, get up so your father can sit." Then she clasps his wrist and leads him across the bed. "Sit down, habibi," she tells him, but now the love in her voice sounds strained, like it's been worn down from years of no tuning.

His soft eyes glare at her with intensity posing as warmth, but he then does as she asks.

I stand beside Mama, and we watch Zain's chest rise and fall together. Baba tries to get up and check Zain's vitals, but Mama's stank eye sits him back down.

"I will tell you now," Mama says to Baba, but her words are meant for me. "I spent too long on arguments with Khadija. Those fights gave me a sense of purpose. I thought Khadija still needed to be raised, and that kept me going, but look at her." My parents gaze at me, my mother's eyes welling with tears. Sadness finally replaces anger. "It was a losing battle. She's all grown and she knows what she wants. So she's traveling to Jordan in a few days with her friend. She will need a ride to the airport and enough money to get her through it."

I think of Mustafa, but I see my brother. "I can't go anymore." I reach for her hand, needing comfort.

Mama moves her hand away. As if a touch of comfort would cause her more pain. "I'm sorry, Khadija," she sniffs. "I can't have you here, not while I'm fixing our family."

A Maisa Shaami apology. If it weren't for the circumstances, my jaw would drop. "I'm a part of this family, too. I should be here."

Mama shakes her head. "I gave you all my efforts, and now I need to give Zain one hundred percent of me this summer."

Incredulous, I ask, "Why do you insist on shutting me out?"

"That's what you've been asking me to do, haven't you?"

Mama has always been full of contradictions. And I am an apple still too close to the tree, too afraid to roll away.

"Is that still what you think I want?" I say, holding back the thickness in my voice. "You think Zain is here because he needed you *more*? You're always around, you're always asking, pestering, *lurking*."

Mama's eyes light up with fire. "Watch it."

But I can't. "Zain doesn't need you more available than you already are. We need you to actually listen."

"I listen."

"But do you actually hear us?" I blink at the tears in my eyes. "I've been asking for simple freedoms for years. And you listen to me go off, but all you hear is that I want to leave you. And Zain, he mentioned he doesn't want to go to summer school. Does he even want to go to RHHS? Has he asked you to get away from those boys who bully him? Did you hear him when he said that, or did you just blame him for not being the son you wished he would be?"

"I don't wish him to be anyone else," Mama says flatly. "I love you two exactly the way you are."

"That's not how it feels."

"Why don't you share your feelings, then?" she challenges.

This is not a real challenge. She does not mean for me to meet her with the truth. Still, I say, "Because no matter what I say, it will never be enough. It feels like you've always wanted me to be the next new Syrian girl who comes into Rochester Heights. I couldn't be Leene, and I'll probably never live that one down."

"I don't want you to be Leene," she says, her offensive front completely lowered. "Leene is the way that she is because she's experienced things that you will never. Some things made her stronger, and I wish you had them, but other things only give her pain."

"She makes herself strong," I say. "And I make myself strong. I don't need your validation and I don't need to be a refugee or a boxer or anything to be strong. I don't need to travel across the world and witness starvation to prove anything to you or to myself. I have a brother right here who needs me right now, and helping him is as worthy as anything I can do thousands of miles away."

Mama's face twitches. "So don't go."

I grimace. Though I've come to the realization that my guilt cannot and is not my motivator, I'm not ready to back out. I think about Leene and Mustafa. I glance down at my brother, who sleeps through all of this unknowingly. Baba has had nothing to say.

These problems with my family will not go away just because I choose to stay in this hospital room with my parents.

Staring back at Mama, I say, "I have to go."

"So go," she says with indifference. "If Leene needs you, you should go."

Shocked, I search for ways she could know of our plans. "You know about Mustafa?"

Mama shrugs, unfazed by the name. "Your change of location? Leene instead of Nassima? You aren't going on vacation;

you have a reason. Maybe whatever you learn from this will help you realize your life is not all that you say it is."

With that, Mama takes Zain's hand in hers, and we settle into a silence that grants no real victors.

~~~

The monitors beep, but otherwise it's quiet. Zain looks like any other sixteen-year-old power napping, except he's been sleeping for twenty-four hours and can't wake up.

"Comatose," the doctor had said. "It's not uncommon after such a traumatic overdose. It shouldn't last a month."

A month. I only had a few days to say goodbye.

Mama was disagreeable. "Coma? He's sixteen years old. I want another doctor's opinion."

"Talk to him, play his favorite songs," the doctor advised after failing to calm her down. "For now, there's nothing we can do."

"Play his favorite songs," Mama grumbled.

Despite her qualms, Mama's preferred song, Fairuz's "I Write Your Name, Oh Love," plays in Zain's hospital room as Mama sings to him. Fairuz's falsetto soars over Mama's tenor. It is a sad song about a woman who loves someone fully while his love is only temporary.

It is an inexplicably beautiful song.

"I'm getting coffee," Mama murmurs. "Walk with me, Abu Zain."

Baba rises to go with her. I take a seat beside Zain and place my hand in his. For the first time, we're alone. His skin glows, his eyelashes fan up and out, but he lies motionless. He is alive yet spiritless.

I take a deep, jagged breath. "I have a feeling you won't be seeing me before I go. Mama wants you all to herself, so that should be a special kind of fun." I fidget. "I want you to know that I was here, that I haven't left your side. I almost gave up on finding you. Actually, I did give up. It's Leene who didn't give up, but she knows what it's like to give up and regret it. She pushed me to keep going, and it's my turn to help her. To keep pushing until she finds her person. The doctors said if we'd found you ten minutes later that you would have been dead. I guess it's God's plan for you to get a second shot at this life."

I blink back tears. "It is hard, Zain. You're a double agent just like me. We're stuck in no-man's-land, trying to be all parts of ourselves yet not allowed to be either or all at the same time. We're stuck between a rock and a hard place, and we aren't given any tools to carve out a place to belong. I had a feeling, that night after the movie when you spoke to me, that there was something wrong. I didn't want to admit that I feel the same way. I live with the constant guilt that I was chosen to be born here, that I get the comfort of being with my family, while our cousins and friends like Leene don't. It's why I avoided Leene, and it's why I can't talk to our family. I even avoid thinking about them." My voice trembles. "Even *thinking* about our cousins hurts. And I know you feel more than me, and that's why it's harder for you."

I lean close to my brother, resting my chin beside his cheek, mesmerized by how much he's grown. For too long I focused on how small he seemed rather than the person he was becoming.

"When you wake up, I want you to know that I'll be the Sam to your Frodo. If you'll let me, I want to try," I whisper.

When Zain wakes up, he will have to decide what it is that's worth living for. My help, Mama's attention, Baba's changes, they only mean something if Zain accepts them. Before I can expect him to do that, I have to embrace what's been given to me. I grab my phone to send a few texts. The first to Leene, to settle her nerves and gear her up for travel. And the next:

Meet me tonight at the riverfront?

44

Khadija

*A*t the riverfront, I face the glistening water. Clouds haze the sun as it dips behind the river's horizon. A slice of sunlight colors the sky in oranges and pinks. The soft hues remind me of the warmth I feel when I'm with Younes.

On the other side, Canada flickers its lights on as twilight envelops the two cities. Windsor and Detroit touch at this place, settled close together yet so different from each other. Colors and colours. Miles and kilometers. Restrooms and water closets.

A cyclist nearly tramples over me, and I stumble toward the rails. The water lapping at stones below hypnotizes me. The river could suck me in on a day like this.

Days like an orange and pink creamsicle spreading across the sky. Warm nights visited by a breeze that plays between branches, swirling pollen to mystify lovers.

Younes calls my name and locks the doors of his Jeep

Wrangler from afar. He runs over and comes to a halt a few feet in front of me.

I take a deep breath. I take a leap of faith. "Hi, Ness."

"Hi, Kadi." Younes's voice is almost undetectable, his face split between hurt and kindness. Then, more quickly, "I heard about Zain, and I wanted to call you. I just...I didn't know if you'd want me to."

"Actually," I start wistfully, "Zain is why I'm here."

He presses his lips together, waiting. It's my turn to show up, or I risk losing my chance.

"Zain," I begin, voice cracking. "Maybe Zain did what he did because he was desperate for some control. He felt he had no choice. Or maybe that's only the way I see things from my end. Maybe Zain's battle is something else entirely. For me, I've avoided us because I thought I didn't have a choice, but now I know I do."

I like him so much I would cry to see him hurt. I like him so much I'm willing to feel vulnerable with him in every way.

I can't hold it in anymore. "I choose us, Ness."

Hundreds of lights swim in his deep eyes. "You're sure? And we won't worry about what it means for our future."

"I mean, we have to think about it, don't we? What dating means for both of our futures. But I also know that the future isn't set. All I can do right now is live in our present."

There's no sense dwelling on *what-ifs*. Most people wouldn't have believed a little boy's surviving a cold, harsh sea. Even I know of a boy who did survive, and there are days when I can't believe it.

Some things, like a first love, are like miracles.

"So why'd you call me here?" he asks, stepping toward me so that I have to look directly up to lock eyes with him.

"We're on a date," I announce. "We're on our first official date of our very real and public relationship." A smile dances on my lips, and though it has cracks in it, it's a smile nonetheless. "We have to call it courting in front of my parents, though, since they don't like the word *dating*."

Younes smiles, and I can exhale. I look out over the water. "No one says *courting* anymore," he says. His hand rests on the rail and I want to reach out and hold it. The overcast that settled above my life spreads over to him, and its physical weight dips our heads down.

All of a sudden, Younes climbs on top of the railing, guffawing.

"Ohmygod, you'll fall in!" I exclaim with a wide smile.

He looks down at me and offers his hand. "Come up here." Gingerly, I place my hand in his and he helps me up. The light breeze is stronger up here, and I almost fall. My grip on his hand tightens.

The air is pure, and the chirping of insects is like music.

A delicate happiness restores itself. It's fragile, and it may burst at any moment, but I hold this moment close between Younes and me because between us it's safe.

45

Leene

The morning of our flight, I'm stuck behind the counter at Falafel Guys.

Amal called in sick, and with no one to cover, I came in for just a few hours before Khadija and I have to be on our way to the airport. But I'm grateful for it. The buzz of the restaurant barely masks my nerves. My hands tremble, and I choke on most of my words. Forget speaking English, I can barely think in Arabic.

Mustafa.

His name runs on a loop in my head.

I don't register when I get into Tank and arrive at the airport. Khadija is in the periphery checking bags in and leading our carry-ons to the airport security.

Zain.

I should ask about her brother. It is a precious thing, to have a brother. A beautiful, precious thing. Brothers always want to be elsewhere when we desperately wish them to stay with us. Watch them too closely or don't watch closely enough, and you might lose them.

I exit through the whooshing security machine. "I'm just going to pat you down," a woman in uniform says and jerks the bun of hair beneath my hijab. She pats me down the front of my chest, down the middle and under my breasts, and under my butt and inner thighs. Ahead, Khadija glares at the female officer. I can't think about how uncomfortable I feel.

Mustafa.

I'm led to the gate, where I have a seat. As I look at the flight number and the destination, our connection in Paris, the other thoughts come.

Mustafa. I wonder how he will look. More like Abood and Baba? Or like me? Or will he look every bit like Mama, as he did before?

I wonder what he will think of me. It's hard to say that he will remember me. How will I convince him that I am his sister? How will I get my little brother to love me again?

Brother and sister. Arguably, the most fragile of relationships.

When he's older, will I tell Mustafa how I lost him? Will I have the courage?

My arm steadies, and when I look down, Khadija releases my forearm. She lets out a relieved sigh. "I'm gonna need you to speak every few hours so I know you're alive," she says. "You look like a ghost again."

I hiss out a long hot breath. "Again?"

"When I first met you, you looked like a ghost. And a few times after that. It really just depends on the day."

"I don't feel real." I feel like I'm floating.

Khadija smiles. "I know, right? I can't believe we're going to be in Paris for a full five hours before our next flight."

I shake my head. It makes sense for Khadija to be excited, but I can't feel anything but dread. "Why does it feel like I'm waiting for something to go wrong?"

Khadija's eyes widen. "Oh no, don't start with that. My mom finally stopped praying for this trip to go wrong. Don't manifest it."

I drop my head in my hands. "I couldn't tell my mom the real reason we're going to Jordan. I'm such a coward."

"You're not a coward," she snaps. "You're crossing an ocean to find your baby brother."

"But I'm the reason he needs to be found."

The cracks in my armor are showing. The pity is like a parasite and it's eaten away the Leene I was, and all that's left is Leene the refugee.

But what can I do to stop this transformation? I am a refugee. Syria is my home, and it was taken from me. I was forced to find shelter elsewhere, in a place that will never be my true home. I can do my best with it, but America can never truly be home. Context be damned.

Yes, I am a refugee, and there is nothing wrong with that. Crying at the gate of my flight, scaring the white people who are preparing to vacation in Paris, I am a refugee. Traveling across the world to find the brother that I lost, I am a refugee. And he, my brother whom I will find, will be a refugee, too.

People will pity us for our suffering. But when I bring Mustafa to this state that will be his new shelter, I will teach him that there is nothing to pity. We are not our suffering. We are the strength that got us through it all.

46

Khadija

$\mathcal{L}$eene lost it.

Without a word, I sit next to her as she cries, but I have to admit that this is an improvement. Her eerie silence was freaking me out—at least now I know what she's feeling.

I stare at the tunnel that'll take us into the plane, but that's only the first step. There's another eight hours to go until the layover in Paris, and a bunch more after that before we land in Jordan. The line moves slowly, and I establish a four-foot bubble between us and the traveler ahead of us, who keeps stealing peeks at Leene, who's still a bundle of sniffles. When our eyes lock, I turn the corners of my mouth upward, the obligatory smile for strangers. It's the I'm-safe-and-friendly-so-please-don't-be-scared-of-me smile. He does a double take. He is the kind of traveler who wears slacks and a button-up on a ten-hour flight.

He huffs loudly. He's clearly going to Paris for vacation and doesn't like that we're sharing a plane.

The line moves forward, and Leene, a mess of emotions, rolls her carry-on and punctures her way straight through the courtesy space bubble. Her teetering luggage smashes into his and the long handlebars tangle and tumble to the ground. He grunts loudly as he and Leene squat for their bags.

Leene apologizes profusely, but the guy edges her away from the luggage. "Don't touch my bag," he barks angrily before adding, "I'm making a complaint."

I turn red from embarrassment. He pulls the carry-ons apart and dumps Leene's at her feet. In a rage, he calls up to the gate desk and I tail him.

He's fuming at the desk to the unassuming employees. "I am not comfortable traveling with these—these—" The employees spot me.

The young female employee levels with the guy. "These what, sir?"

"You see them!"

I keep my mouth shut, waiting for his response. Whatever I have to say won't go over well with this irate man.

"You're upsetting other travelers, sir," the male employee says.

"They touched my luggage! I will not get on this plane with these two!" The guy's voice travels to other gates.

I avert my eyes from the raised cellphones recording the spectacle.

"If you won't board, I'm afraid you're not a passenger." The female employee's jaw sets. "If that's the case, I'm required to call security to remove you from this gate."

"Remove me? Remove them!"

The female employee types away on the keyboard. "I'm going to upgrade these two so they won't have to sit in the same cabin as you. If you decide to calm down and cooperate, you may board, sir. As of right now, you're a threat to the aircraft."

"They're the threat!" the man insists. The male employee nods at another, who calls security. Security comes in no time, proceeding to resolve the man's issue on their own.

"Thank you," I tell the employee who commandeered the operation.

"It's my pleasure." She hands me two first-class boarding passes.

I could let the whole scene ruin my mood. *I could.* But right now, I have to choose what will bother me for the next eight hours until we land in Paris, and I choose to let it pass, because I have two first-class tickets and a whole lot of experience with the wrongs of the world. Yes, it's a Band-Aid on a gaping wound, but who am I to tell people not to try to right those wrongs one upgrade at a time.

47

Leene

*K*hadija?"

"Mm-hmm?" she hums from beneath her blanket. These first-class seats recline into beds, and their blankets are like cashmere. We lie with our heads where our feet should be in our chairs so we can see each other from across the aisle.

"Are you sleeping?"

She tosses and turns for the thousandth time on this flight. "Nope."

My chest feels unbearably heavy. The tears at the gate helped a little, but a question cages me.

"What happens if we don't find him?"

She tosses again. "He's at the orphanage. We saw his picture. The director invited us herself."

I cross my arms over my chest, holding myself. "It all feels imaginary. The orphanage, the director, Mustafa. Even Jordan doesn't feel like it's going to be there when we land."

"I can't believe it, either." She turns toward me and pulls

the blanket off her face. Across the aisle, her hijab is half off, but she's out of anyone's view except mine. She bites her lip. "Mafraq is five miles from Syria. I googled it. It's ninety miles to Damascus. I could drive to it in an hour and fifteen minutes to be with my teteh and my cousins in no time."

Her eyes light up in the dim reading light above her. I had been so focused on Mustafa I didn't realize visiting Jordan would be a milestone for Khadija, too.

"An hour and fifteen minutes maybe seven years ago. There are destroyed roads and checkpoints everywhere," I break it to her. "It would take hours to get to the Midan."

A blaze smolders in her eyes. "Is it really that different?"

With closed eyes, I try to picture 2010 Syria, but the smell of gunfire and smoke and the sounds of bombs and bullets ward off the memories. I don't want to kill off her Syria, too.

"How do you remember it?" I ask her.

The blaze glows as she says, "Orchards and gardens and ice-cold swimming pools. Summers running barefoot between fruit trees. Hoarding the sweetest apricots I've ever had in my life. Bargaining for candy and playing in the streets, where my cousins and I made the rules. Waking up to roosters crowing and vendors yelling trade songs. Standing on the balcony at sunset waiting to hear every mosque send out the call to prayer seconds after each other. Those few minutes before sunset when the city was the quietest.

"I remember the family trips to Slunfeh in the mountains

and the Sea of Latakia and the first-ever shopping centers of Damascus. Shaam Center was the biggest building to me. There were traffic circles and huge buildings and malls, and I remember thinking that Syria wasn't 'third world' anymore. And I won't even talk about how I only had that thought because my brain lost a battle with American propaganda of what is 'third world.' Point is, we'd finally be able to go to Syria often without making a big fuss about it. It would be like any other vacation. But my favorite part of Syria will always be the reunions at my grandfather's old Midani house."

"Like the *Bab al Hara* houses?" I ask. Not many Syrians get to experience living in those open-roofed houses built tile by tile.

She relishes in the memories. "Yup. The ones made of tile and stone that let the sun shine down on the inside courtyard so even hijabis can suntan without leaving the house. The houses in the old city that were just extensions of the streets. They wouldn't lock the doors because kids would run in and out all day long. I think Zain was his freest then."

The portrait of Khadija's Syria takes shape in my brain like a postcard sent from a paradise. It's vivid with beauty and reminiscent of the prosperity that could have existed in Syria. The average person might think Syria is a desert, but it was an oasis.

"If that is your Syria," I whisper, "then I don't want you to go back."

My Syria is collapsed buildings and destructive tanks. A

stream of blood trickling from a bullet wound. A hospital of corpses with no doctor in sight. Where her Syria is family, mine is death. Where hers is freedom, mine is a prison. Where hers breathes, mine suffocates.

The two Syrias we each have in our minds don't coexist. Mine is the present and hers is a memory. Only one can be the future.

When I look at Khadija now, I see a girl of many lives. She's seen the Syria I can't remember: a place of rich history and natural beauty and the unbreakable bond of family. She carries it with her. One day, she will paint canvases of its beaches and write books of its traditions and record its songs to share with the world.

"I used to call you 'the American' in my head," I confess. "I admired you for putting Syria in the past where I thought it belonged and embracing your American lifestyle. I admired that you could forget it like that."

Khadija sighs and says, "That's why being around you reminded me that I wasn't Syrian enough...."

"But you were so confident."

"I was so full of it that I didn't realize who I had become. Life is too short to flip-flop between being American or being Syrian. Being in love or loving myself. Being independent or standing by my family. Seeing the world or having a home. I can be all of them at once. I can have all of them, too."

We listen to the engine whirring and my ears pressurize.

Turbulence shakes the other passengers in first class, and they stir. A question that had planted itself in the back of my mind surfaces.

"Why did you decide to help me?"

Khadija's answer isn't immediate. "At first, I thought it was impossible to be friends. You were everything my mom wanted in a daughter, and maybe I was a little jealous."

"Jealous of me? Impossible."

"Uff, I'm not proud of it," she admits with a sly smile. "I also didn't understand why my mom wanted to help you. I thought we should help others who needed it more than you, since you're the lucky ones who made it to America. You were able to seek asylum while other Syrians are stuck in war zones or a refugee camp. It was easier to think of you that way. I didn't realize how hard you worked to get there. Everyone has a story. I just needed to hear yours. Once I did, I felt I should do everything I could to help you."

Khadija's first impression was right. We are the fortunate ones, but fortune is relative. At least we had a Maisa and a Khadija. There are Syrians whose stories no one will hear, and whom no one will save from their ill fate.

"Thank you for hearing my story," I whisper, my eyes filling with tears. "And for helping me rewrite the end of it."

48

Khadija

*F*irst time in Amman and the city hits me with a mean left hook right in the jaw. It shrinks behind us as our mikro rumbles toward Mafraq.

Mikro—(vehicle)—meek-ro—/mikro/: a microbus or a minibus no larger than a Chevy truck that can jam fourteen or more passengers inside.

Mikro driver—Death's right-hand man—/mikro draɪvə/: the driver of a mikro's only credentials are that they own a mikro with dodgy brakes and they drive it like it's a sports car.

Accepting the way of the mikro also means claustrophobia is a Western notion that has no place here. I jostle around in the back row between a mother, her two infants, and Leene. Naturally, the AC is broken; the aromas are fatal. I hold my nose and breathe through my mouth, inducing nausea. I cast a look outside the window, hoping we're any closer to Mafraq, but we may never arrive. The barren desert landscape outside taunts me. If the ride lasts much longer, my sweat will cement me to this seat, and the mikro and I will become one for real.

The slobbering baby in his mother's arms stares at me with wide gray eyes, and when I stare back, he fusses and squirms. God bless, I've horrified him. I wipe the sweat on my upper lip and smooth out my wrinkled shirt.

The mother shushes her baby and bounces him up and down. "We're almost there," she says to comfort him.

"Really?" I rejoice. "How much more to go?"

The mother glances at me dismissively. "Don't be so eager. I live for my doctor's appointments in the city."

I can tell by her Arabic dialect that she's Syrian though not Damascene. She's also a young mother, perhaps my age, or a year or two older. When her baby resorts to crying, she vigorously bounces him on her knee. I'm tempted to snatch him from her to quiet him, but I'd probably start crying, too.

"There's our home," she groans.

In the distance, a town of short beige stone buildings and a turquoise dome marking the mosque breaks through like a hazy mirage. The driver slows down for pedestrians, preteen boys kicking a soccer ball across the road into the city. He drives past them but comes to a complete stop meters away from the town.

Grumbling commences. The Jordanian driver will hear none of it. "I'm not driving into town! This is as far as your fare pays you."

Doors open and passengers hop out, and the younger ones sprint in the heat to make their shift or to locate breakfast. The mother beside me doesn't budge. "I have two kids, akhi! I need a short drive into town. Please, brother."

"I can give no more free rides, ikhti," he says. "They will ask me for rides if I drive into town and I cannot say no to the grandmother with a walking stick or the young men looking for jobs. I have to make a living, too."

Grumbling to herself, she shifts the seats in front of us to access the door. She lets her toddler out first and follows with her baby on her hip. Leene and I follow, and I stop myself from giving the driver a tip.

He drives off in a cloud of dust and I expect Leene to sprint into town, but she doesn't. Instead, she chases the toddler, who has escaped his mother's grasp, and collects him in her arms.

"What's your name?" Leene asks the child as we join his mother on our way into town.

"Abood!" he screams at the top of his lungs.

"Abood?" She walks ahead of us, quickening her pace to keep up with him. "My brother's nickname was Abood, too."

"Abdul-Karim!" the mother calls after her son, using his full name. He runs farther ahead, and Leene races to catch up. "Be good to Khaleh!"

I snicker. Leene's a khaleh. The young mother eyes me. "What part of Syria are you two from?"

"Al-Midan," I say, and though I can tell by her regional accent, I still ask, "And you?"

"Homs," she answers. "Are you a refugee?"

I shake my head.

"I knew it. You don't look like one. New people are always showing up in Mafraq, but they're always looking worse for wear. You dress too nicely. You look ajnabiya. Why are you coming into Mafraq?"

"I'm visiting the orphanage. It's called Ibtisami—"

"Ya Shaami," she completes. "It's a good orphanage. A nice British lady directs it. Are you looking for someone there?"

"How did you know?"

"Strangers come by to visit the orphanage looking for a brother, a sister, a cousin. They stay for the Syrian food, but they leave in a few days. Nothing could keep you here."

We approach the buildings, and Leene catches our eye and points into a shop before entering it with little Abood. Ahead, where the alley breaks off into a main street, the hustle and bustle of an overpopulated city resembles a stampede. A dust cloud from the foot traffic floats above heads.

"I didn't catch your name," I say, and then tell her mine.

"I used to be called Hanya in Homs, but that was another lifetime. You can call me Umm Abood." Mother of Abood. Like Khaleh Rana. As if on cue, little Abood runs out of the shop with a pink and white bunny creamsicle in his hand. He's looking at it like he's in love.

"Thank you," Umm Abood says to Leene. She looks back at me. "I told you I knew you weren't from around here."

Leene curses, "How does that crook sell any ice cream at that price?"

"He probably charged you about four times what he'd charge me because you're sweet enough to buy it," Umm Abood teases.

"But I even bargained for it," Leene shoots back. Umm Abood graciously concedes.

"We'll get trampled if we use the main road," Umm Abood tells us. "I'll take you around to the orphanage."

"Are we nearby?" Leene asks.

"A ten-minute walk or so."

Leene clings to me. The blistering sun beats down on us and moisture accumulates in places on my body I didn't know could sweat. Mafraq rots in the sun. The trash lining the streets ferments despite hordes of people trying to find work to clean it up. Boarded-up shops that are held together by a dozen nails are open for dining. There are more people selling pens and homemade crafts in the street than there are people to buy them. Beggars and peddlers bombard us with a complete disregard for personal space.

"Stop looking at them," Leene instructs. I drop my gaze to the ground, breaking the connection we make when our eyes meet. Little by little, the harassment abates.

"Kids aren't even out of school yet. The crowds will grow,"

Umm Abood tells us. We reach a crossroads. "The orphanage is down that way and I'm down the other way. I live in the barn on the edge of town if you need anything. It's the only one with lights; shouldn't be hard to find."

She vanishes with her children before I can thank her. If I never see her again, she lives in my memory. Not as a statistic, but as a person, a sister, a mother.

Leene faces the direction of the orphanage and I shift gears. "This is it," she says without certainty. Then, with a shake of her head as if to banish ill thoughts, she adds, "I'm ready."

49

Leene

ustafa has to be here. He has to be.

I inhale deeply, staring up at the wooden sign that marks the orphanage's entrance: Ibtisami Ya Shaami. It's carved in Arabic calligraphy. A brick holds the door open, so we enter down the long corridor that leads to a dingy room with an empty desk.

"Hello?" Khadija calls. I relieve my weak knees by sitting on one of the white plastic chairs in the tiny foyer. "Anyone here?" There are no sounds of crying babies or playing children. "Hello?"

My nerves make me feel like I'm on the verge of throwing up. Khadija peers at me and tries the other door in the room, the one with the chipped painting of a child's smiling face. It's locked. I groan. Khadija knocks once politely, and when there's no answer, I bend over myself while Khadija bangs on the door. The heat makes my eyes see halos. Mustafa is here. He breathes, talks, laughs, plays, learns. I compose myself for him.

The door swings open, and a thin woman with a straight brown bob enters the waiting room. "Merhaba. I'm Charlotte, the director of this orphanage. How can I help you?" Her Arabic is heavily accented.

Khadija responds in English, "We're looking for a boy. We—"

"Americans, great!" Khaleh Charlotte clasps her hands together, dumping the diapers from her arms onto a chair. "I'll show you around."

I stand on wobbly legs. Khaleh Charlotte talks for an entire country, and Khadija and I can't get a word in. She leads us into the orphanage, her tour begins, and she fills in every pause, period, and comma.

"I'll show you where the kids sleep, or where they try to sleep anyway. A lot of them have nightmares and can't sleep until exhaustion tucks them in for the night." Khaleh Charlotte guides us away from the kid-sized cafeteria, the central bathrooms, and the play area. If the next stop of the tour isn't to the children, I'm going to burst.

"Does she not recognize us?" I whisper to Khadija. She shrugs back. After the email correspondences and the dates Khadija told her we would visit, I thought she would know it was us.

In the sleeping area, what appear to be windows on the far side of the room are boarded up by plywood. Metal-frame bunk beds maze the room, cushioned by thin mattresses and blankets. Teddy bears or small toys personalize some beds. I scan the room for Mustafa's blanket, but all I see are rows and rows of beds. My vision blurs.

Khaleh Charlotte babbles on, "At the moment all of our beds are filled, so we have siblings sleep with each other. Unfortunately, the room capacity—"

"Where's Mustafa?" I interrupt her, my patience running clear out.

"Pardon?"

"My brother. The emails? Are you the director or not?"

"Leene." Khadija tugs my elbow.

"I'm sorry, I didn't realize you were looking for someone," Khaleh Charlotte says.

My head spins. "Khadija told you. We emailed you. We sent the picture. You invited us to come find him."

Khaleh Charlotte widens her eyes innocently. "Oh, I thought you were here for a tour. Sponsors from America or Europe sometimes drop by. I have an office that deals with emails and inquiries since our internet can be unreliable out here. I apologize I wasn't notified, but we can go to the children right away. What was your brother's name?"

"Mustafa. Mustafa Taher. He's five years old now."

Khaleh Charlotte pauses like a buffering video, and I want to shake her into action. "Let's go to the classroom—I could be mistaken."

My stomach flips. "Mistaken?"

"Sometimes the young children arrive and they're not

familiar with their names. They know a nickname, or they can only say a part of their name. I don't want to alarm you—"

"Too late," Khadija interjects.

"—so let's go to the reception classroom. Kindergarten for you Americans."

My breathing sounds like a carburetor. I pull up Mustafa's picture. "Here, look at this. This is my brother. This picture is off your website."

Khaleh Charlotte doesn't look at it because she's speeding down the rows of beds and out of the room. She takes us out a back door in a courtyard surrounded by three other buildings. A legion of Syrian children line up in the dirt with a single teacher leading them in stretches. The children shriek the royal anthem of Jordan.

Long live the King!

Long live the King...

"The classroom is up ahead."

"I'm positive we have a boy named Musa in reception. Naming him Musa instead of Mustafa could have been a guess on our part. We have to do that sometimes when they arrive young."

The kids' singing and Khaleh Charlotte's speculations take a back seat to my loud heartbeats. The King-glorifying anthem continues.

The singing ends and a lull falls upon the children. Khaleh Charlotte glances back at us. "They'll start with the Syrian anthem soon, of course. We want them to remember where they're from."

"When will we get to this classroom?" Khadija hisses.

Khaleh Charlotte turns into a classroom and I freeze. Khadija steps in, then steps back out to where I've cemented my feet.

"Mustafa," I mouth, my voice evading me. I try again. "Mustafa is in there?"

"Yes, Leene, yes!" Khadija drags me forward. "Come on. We came all this way to find him. He's here!"

I take a deep breath and enter, bracing myself to meet my brother again.

50

Leene

Thirty children wage a battle in their classroom.

Khaleh Charlotte pushes through to a little boy facing away from me. She carries him back through the battlefield. "This is Musa," Khaleh Charlotte says, introducing him to me. His hazy green eyes gape at me. A bald scar bisects his dark-brown buzzed hair.

My cheeks are sore from salivation. My chin quivers. My eyes are peeled so far back I can't blink.

"That's not Mustafa."

I scan the children's faces. Even older, I'd be able to recognize Mustafa among these faces, but I can't.

Because he isn't here.

51

Khadija

*L*eene's phone drops from her hand, and I lunge for it. Her body collapses over mine and my unsuspecting knees buckle. The two of us crash into the miniature desks and chairs. The kids holler and dogpile over us. Their stubby hands and ashen faces mob us.

"He's not here, he's not here," Leene mumbles in a stupor. The children seem to multiply with every passing second as I lift Leene off of me.

"He has to be here," I say back. I whip my head around the room. "Kids! Where's Mustafa?"

Like little broken tape recorders, the kids, all in faded pants and frayed T-shirts, yell Mustafa's name at the top of their lungs.

"Mustafa! Where are you, ya Mustafa?" they sing.

Among the wide muddy-brown and green eyes and long lashes and brown faces, the eyebrows dipping softly in the middle and the dark lips, the tickling lisps and missing front teeth, not one among them belongs to Mustafa.

Leene's dry sobs last a minute before she dry heaves, gripping the desk and repelling the kids away from her. Paralyzed, I place my hand on her back and turn to ask Charlotte what the hell is going on, but she's gone.

Just like that, my legs march me out of the classroom and through the courtyard after the director. She dips into a room, and I stomp in after her.

She rummages behind her desk, files upon files splayed across the top of it. I shove the picture of Mustafa in her face. "Could you stop for one second and explain this picture to me?"

She barely glances at it, as she's taken to scouring a drawer for papers. "That's the front of the orphanage."

I point at Mustafa. "And that is my friend's little brother. He has a blue blanket with his name sewn into it in Arabic. If you say you make educated guesses, that's about as clear as you can get."

"I know."

"Then where is he? Do you post photos of little boys on your site that aren't orphans here? Why did your office lead us to believe he may still be here? Why put us through all that?"

Charlotte slams a drawer closed. "I remember that boy's blanket. I remember thinking how brilliant it was for his parents to sew his name into his blanket. I need you to take a deep breath while I find his records."

"Finding his records won't make him materialize." I have an attitude and I can't dial it down.

"This isn't America," Charlotte snaps. "We're a few miles away from a dangerous border. Children come and children go. I have enough on my hands changing babies' diapers and explaining to these kids why their parents aren't here. I can't possibly memorize every child's file."

"Why are you even here?" I ask defensively. "You're not even Syrian."

Charlotte stiffens. "I don't know where you're from, but I know that I'm here with my Syrian husband teaching classes for hours a day and granting these kids some semblance of normal. Don't ask me why I'm here if these kids need someone with a good heart to help them. Who cares where I'm from? These kids definitely don't."

I flop into the chair parallel to her desk. I'm yanked between my Syrian side that suffers and the American side that can live autonomously of all that is here.

Sometimes the two parts of me are stitched together. Other times, an axe hacks at the connecting fibers mercilessly. When will I be able to rewire them to find peace with both parts of me?

"Here!" Charlotte wags a paper at me and places it on the desk between us. She points at what looks like Mustafa's mugshot, a different picture from the one online. "We send the children's photos to other organizations to see if they have any family left who'll claim them. Someone in Zaatari claimed him."

"He's at the camp? Isn't it dangerous there? Who claimed him?"

"It's more of a bleak settlement now, but being with family there is better than not having any family at all. Trust me, I know."

The sounds of children stomping and shrieking raise us out of our seats and we race into the courtyard. Leene slams into me, sending me staggering over Charlotte, but a buffer of five-year-olds keeps us upright. Leene doesn't relent. She brings a little boy and girl with matching bowl cuts to the front of the procession.

"Tell them what you told me!" Leene's eyes are bugging out of her head.

The girl with a bowl cut cackles from the spotlight shining on her. "We remember Mustafa!"

52

Leene

MINUTES EARLIER

J feel Khadija's hand leave my shoulder, then she rushes out of the room. I hyperventilate in the classroom without her to steady me. The kids stare at me with their thickly lashed eyes.

"Khaleh, are you okay?"

The room spins in and out of focus. The children lift their voices in a chorus, swarming me with questions.

Their singing augments my nausea and torments me. Was Mustafa ever here? I desperately yearn for his peace. A peace where he isn't floating in a sea or forgotten in an orphanage.

"Mustafa," I lament, his name escaping my lips over and over.

In sweet tunes, the children implore me to stay.

"Looking for Mustafa, where is he? Missing school, where is he? Bunny rabbit Mustafa, where is he?"

"Hey!" a little girl with a mushroom haircut screams to capture everyone's attention. She jumps on a desk and commands the classroom. "Let's sing Mustafa's favorite song for Khaleh! Mustafa will come when he hears his song."

All together in a high-pitched chorus, their voices rattle the walls.

The bunny rabbit said to his mo-om,
"Will you let me go out and play, Mama?"

I wildly wipe the tears off my face. The beat is cheerful this time, and the whole class has the words and movements memorized. Shaking their shoulders and picking the pretend flowers and smelling them just like Mustafa used to. They sing the lyrics I could not remember.

The wolf saw him and attacked him!
The bunny rabbit ran, all scared!
He hid in a tiny hole,
And the wolf got lost in the pen!
Then the bunny rabbit returned to his mo-om,
With his eyes full of tears,
She told him for the next ti-ime,
Make sure you listen to me in your little years!

"You know Mustafa!" My heart surges out of my chest.

"Yes, we remember Mustafa!" A little boy in an identical mushroom haircut jumps on the desk with the girl and bounces up and down. "Mustafa the bunny rabbit!"

"Mustafa the bunny rabbit!" the class echoes.

I take their little hands in mine, and they jump down. I sprint out of the room practically dragging the mushroom-headed children by their shoulders. The class follows us in a mob, yelping and squealing in delight.

"It's a race, it's a race!"

I look down to check that the mushroom twins' arms are still attached to them when I crash into Khadija.

"Tell them what you told me!" I gasp for air.

"We remember Mustafa!" the girl screeches, her twin echoing her.

"He's here," I say to Khadija. "They remember him. Sing his song," I order the kids. They start again, breaking off into playtime, holding hands and twirling in circles, and missing every note.

"Listen to me." Khadija seizes me by the shoulders. "I need you to take a deep breath. Mustafa was sent to Zaatari. He's not far now. We'll find him. Leene, we'll find…"

Her words dissipate. The children's singing muffles.

Zaatari refugee camp.

Mustafa hasn't traveled at all. While I was moving farther from Syria, Mustafa was moving closer to it.

Umm Abood serves us dinner of shorbat addas, a lentil soup flavored by onion and carrots. I take it out of politeness, but it just sits in my hands, the bottom of the bowl burning the skin of my fingers.

Little Abood toddles over to me and sits in the crook of my arm. I give him my spoon and he blows on a spoonful of soup before clamping his jaw on it.

"You two must sleep here," Umm Abood offers.

"We couldn't," Khadija says. But we both know we have nowhere to go. We were supposed to be in Mafraq for the day, pick up Mustafa, and go back to our hotel in Amman with him in my arms. I'm not even sure this town has an inn. It wouldn't matter anyway; I could sleep on the streets for all I care.

"You must," Umm Abood insists. "I've already kicked my husband out for the night for your comfort. Please, stay the night in my home. It's the least I can do for the joy you brought Abood today."

Little Abood can feel joy, but all I feel is the disappointment of my failure. Khadija gives Umm Abood a rundown of the day in hushed tones. Rehashing it doesn't make it hurt more, but it does make me muter to the world.

"But that means you have family in Zaatari," Umm Abood deduces. "Praise God, you might find more people than you were looking for."

"That's what I keep telling her," Khadija says.

"Do you have an idea of who claimed Mustafa?"

My grandma has bad hips, and my aunts and uncles would never leave her in Syria. I can't be sure this person who claimed Mustafa exists, and I won't let myself believe in more false hope.

Umm Abood continues, "Stories of people coming back from the dead are always making their way here from Zaatari. A brother in Halab left the city when his building was bombed, and his wife and kids were buried in the rubble. A year later his entire family arrived in Zaatari and they were reunited."

How much guilt must that man live with every day of his life? I must feel only a fraction of what he does.

Umm Abood recounts story after story. "A woman survived a shoot-out and waltzed into her family's home like a ghost months later. She'd been gathering her strength for months before she could go back. Her family was going to leave, but some feeling kept them there. She arrived two days before their final departure date."

"Leene?" Khadija calls, and I hear the optimism in her voice.

"Stop," I murmur. Little Abood stares up at me. I bite down on my tongue hoping it'll bleed.

"Leene, do you think—"

"Stop," I repeat forcefully. Little Abood flinches.

"But you never know—"

"Stop! Stop!" I yell, sending little Abood wailing to his mother. Khadija is stunned into silence, but Umm Abood just gazes at me while embracing her crying son. "Is this what you expected, Khadija? The revolution died a long time ago. There's nothing left but killing and running. I should never have come back here. Not for rumors of Mustafa's survival, not for delusions that anyone in my family is alive. I was beginning to forget."

"You can't—"

"Let me forget." I hold my head in my hands.

"We can't forget," Khadija presses. "We're the last ones who will remember. The last ones who will know what it was like before."

"Pull yourself together," Umm Abood says. "You've already been through the thicket, and the wolf won't follow you out of the woods."

I rock myself until I'm lying on the cushions willing myself to surrender to sleep. I will myself to forget like I used to. Except I can't because now I am too close to the memories.

53

Khadija

I hand Leene her jeans and tunic as I monitor her. "Get dressed, please."

Her eyes are swollen and ringed in dark shadows. Her skin is a sickly color. The sunburn from yesterday brands her forehead, lending her a ghastly streak of color. She drops her cheetah-print sweats and undresses in front of me, leaving her standing in her bra and underwear.

I pull the gray tunic over her head and insert her arms into the correct holes like I'm dressing a baby. I situate the jeans on the ground for her to step into. She does.

"Why are we going?" she asks flatly.

I pull them up for her. "Because Mustafa is waiting for you."

"Why would he wait for me?"

"Because you're his sister." I button her jeans. "And don't ask me what kind of sister you are. I'm not high on that list, either."

"What kind of sisters are we?"

I pause, crouching by her bag and rummaging for her hijab. The poor lighting in the barn gives Leene two black eyes. A few months ago, my temper would dictate that I tell her off and then storm away. A few months ago, Leene's words would have felt like an attack rather than the truth.

"Zain and Mustafa, lucky little devils," I say, trying my best to keep my tone light. "We messed up pretty badly with our brothers, but we're gonna get our second chances. We're going to find Mustafa. It's just taking us a little while longer, but the world isn't over. It's still going."

"People don't go to Zaatari to be found. My world is over." She holds back a cry.

"Umm Abood was right, Leene. The worst is over and maybe your world did fall apart yesterday. But we're going to put it back together, and when we do, you'll have Mustafa and me with you."

Leene is silent the rest of the morning. Before we leave, I wad up roughly fifty dinar and drop it in an unused diaper for Umm Abood and her family.

And it doesn't relieve me from any guilt. It just is what it is. A cash gift she would never accept if I didn't hide it for her to find later, once I am miles away.

❧

Leene is a fading light of the girl I have known, yet behind her eyes is a fire. Wiped away are her pleasantries and pep, and in their place lies fortitude.

The beige desert horizon sheds into white. The white tarpaulin of the Zaatari camp stretches across the landscape. Our driver parks his mikro, and Leene, Charlotte, and I pile out and make our way to the administration building.

Charlotte sweet-talks her way in with the authorities. They lead us outside and begin a camp search for the boy in the picture. With every step we take toward the camp, Leene uncovers resolve, and it hardens like marble. Like the Leene that I first met, she finds the strength to face her future.

Waiting is the hardest part. The unknown stretches before us, giving time a boundless quality. We approach the fence at the junction between the rows of tents. I watch as women in jilbab enter tents, holding children's hands, their skin darkened from the sun and weathered from their travels. I watch as men, thin and dressed in scrappy clothes, deliver packages of food outside tents. Some tents are newer, some old, others soiled, others torn. I try to imagine how many people live in each of them and how many stories each holds.

We garner attention quickly, mostly from the children. We're ordered to stay close to the administration building and not enter the camp, but that doesn't stop the kids from flocking toward us. Some of them want to play, others want to talk, but the majority just stare at us. Or perhaps, they're imploring me to look at them, to have someone from the outside see them.

Leene examines each child, tears in her eyes, as she sends them off for another. None of them are Mustafa, but all of them wish they were the ones the ladies from America are searching for.

"Amrika Khaleh," the kids call over to me. It's only been a day, but the kids have figured me out. I am the American Khaleh. They look at me with shining eyes. "Can you watch us play?"

I hold my breath and lean against a tent post, stationing Leene beside me in the shade. I watch them as they jump rope made of tied plastic bags. I don't know how long we wait. Long enough for me to wonder how old my youngest cousin has gotten and how many new cousins I haven't met yet. I wonder if they'll ask me to watch them play as easily as these children do, if they'll still feel the familial bond that connects us by our shared name.

The next time I return to Syria, I might be much older than I am now. It might be after I graduate college; it might be even later. And if it's later, will our shared name be enough to keep us feeling like family?

Mama says I can call them. A phone call sounds easy. In theory, it's clicking a few buttons, bringing the phone to my ear. But then the person on the other side speaks, and my throat closes. It physically hurts me to hear my family's voices on the other side. I look at these children who ask nothing of me but to watch them. I suppose a phone call shouldn't be that daunting. Maybe all my family wants is to know that I'm on the other side, listening and breathing and present.

I suppose I can learn not to fear a phone call like I learned to open up to Leene.

The sun burns high in the sky by the time an administrator returns. I make sure Leene is out of earshot.

"We found several Tahers," he says. "It's a common last name, and many of those we asked claim their relation to her. We have some waiting to see you."

"I'll go," I say. I don't want Leene to be crushed if she doesn't find him there again. "I'll be back," I tell her. Leene presses her lips together, looking faint.

The administrator leads me to a group of ten refugees, several of them clinging to each other, praying with each other, hoping I'm here to take them away. I don't find Mustafa. I do see a boy not many years older than me with angled eyebrows painted sharply against his skin, and my heart beats faster. The man's black curls remind me instantly of Leene's photos. I hold my breath.

When he sees me, disappointment dashes across his face. I'm not his sister. But I know him.

54

Leene

Khadija reemerges empty-handed. My knees buckle, but she reaches me in time to catch me.

"He's not here." My lips move, but my voice is gone.

Khadija eyes are rimmed red. She shakes her head at me. "Don't lose hope just yet, Leene Taher."

Two full heads of Baba's black curls bob in the distance. They sprint toward me. I let go of Khadija's hand, but I don't dare move. Khadija urges me toward them.

"Abood?"

I don't embrace him immediately. I squint at him, gasping for breath. We strain our eyes to believe what we're seeing, clutching each other's arms, anchoring ourselves to what our brains say are illusions. Abdul Rahman's existence defies all logic. My Abood is alive.

He drops Mustafa from his back.

My brothers are alive.

Abood was the first brother I mourned. The first brother I left behind.

I cry, and my older brother embraces me, lifting me up. The older brother whom I cried for, whom I wished I could cry to, whom I wished I could hold one more time, has his arms around me.

"How?" The word is strangled. "We thought you died in the attacks."

"I had a delivery outside the city when the attacks hit." His voice is thick with regret and sorrow. "Douma was destroyed when I tried to go back. The streets were filled with the dead. When I was finally allowed to enter the city, you and Mama and Mustafa were gone."

We never saw Abood's name on the lists of the dead that are posted online. We trusted word of mouth, and our brains were trained to assume the worst.

I wipe my tears and pull away.

"I tried to find you," Abood says. The lines of his face are deep when he frowns. His stubble is thick. He's changed so much. "It was impossible to track you from here."

His heart must have felt as heavy as mine with Mustafa, but it doesn't matter anymore. We're together. I make sure to keep one hand on him, as not to let him disappear like an apparition. I glance down at Mustafa, who stares at me, bewildered at his siblings' reunion. His eyebrow scar has grown with him, and his skin is a dark tan. A most beautiful shade. His little hand latches onto Abood's pant leg.

After Abood, I grieved for Mustafa next. I was ready to grieve for an eternity.

When I bend down beside him, he evades my gaze behind Abood's leg. I draw my free hand to my chest. "Do you remember me?"

Mustafa shakes his head.

The pain I feel is more than the news of Baba's death. More than losing Abood. More than reliving Mustafa's last breaths in the Mediterranean. More than the blame knowing I abandoned Mustafa alive.

The death of a memory is agonizing. It's an extraction of a thread in the brain that happens slowly over time with nothing to numb the pain. Forgetting Mama and me etches betrayal onto Mustafa's face. He recoils at my touch from its lasting effects. I glance at Khadija, the memory of Syria dying in her every day. I know the fight she puts up against it.

I was wrong. Lost is better than gone. Because there is always, *always* a chance to find what is lost.

Abood ushers Mustafa out from behind him. We're crouched together, Mustafa between us.

I wave Khadija over to us. She should be here; this is hers to experience, too. She stands around us, and I sniffle. "I'm your sister, Mustafa."

His eyes glint in the sun. "I don't have a sister."

"You do," I lament. "You have a mama, too."

His knuckles turn white from his grip on Abood. Our older brother tries to convince him as well, but he's wildly against it. To him, I am a stranger. Mustafa's disbelief shatters my last shred of composure. I want to crumble.

Then Khadija crouches beside us. She smiles, but her eyes are downcast.

"Salaam, kid," she starts.

Mustafa pouts. "I'm not a kid, I'm Mustafa." I blubber a small laugh.

"Fair enough," Khadija says. "Salaam, Mustafa, my name is Khadija. I got on a big plane, and I crossed an ocean and Europe to come meet you." Mustafa peeks at her, his grip on Abood loosening with her every word. "It took us a long time to get here. We're very stubborn, and we had to fight a lot of monsters, like weird, invisible monsters inside of us, before we could come get you."

Mustafa's eyes widen. "You had monsters *inside* of you?"

"Unfortunately. But we vanquished them for now. Isn't that cool?" She smiles. "We came to you all the way from a faraway land. It's very different from here."

He emerges from behind Abood's leg. My tear ducts refuse to dry up.

"It's a place with lakes and parks and school..."

I want to tell Khadija that Mustafa probably can't remember parks, he hasn't been to school, and lakes only exist in his imagination. I want to protect him from knowing how much he missed in the world.

"...and soccer fields and pools and movies..."

Khadija coaxes him out of his shyness. Brief excitement replaces it.

"Is it Syria?" Mustafa asks. His voice is expectant, yearning for a place in Khadija's memory, hoping for a land of his dreams.

Khadija purses her lips, and her eyes gleam with moisture. Abood's eyes flash with unspoken wounds.

"One day." My voice quivers.

Khadija swallows hard. "But for now, you have to trust us. Abdul Rahman is your brother, right?"

Mustafa nods.

"Then you can trust him."

Mustafa checks with Abood, who affirms that we are a family. Mustafa examines me. I barely compose myself, trying not to scare him with my tears.

"I'm your sister, Leene," I say to formally introduce myself. "And I will never leave your side."

55

Khadija

I swing Mustafa's chubby hand while Leene holds the other. It's only been two days, but he's warmed up to us quickly, and he hasn't looked back since we left Zaatari for Amman. He sings his bunny rabbit song in the smoke-filled streets, stomping about, his body twisting in a little dance. Leene would be singing along but worry distracts her.

"Leene?" Mustafa chirps. "When will we see Mama?"

"Soon," she mutters, cutting me a look full of apprehension. Leene needed time to prepare for her call with her mama. Today, we'll be in a hotel with good Wi-Fi, and she'll have to tell her, ready or not.

We meet up with Abdul Rahman as Friday prayer ends. It takes forever to hail a taxi.

Before we get in, I give the driver our destination to check whether he'll take us there. His face sours and he asks, "Where are you from?"

"Syria," I say to spare us from an American's overpriced ride.

He kisses his teeth, aggressive Arab style. "I don't take Syrians in my taxi."

His car screeches away, leaving smog in its wake.

The next two empty cabs don't take us. We walk farther down the street before we hail another. Abdul Rahman gives the hotel name with his well-oiled fake Jordanian accent and tells us not to speak a word.

As I look out at the Jordanian streets passing by, I pull out Merriam-Webster one last time.

Merriam-Webster's *refugee*—a person who flees to a foreign country to escape danger or persecution.

Again, that definition doesn't pack a punch. In terms of description, it's poor to say the least.

Months ago, my version of *refugee* was a person who flees persecution in their country and lives in a desert camp surrounded by waste. I learned that I was wrong about that the hard way. I guess I had more in common with Merriam-Webster than I thought.

There's more to the word. A refugee in Jordan is a person who flees persecution in their country to live in overcrowded apartments, to be discriminated against in the streets, and to fear imprisonment for holding a job. A refugee in Detroit is a girl like Leene, coping with loss quietly, convinced that the world doesn't want to hear about it.

A refugee's existence is too complicated to be encompassed by one of Merriam-Webster's definitions. Like Leene would say, context is everything.

When we arrive at the hotel, Leene wrings her hands. In the room, we sit in front of my laptop. Abdul Rahman and Mustafa remain offscreen as I Skype call Mama, who brought Khaleh Rana over to our house. We thought it best that Khaleh Rana wasn't alone when she got the news.

"You have to be really quiet, Mustafa," Leene says. Mustafa puts his finger to his mouth and grins. Abdul Rahman scoops him up into his lap.

"Allo?" Mama answers. The audio and video don't quite match up. We exchange salaams, and she updates me on Zain's recovery. He's since woken from the coma, so I ask to speak with him.

"He's resting now," Mama says, though she heartens. "He's doing better, but he's still tired."

Mama brings Khaleh Rana into the frame, and Khaleh Rana's smile radiates a found comfort. Leene's breath hitches, but it steadies when I link my arm through my Syrian sister's.

"Mama," Leene starts shakily, "I want to show you who we found, but I need you to promise me something."

Khaleh Rana laughs with uncertainty. "What mess did they get themselves into, ah, Maisa?"

"Please don't blame yourself," Leene says. "I want you to know that it wasn't your fault. We couldn't control our fate."

I look at Leene, a girl who has had a reckoning with fate. I see someone strong, someone resilient. This girl who has made a future out of the hand that fate has dealt her.

"We couldn't have known Abood was still alive. We couldn't—" Leene struggles to keep it together. Mustafa squirms out of his brother's lap. He runs into his sister's arms.

"Who is that kid?" Khaleh Rana asks, an upward angle of her face taking up the screen.

"I'm not a kid. I'm Mustafa!"

"Mustafa?" Khaleh Rana's eyes are wide. "Leene, what is happening?"

So Leene tells her story, with tears and regret. Abdul Rahman joins to tell his. Mustafa meets his mom cheerily, but shyly, unaccustomed to the Taher family crying fests. Khaleh Rana thinks it's a dream, that she may have fainted—that part still isn't clear. Mama supports her on her side of the world. It stings to watch the way the return of two ghosts uproots Khaleh Rana's reality.

Just like at the camp, I push myself out of frame.

I excuse myself from the room. Almost instantly my phone rings, and I answer it.

"Allo, Khadija?" Mama's voice is a whisper.

"Allo, Mama," I say, anticipating the worst.

"I'm so proud of you, habibti."

I nearly choke. I tell her what matters. "I'm proud of myself."

"Do you see how the Syrians live?" She says the word *live* like it means *suffer*.

"I saw how they live." I say the word like it means *endure*.

"Don't worry too much about our family there," she murmurs. "I know you and Zain worry about them."

I swallow the ball in my throat that has been there since I left Detroit. Finally, *finally*, Mama is right about me, and it opens up the possibility that one day, maybe not so soon, I will be able to return to Syria and feel like I belong.

Finally, *finally*, even if for just a moment, the two halves of me click into place.

EPILOGUE

Khadija

TWO MONTHS LATER

The sun nests in the sky where it hangs the longest, like a God-blessed tease. The sparkling water twinkles in the light breeze, marking the end of summer. I rummage around the stones at the edge of the lake with my bare toes.

"Flat and smooth?" I call out.

"Like Zain's abs," Younes replies with a grin. A rush of color bursts onto Zain's cheeks. Younes pokes at him and Zain flexes while avoiding Younes's reach at the same time. Zain's been training at Jerr's with Younes ever since he got out of the hospital. He's put on some weight from it, his posture has improved, and he's being more social—I barely recognize him. He reminds me more and more of the Zain he was when we were kids. I can thank Younes for a lot of the changes.

I collect a handful of stones and throw them into the water with little luck.

"Flick your wrist," Zain instructs.

I try it, but no dice.

Zain flicks one of his stones, which zooms through the air and skips across the water ten times. Who knew this was his secret talent. He gives me one of his stones, aerodynamically superior to mine in every way.

"Use all your power when you throw. Tilt a little from the force you put into it. The rest is in the wrist," Zain says. He takes my hand and pulls back, guiding my wrist into the throw. I release, and the stone skips an outstanding three times before plummeting to the bottom.

I yelp in delight, "I did it!" I shake him a little to get out that smile he's suppressing. The wider his smile, the farther his head dips toward the ground. It's a beautiful smile he has. I notice the little things more now, like when he leaves to go to therapy or when he's holed up in his room for too long, because it's easy to get caught up in life and forget to check on others. I don't want my brother to be forgotten.

I beam at Zain and let my hand fall to my side, the itsy stone on my ring finger twinkling as the sun hits it.

Younes had tried to get on his knee, but I didn't let him. Eye to eye, we promised to keep striving for happiness for ourselves, together. The official proposal could wait a few years, but a promise ring never killed anyone.

Younes, Zain, and I trek up the slope to our back patio, where Mama, Nassima, Younes's family, and Leene and her family wait on Baba's barbecuing. Among the others, I spot Khaleh Rana's and Leene's grins from a mile away. Abdul Rahman and Mustafa arrived a few days ago after they were approved for expedited visas they give to separated families, courtesy of Mama pulling strings with the right officials. It turns out Mama is the queen of a lot more than Rochester Heights.

I plop down between Nassima and Leene, and Leene extracts Mustafa off her to hook her arm with mine. Nassima leans her head on my shoulder, and they sandwich me, two friends from different lifelines meeting me in the middle.

"Tonight is a celebration," Baba declares from behind the grill. Zain keeps away, and I have to adjust my ears. Baba's newly obligatory Sundays at home don't feel natural yet.

"That's right," Mama agrees. "For the reunited Taher family."

Khaleh Rana giggles from across the table. Mustafa clings onto her now. He's a proper mama's boy after all that he's been through. Khaleh Rana cried for days after her boys arrived in Detroit, and since then she's been a totally different person. She's more carefree, almost teenager-like, making Leene and Abdul Rahman the adults in their house. While her childhood wasn't destroyed in Syria, Leene's and Abdul Rahman's were. She still remembers what it's like to be a kid.

Abdul Rahman stands behind Baba with his arms on his hips Arab-style, watching the meat cook and giving pointers about the amount of smoke and heat level. Serious and stern, jaded by a war he never asked for.

As we eat, Leene tells the story of our journey to finding Mustafa and Abdul Rahman, starting at the very, very beginning.

"Khadija couldn't stand me at first!" she squeals.

"I don't know how *you* could stand *me*," I say back.

Nassima snickers while Mama attempts to take all the credit for instigating my friendship with Leene. Arabs always try to find a way to steal credit for things they didn't have any business in to begin with.

Leene continues modestly, but we both know she was the hero of the journey. She traveled across the ocean, holding on to the hope that her mother had lost, and fought her way back to her brothers.

The day folds into night, and fireflies rise from the grass, shaking their lights around us. We sit around the firepit as Leene's story comes to an end. I slide into the background of the tale until we settle into a silence listening to the sound of grasshoppers around us.

Leene whispers into Mustafa's ear, and he jumps down from her lap theatrically. He's growing fast, looking more like Leene's father zapped into a gremlin-sized body. He waddles like a penguin until he's blocking the heat of the fire from me and gazing at me with his round brown eyes.

"I've been chosen," I declare dramatically. My hand flutters to my heart as he climbs into my lap. Since his arrival, he hasn't been so trusting of anyone other than Leene, Khaleh Rana, and Abdul Rahman.

"I'm supposed to give you something," Mustafa tells me in his chirpy Arabic. "Boseh," he repeats. A kiss.

I lean forward for him, and he smushes my cheeks with his sticky hands. He gives me a fat slobbery one on the cheek.

"Awesome," I say sarcastically, wiping off his saliva.

"I'm supposed to tell you why I gave you a kiss," he reports. I look over his shoulder at Leene, whose hand is clamped down on her mouth to hide her quivering chin. Her eyes are moist.

"Why?" I ask.

"Because you helped save me," he proclaims brazenly. He doesn't know what he's saying—he's only repeating his sister's words.

I don't accept it. "Nu-uh. Not true. See that girl over there?" I point to his sister, whose eyes glisten. "She saved you."

Mustafa immediately jumps out of my arms. "I told you!" He runs back to Leene like I'm objectionable.

Leene shakes her head profusely. "I'm telling the truth!" Leene whispers in Mustafa's ear loud enough for all of us to hear. "She's a superhero."

"She can't be. She's too scary." Mustafa shakes his head in an effort to rid his mind of me. The kid forgot about our friendly talk at the camp, and he's moved on. The laughter from around the fire is so uproarious it's insulting, but I join in. The kid's not wrong.

"Boo!" I jump up at him, knowing well the devilish shine that reflects from the fire into my eyes. He shrieks into a fit of giggles.

Leene clears her throat, and I worry she's gearing up for a sappy toast. But she drops it, squeezing her eyes to stop any tears from escaping. And I'm glad she does. There's no need for a toast or a speech or recognition tonight.

Leene and I don't need any of that because we know each other enough to be understood without words.

ACKNOWLEDGMENTS

This book is possible because I come from a place of immeasurable beauty, with a culture so rich and a people so strong. This story is of my tetehs and jidos, my ammehs and ammos, my khaltis and khalos, and my cousins. The Syria I know, the backdrop of my childhood, exists because you filled it with laughter and love.

The path to making this book has been wild, and I'm grateful to everyone who took part in it. To my agent, Serene Hakim: Thank you for believing in this book and advocating for it when I couldn't see a way forward. We make an incredible team. To Ruqayyah Daud: Thank you for connecting with my words, preserving the heart of this story, and bringing out the best in it. Thank you to my entire team at Little, Brown and Company: Marisa Finkelstein, Virginia Lawther, Stefanie Hoffman, Shanese Mullins, Savannah Kennelly, Cassie Malmo, Victoria Stapleton, Amber Mercado, Shawn Foster, and Danielle Canterella. Special thanks to Jenny Kimura and Sasha Illingworth for designing the most gorgeous cover that makes so many feel seen. And to Pollyanna Dee for illustrating the girls so beautifully.

For one as impatient as I, I am eternally grateful for the lovely authors and writers who gave me their support, guidance, and friendship. S. K. Ali, Tina Ehsanipour, Shannon C. F. Rogers, Sara Hashem, and Mallory Jones. Thank you to my wonderful sensitivity readers. To Maeeda Khan: We went from aspiring authors to baby authors together; we've debuted, and we did it fabulously. To Emily Miner: Your support saved me many times over; I can't thank you enough. To Zoulfa Katouh: Our words will lift up Syrians; I'm so proud of us.

Most of all, to my family: You are the reason I can write. My parents, for nurturing my relationship with Syria, for teaching me its language and its culture so that I wouldn't be lost. My sisters, for being my fiercest supporters.

Mama, you are the tenderest parts of this book. Baba, your strength holds this book together. Noor, this book is our childhood, one I hope we'll always cherish. My marvelous sisters, Bushra and Tessniem, this book has personality because of you. How blessed we are to share our lives and dreams as sisters. I adore you. And, Omar, my precious little brother, you are the heart of this book. And you have my whole heart.

Tessniem, again and again and again, your notes, your pep talks, and our sisterhood keep me from drowning. Sundos, our friendship means the world to me, so I call you sister and soulmate. May we travel the world together like we say we will.

Safa, I treasure our time in Boston; I survived it because of you. You're brilliant and wherever you go, you shine.

Ammo Khaled and my family in Michigan, my memories with you keep Syria alive even when we're so far away. It's impossible to list every cousin, family member, and friend who believed in me and to whom I'm incredibly grateful; the list would be pages and pages long. Know that I have my own running acknowledgments where each of your names are listed. I've never forgotten a word of your support.

My dear friend Dahlia: Thank you for your unwavering trust that this book would one day be on shelves. Mona and every Syrian refugee who shared their story with me: You were and are brave.

To every Syrian and Arab, full, half, or any kind of fraction: I hope you see yourself in my words. Your joy, your home, your grief, your peace. Whether my words unraveled or recovered parts of you, I'm blessed that they are a part of your journey. To my niece, nephew, and every child born in Syria or born to her: We will return and she will be free.

And to you, reader, thank you for caring. It means more than you know.

Above all, I praise Allah for giving me this life and all its blessings. Patience is beautiful.